"The literary equivalent of smashing a beer sign with a pool cue. It's a story that swirls with grit and glitter, God and pork butt, stale cigarettes and fresh wounds. Parker's Oklahoma buzzes with tension, a fitting backdrop for his idiosyncratic personas and their bad, bad choices. But however gnarly, Parker has also graced his characters with a childlike tenderness. Meaning, you'll be quickly smitten with these earnest weirdos as they love, lose, and grapple with the fallout from catastrophes of their own making. Bonus: It's also damn funny."

—Ariel Dumas, Head Writer and Supervising Producer, *The Late Show with Stephen Colbert*

"For as long as I can remember, I've been a hopeless book addict. A good book is one of life's special pleasures. Tyler Parker has gone and written a great book and I will never forgive him for enabling my addiction."

—Jason Concepcion, writer, host of *X-Ray Vision*

"In *A Little Blood and Dancing*, [Parker] takes a landscape most often seen through the passenger window of a speeding car and carves it up like a Jack-o-Lantern. The banality of familiarity is transformed into something grinning, haunting, hilarious, and new. These characters are as bombastic as they are believable, crafted with love, a deft hand and true empathy down to the very last scheme. Tyler Parker is Elmore Leonard with a Dream Shake and a cracked iPod Nano."

—Ian Karmel, head writer of *The Late Late Show with James Corden*

"Tyler Parker shows us how the weird, the beautiful, the terrible, and the generous all nestle up together inside a human heart. And he's also very, very funny. I love every page of this novel."

—Rivka Galchen, author of *Everyone Knows Your Mother Is a Witch*

Praise for *A Little Blood and Dancing*

"Tyler Parker rhapsodizes a lush electric yarn of pop culture, basketball, neon-Jesus, and a simmering violence that is distinctly American. *A Little Blood and Dancing* is an everlasting gobstopper of a book!"

—Lilly Wachowski, filmmaker, *The Matrix*

"*A Little Blood and Dancing* is majestic and down-and-dirty and unstoppably funny and deeply sad. Tyler Parker is what they call in basketball a unicorn: he can do it all. I haven't been this riveted, thrilled and broken open by a novel in a long time."

—Sam Lipsyte, author of *No One Left to Come Looking for You* and *The Ask*

"Tyler Parker is one of the funniest writers alive, but *A Little Blood and Dancing* is also a book of deep and surprising tenderness. The best comic novelists know how to laugh at their characters without belittling them, and if this book is anything to go by, Parker has mastered this magic trick. His cast of screwball Oklahomans is so weird, vulnerable, gentle, violent, hopeful, and lost that it wouldn't be out of place in real life. I loved it."

—Brian Phillips, author of *Impossible Owls*

"The hardest task in literature is writing a truly funny book that makes you feel something, not just from the characters and what they do and say, but also from the sentences and how they feel new and full of energy. Only the most ambitious writers even try to do this and it's remarkable and even edifying to see a writer like Tyler Parker do it all with such style."

—Jay Caspian Kang, author of *The Dead Do Not Improve* and *The Loneliest Americans*, staff writer at *The New Yorker*

"Broke my heart and hurt my stomach. And I laughed the whole time. Can't stop thinking about it."

—E.R. Fightmaster, *Grey's Anatomy*, *Shrill*

A LITTLE BLOOD AND DANCING

A NOVEL

TYLER PARKER

STRANGE
LIGHT

Library and Archives Canada Cataloguing in Publication
Title: A little blood and dancing : a novel / Tyler Parker.
Names: Parker, Tyler (Author), author.
Identifiers: Canadiana 20220469253 |
ISBN 9780771002090 (hardcover) | ISBN 9780771002106 (EPUB)
Subjects: LCGFT: Novels.
Classification: LCC PS3616.A7463 L58 2023 | DDC 813/.6—dc23

Book design by Andrew Roberts
Jacket art: (neon letters) Sebestyen Balint / Shutterstock;
(asphalt) Artem Hvozdkov / Moment / Getty Images;
Back cover (flamingos) Frans Lemmens / Corbis Documentary / Getty images;
(tv static) Nikolay N. Antonov / stock.adobe.com

Printed in Canada

Published by Strange Light,
an imprint of Penguin Random House Canada Limited,
a Penguin Random House Company
www.penguinrandomhouse.ca

10 9 8 7 6 5 4 3 2 1

Penguin
Random House
Canada

For Blythe, June, and Adelaide

You treat me badly / I love you madly

—SMOKEY ROBINSON, "You've Really Got A Hold On Me"

Anything can have happened in Oklahoma.
Practically everything has.

—EDNA FERBER, "Preface," *Cimarron*

...gator skin seats, call me Dundee

—RICH BOY, "Throw Some D's"

Don't you see me down here prayin'?

—NINA SIMONE, "Sinnerman"

I love design, architecture, the feel of certain rooms.

—HAKEEM OLAJUWON, "Dream Machine," *Houstonia Magazine*

Prone to wonder, Lord, I feel it

—ROBERT ROBINSON, "Come, Thou Fount of Every Blessing"

You can't eat an air conditioner.

—PAULETTE MARRON as Air Conditioner Girl, *Putney Swope*

And it never did occur to me to leave 'til tonight

—JASON ISBELL, "Speed Trap Town"

Enough of these fairytales.

—WES STUDI, *Unreserved*

...do I deserve to live? / Or am I gonna burn in Hell for all the things I did?

—HAVOC, MOBB DEEP, "Shook Ones, Pt. II"

HOT PURPLE WATER GUN

THE FLAMINGOS JUST STOOD THERE. Pink and plastic on the lawn, a flamboyance of sun-faded ornaments in the Blackwood backyard. Priscilla Blackwood sat in a small rocking chair with her hands behind her back and a Twizzler in her mouth. The licorice hung off her lip like a scarlet car tassel and she screamed the word *dad*. Her father, Solomon, held a hot-purple water gun the size of a fat cat against her temple. His boots were gator and sunglasses orange—tactical shooting specs he wore like readers. A tank-shouldered refrigerator of a man in an Akeem Olajuwon T-shirt and coveralls zipped to his waist. Priscilla wore a lime swimsuit under a blue sweatshirt under an Oakland Raiders Starter jacket and her gray baseball cap was backwards. Oklahoma sun on her face, a prisoner in her own backyard. She heard music and turned. A turquoise Ford Falcon came down Thrasher blasting a song she didn't know, some sad woman begging Break my mind. There was a stripe of pain in Priscilla's jaw and she touched her cheek. Her hands were cold. The Falcon turned down Manegloss, the voice fading into oblivion: you're gonna leave a babbling fool behind. Priscilla looked back at her dad. He screamed Come get this work and shot her in the face. She was drenched. She spit at him. Her Twizzler fell.

Oh, man, my special treat died, she said.

The king is very alive, Solomon said. Broncho County's finest. Spit is nothing to me. I have it in my mouth all the time. Answer my questions. First, what's your name?

Priscilla July Blackwood.

I've inquiries about each aspect of that name.

What?

Priscilla? Parents must've been Elvis fans. What a couple weirdos. Elvis sucks. He's a dork. You're a dork.

Don't talk to me that way.

Don't be that way.

Daddy, I'm wanting to not sit here.

Solomon pressed his forehead to hers and screamed Ahhhhh. Priscilla matched it, tried to disarm him. He stepped back and shot twice in the air.

I have unbelievable spatial awareness, Solomon said. Next question. Your middle name's July? It's a fool that names a child after a sweltering month. November would've been better. You'd be cool if you were November.

I'm cool.

You're not. You're July. July's hot. Not cool. What do you have to say for yourself?

I was just named Priscilla July Blackwood.

What's Blackwood?

My last name.

How do you spell it?

With letters.

Solomon took his glasses off and rubbed his face.

Jesus, he said. I'm naming you Farts.

Oh, Daddy, I don't want to be named no Farts, Priscilla said.

Do you know why you're here, Farts? Why I've captured you?

Priscilla rolled her eyes.

Yes, she said. 'Cause I'm a secret spy and I saved the whole world.

For now, he said. The world is safe for now. But you are not. You are my prisoner and you will answer my questions. How old are you?

Five.

Five? Stop playing. Be serious.

I'm serious. I'm five years old.

Could've swore you were at least forty. Who's the president?

Akeem Olajuwon.

No. He's Master of the Universe. Who's President of the United States?

I don't know.

What?

She put her hands on her hips and shouted.

I don't know, I said.

Answer's Ronnie Reagan. Would've also accepted former University of Oklahoma running back Joe Washington, who is the man. A young Native woman such as yourself should— Wait, where you live?

Yaya, Oklahoma.

So, these United States?

Yes.

Oh, no. I thought so. A Cherokee girl like you should always be informed on the country in which she lives because hear me: they will fuck you over in a hurry. It's one of their favorite pastimes, right up there with killing people. How many stars are on their ugly rag?

One hundred sixty-three.

Wow. No. Fifty. How many stripes?

Fifty.

No. Thirteen. Thirteen dumb stripes. Fifty stupid stars. The most interesting thing about the American rag is it sucks. Tacky little towel. They blew it with the red, white, and blue. No sauce. Just copied England and France. Dull from the jump. They chose as their symbol a yawn. If their precious founding fathers were worth a damn, they'd have used fun colors. Purple and orange or something. Green and pink. I mean, white? How do you pick white? You got all the colors of the rainbow at your disposal, the full Roy G. Biv, and you go with white? Are your lily-white wigs cutting off the circulation to your lily-white brains? Embarrassing display. Cookie-cutter. Bunch of unoriginal clowns. Put some pictures on it, Georgie, shit. Give me a story. A crest. Something. Angola's has a machete. Belize, that new one, they put two shirtless dudes on theirs. Nobody's done that before. That's real invention. But stars? Stripes? Snooze. They're not intimidating and they do not dazzle. Tasteless dogs. I apologize for the digression and I love you so much.

He hugged her tight.

Oh, I'm giving her a big ole smooch, he said.

He blew a raspberry on her cheek and she laughed.

Daddy, she said. Keep playing please.

He lowered his eyebrows, got back in character.

Now then, Farts, I'll have to squirt you with Big Scary for your lack of knowledge. Sit up straight. And your hands should be behind your back. I tied them with the magic unbreakable rope that only I have access to.

Daddy, I'm supposed to win.

No, it's okay. I'll win. I have to. I'm King Champion.

She sat back confused.

Who? she asked.

King Champion, he said. Strongest, most powerful king in the world. The king of kings, really.

You're not King Champion. You're just the king. That's how the game was. It's not King Champion. That's not your game name.

Look, Farts, I don't know what to tell you except I'm King Champion and you're my prisoner who has to make me a bunch of, like, snacks and treats. Assorted pastries. Let's just move on.

Your name's Mr. Titty Baby.

Solomon smiled.

I'm sorry, he said. What'd you call me?

Priscilla smiled.

I know you heard my words, she said.

You better take that back, he said.

Daddy, I'm having fun.

Solomon laughed. Priscilla started giggling.

Me too, smart girl, he said.

He gave her another hug, kissed the top of her head, and lowered his eyebrows again.

Hey, I'm not Mr. Titty Baby, he said. Take that back right now.

I don't think so, Mr. Titty Baby, she said.

No, you must do what I say. You're my prisoner.

I am a piece of work.

Solomon stifled a laugh and faked a scowl.

Take it back, Farts, he said.

Never, she said.

Take it back right now or I let Big Scary off the chain. Repent.

Hey animals and trees and flowers and my house, my daddy is named Mr. Titty Baby.

He shot her in the mouth. Priscilla screamed and fell back, landed laughing in the grass. She wiped her face and looked around the yard. Butterfly bush clung to the chain-link fence in fuzzed lavender beams. And there was the picnic table and the redbud tree and a butter-colored Kawasaki Jet Ski. The flamingos and the hula hoop and a dead Mercury Comet. A blond stick horse lay on the ground beside Priscilla. She said Clementine and ran with it. Leaves flew off the mane. Priscilla's mother, Amma, came to the back porch in blue sweats and a yellow sweatshirt. She held the phone against her thigh and said Black.

Black. Hey, Priscilla, don't be screaming in that hawk sort of way. Makes me want to go lie down. Black, here go somebody called Table talking about Charlie's tonight.

What time's he want to meet? Solomon asked.

What time you trying to meet? she asked. Nine?

Nine works, Solomon said.

Nine works, Amma said. I don't know, walk outside and figure that out yourself.

What's up? Solomon asked.

He's asking what the weather's like, Amma said. If he should wear a sweater.

Supposed to get cold later, Solomon said. Might need a jacket. What I do, I dress in layers.

I ain't relaying that shit, Amma said. I won't tell you what he said. I won't tell you what he said. Ain't no secretary. He'll see you at nine.

She hung up, shook her head. Solomon put the water gun on the ground.

Shit, Amma said. Got me fucked up. He's like Would I be okay in a winter vest? Dumbass. His name really Table?

Yeah. I couldn't believe it either.

That's a stupid-ass name. Oh, Viv said Tucson was going to call you?

He's supposed to holler after practice. Gotta talk logistics for the library car wash. The wait was way too long last year. Left too much money on the table. Could've raised more if we had our shit together. What's up?

Well, I told Viv we'd go over there Saturday after the game. They're taping *Golden Girls*. She's doing her ribs. We're in charge of dessert.

Sounds like time for another rousing edition of Chef Solomon's Churro Supreme, Solomon said.

Priscilla started jumping up and down.

Your schedule open enough for that? Amma asked.

I got work shit tomorrow and Friday's my morning at the shelter but the afternoon's clean. It's churro time.

That's my favorite time, Priscilla screamed.

Mine too, Solomon screamed.

Amma smirked, lit a cigarette, and went back inside. Priscilla smirked, picked up the water gun, and shot Solomon in the face.

I'm in charge, she screamed.

He looked at her.

Want to come to work with me tonight? he asked.

Solomon sat in a booth at Charlie's Chicken fiddling with an empty Ziploc in his jacket pocket. In front of him were three fried chicken breasts, mashed potatoes and gravy, fried okra, and two rolls. It was 9:07 p.m. and the restaurant was empty save the man working the register. Priscilla sat on the floor playing with salt shakers and an Akeem Olajuwon action figure. There were tiger stickers on the backs of her hands. Her Sambas were off. She weaved Olajuwon between the shakers, called him Dream. Solomon gave her the toy on her last birthday. He'd fallen for the University of Houston Phi Slama Jama teams Olajuwon led, thought he played with incredible elegance, force, grace. His rookie year in the NBA had just begun and Solomon was excited to watch him develop. The week before, he'd let Priscilla stay up late to watch the Rockets' third game of the season. They sat on the couch, ate popcorn, saw Houston beat

the Kings on tape delay. Olajuwon put up 25 and 13, plus six
blocks, three assists, and a couple steals. Solomon narrated the
game sparingly, whispered observations. Things about
Olajuwon's footwork or his defensive instincts or how soft his
hands were. Priscilla loved feeling grown and being with her
dad. He put his arm around her as they watched. She felt safe.

Table walked into the restaurant with his head down. He wore
blue jeans, a black jacket, and a St. Louis Cardinals baseball cap.
Priscilla watched him step over her and sit opposite Solomon.
He took his hat off. They saw his face. Plumb circles around his
eyes faded into bruised cheeks and there were lacerations spread
on his mug and a shard of a scab falling from his hairline.
Prematurely gray, the color of oatmeal, a fat skinny. Table put his
hands on the table. They were red. Open cuts ribboned his fingers. Priscilla sat beside her dad. Table pointed at her.

Yours? he asked.

Yeah, Solomon said.

What do you say, little lady? Table asked.

You should see a hospital, Priscilla said.

What's your name? Table asked.

You look like a sad boy, Priscilla said. You were crying.

Umm, okay, well, swing and miss, little girl, Table said. Not
at all. Wow. That's hilarious. Truly, one of the funniest things
I've ever heard, okay, and I pay close attention to the comedy
space. Stand-ups. Late night talk shows. Sitcoms. A lot of movies
are comedies. What's her name?

Don't talk like she's not here, Solomon said.

She didn't answer before, Table said.

Admit you've been crying, Solomon said. Nothing wrong with
showing emotion. It's good to cry. Makes a man stronger.

I've cried once in my life, Table said. First time I saw *Chariots of Fire*. At the end. With the music.

Solomon didn't respond, just stared at the wounds on Table's face. Table wouldn't look at him. He shifted his weight and kept his eyes on Solomon's tray. Priscilla watched Table fidget, thought he looked weak, boring. When he walked past, she'd gotten a whiff of him, some freak-of-nature skunk vinegar, and now the stink had settled in the space between them.

You smell like fireworks and ass, boy, Solomon said.

Ain't got a chance to shower yet today, Table said.

Might make that a priority when you get home, Solomon said.

Appreciate the advice, Table said.

Seems like a mess for such an easy task, Solomon said.

The chicken here's good, Table said.

I know, Solomon said. I'm smart and have great taste . . . Guess the bag's in the car?

It's not, Table said.

Daddy, may I have a roll? Priscilla asked.

Solomon nodded, kept his eyes on Table.

Thank you, my dearling, Priscilla said.

She took a bite.

Where is it? Solomon asked.

Don't have it at the moment, Table said.

You know, I have to say, of all the answers, in all the world, that might be the worst, Solomon said.

I'm sorry, Table said. I was—

Go ahead and dance for me, Solomon said.

What? Table asked.

Stand and dance and be embarrassed, Solomon said.

You want— Table said.

Dance, Solomon screamed. Dance, dance, dance.

Table leapt up and spun like a ballerina, chasséd. Solomon tapped his foot, hummed "The Blue Danube," felt like God. Priscilla watched Table twirl and hissed. She didn't like his face. His eyes were too small, his teeth too bright. They looked like empty rooms and upset her, made her feel alone. Solomon hummed louder. Priscilla looked at him and smiled. Solomon smiled back. Table saw them looking at each other and stopped dancing. Priscilla pointed Olajuwon at him and screamed Dance. Even though you're ugly, you should still dance.

I know you heard her, Solomon said.

Dance pretty with your hands, Priscilla said. Not just your feet.

You hear that? Solomon shouted. Dance pretty with your hands. Feet aren't enough. Hands got to be pretty too. Hey, I don't know. Whatever that means to you.

Table obeyed. His fingers framed his face and waved. Solomon popped, locked, and dime-stopped, hummed more of the Strauss. Priscilla held up Olajuwon and shimmied. She said the word *shimmy*. Table pushed the air in front of him, cupped his hands, brought the space back to his chest. Priscilla started giggling. The giggle grew to a laugh and the laugh grew to a cackle. She was in hysterics. Table did an arabesque. He said the word *arabesque*. Priscilla looked at Olajuwon and fell silent, raised him to her ear. She screamed.

Dream wants him to stop. Stop right now.

Solomon slammed his hand on the table. Table flinched.

Right now, Solomon screamed. Sit down. Sit the fuck down.

He's a bad dancer, Daddy, Priscilla said. Looks like a fish dying. Flopping around. Nerd.

That's a great observation, honey. He is a nerd. Look at him over there. You nerd. Sit up straight. Got the posture of a blanket. Get your dirty little elbows off my table. What happened?

It all sold how I said it would, Table said. More even. The Zo was hitting. Gone by one. Set that hook deep. Got a drink after at that circus bar over there.

Barnumb, Solomon said.

Right, Table said. Just trying to celebrate. Body kind of got away from me. There was a lady there. We kept on, and—she put this song on people didn't like.

What song? Solomon asked.

"Jesus Was a Capricorn," Table said. Played it over and over. She'd put, like, a ten in the jukebox. Just kept repeating. Made people so mad. Some guy started shouting after a while That ain't how Jesus is. Half the room's yelling at her. I get pissed. Yell back. And some of them start to come at me, but one of the fellas there talks them off. I'm trying to pay fast as I can. Had the bag there with me. Reached for the money. Just taking some out of my cut. Bag tipped. Couple rolls came out.

You had the bag in the bar? Solomon asked.

I'm not leaving it in the car by itself, Table said.

Solomon rubbed his face, looked at Table. He wondered if he should kill him. He knew where he lived. He could go over there while he was sleeping, handle it.

What's a dumb animal? Solomon asked.

Um, Table said. I guess pandas are supposed to be pretty stupid.

Then you're a panda, you little dumbass pussy ass panda ass shit, Solomon said.

That's—yeah, all right, Table said.

Keep going, Solomon said.

Tried to put the cash back in quick as I could, but people had seen it, Table said. And they come at me. I'm obviously physically gifted, but there was just too many. Losers is what they were. Taints. Throwing bottles. Got me on the ground. Stomped upon my penis and testicles. One of them was clearly a karate guy. Kicked me in the face three times in the span of like two seconds. Got chucked through a window. Some hayseed Goliath broke a chair over my back so, you know, bad times all around. They took everything.

Everything? Solomon asked.

Table nodded.

He's about to cry again, Priscilla said.

No, I'm not, Table said.

It's clear you are, Solomon said. It's cool. Just cry. You'll feel better.

Sometimes I watch myself cry in the mirror because I'm so good at it, Priscilla said. Daddy, I've finished this roll. May I have the other?

He handed her the bread.

Thank you, my dearling, Priscilla said.

She took a bite, fed a piece to Olajuwon.

Who was it? Solomon asked.

Who? Table asked.

People that jumped you, Solomon said.

Oh, I don't know, Table said. Dudes.

You ain't seen them before? Solomon asked.

Total strangers, Table said.

Solomon said I would never write home about you, and looked out the window. Stouts Bank across the street had a lime E21 at the edge of the lot. Shoe polish on the windshield read PROCUR-ABLE. Solomon shook his head.

What you want me to say? he asked.

Table said nothing.

I actually want you to answer, Solomon said. Tell me what you'd want me to say.

Um, Table said. Shit. Well, hey man, least you're okay, you know? Thank God. Thank Jesus Christ. You still got your health and that's the most important thing. It's health and then right below that's respect. Think we all know family's crucial as well. And I love you like a brother—

Shut the fuck up, Solomon said.

Roger that, Table said.

In 1976, a jaguar put me in a trance, Solomon said. I was at the zoo—

You've told me this story, Table said.

I have? Solomon asked.

Yeah, Table said. Known you six months and you've told me this story three times.

So you understand not to fuck with majesty, Solomon said. Have I told you I find your soul ugly?

You hadn't got around to that yet, no, Table said.

On the inside, he is ugly like a pig, Priscilla said.

Aesthetically speaking, a pretty soul's better than an ugly one, Solomon said.

Priscilla saw her father was upset and wanted him to feel better. She held up Olajuwon.

Dream says he thinks he's really gross too. And he probably don't get no hugs or kisses.

Dream's very wise, Solomon said.

I'm getting kisses and hugs all the time, thank you very much, Table said. I'm swarmed by love constantly because of how hot

I am. Olajuwon will amount to nothing. Got bust written all over him.

He's averaging a double-double right now, dumbass, but good call, Solomon said.

Rookie luck, Table said. Be out the league in two years. That's a Table guarantee. Let's go Wolfpack. Let's go Jimmy V.

Good lord, Solomon said. How old are you?

Thirty-two, Table said.

Thirty-two going on six, Solomon said. Fragile little thing. Built on sand.

Please don't parable at me, Table said.

Pretty wins, my man, Solomon said.

I'm really sorry about the money, Table said.

Well no shit, mooncalf, Solomon said. You lost my money. The least you could possibly do is be sorry. It's not special to be sorry when you do something wrong. It's the bare minimum. You told me you could provide a service and that service wasn't provided. I showed faith in you, gave you an opportunity, and as it stands right now, I don't have my money. And the time's up.

What time? Table asked.

Since you came in and said what you said, I've been giving thought to the idea that maybe you're just too stupid to survive, Solomon said. And it's my duty as a functioning member of society to make sure you can't hurt anybody else, make sure you can't piss away someone else's hard-earned bread.

Hold up, Table said. I can pay you back.

What do you have? Solomon asked.

The Crown Vic, Table said.

That ain't enough and you know that and you knew I'd know that so now I'm even angrier, Solomon said.

I'll owe, Table said. You get the Vic. Then $100 a month till we're square. That includes my cut.

Why would I do that? Solomon asked.

Because of kindness, Table said. Show your daughter the value of mercy, forgiveness.

Don't talk about me, Priscilla said. Your ears are too big for your head.

Solomon slapped Table in the face. A sound like a baseball hitting a glove. Priscilla smiled. Table closed his eyes, rolled his neck from side to side. Solomon flexed his back.

I love to hit y'all grody little country dudes, Solomon said. Y'all are very accommodating, very user friendly.

Table opened his mouth to stretch his face. Church bells ringing. His eyes were dingy and gray. Solomon's hand tingled. Priscilla took a bite of chicken. Sometimes she felt bad when her father hurt people. It made her want to apologize, say I'm sorry about Daddy but I promise he's nice. But she looked at Table and knew he was wrong and weak and sour. He'd failed her family. Solomon took a bite of chicken, talked with his mouth full.

Listen, homey, you're horseshit, okay, and, personally, I'd encourage you to realize that. I'm an incredible father. I don't need parenting lessons from Bobo the Dancing Scrote. Shut your mouth and look at this angel. Look at what a good job her mother and I are doing. She's amazing. She hung the sun.

Love you, Daddy, Priscilla said.

Love you, baby, Solomon said.

I'm sorry, Table said. I know you said not t—I'm just sorry.

Solomon's eyes went from Table to the table to the window. A man and woman had pulled into the bank parking lot to look at the BMW. They shared a cigarette beside the vehicle. The orange end ponged back and forth in the dark. Solomon looked back at Table.

The Crown Vic, Solomon said. Your half, my half, plus a couple bricks for the trouble. One favor to redeem later. Obviously, you won't be able to go to Lasso no more. Same with Santon's. Really, for you, across the board, Broncho County's a no go. Find somewhere else to drink. And it'll be $200.

I can't do $200, Table said. I could do $150. The Vic, the favor, no Lasso, no Santon's, $150, and I stay out of Bronc.

Solomon slapped him again. Flush on the cheek. A thick snap out into the restaurant. Table rocked to the right and his face hit the wall. Priscilla's knee bounced.

This ain't a pawnshop, Solomon said.

Table sat up. His lip was busted. Another slap from Solomon. Priscilla was excited to be with her father. She loved to share things with him, loved watching him dominate. He made her feel strong. Another slap from Solomon. Another slap from Solomon.

Okay to two, Table said. Okay to two. Okay to two.

The man working the register shouted.

Yo. No. You can have him dancing all you want, but please leave if you're gonna play Hit Me in the Face. I hate that game. Been on the crap end of it too many times.

They went outside. Table had parked his Vic next to Solomon's Ram. Theirs were the only two vehicles left. The town was quiet. Priscilla could see the highway. Nothing moved. The Charlie's Chicken sign glowed with the cartoon poultry in boxing gloves mean-mugging the ground, the three of them awash in candy reds, lemon yellows. Solomon looked at Table.

Let me get her in the truck, Solomon said. Stand there and be still, Solomon said.

Let me go back in right quick? Table asked. Meant to get a to-go drink.

Why you ain't get one when we were in there? Solomon asked.

I was going to, but you started hitting me, Table said.

Boy, Solomon said.

I'm saying, I was planning on getting one on the way out but—

Stop talking, Solomon said.

It'll take two seconds.

Dude. Let me get my girl set up.

Black, it ain't—

Black? Fuck your familiarity, shit brick. Look like a fucking . . . you got a weird . . . you look weird, man. Straight up. You got a weird, punchable face. And it's a conversation piece for everybody in your general area. People bond over it. They form deeper relationships with one another based solely off the fact that you're funny-looking.

Wh—that's not—first of all, we've already established I'm hot, Table said. Can I just please go inside and get a drink?

I will hoist you onto the tip of my gun and empty the clip into your asshole, you dork. Stork. Make you mesh. Just stand there beneath me and be quiet while I talk to my daughter.

Table stared at the ground. Solomon turned, looked at Priscilla. Her hand covered her mouth. He smiled, stuck his tongue out. They high-fived silently and went around to the other side of the truck. He sat her shotgun.

All right, smart girl, Solomon said. I'll be out here dealing with Stupid. Love you. Be done soon. Play with Dream. Go get buckets.

He kissed her and shut the door. Priscilla stood Olajuwon on the dash. Her hair was in a bun and she let it down. She touched the window. The window was cool. She watched her fingerprints disappear.

Okay, dipshit, I'll take the Vic now, Solomon said. The favor will come one day. And $200 a month. You skip town, I'll thank you when I find you. Love me a good hunting trip and pecker-head season's year-round. You miss a payment, done. This the one chance.

Appreciate you, Table said.

Give me the keys, Solomon said. Get your shit. You can walk.

Table stepped toward the car.

Man, I should just off you, Solomon said. Folks hear about this . . . gonna think I've lost my juice.

Priscilla had Olajuwon doing tomahawks off the door handle.

Bucket, she said. Bucket. Akeeeem the Dreeeeeeeam. This is boring.

She took Olajuwon and got out of the truck. Boots shuffled on the pavement and Solomon screamed the word *dead*. More yelling. She ran to the noise.

On the other side of the Vic she saw her dad and Table on the ground. They rolled. The jangle of broken glass beneath them. Solomon grabbed one of Table's arms and she saw the gun in Table's hand. In the light of the night the Colt six-shooter shone pale gray and there was a laying of silver like glowing branches across her eyes. She did not feel there. Her dad's pocketknife was on the concrete a few feet away. In her head was a waving. Solomon mounted Table. One hand was around his throat. The other pinned his gun hand to the ground. Blood dripped from Solomon's face onto Table's.

No, Table said.

Another drop.

Soft as the day is long with your bitch ass, Solomon said.

Daddy, Priscilla said.

The men looked at her. She wanted them to stop.

P, Solomon said. No.

Table used the distraction, freed his arm. Solomon said Oh and lunged for the gun. He missed. And there was a boom and another and another and the booms shook Priscilla and her whole body arched. She spun away from the sound and stared at the restaurant. It seemed to heave and the bricks went blue. She tasted smoke. Tears melted the building. She turned back to see her father on his stomach and still. A violent wrenching in her chest. Her eyes were like warped crystals. She looked at Table. His face was bent and his hat was at his feet. Some of the cuts on his forehead had reopened and blood ran down and checkered his cheeks. His eyes were wild and iced and un-occupied and he stared at Solomon's back. The man working the register sprinted outside and screamed Get away from her. Table put his hands up.

Self-defense, he said. He tried to choke me. He pulled a knife. I was just protecting myself. I couldn't breathe. I wasn't doing shit and he came at me and tried to choke me and stab me and I used this gun to defend myself.

The man working the register picked Priscilla up and asked Are you okay? Are you hit? My name's Jason. I'm nice. I'm a good guy.

He walked backwards with her. She held on to his shirt. There was a stain the shape of Florida on the collar and she stared at it, tried to think of the ocean. Her feet were limp and bouncing. She could not feel her head. There was a wailing in her mouth. Her fingers burned, pale at their tips. She let his shirt go. Her fingers buzzed. She did not know what to do.

I need you to not look back, Jason said. You could look in my eyes, hi, yeah, or the restaurant, or the ground. You could look at the sky. Outer space. Why don't you look into outer space? The moon. People been there. No.

Priscilla turned and saw her father again, wanted to go to him. Table hadn't moved. He rubbed his throat and stared at Solomon. Priscilla made Jason put her down and went to her father. The back of his jacket was wrinkled and there were holes in the fabric. A Gaucho Light bottle had shattered in the lot and green shards caught glows on the back of his jeans. She went to her knees and rolled him over. His eyes were open and frozen and bronze. When he fell, he'd led with his right cheek and there were stripes of blood there and bits of asphalt. Her head thumped and it was like the pores in her face were being burned. Rumbles in her mouth. Her whole body tightened. Table stomped in circles. Green glass jingled off his back and he sounded like a change machine. He shouted to no one.

A man tries to take your life, you have every right to take his.

He waved his gun as he spoke. The light behind him was red. The light behind him was yellow. His hair was like vines and lightning. The barrel winked. She looked back at her father. He looked like he was daydreaming. She touched his chest. Blood on her hand. Her brain fluttered and there was a pang where her spine met her neck. She palmed her nape, stood, and looked at the Vic. Blood had sprayed onto the back door and speckled the gas cap. Blood on her neck. She looked at the stars. They were gaudy and low. More shouting from Table.

Soft ain't me, he screamed. I'm deathless. I'm the goddamn ocean.

SHORTHORNS / OXBLOOD GATOR SKIN SEATS

LADY COULD NOT AFFORD SKATES so she walked to the vehicle carrying the red tray with the Sonic bacon cheeseburger. Table smiled.

What's your name? he asked.

Lady, she said. Careful. Hot.

The fluorescent light over the car had a seizure, her face framed by the glowing square of the menu. Along the exterior of the building a sign featured heart-shaped stacks of chicken tenders pierced by arrows made of french fries. And in the same font used in the original poster for *Cimarron* were the words LOVE ME, TENDERS. Table rubbed his right arm, felt beautiful, said her name to his lap.

Lady, he said. That's regal. You're royalty?

Used to be, she said.

Yeah? What were you?

A princess.

What happened?

I don't know. Woke up.

He held a twenty out the window. The Oklahoma wind made the bill bend. There was a tattoo of a tiger barb on his left arm. Black quasars surrounded the fish. Lady gave him his change, touched her bangs. They stared at one another. Heavy blush caked her cheek, black hair at her shoulders, and her eyelids were violet. She was powerfully built, compact, well-knit. Round face almost a perfect circle, made him see stars. Her clothes she wore loose, always black jeans with a red Sonic polo or a white T-shirt. Around her neck was a thin gold necklace with a silver elephant attached. Lady would often touch the charm, run the animal on the chain. She pursed her lips when she did this, trumpeted for the beast, sometimes adding quietly, to herself,

You know, Lady, I ain't trying to start nothing, but a bunch of people's saying you're the best thing breathing.

His hair was pearl silver now but still full, stainless-steel mustache connected to fluffed sideburns coming down in heavy Ulysses S. Grant chops, a U on his face. He'd gotten lankier and ropy with a flat head wider than it was tall. His jeans were the color of Neptune and starched rigid. A middle crease tented each pant leg. His teeth were perfect, little white piano keys showing when he smiled. On warm nights he'd sit in his yard, get drunk on Red Pigeon, and scream at crickets, give them advice on how to live: Tell you what, my bugs, thing I wished I'd done? Real estate. Land. They ain't making no more of that shit.

Lady studied his car: a 1968 seafoam-green Ranchero, upside-down longhorn rack on the grille, the horns crimson, and in white paint along them DEATH CAME FOR BEVO. Table stared at her and stretched his neck.

You like the horns? he asked. Guess I messed with the bull a little bit.

Bevo's a steer, though.

I'm aware, but Guess I messed with the steer a little bit doesn't sing as nice.

It's a pretty red, she said. Reminds me of apples. Also oranges.

Those from the real-life Bevo. Or used to be real life, now my man's just real dead. Snuck into the Texas State Fair and knocked his handlers unconscious with my physical abilities. Crushed their Stetsons with my boots. It was awesome. You'd have loved it. Cut his head off with a sword. I own a sword. It's badass. Used to belong to a great champion. Still does.

Lady saw how hard he was trying and felt flattered by the lie, decided to let it go.

Goes nice with the green, she said.

Crimson's often regarded as a symbol of vigor, passion, and courage, he said.

She looked inside the cab. Oxblood gator skin seats, plastic mold of a mini 1886 Winchester on the outside of the glove box, shellacked rose rock knob on the shifter, sycamore steering wheel. There was a hand-stitched quilt spread over the seat featuring Sissy Spacek and Tommy Lee Jones as Loretta and Mooney Lynn. They lay on a beach between a palm tree and an Italian ice vendor. The state flag of Oklahoma was thumbtacked to the ceiling and the driver's section of the bench seat had been ripped out and replaced with a western saddle, its horn silver and bearing an image of a horse on its hind legs playing a Telecaster. He watched her look at it all, fiddled with his mustaches.

Would it be dumb to say I was a tramp and we should hang out? he asked. Some dummy stuff, wouldn't it? And you seem like you wouldn't fall for no dummy. But then I also feel good about this flirt and I'm trying to figure out if you do too.

You're trying, she said.

Got me sweating, girl. About to start cramping. Should've stretched before I drove over. Y'all got bananas in there?

She smiled, started walking away.

Drink a Gatorade when you get back to the house, she said.

You don't understand, he said. I'm interesting.

Sonic closed at midnight. She went to the bathroom before she left. There were writings on the walls: TZA; *hoss*; *Jordan in Spain*. She rubbed water on her face and heard clicks above her. Live crickets bounced in the lights. She stared at her reflection, lit a Newport, watched smoke leave her mouth.

Outside, the town was all hushed. She put her visor in her purse, walked down the empty row. Light stretched out on the pavement ahead of her and Table pulled up cheesing. She was surprised she was happy to see him. He rolled his window down.

You want to drive around and look at shit? he asked.

He took her to Yellowtree, in the woods by the Big Pin, near Lake Florra. She sat beside him in the dirt with a handle of Osto between her legs. He smoked a Camel and talked about his car.

Certainly, the saddle's impractical. If it weren't so badass I'd get rid of it, but it's just so badass.

It is certainly ass.

He smiled and held the cigarette to her lips. She hated it, kept her face straight, took a pull.

How old are you? he asked.

Twenty-seven, she said. You?

Forty-two. Where you stay?

Sparrows over there across from Church of Christ. Little apartment. Where you at?

6 Mile. Twelve acres out there. Nice little, what's the fun word?—can't remember. You from here?

She nodded yes. He held the cigarette to her lips again. She shook her head. Her earrings chimed.

Only once I do that, she said. I think it's stupid.

They smiled.

Ten four, he said.

Lady took the Camel and placed it between her lips. Table's sunglasses were in the front pocket of his shirt and she grabbed them and put them on. Smoke corkscrewed off the cigarette and she could see he wanted her.

Table was relaxed. Her voice calmed him. There was no effort to it. He felt like she could roast him at any moment. This terrified him, thrilled him. He wanted to talk to her all night.

So, he said. Florra girl. Ever leave?

No, she said. Well, seen cousins in Arkansas once.

How was that?

Fine. Everything red. You gone places?

Bunch. Forty-one of the states. Mexico twice. They got the sea down there. Left Oklahoma for a minute a few years ago. Well, a decade ago. Stayed gone awhile. Needed to let some shit breathe.

The past snuck up. Solomon on the ground. His daughter beside him. Shattered glass glazed his back acid green. Table did all he could to keep that night out of his head, but his memory was creative and his brain easily fooled. The killing always found new ways to crop up again, reveal itself, claw at his eyes.

And now you're back, Lady said.

From outer space, Table said. The cowdude has returned.

Lady lay back and stared at the sky, cantaloupe moon hanging. She held the cigarette up, touched stars, found Pavo.

There's the peacock, she said.

Mom used to say I was peacocking all the time, he said.

Were you?

I have ostentatious tendencies.

I've seen your vehicle. I'm aware.

You should go more places. See things.

She grabbed at grass, watched his boots.

I'm good, she said. I like it here. I want to stay here.

Why? he asked. You taking care of your parents or something?

They been dead for a minute now.

Oh, I'm sor—

You're good. Ain't no deep reason. It's like, people spread their minds out. Get fucked up.

Got big plans? he asked.

I got plans to go to work tomorrow.

Ain't nothing you want to do?

I'm supposed to have some big answer? Open a salon? Build computers? Be a lawyer? What do you want to do?

He wiggled his eyebrows and took a drink.

Want to get my own line of tables. Brand that shit. Table's Tables. You don't be seeing people with their own line of tables. Just doesn't happen. God gave me the ability to have a recognizable sort of what's it . . . unique brand in that field. It's like Oh I could buy a table from a guy named John or a guy named Table. Which will I choose? The guy named Table of course. I'll dominate the market.

What do you do now?

Betwixt gigs currently, but what'd Lincoln say? I can do anything. Last year it was construction. Roofing houses. Year before that I came into some copper. Let me tell you, if you ever find yourself with an opportunity to acquire a large amount copper, highly recommend. Windfall. The harvest was bountiful. I bought a boat. It's no longer in my possession at this time, but that was a fun two months. Where else? Worked maintenance at Kenzerver Downs in Cactus Hollow for a few years. You would not believe the amount of shit these thoroughbreds are pumping out. It's, you're almost in awe at a certain point, you know? Horses rule. I drove trucks for a little while. Bartended. I'll do whatever. Don't really like working, though. Don't like being tired.

The breeze picked up and batted her ponytail. She put her

arms inside her shirt. Coyotes howled in the hills. Owls in the trees overhead. He got the quilt from the car and wrapped it around her. She looked up, extended her arm, held the blanket open. He shook his head.

I run hot, he said.

She fought off a laugh, felt thrown. He lit another cigarette.

I like tables, she said.

Tables are great, he said. You can put stuff on them. Plates. Goblets.

Table's your first name?

Last. What's yours?

Sixkiller. What's your first name?

Sylvia. Sylvia Carl Table.

She tilted her head down and looked at him over the tops of his sunglasses. He smelled like Pine-Sol.

She Boy Name Sue'd you? she asked. Toughen you up?

No, he said. She just really wanted a girl.

Must've been rough.

Nah. Fighting's fun. You can call me Sylvia if you want.

You'd hit me if I did?

Doubt it. I'm not too big on hitting pretty things.

On, uh, what's it? All cylinders. Boom boom.

I got no idea what you're talking about, but I just remembered the word I wanted to say earlier was *nest*.

Some hours later they were drunk with the sun coming in thin, golden Wonka tickets between the possumhaw. He peed against the huge pin oak as the sky took on color. She sat on the hood of the Ranchero, traced sevens in gathered dirt.

———

On their second date he took her to the Arby's in Ox for an early dinner. They sat in a booth by the window and discussed the ethics of stealing from department stores. The pads of Lady's feet rested on the heels of her sandals and Table's knee bounced. She saw for the first time, on his right arm, *Jeremiah Johnson is my favorite movie*. He dipped his hand into his water and rubbed the liquid on his face.

But yeah, they ain't expecting you to pay for small stuff, he said. Like a TV, yeah, you got to pay. But you go in a Kmart and get a watch? Like, not a nice one. One with the what's it. How it's not. You know. It don't got any—

Numbers, she said.

No. It's a watch. Watches got numbers.

Some don't. Some just have lines.

He sat and stared at his roast beef, thought about if she was right. She took a drink of her tea, knew she was. Laundry list of watches in his head. He realized she was correct.

I've given it some thought and you're right, he said. Some are just lines. But I'm talking about like it's only electronics. It don't have the hands.

Digital, she said.

Digital. Shit. Digital. But yeah, a toothbrush? Nails? Pens? Ain't got to pay for that shit. Catch me paying for rain before I pay for some motherfucking pens.

That just sounds wrong, though.

It's not. They account for it with their prices. They know people steal 'cause they know some people need to so they charge too much for big stuff. Like, you go in there to get a bicycle, ain't no reason a bike would cost more than, shit, $50? But you see some bikes in there, they're like a hundred bucks.

Ridiculous. They're charging that to account for folks taking tape or Q-tips or whatever.

I ain't, like, I don't believe you, she said. But that's all right.

Neither were fazed by the disagreement. Neither understood why. Lady took a bite of her sandwich and looked around. On the opposite wall were white Christmas lights strung in the shape of palm trees. Papier-mâché Jamocha Shakes hung from them like ornaments. Table's right elbow was on the table and his right hand was under his chin. He reminded her of school pictures.

Meant to say I'm real into you, though, he said. You got a dynamic personality and a interesting mind. Clearly intelligent. I like how you talk. Your body's radical. I'm into it all.

You, too, she said.

She wore her only dress—yellow with bellflowers on the collar. Her earrings were golden horses hidden by her hair and still she wore the elephant around her neck. He wore black jeans, a white button-up, and a black duster vest. She took a napkin from her tray and wiped her mouth.

Smells good in here, he said. Arby's smells good. These curly fries are talented. It's a big-time fry. What were you like as a kid?

He would change subjects quickly, without warning. Her days were monotonous, filled sameness. Apartment, work. Apartment, work. Apartment, work. It was exciting to not know what was coming.

I don't know, she said. I was a kid.

You're still a kid, huh? he asked.

No. You're just a geezer.

What'd you do for fun?

You want kids?

Not really. Do you?

Yeah.

Maybe they wouldn't be so bad. What'd you do for fun?

Um. Didn't have no TV. Went outside a bunch. Used to swim in this pond by our place. Climb trees. Would just climb up there, talk to myself. They worked all the time so I was alone a lot. Didn't love it. Grammo had one of them little Ford Couriers. Do errands with her sometimes, ride in the bed. I liked that. We had a one-eyed Yorkie named Edna. She was very difficult. And yet I would've died for her. Um, what else? Sneak in movies. I love movies. I don't know. Normal stuff. What'd you do?

Had some friends. Used to drive around, too. Throw rocks at nice cars. Get in fights with gas station attendants. We'd hang out in the old, you know Vernon's? May have been before your time, but they had a bigger parking lot. Was off Rivaldi over there before the old elementary school. Right up against where Cheeseburger Lomney's Laundromat was, before she got famous. We'd sit out there. Mess around. Kiss on girls.

You're wanting to impress me more than anything in the world.

Kind of music you like?

Country, but I like pop stuff too. Rap.

What country?

Reba, who I'd commit any number of crimes for. Slimy Willow and the Hogs. Wanda Jackson. Gudd Davis.

"Junior Takes a Pill."

So good. What about you?

Table reached into his vest and pulled out his flask. Airbrushed on the back was a white woman in a purple bikini with a tiger beside her. He drank the rest of his water, poured the whiskey into the cup, and took a drink. Lady ate a fry and raised her eyebrows, added some to her tea.

I skew, uh, older? he said. Merle. Charles Church. Duppy. George. The Band's my favorite band. I don't know. The boring answers, I guess. Ralph Stanley. Actually worked for him in Virginia one winter. Got a picture with him. He signed it and everything. To my good friend Table. Thanks for being so interesting and thoughtful about my work. And for helping me with my lyrics as well. You got the gift. It was a Polaroid. I lost it, though.

He braced for impact, felt nothing. She let that lie go too. He was still working hard. She felt complimented. She was worth lying to, worth him pretending he was cooler than he was to secure her affections. He was worried he wasn't enough. She loved that, fell harder.

Remind me to tell you my Marty Chisholm story, she said.

Okay, he said. But yeah, I know a lot about music. I like it. I think it's compelling. You know Hutch Suggs.

"If You're Drunk Then Planes Look Like Shooting Stars."

Beautiful song.

I love Hutch. I'm bored a lot lately. Don't nobody have fun like that no more.

You'd have some fun with me?

I would.

You look just as nice with your hair down as you do with it up. Have you completed your Beef 'N Cheddar?

He took her to his place: a two-bedroom, two-bath red brick out in the sticks five miles west of town. They parked in the driveway.

Here she be, he said. The Palazzo at Pink Creek.

In the front yard were two blue folding chairs with a cinder block in each seat so they didn't fly away. Eight plastic flamingos on the lawn, four on either side of the front door, Oklahoma Sooners caps stapled onto each of their heads. A basketball hoop had been cemented into the ground in the side yard south of the house, a half court of naked concrete jutting out toward the pasture.

Pink Creek ran along the back of the house. The car windows were down and they heard the water. Table got out. Lady stared at the drive they'd come down, felt warm. In the west the sky was huge and alien, polished lava spread over pink attic insulation, purple-and-blue bulbs leaking through silver clouds. She got out and sat on the hood. He leaned against the driver's side door. His jaw was tight. There was no wind. She looked perfect and he was proud of himself. Lady heard his feet in the gravel. Her jaw was tight. He touched her knee, put his mouth by her ear. She kissed his shoulder.

I could kiss your face? Table asked.

You can explore some, Lady said.

He started on her right cheek. She felt his mustache first and smiled. He kissed her lips, held there. She kissed him back. After a minute they stopped.

Every day you can do that to me, she said.

Your tour begins now, he said.

Table opened the front door and Lady stood on the welcome mat, looked down at the turquoise carpet.

You could take your shoes off? he asked. Like my turquoise turquoise.

Ain't no mud on me, she said.

Shoes are rude to carpet. Take them off.

Thought only white folks with money had people do that?

You don't know what's buried in the yard.

Okay, Arby's.

Shots fired.

Folgers can with a bunch of lies.

She stepped out of her sandals.

We must be stewards of our shit, you know? he said. Make you more comfortable anyway. Let the toesies breathe. If you'll turn around, 'tween the door and transom you'll see the afore-mentioned sword aka Bevo's Worst Nightmare aka the Beef Slayer aka Switzer's Delight. Cool as hell. Sharpen it once every couple weeks. Gets all shiny and deadly and shit. Slices bricks easily. Swear to Jesus. There go the TV. Fella I bought it off said it was the largest he ever sold. Very cool guy. Name was Gabriel. He wore white jeans. Only get the three out here, but then I do a bunch of movie marathons where I just sit on the couch and watch pictures and films and cinema and cinema verité as well. Cinema verité's probably my favorite just in terms of emotional filmmaking, but yeah. VCR. You ever want me to record anything, just ask. Don't even need to provide a tape. I'll take care of that for you. I'll always take care of you. What else? Coffee table. That's real wood. Couch was Mom's.

The sofa was along the wall opposite the front door, six feet long and cloth, printed up with purple hydrangea vines, a pillow at each end. The one up against the left armrest said LIFE. The one up against the right armrest said COUNTRY. Table said Damn it and switched them.

Meth trying to piss me off, he said.

Meth? she asked.

Methuselah. My uncle. He was visiting from St. Louis. He left today. Must've changed them when I took off to meet you. He knows it bothers me.

So embarrassing.

I'm particular.

Think you mean dramatic.

On the coffee table was a wooden mallard sitting on last month's *Cattlemen of the Great American Plains*. There was a Crimson Outdoors baseball cap on the floor, to-go box of brisket on an end table, and the *Ox News Sentinel* on a footstool near the door. A twenty-gallon aquarium hummed behind the couch, bed covered in teal pebbles, rowboat at the bottom. A Larry Bird action figure stood inside. He had small holes drilled in his back, wore an eye patch and Converse Weapons. Violet archways like purple mountains in the tank. A tiger barb swam its infinities.

I see you seeing the tank, he said. Sexy, huh? Basketball Jesus right there. I praise his holy name. That's my fish. Her name's Fish. Named her that 'cause she's boring as hell. But yeah, there's the kitchen. I'll fry you up some catfish sometime. You like catfish?

She nodded.

Cowabunga, he said. Um. Dining table. An Italian piece, actually. Beautiful construction with regard to detail and structure as well.

The table was a brown rectangle. On it, the September *Arcadian Man*, a pitcher of lemonade, and a to-do list:

1. ~~tp~~
2. sea dragons (can they breathe fire? How's that work?)
3. no nightmares
4. ~~call Dillard's about that shirt~~

Table drank from the pitcher and waved her toward the hallway. What's there? she asked.

Lions and tigers, he said.

No bears?

I wish, but no. That'd be unsafe.

She followed him into the hall, three framed pictures there.

So, this first one is Little Table, he said. Think I'm about five there. That's the old place. Was over there behind Harp's.

He sat in his underwear, face blocked by a watermelon. His hair rose above the rind in sprayed curls like blond Slinkys.

Then here's Mom, he said. She's about thirty-five, thirty-six there.

Profile shot at the kitchen table: camellias on her blouse, Gaucho Light, ashtray.

Then us later on, he said.

She had white hair and square glasses. The front of her shirt said I HAVE MIXED DRINKS ABOUT FEELINGS. His arm was around her. Neither smiled.

What was her name? Lady asked.

Kay, he said.

They're all real nice pictures.

Thank you, my dearling.

They grabbed beers and went outside. He took the cinder blocks off the chairs and set them on the lawn.

Footrests, he said.

Multicolored Christmas lights lit up along the roof and railing of the porch, spiraled around wooden beams at either end. Table used his shirt pocket as a cup holder and put his hands behind his head.

This is cool, he said. Hang out. Kick back. Couple cool kids.

Your flamingos are nice.

Thanks. You remind me of a girl I went to high school with.

I stayed up the other night 'cause in my head I met you before.

Where?

I didn't.

Her feet were on the cinder block. Her beer was in her lap. Clouds made mouths in the sky. He looked at her.

You good? he asked.

She nodded, closed her eyes, moved her hair so it fell over the chair.

This is all very fine, she said.

It's wild, he said. People think there's shit better than this.

A month later she was at his house again. It was the fourteenth time she'd been there. They lay on the couch and watched *McCabe & Mrs. Miller*, talked Warren Beatty's coat, Julie Christie's hair. After it was over, Table drove to get pizza for dinner. Before he left he told her Stay. Imagine living here.

Lady went to the kitchen table and pretended to eat a sandwich. She took her time with it, savored the dream. Then she went to the bathroom, pretended to shave her legs, brush her teeth. She walked into the bedroom and got under the covers. The bedspread was white with rose rocks on it. The creek was loud. His sheets always smelled like Tide and sweat. She looked at the bedroom door and lit up.

My babies! she shouted.

She leapt out of bed and went to her knees, hugged her imaginary children. Table's headlights ended the fantasy.

They sat on the couch with the pizza in their laps, drank Gauchos out of Dallas Cowboys souvenir cups, ashed cigarettes into an old Cool Whip container. Lady ate Table's crust. He rambled on about pizza buffets.

I'm telling you, you go to the right buffet you can almost always get out without paying. They're too busy to tend to everybody. Just walk in, get a plate. They'll ask if you want anything to drink. Water, please. Nondescript, you know. Ho hum. They bring it and you just make that last. Waitress having to deal with so many people somebody she come across once may as well be a ghost. Just make sure you leave when it's still busy. Pizza Inn's perfect. I go there every Sunday anymore. Just arrive with the white church crowd and leave when the Black churches start showing up. Pizza Hut in Ox is nice on Tuesdays 'cause they'll put pasta out and more people come and you want chaos around that buffet. Shitstorm of plates and tongs. Make love to the mayhem, stock up, and disappear. Mazzio's any weekday. All them construction guys and people finishing the four-to-twelve at Bluelake come through. Wear clothes with lots of pockets, you can take croutons home. I recommend cargo pants if you can afford them. They can be quite clutch. Don't go to a CiCi's. They make you pay beforehand. Shame, 'cause it's a high-quality slice and they have great dessert pizzas. Ideal scenario's one where you pay after and get your own refills. That way, you want pop or something, no problem. Waitress just comes around at the beginning to see if you want something other than the buffet and I ask you, my Lady, what kind of clown wants something other than the buffet?

Later, they were in his bedroom, her cheek on his stomach. She wore his T-shirt from the 7th Annual Tunero Car Show. He wore purple briefs. She brought her fingers together at the center of his kneecap, took them slowly away from each other. Lamplight made the ceiling yellow. He scratched her back. They ate grapes and drank lemonade.

Just remembered I was supposed to remind you to tell me your Marty Chisholm story, he said.

Oh, yeah, she said. Martypants. Went to see him at the Yapley in Corder when I was, like, twelve? Daddy took me.

He play "Outlaw's Trick"?

Don't remember.

What?

I can't recall.

Must not have.

I don't know. He might've. I slept a bunch since then.

Hearing OT live would've been too monumental to forget.

Lady rolled her eyes.

Whatever, she said. We went out back to wait on him after the show, trying to get him to sign a shirt, Daddy bought me a shirt, had Marty's little face on it, and we were waiting awhile, and it's cold, so people are wanting to be there if they're there, you know? It was like an hour before he walked out. No shirt. Just shorts. Tennessee hat. Said VOLS on there.

Yeah, I guess him and Bill Dance are boys. How was his body?

He treated himself well. Had that V that come down toward home. But he's signing stuff and I'm watching like There's Marty, you know? And sort of out of nowhere he goes over to this woman, found out later it was his wife, pretty lady, not even blond but, honestly, yellow hair. Still the shiniest dress I've ever seen. It was like silver and gold at the same time. Had this beaded fringe. Sequins. Marty grabs her up. Pulls her to him. Kisses her. And she's into it, now, she likes it, kisses back. I remember he had that big mustache then and it was just coming after her. But he stops for a bit and signs some more stuff and people's like That was weird but whatever, it's Marty, we won't fuss. He's being cool while he's signing. Takes pictures with some kids. Somebody asked him to sign their dog.

What kind of dog?

Ugly.

That's not a kind.

I don't know kinds.

Well, shit.

But then he goes back to kiss ole girl some more and I'm like All right, I see Daddy's irritated now, 'cause it'd been a long day. He had to open the shop that morning which meant I had to go in with him, wait for school. Wake-ups on those days were at five so, all told, you're talking about, like, thirteen-hour day? We're worn out, mad, tired of waiting. Marty's just smooching away. And they're getting active. Using both hands.

Martine copping a feel.

Very much. And we don't know it's the wife, you know, we think it's just some random—not that it would've even mattered, crazy's crazy, but we're all just watching them make out. Then he sort of, like, takes the top of her dress and moves it to her waist.

Table raised his eyebrows and took a drink of lemonade.

Right? Lady asked. I'm saying. Bright-orange bra and Marty's all over it. One of his security nudges him, though, and he stops and turns back to us. Marty's just shaking his head. Smiling. Starts signing again. And people are looking around now, confused, but nobody's leaving—

Got to get the autograph, Table said.

Got to. Been waiting too long not to. And so he's signing again, you know, signing for a while, and there's banter, line banter. I like such and such song. Glad I wrote it then. And the line keeps moving, wife still there in her bra, and we're one from the front now, the front, but ole girl's still wanting more. She can't help herself. There's just something about Marty. She touches his arm again and boom—they're at it again. Marty's dropped the pen. She don't have no shoes on. And it's this deep kissing, rubbing everywhere, grabbing. Daddy's furious. It'll just be another moment. He's shouting that. It'll just be another moment, Lady baby. It'll just be another moment. Then Marty starts feeling her up underneath her bra.

Dude. Sneak attack. Subterranean.

Daddy tells me quit watching but I keep looking 'cause it's a nuts thing to see. He's so heated, shouting more, security just watching. One of them said Go on then, Marty. Then off went the dress.

Goodness.

And she ain't got no panties on, Table.

Pantie free?

Without undies.

Good for her.

So, she's bra and nothing else. And Daddy says to me again 'cause, you know, you're not gonna stop watching this stuff, when do you see *this* stuff? He goes Shut them eyes, Lady. Fuck, he goes. Fuck! He's shouting it at Marty and the wife and security and he don't mean it like Please have sex. He means it like Come on! It's like a Come on! kind of fuck.

I understand completely.

Not that they needed help, but Daddy saying it over and over, I mean, they might've confused his hating it for liking it, you know? Wanting more? Daddy's in a loop, mind fried—Fuck, Fuck, Fuck—then Marty drops his shorts.

Martimer.

Lady held up her right pointer finger and imitated a penis.

And he's got boxers on but his thing's just sticking out the hole, she said. You know how boxers have those holes?

As you know, I'm a briefs boy, but I've seen boxers and know what you're talking about, Table said.

First dick I ever saw. Didn't really look how I thought it would.

What were you expecting?

Like a . . . one of them big erasers.

Oh. Well, no.

And Marty screams This is my wife and she is perfect. Always there. Always true. He's hollering all this. People are paralyzed. Don't know what to do. Then bang. He starts to drop the boxers. That's when Daddy tackles him.

Table put his hands on his head.

Mr. Sixkiller, he said.

Lady popped a grape in her mouth and snapped her fingers.

Security snapped out the trance but Daddy and him were already on the ground. Remember Daddy being real close to it, Marty's little Snausage. It was like right here. Mrs. Marty's screaming. Marty's all, you know, he's picking up his hat. What's the issue, man? What's the issue? Daddy starts shouting Don't fuck on my time. Don't fuck on my time. Security got him around the neck, dragging him off. Daddy keeps screaming. Sign something for my little girl, Marty. Sign something for my little girl. I turn back and Marty's just there at attention, little wiener straight out. He pulled his shorts on and walked over. He goes You his? I said Yeah. He said What I'm signing? I said This shirt. He said You like the show? I said Yes, sir. He said Yeah, I had y'all melting. Signed it huge. Took up the whole back. Said on there I am Marty Chisholm. Think that was the first time I ever saw someone truly do whatever they wanted.

When Table stirred the next morning, Lady was already awake. She ran her finger on the comforter, traced the outlines of the rose rocks. He touched her back. She rolled over. His mustache was everywhere and she combed it with her thumbs. They stared at each other and smiled. Sometimes she looked at him and forgot her body, her brain, her life. Sometimes he looked at her and felt immortal, perfect, above time. He kissed her hands.

I'm surprised I like you, she said.

Why? he asked.

You're not what was in my head.

What was there?

Carl Weathers.

What happened? Was it my pretty smile?

You're ridiculous.

Look at it. You sure? Might be the smile. I got nice teeth. They're all very up and down.

You're a type. Like, you think you should have a good life.

I should. You should too.

Are you a good person?

Not traditionally.

I don't have many friends, really.

I know. I'm not swimming in them either.

I'm alone a lot. I don't like it.

Me neither.

Will you be good to me?

I'll try.

———

They were married at the courthouse in Ox, sun-bleached paintings of dead judges staring at them. They'd known each other
two months. Table's hair was slicked back and moussed, a
Travolta comb having made lines in it, and in the Ranchero on
the way there he found himself in the rearview and screamed Pat
Riley. He was in a pair of pleated khakis and a navy blazer he'd
bought that morning. She wore a white dress with suns on it.

Okeydoke, the judge said. Say what I say.

Table raised his hand.

Actually, squire, we worked it out where we'd say our own,
Table said.

With who? the judge asked.

What's up? Table asked.

Ain't work it out with me, the judge said.

I'm saying we worked it out with each other, Table said.

That's wildly irregular and honestly makes me hate y'all, the
judge said.

They're both quick, Lady said.

Typically, we just get in and out and keep it standard, especially this close to lunch . . . please, just, hey, Kath? Call
Rhodette and tell her I'll be late 'cause I got two people here
who want to be unique. Make sure she gets me the burger with
cheese. She's got a real laissez-faire attitude when it comes to
ordering. All right, giddyup. Say your stuff.

Table pulled out a sticky note and put on his readers. He
looked at Lady, then the words.

*Lady, I'll love you till the galaxy breaks and the universe ends. And
if it all did wind up collapsing while we were alive, I'd be there like Hey
I'm here. I don't care how devastating the apocalypse is. I'll love you
when the Earth's dead. I think about trying to take over the whole*

world so I can give it to you. I feel good around you and I love you. Thanks for loving me.

Lady smiled, wiped her eyes, took out an index card.

Sylvia, you're not real. I feel so good when I'm with you. You make me feel that way. And you make me feel smart and strong. Everything's real close now. I'll never leave and I'll always be nice, even when I don't feel like it. Thanks for the sweet things you say. I love you so.

When the judge pronounced them man and wife, Table kissed her hard for thirty seconds then sprinted out of the courtroom and into the bathroom. Lady stood by herself, smiled with her teeth, cried. She started clapping. The bailiff and judge just stared. Her claps were quick and loud and she shouted Yeah, Lady. She raised her arms over her head, pumped her fists, and started to roar.

Congratulations, she shouted. We love you.

She ran to her purse, took out a bottle of Taureau Brut, and popped the cork. The thud echoed off the walls and she sprayed the room with champagne. The air was gold. She took a drink. The bailiff reached for his walkie-talkie and said Yeah somebody in maintenance come with a mop on account of a lunatic with no wedding attendees celebrating herself.

We're stoked for you, she shouted. You rule.

Lady was on her knees, her knees in the Taureau. She put her hands over her heart and prayed out loud.

Oh, I feel very good, Lady said. This is the happiest I've ever been. I don't know who I'm talking to, but I want to talk to you right now. Thanks for him. Please keep him safe. Please give us fun lives. Let us be kind to each other. Man, I'm lit up. I'm in the zone. I'm in the zone. I'm in the zone.

She waited on Table outside the restrooms. When he appeared, he was out of breath. She looked past him to the closing door and beyond it saw the trash can dented and turned over. Glass had webbed on the mirror and wadded paper towels were scattered on the wet floor around the sink. A stall door leaned against the hand dryer and the water still ran. His knuckles were open and bleeding, bursts of red smeared on his thighs.

You okay? she asked.

Yeah, he said. Ain't know how to—I don't know—just happy.

NAKED AS A
PICKED BIRD

LADY SAT ON THE COUCH and watched *Broadcast News* on VHS. Her feet were on the coffee table and the remote was on her thigh. Joan Cusack looked lovingly at Holly Hunter and said Executive producer, wow. Table appeared in the hall, swaggered naked into the room. Lady wolf-whistled. He stopped in front of the television and did the Running Man. She smirked. He whirled his penis around like a propeller and screamed the word *helicopter*, made chopper sounds with his mouth.

My God, she screamed. It's hideous. Someone kill it. We can't let it reach the city.

Look at the raw power and energy, he screamed. That's good old-fashioned American ingenuity right there. Type of shit they use on the space shuttles.

Enough. I boo you. Boo. Can you please move?

What? I'm putting on a show for my Lady love, au naturel.

I appreciate the effort but, as I stated previously, I must boo you.

Well, I boo you.

What a wordsmith.

Table went to the kitchen and Lady looked back at the movie. Hunter screamed Do it or I'll fry your fat ass, Estelle.

Want some Cheetos? Table asked. I'm about to go to work on some Cheetos.

No, Lady said. My hands smell all day after I eat Cheetos.

Think that's a testament to the power of the Cheeto. I've always said that.

Table got the bag from the pantry and put a handful of orange in his mouth. Lady watched him chew. He chewed with intensity. He chewed with pace. Cheetos smithereens flew from his lips like buckshot and he blew kisses. Puckered mouth like a mandarin slice. He spun and remembered dancing in Charlie's.

His face wanted to drop. He overcompensated for the memory, smiled huge. The taste of blood in his mouth. Lady rolled her eyes. He used the Cheetos bag as a maraca and danced to William Hurt saying The Libyan government has disavowed any prior knowledge of the attack.

Once we got some little ones we'll need to do something about you walking around naked as a picked bird all the time, she said.

I like being naked, he said. I like the air.

Kids can't be seeing Daddy's wieners flopping around.

Wieners?

Wiener. Not sure why the s wanted in there.

Probably 'cause I got me a big ole horse cock and when experienced it's like there are many of them.

Whatever you say, little man. Just cover it up.

I'll get a sock. Some duct tape.

The butt don't work either.

I'll figure out a contraption. Some sort of modern Adam look. Sock over the crack. Something with string.

You do have a very long crack. It's very tall.

Right? About as high up as my belly button. What can I say? God is good.

Table sat in the recliner and covered himself with a blanket. Lady looked back at the movie. Robert Prosky told Hunter she was brilliant. Table saw flecks of green on the television and blinked several times. He touched his stomach. His stomach was cold. Lady had an idea and glanced at him, tried to make herself cry. The nerves at the front of her face strained and heated and her nose burned and she ground her teeth. Table heard a sniffle and looked up. Tears ran down her face.

You good, baby? he asked. What's wrong?

And scene, she said.

She wiped her eyes and smiled. He was confused.

I was acting, Lady said. I never told you I used to want to be an actress?

He tilted his head to the right.

No, Table said. That's awesome. When?

When I was little, she said. In my room. Put on little plays, be a movie star. Took drama in high school even. Got a monologue and everything.

That's wild. You still have any interest in it?

Hell no. Hated people looking at me. Too self-conscious. I'd be all in my head, clam up. I was unbelievable when it was just me, though.

You remember the monologue?

Yeah.

Can I hear it?

For real?

He nodded. She clapped once, turned down the movie, and went to the center of the room.

Okay, she said. Sit like you're sitting. I have to . . . You're supposed to walk in and announce yourself. So it's like, My name's Lady Sixkiller-Table. I'll be performing one of Myra's monologues from Darlene Scarataza's *Pape*.

Pape? he asked. That's a movie?

A play.

Gross. Disgusting.

They have to be from plays if it's a theater thing. So you say when you're ready.

What?

When you're ready.

For what?

No. That's what you say.

I'm ready for you to start.

No. You say to me the words *When you're ready*.

What words?

When you're ready.

Jesus Christ.

Dude. This is not hard. Say this exact thing. Say When you're ready.

Oh, just those last three words?

Yeah.

Wow. You explained that horribly.

I think I explained it very well.

Want me to say it now?

Hold on.

She turned around and gathered herself. He remembered he was excited. She rubbed her palms on her thighs. He did not hear her whisper Feel it.

Now, she said.

When you're ready, he said.

She licked her lips and spun.

I eat aged swan nightly, which isn't easy to find. You must have friends who understand you are God and impart that knowledge with passion whenever necessary. I require the bird grilled. Keeps things tight. Taut. Right. My vanity demands I enchant. A scant Russian man carves it for me. I found his name strenuous to pronounce—there were an overwhelming number of *k*'s involved—so I named him Bartimaeus. Bartimaeus. A treat to say. I did well choosing it and make him thank me every day.

Now, my Bartimaeus is an honorable man and gentle, but he tires quickly. There have been occasions I've had to beat him with a fire poker, force him to the ground, shave him with a cactus. Understand, this is to discipline him. I could have someone else do it. I could pass the buck. Presently, I employ eighty-three full-time guards. But here I say my truth: I enjoy hurting people. It gives me strength. When I see his face blood in sprays against my de Koonings, I feel I'm pirouetting in the stars. I stay in the finest hotels and eat $50 salads, bitch. My life is a ball. A beautiful, never-ending ball. Oh, me! I'm so happy I'm me! Bartimaeus slices the swan into bites exactly one inch by one inch by one inch. Any error and he's not allowed to eat for a week. I make him watch me swim, discuss current events, compliment me on my personality as well as my breasts and stomach. Thankfully, when his performance is taken in its entirety, Bartimaeus is an extraordinary servant and I love him dearly. For him, I would kill thousands. He gets me going, comforts me, his sporting tongue. Makes me feel safe and dominant. He is the best friend I've ever had. The sweetest man in all the world. And I will lick him tonight.

Lady looked at Table. His orange mouth was open and his eyes were full of light. She put her hands on her hips. His cheeks were flush.

Holy shit, he said.

Told you, she said. Went longer than normal but—

Table stood and screamed This is my wife and she is perfect. He held her cheeks in his hands, kissed her lips. She tasted the Cheetos.

Babe, he said. Best performance ever. You acted the shit out of that. I about called the cops. Swear to God. Thought I had an intruder.

Shut up, she said.

He jumped on the couch. The springs squealed and the blanket fell.

Glenn Close ain't shit! he screamed. Judi Dench ain't shit! My Lady is the shit!

Quit flexing, she said. Judi Dench is unbelievable.

Fuck her. She's worthless compared to you. She's horrible at her job compared to you.

Speaking of jobs, you look for one today?

No. Chill out. This is just a casual conversation.

Don't tell me chill out.

Not yet, I mean. Haven't looked yet, but I will. Sorry.

You told me you'd get a job after the wedding.

And I will. I've just been in honeymoon mode.

Yeah, honeymoons aren't usually a month.

You're right. I'm sorry. I'm being a butt. I'll look at it tonight.

It's okay. There's a bunch in there. Should be able to find something.

A folded stack of darks sat under the coffee table, pair of briefs covered in Gaucho logos. Table slipped them on and sat back down.

Babe, I got you. That's my toilet reading this week. Promise. Besides, I can get pretty much any job I want. I'm great with my hands and brain as well. My brain's actually super advanced.

You work so hard on such mediocre jokes.

She went to the fridge and got a Dr. Pepper, pointed at the can. He nodded. She grabbed another and tossed it to him.

You really don't need to be worrying about money like that, he said.

I think I do, she said. We don't have any.

So, yeah, that. Look. Didn't want to tell you during the wooing period because I wanted you to like me for me, but here in a few years I stand to receive a sizable chunk of change.

She stood up straight, squinted, tried to read him. He raised his eyebrows.

What's that mean? she asked.

I told you about Methuselah? he asked.

Mentioned him a few times. He's your uncle?

Yeah. Methuselah Silk. My mom's little brother. Lives in St. Louis.

Okay. So?

Well, he's loaded.

They stared at each other. She looked at him, half smile on his face. His stomach was tusk-colored. Tufts of gray hair on his shoulders like carpet samples.

. . . okay? she said.

I'm saying, he's rich, he said.

I know what *loaded* means. What's that got to do with you?

He scooted forward in the recliner and straddled the footrest. The outer reaches of his scrotum stretched beyond the edges of the cotton.

Thing about Meth . . . Table said. He's old. Or not *old* old. But older. Seventy-two. Wife died awhile back and they never had no kids. Silk-wise it was just him and Mom. I'm the only blood he's got left. When he dies, I get it all.

You're being for real?

Completely.

What's he do?

He was in the oil business for a minute, but the thing that really set him up—he bought a bunch of Wal-Mart stock when they first went public in '70 or whenever it was. Hooked up with a Busch. Budweiser, not Texas. Now he's got an indoor swimming pool.

Oh. Wow. Okay, so you're going to inherit a bunch of money?

Affirmative. He's got one of those houses so fancy they named it.

What do you mean?

You know how some houses are so fancy they have names? Biltmore Estate. Fallingwater. The Breakers . . .

Graceland?

Sure. Meth did that with his. Named it Silkhaven.

Silkhaven?

There's a movie theater in there, sauna, sixteen-car garage.

She lay on the couch and looked at the television, the room reflected in the screen. Her face was warm. This was nothing she expected to hear and she didn't know how to respond. If true, it didn't change much in the immediate. It was exciting maybe one day she wouldn't have to work as much, but it meant nothing now, and there was something off-putting about him viewing a family member's demise in this light. She also wasn't sure she believed him.

Little morbid rooting for somebody's death, Lady said.

I'm not out here praying for him to die, Table said. I'm just saying, when he does, we'll be rich. We can buy fun things like pontoons and fucking . . . myrrh.

Sounds like you're rooting for it.

I'm really not.

And you promise this is real?

It honestly is. I get it. But it's real.

Well, just 'cause you're getting money later don't mean we shouldn't worry about not having any right now.

Babe. Loud and clear. I'll find something. I'll look in the paper tomorrow. For real. I'm being serious. I'm sorry. I see you're worried.

Thank you.

Lady turned up the movie. Hunter wept at her desk, covered her face with a tissue, and whispered God help me. The cloth of the couch felt cool to Lady and she tucked her feet under the Life pillow. Table tried to get her attention, flexed again.

Just go put some clothes on, Lady said.

My bod turns heads, Table said.

So does a car accident.

You could've done better than that. Should've been more patient, let the joke come to you instead of just attacking all willy-nilly without putting any thought—

One of your balls is hanging out.

Lady watched the Ranchero from a lawn chair. Plumes of dirt shot up behind the coupe and Table tore down the drive. He hung out the window, honked the whole way. She smiled at the horn, watched the car slide to a stop. He'd just finished his final interview with the Oklahoma Treasures Outfit, got out holding a bouquet of cosmos and a bottle of Taureau.

There he is! he yelled. Start Monday.

She screamed and ran to him, jumped in the air. He dropped the flowers and caught her. They kissed. She wrapped her legs around him. He took her to her chair, ran back for the cosmos.

She lit a cigarette and watched him pick up the bouquet. The sun was behind him. He took a step a second, acted like a bridesmaid. Her nails were purple and he watched them on the cigarette. He got to her. They high-fived the way bikers do.

I'm so happy for you, she said. How do you feel?

Unbeatable, he said. They said I get business cards of my very own.

Business cards for the businessman. You can do the thing at restaurants where you drop one in the bowl for a free lunch.

That was the first thing I thought too. Would be a dream.

She pointed at the flowers.

Who those for? she asked.

Not sure, he said. Is there a card?

She plucked the note.

To: My Lady

Love: Me

Thanks for shaking me awake.

They sat in the front yard, the champagne and a bag of popcorn on a tray between them. It was a calm evening with a small breeze and the western sky yawned, crushed orange on the clouds like broken mangoes. Table took a drink and patted his thighs. She put her feet in his lap.

It's wild, he said. Never even crossed my mind there's somebody that puts the prizes in the crane games, but it totally makes sense. Not just magic a teddy bear gets in there. Robots can't do that. Least not yet.

He grabbed a fistful of popcorn and put the bag back on the tray.

Making fifteen an hour, he said.

That's huge, she said.

Right? And he was, like, being all nice and saying I was exactly the type of guy they were looking for. Smart. Good hang. Courageous.

I'm so proud of you, baby.

Did want to say thanks for your help. Finding it. Talking me through everything.

You're welcome. I like helping you. I like you.

Oh, and I'm not saying I want to tomorrow or anything, but after we save some, I want to get a custom decal on the back of the vehicle.

Of what?

Want a fucking bald eagle staring at people behind me. Wings spread. And it's like a angry eagle. Maybe give it muscles if it's possible to do that. Like its wings are jacked. And it has the words MY ENEMIES in its beak and the words are, like, broke in half. Get a cross rising up behind the bird. Golden cross, for spirituality. Then behind all that's the ocean. And the sun's setting but you can't see none of the actual sun so the sky's, like, not pink pink, but pinkish. And I want the wings blood-soaked.

The job was uncomplicated. From 7:30 a.m. to 6 p.m. he rode around with his immediate superior, Ignacio, and stocked crane games and sticker/temp-tattoo vending machines in the area. OTO serviced businesses in seventeen different counties in and around northeast Oklahoma and had recently expanded into parts of northwest Arkansas and southern Missouri. Their truck was loaded with a medley of plush toys: dinosaurs, farm animals, race cars, footballs, Muppets, so on. A couple Santas crisscrossing the countryside.

Table liked Ignacio. He stayed on time but wasn't trying to be a hero about it. They got along well, ate lunch together, talked fishing. It was steady, humdrum work. Initially, Table enjoyed the repetitiveness. Ride around. Load, unload, load. The schedule allowed him plenty of time to think and the work was involved enough that his body got solid from all the lifting and there were days he left feeling gifted and unbreakable. He loved that he didn't have to take the job home with him. When he wasn't at work he didn't think about work. It didn't interfere with his dreaming.

Things first went bad when Ignacio started fly-fishing. Table thought fly-fishing was elitist. He loathed hearing about the tying of different flies, nymphs and caddis and woolly buggers and quick upstream mends and proper fly presentation when fishing for brown trout in the sun in the spring in the morning, Ignacio yammering on and on about the purity of the sport and how close to God he feels when he's in the water. Then he started eating cabbage for lunch. It was part of a new diet he was trying where he had to eat cabbage for lunch. The smell would live in the truck, on their clothes, and in their hair. People stared when they walked in restaurants. In the evenings, Lady made him air out in the backyard before she let him inside. Load, unload, load.

The monotony wore him down. He grew bored, lazy. His body started retaliating. First, his lower back, little stabs of pain that morphed into full-on aches. He stretched every morning, spent entire evenings icing it. It didn't help. Then his knees started giving him trouble. Then his hands. And the injuries were the only new things. Load, unload, load. He would sit in the same truck every day and stare at the same land every day and go to the same places every day and he started to hate trucks and roads and stuffed animals and Ignacio got into trotlining and would want to wax on about some fifty-five-pounder that about snapped his net at the handle and his breath would be dank and Table would have this feeling like there were bats flying around inside him, landing on his organs, shrieking, eating their way out.

It was early evening and they were drinking and cleaning the house. Table rearranged the magazines on the coffee table, sipped his Gaucho. Lady took a glass of Hatta into the kitchen and wiped down countertops. She asked Table if he'd done the laundry. He didn't hear her. The radio was on *Coast to Coast AM*. A caller told a story about snow skiing with Bigfoot.

He had no poles, a high voice, and said I've lived five eternities and you're the most beautiful thing I've ever seen. Then he skied off a ledge to his death. I was able to ski down the mountain and recover some of the beast's remains before the wolves arrived. His brain was the size of a loaf of sourdough and the fur cashmere soft.

Liar, Table said. I've seen Bigfoot. In the woods, down near the Texas line. Our side. Just a ways from Auna. Followed him for six hours. Watched him rub one out in the Red. He was furious. Ate a squirrel whole and danced to the forest sounds for like half an hour. He has rhythm. Doesn't look how the shows say, though. It's actually a lot more like André the Giant. Not near as much hair. And I'll tell you what. Don't know about the brain but dude got him a big ole dick. Good golly. Dadgum pool noodle.

Did you do the laundry, though? she asked.

Not yet. Gonna do it tonight before bed.

Please do, she said. You said you wanted to help more.

I promise I will. I'm sorry.

He ran his foot over the carpet, made a darker turquoise. She watched him scratch his face, put his hands on his hips. His shoulders drooped and his eyes moved across the floor in a blue gloom. She tilted her head to the side.

What's up? she asked.

Just kind of a shit day, he said. Wasn't trying to do much when I got back.

Oh, no. You didn't say anything. What happened?

Restock at Party Beach.

Oh.

Right, so we're having to navigate all that. Tons of school groups there. Kids treating us like shit. Grabbing at prizes. Bunch of little Satans. They fucking read books so they get to come here during school? Reading is easy. They should not be rewarded for it.

Shit. That's rough. I'm sorry, baby.

He shook his head, thumbed the stay-tab, made it buzz.

You should get to call kids names, he said. That should be totally fine.

There was a bowl of apples on the counter. Lady washed one and took a bite. Her reflection hung in the window above the sink. When he got to moaning, he'd try to get everything in their world to stop while he complained. He needed an audience. She mainly didn't mind—she loved him, he was upset—but some-times the doom and gloom grated her. Her feet hurt. She wanted to sit down.

What were you restocking? she asked.

Couple sports packages, he said. Those balls that're, like, NBA themed. Rockets or Bulls or whoever. Had to put necklaces in one of the new ones. Believe that? Necklaces. Fancy silver ones. Some of the most breathtaking jewelry I've ever seen. Frustrating to load. Impossible to win. But yeah, just kid after kid pestering, asking if they can pay me for the stuff. One came up talking about he'd pay $5 for a Mavericks ball. Told him no. He went and got his mom. Brought her over. They yelled at me together.

What'd they say?

Just that I have no life.

I'm sorry, babe.

Table finished his Gaucho and put the empty on the coffee table.

Meth needs to die for me so I can quit this bullshit, he said.

Don't be saying that, she said.

She went into the living room and laid on the floor, pointed at the COUNTRY pillow. He Frisbeed it to her.

How was your day? he asked.

Same ole, Lady said.

Tracy call in again?

Yeah. It's over for her.

She's the worst.

I feel bad for her.

You all right? They give you help?

Yeah. Corrine wound up staying.

How're your feet?

Good.

Foot rub?

No, but you can get me a refill.

He went to the kitchen, topped her off, brought it back. She took the drink and pretended to bite his hand. He sat in the recliner, looked out the window. The pasture was an extreme lime from the recent rain and the yard was thick and glossed and sharp-looking, like green spikes. He thought of Solomon, face down on the concrete, jagged shards on his jeans. Shaking gray in his head. Stinging in his temples. His throat felt full and the recliner stabbed him. The late light caught the flamingos, pink-and-crimson halos over the birds.

Lady sat up and looked at Table. He didn't notice. She wanted to talk with him about kids, had been planning to all day. It was time. Her pulse knocked at the ends of her fingers. She'd start by calling him babe, to lower his defenses and remind him they were in love.

Hey babe, she said. I was thinking about our conversation this morning on my way home. Let my mind go there, I guess.

Yeah? he asked.

Would you want a boy or a girl first?

Table sighed and looked toward the hallway. Her head went back and she narrowed her eyes. A caller on the radio said Jurassic Park is real and it's actually pretty cool. Lady tried to relax her face.

I don't know, Table said.

I'd be happy with either, Lady said. A boy would be neat. A girl would be—

Sorry, can we talk about this later?

She let him see her frown.

I'd just really rather talk about this later, he said. I'm sorry.

Why not now? she asked.

Do you not remember the whole first part of this conversation?

I understand that's annoying. I don't like rude people either, but that ain't nothing to wallow in. Feels like you're just avoiding me. I meant what I said. You'll be a great dad.

Babe, how many more ways—? I don't want to talk about it.

Table.

He raised his voice.

Stop.

She flinched and felt embarrassed.

Don't tell me stop, she said.

Don't be trying to rile me up, he said.

I'm asking you about our family.

Fam—

You know what I—

Shit, girl. You're being an asshole.

No no no, boy.

She went outside and smoked beside the lawn mower. Rags and tatters of violets at the rim of the western sky. Her shoulders were tight. Fuzz in her head. She did not feel known.

They grew shorter with one another. Talks late into the night about how they should treat each other. More arguing. More discussions about children. Methuselah had a stroke and lost partial use of the right side of his body. Table took a few days off, drove to St. Louis, visited him in the hospital. When he got back, he told Lady the doctors were worried about a second stroke hitting Methuselah in his weakened state.

What they told me was he's way higher risk now to have another one sometime in the next six months. They said if that happened, it would be bad. If that happened, that'd probably be it.

She didn't believe him.

———

One cold Saturday they drove out east of Tunero to Nancy Meats, ate in the Ranchero at the edge of the lot. Four Black boys played jackpot in the field behind the restaurant and cattle grazed across the road. Lady sat shotgun, Styrofoam containers on the seat between them—pork butt, onion rings, and deep-fried cinnamon biscuits. A six-pack of Gauchos chilled in a cooler on the floorboard. Lady opened one and took a drink. She was undeterred by the uptick in arguments, felt like she'd always been open with him, wasn't going to stop now. He stared bored at telephone wires and said This is Peter Gammons, ESPN.

Thought any more about kids? she asked.

He yawned, held a fist over his mouth, nodded.

Sorry, he said. Some.

Let's talk then, she said.

His knee bounced. He'd wanted a break from these discussions, was looking forward to eating pork and relaxing. Lady saw he was anxious and touched his knee. He stopped moving. One of the kids wore a Ken Griffey Jr. Mariners jersey and laid out for the ball, full extension, brought it in with one hand. Table pointed out the window with his chin.

What a snag, he said. Kid's going Largent out there.

Table, Lady said. Meet me here.

Sorry. You start.

I'd like you to.

All right. So, I love you. I don't want to make you sad. I'm just not sure now's the right time.

She was so confused by his hesitancy. He was almost fifty. She'd been patient. She didn't have forever. She was ready.

You knew I wanted them, she said.

Just a few more months, he said.

What're you waiting on?

Oh, wow.

He turned and looked out the back window. An orange Typhoon strutted through the lot playing Mobb Deep's "Shook Ones, Pt. II." Prodigy: When the slugs penetrate, you feel a burnin' sensation. Gettin' closer to God in a tight situation now.

What a beautiful truck, Table said.

There was the feeling of nails scraping her neck and her chest was hot. She set her jaw. The Typhoon stomped around the corner and the lot froze again. Table took a bite of a biscuit, noticed the silence, looked at Lady. Her eyebrows spiked down. His hands were closed. He opened them.

Come on, man, she said.

What? he asked.

You know what you're doing.

I don't.

She took a bite of pork. There were dead flakes of yellowed grass at her feet and she moved them with her shoe. The boys stopped playing jackpot and started playing Tackle the Man with the Football. One wore a Ric Flair sweatshirt. He tore through the field like a bull hollering Woooo, sounded like a train. It took all three of the others to bring him down.

I don't understand you, Lady said. Ignoring me. Like you're trying to make me sad.

That ain't true at all, he said. I'm big and strong and pure of heart.

She rolled her eyes.

Pure of heart, she said. Wow.

Table tried to rip open his T-shirt. He struggled with the neck, fought with the collar. After twenty seconds he just took it off.

His alabaster stomach looked like a dying tooth. He pounded his heart.

I'll cut open my chest right now and show it to you, he said.

Did you shave your stomach? she asked.

I swear to God, if you make fun of me . . . Let me be how I want to be.

What're you talking about? When do I make fun of you?

You know what, Lady? If you must know, a pretty remarkable amount of lint was starting to collect in my belly button throughout the day and it was really annoying so I shaved my stomach thinking that'd help. Why don't we call a press conference and alert the nation?

Did it work?

Table put his head on the steering wheel.

Not at all, he said. Somehow more gets in there now.

I can see inside your veins.

And you're a goddamn biscuit hoarder. Hoarding biscuits over there. Biscuit hoarder.

Such a dick.

They looked out their respective windows. Lady stretched her neck, tried to calm down. A black Grandeur parked beside them and the driver stepped out. He wore a Hakeem Olajuwon Rockets jersey and Adidas slides.

Need to get me one of them, Lady said. I love Hakeem.

Olajuwon sucks taint and so does anybody who likes him, Table said. One-letter name change. Who cares. Loser.

Lady smiled and shook her head.

What's wrong with you? she asked.

Nothing wrong with me, he said. Something wrong with Olajuwon's bitch ass. Something wrong with you.

I'm trying to let the bad parts of you go, but you get worse by the day.

Shut up.

Are you gonna have a kid with me? You need to tell me if you're not gonna have a kid with me.

I will. Just not right now. Sorry you don't get everything you want the moment you want it. Act so spoiled sometimes.

She got close to him. Her finger stabbed his chest.

Spoiled? she asked. Who's spoiling me? You're not showering me with diamonds, baby.

I don't take care of you?

Are you doing your best?

He put his hands on his head and squeezed his skull. His throat felt tight.

Am I doing—Wow, okay, you can go fuck yourself.

Thanks for your permission, but I been doing that a while now, she said.

Awesome. Awesome masturbation joke.

Gracias.

No. No de nada to you. You've ruined my Nancy Meats trip. Shut up. Stop poking me.

No, I want to tell you about it. I wait till you leave for work, then go into the living room and turn on *Money Train*. I light candles. Lie on the couch. Fast-forward to when it's New Year's and J.Lo shows up at Wesley Snipes's apartment—

She was in his face, her breath all over him. He could smell the cinnamon with the pork and the Gauchos and she wouldn't stop. He felt overwhelmed. His ears rang. Thunder in his chest. She felt lied to, on a roll.

Quit, Lady, Table said.

—and he is all over her. Handling his business. And I am *jealous*. I love that scene. How he looks. That back. My God. He's so beautiful in that scene. I want to be her so badly when I watch that scene. I want to touch him so badly when I watch that scene.

I'm telling you. Stop right now.

Lady made her voice soft.

Sometimes I'll sort of talk to him on the TV and say You know what, Wesley, you're much prettier than Table, she said.

Quit, he said. No more.

And I'm watching him, and he's affecting me, and my hand goes down, AND I GO. TO. WORK.

Table reared back and her eyes got huge.

What? she screamed.

He brought his fist forward. Solomon's jeans appeared. They hung in the Ranchero between them. Green shards of glass coated the denim like mossed ice. Table smelled chicken. Lady covered her face, moved back, and slammed her head against the window. The biscuits fell. Flakes of cinnamon sleeted out of the box. He stopped before he connected, fist just shy of her nose. She held the back of her head. Her eyes were closed. He blinked. The jeans were gone.

Oh, my God, Lady said. You're so done.

I didn't hit you, Table said.

She slapped him twice.

You damn near did, she screamed.

I didn't, though, he screamed. Calm down.

You hurt me.

You hurt yourself.

You made me hurt myself.

I only lost my head for a sec 'cause you were saying vulgar, hurtful sex stuff trying to rile me up.

This is your fault.

You should have trusted me more to know I would never hit you. I'm a good—I'm a great guy. Probably one of the top ten guys of all time.

Lady's face bent. She looked at the floorboard. The back of her skull thumped. The edges of the pores in her cheeks waved. She held her hands up and shook her head.

That is absolutely, positively the most insane thing I've ever heard and I look forward to telling people you said it.

He got fired on a Thursday, broke the news to her in the backyard. It was summer and roasting, her back soaked and sore from landscaping, pulling weeds. She was worried for him. She was exhausted. His eyes were jittery and red with purses under them and his head seemed longer, stretched out. Table had broken his wrist a few weeks prior and wore an orange cast. There was one signature on it—Lady's. She watched him pace.

Fucking Ignacio, Table said. Little shit said I was stealing quarters.

Were you? Lady asked.

Well, yeah. But not all of them. And he was just guessing. It's a cashbox, you need a key. Could've been anybody with a key.

Who all's got a key?

Me and him.

So, then it obviously has to be you.

No. Not obviously. He's living life. Man about town. Who's to say someone didn't steal his key, or even mine—I make mistakes—make a copy, put the original back before we realized it was gone, and it's them who perpetrated the crime. That could happen easily.

You know, I knew you weren't smart. I knew that after probably two weeks. But I didn't care. I was like No, I love this man. He's dumber than sand but somehow, miraculously, for reasons beyond my comprehension, I love him. Got to say, though— you've outdone yourself.

That's horrible of you to say. He had no evidence, Lady. None.

Well, detective, seems like he did.

It wasn't good evidence, though. No footage. No witnesses. He's just trusting his math more than mine. I know I'm lying, but let's say I'm not. His math is always perfect? He can't forget to carry a one? He trusts himself that much? It's honestly arrogance on his part. Pure, unbridled hubris. You'd think he cured cancer. He needs to look inward. There was no hair or DNA present. I wore gloves and a mask and took care to clean up after myself. I was real careful. He should've trusted me.

I mean clearly he shouldn't've.

Table jumped and made a noise like an elephant. Spit left his lips in splashes. He barreled toward her. She stood, brushed her knees, put her hands in her back pockets. They were mouth to mouth.

Oh, I'm not trustworthy? he asked. You think I'm a liar?

Are you hearing you say the same things I'm hearing you say? she asked.

You would take his side.

She shook her head.

You're embarrassed and trying to pick a fight to take it out on me, she said. No.

She started toward the back door.

Course you just walk off, he said. You don't give a shit about me.

She threw her hands in the air and turned around.

Fine, she said. Quarters? What? Were you going to take me to an arcade? Were we going to play Skee-Ball while the electric company shut off our power?

You think I want to take you anywhere? he asked. I wouldn't take you to the trash. And I would smoke you in Skee-Ball.

Lady clapped her hands and screamed at herself.

You married a fool, Lady. Why did you do that? Why did you marry such a fool?

She stomped inside with Table at her heels. He caught up to her in the living room, grabbed her shoulder.

Don't you dare touch me, Lady said. Your yucky little hands.

Don't call me a fool, Table said. I'm real smart.

I don't got a clue how to talk to you right now, but you better figure this out. Fixing the car's stretching us as it is.

Don't be telling me what to do.

Don't be a baby and I won't feel like I have to.

Suck my dick.

Suck your own dick, dipshit. Sprain your neck again.

I swear to God, Lady. Stop teasing me. I'm not playing around. I've had enough.

Fuck off. Get a job.

This time, for the first time, he hit her.

VELVET HALF-ZIP

PRISCILLA SAW NO REASON to rush her cigarette. It was 7:06. He'd said seven. There's a three-minute window past an arrival time where any tardiness can be blamed on a bum watch, so it was effectively 7:03. And as long as she walked in the restaurant sometime in the next two minutes, she would basically only be five minutes late. That's practically a blink, especially if he went to the bathroom at some point. And he probably did, Priscilla thought. People go to the bathroom all the time. Usually before sitting down for a while. Plus, she was giving him an opportunity to explore the menu in private in case he wanted something other than the buffet. It can be hard to look at a menu with other people around. Tablemates commenting what looks good, what looks bad, what's a must, what's a never. It's overwhelming. Sometimes someone makes a snide remark about an entrée she was considering and scares her off ordering it entirely. This was a gift she was giving him. He's lucky she's late. He's lucky she's there at all. She shook her head.

Gross, she whispered. Get over yourself, P. *Forgive my smugness, Lord.*

It was Jed who'd suggested Crystal's. Priscilla had eaten here a few times, alone, before a movie. The restaurant was cafeteria-style à la Luby's, a Golden Corral–esque superbuffet in the same mall as the multiplex. It made it easy. She looked through the window for the shirt he said he'd wear.

I'll keep you posted if I audible, but as of right now, the leader in the clubhouse is this velvet half-zip, Jed said. Crimson. Gold zipper of substantial size. High style. Fly as a bird. I also have long brown hair. What will you wear?

Um . . . pants? Priscilla said. A shirts with pant. I mean a pant with shirts. Wow. A pants with pants. Stop, P.

Patrons waiting for tables blocked half the dining floor, but sections of the scrum were scattered enough to see through. Priscilla scanned the room until she saw the shirt. Or at least it looked like the shirt. She couldn't be sure, but a crimson velvet half-zip is not a white oxford. Highly unlikely there were two in the same restaurant. And he had sounded eager on the phone. Those people are always on time, especially if the thing was their idea. His back was to the door, but his hair was long. She guessed it was him.

He was the nephew of one of her church's youth group workers, a middle-aged bag of flour named Maureen. She had permanent eyeliner, brows so tall and plucked they looked like fun-sized Gateway Arches. Maxi dresses in lunatic geometric prints, fringe jackets, clogs with dogs on them. Maureen helped in the eleventh-/twelfth-grade girls' Sunday school class and had bothered Priscilla about going out with Jed for the last three years. Priscilla had always been able to dodge any concrete plans and would have done so in perpetuity had Maureen not plopped down beside her on the bus on the way to Falls Creek the month before. She made her case again, only this time, she could filibuster. Priscilla couldn't slip away under the guise of helping a seventh-grader memorize scripture, couldn't claim she had to use the restroom or set up donuts or stack chairs. Maureen was off her leash, had Priscilla up a tree, and would not stop barking.

I just think you're sweet as all heck and God has always had it on my heart y'all would be great together.

Priscilla loathed confrontation and avoided it whenever possible. She didn't like disappointing people, didn't like watching a face fall when she told it no. Maureen's Jed overtures were so unappealing, though, she hadn't cared. Only when tears arrived did Priscilla finally cave.

Fine, Mo, Priscilla said. You can give him my number.

Priscilla had thought endlessly about the interaction in the days since, decided God must want her to go out with Jed. There had to be a reason the seat beside her was open, a reason Mo continued to ask. Any remotely normal, emotionally intelligent person would've stopped long ago. Surely there was something larger at work. Priscilla checked her watch, tossed her cigarette, and stretched her neck.

Lord, thank You for today. Help me be kind and listen and keep my mind here. I'm trying to figure out what You want. I get distracted by feelings I don't understand. It's like I'm unsettled or something? Restless? I know I'm happy but sometimes it feels like I'm not. Sometimes it feels like something's missing, even though I know that's impossible. You're all I need. It's just there are days, I walk around, it's like there's a rock in my brain. I don't know. I love You. Amen.

When she got beyond the hostess stand, she saw him more clearly, posted up at a two-seater in the middle of the restaurant. Priscilla checked her reflection in the mirror above the booths. Lanky and rawboned, fingers like straws. Lean muscle, body always fading, as if she led with her knees. Hair beyond black, an ink-sable mix thick and at her shoulders. Pale blue floral-printed jeans. Black Watch blouse. Black-cherry ropers. Dime-sized silver hoops in her ears. He stood when he saw her, smiled huge.

Jed? she asked.

Yeah, he said. Priscilla.

Nice to meet you, she said.

They shook hands. He had the nails of a guitarist who did not use a pick and she hated them. His chestnut hair stopped at his shoulders, manicured blond streaks lining the mane. Biscuit-looking and chunky, a sunburnt cherub. He wore dark-wash Parasucos with orange side stripes and black Docs. White-eyed goggle tan from the Oakley Romeos hanging off the neck of his half-zip. Tiny Tic Tac teeth. Many jewelries. Two leather bands on one wrist, WWJD bracelet on the other. Gold cross in his left ear. A smattering of rings. Three necklaces. One with puka shells, one with the Virgin Mary, and one with JED on a grain of rice. He was a golden retriever/American bulldog mix with a nose for attention and no lips whatsoever. She'd have been more attracted to a box of thumbs.

Thanks for coming, he said. So excited to do this. Date it up.

Same here, she said. And the tardy party must say sorry. Hope you weren't waiting long.

Two minutes. No big.

Priscilla respected the lie. She'd have done the same if the roles were reversed, decided to play along.

Okay, good, she said. Whew. I was worried.

Shoot your worries into the sun, he said. Let the chopper spray. I'm glad you came. Happy to have an opportunity to dine with you. This table okay? We can go booth if you'd rather. I like booths and chairs equally. I was led here. I had no say in the matter.

Chairs are cool.

Well said.

Priscilla hung her purse on the back of her seat and looked at the table. Two menus and two waters, plus salt, pepper, and crackers.

Got you a little agua, he said. Didn't know what you'd want but figured nice to arrive to a beverage.

Thanks, she said. Nice of you.

You look nice. You look pretty.

Thank you. You do too. Handsome.

Well, that's good. It'd be a bummer to be ugly. You live close?

Ish. Everything's kind of close to everything here. Seven minutes from the house to the—I don't know which way you came in, but the movie theater is on the other side of the mall from here. I can go door to door, house to theater, in seven minutes.

Very cool. Figured since I didn't know what kind of food you liked a buffet might be wise. Cover as many bases as possible. Thought about taking you to Chili's 'cause, you know, it rules, but I saw in last month's *Arcadian Man* you're supposed to avoid chains on dates just due to uniqueness. Therefore, Crystal's.

How long was the drive?

Forty-five minutes? Ain't no thang but a chicken wang. I love the road. A wonderful venue for thought.

Priscilla wanted to stand and leave.

We could've met halfway, she said.

She did not mean that at all.

I ain't mind, he said. Next time you can come my way.

The back of her head itched and she scratched it. It was early and miracles happen, but she could not imagine driving to the end of the block to see this guy. She took a drink and looked back at him. He smiled again, opened a pack of saltines.

You said that shirt's velvet? she asked.

Indeed, he said. You like?

He put an entire cracker in his mouth. Crumbs swayed to the ground like ash.

Looks comfortable, she said.

Jed hid his chews with a fist, started nodding.

Oh, wow, he said. Thank you. That means a lot. Fashion's a passion and I like getting dressed. Gives me another outlet for my creativity. Love the jeans, by the way. All that and a bag of fries. I know it's chips, but fries are the superior side.

She pretended to curtsy.

Thank you, she said. Got them at Penney's for a song.

Also, he said, while I'm remembering, wanted to say sorry if Mo was being annoying. She seemed pretty set on us hanging.

She's a big Jed fan.

She's kind of a chore.

Since you said that, I can say I know what you mean.

She was pestering you?

Little bit.

Sorry.

It's okay.

What'd she tell you about me?

That you were a good Christian young man. Musician. Sweet. How'd she sell me?

Just said you were smart and kind, pretty, and took your faith seriously.

Well, I don't know about all that, but that's cool of her. She tried to set you up before?

Few times. Aunty Mo loves love.

Nothing stuck?

No, I got a bunch of girlfriends.

That right?

Eighteen, I think?

She watched him smirk and was surprised to like the joke.

Wow, she said. That's almost nineteen.

Close to twenty, he said.

Must be difficult to keep track.

You don't know the half of it. I got four different Jessicas. No. I don't go on many dates. You?

Very few. Been focused on my relationship with God. What kind of musician are you?

Singer-songwriter. I play me a little guitar.

What genre?

Christian. It's really the ultimate way to spread the gospel.

A dumpy white waiter lumbered up. He was in his mid-forties with a handlebar mustache and severe psoriasis. Name tag: Gene. Favorite dish: ham hock.

Howdy, ma'am, and welcome to the party. Y'all riding with water or getting spicy? We've got mixed drinks listed on the little paper there and virgin options for each. Rebas are $4 all night.

Priscilla ordered Diet Coke and Jed Dr. Pepper. Gene sighed and went away. A little white girl ran by holding a toy space shuttle. She made rocket noises and said Hellooooooooooo Mars. Mom, did you know Mars is called the red planet because of it's red?

Priscilla heard Jed giggle and felt his stare. He was looking to see if she'd laugh too. She would not. If she were alone she'd have rolled her eyes so hard they'd have gotten stuck. The girl seemed neither funny nor adorable and Priscilla was glad she was leaving. She wanted to ask a question before he could say something awful like That's hilarious or You hear that? His chuckle was petering. She had to act. Her mind felt scrambled. The room was loud. Mars girl landed the shuttle beside the register and finally Priscilla had her line. She opened her mouth. It was too late.

That was hilarious, he said. Did you hear—

A server dropped a tray of drinks. The commotion turned the noise up even more. Priscilla had not looked at Jed when he started talking and decided to act like she didn't hear the question. She stared at the spill. Jed was undeterred.

Did you hear what that little girl with the rocket said? Jed asked.

She couldn't ignore him twice, but maybe she could misunderstand in such a way that she could keep the conversation moving. If she gave a little juke and continued on with no explanation, there was a chance she could get him to bail on the topic entirely. She pretended he complimented her.

Oh, she said. That's sweet of you to say. I'll have to see about that. What do you think of all this *Pathfinder* stuff? You watch any of that yesterday? Kind of nuts.

That's the first time on Mars? he asked.

An invisible sigh of extreme relief. Celebration inside, an all-out rager, bullet dodged.

Third, she said. *Viking 1* and 2 in June and September of '76. Guess they kind of fell on either side of the bicentennial. Then yesterday. You catch any of it?

Pieces and bits. Dad had it on. I was mainly in the pool. You watched?

Much as I possibly could. Sometimes I get on these kicks where I get really into space. Fun place to think about. But the way they landed it, they said it was protected by air bags. Whole thing was covered in them.

I don't understand how it gets there. How do they navigate? 'Cause I think it's supposed to be confusing once you're in space 'cause it's nighttime everywhere so feels like it would be easy to, you know, get a little wildered. Obviously initially you're just going straight up but at a certain point they have to turn, don't they?

How's it work? They shoot the thing off and type something into the whatever and it's just like a fancy airplane without passengers? How's it fly all throughout the cosmos and hit nothing? Like, when do you get to stars? When do they show up? 'Cause there's supposed to be a bunch of stuff up there, right? With respect to meteors. Asteroids. Various celestial bodies. Moons and such.

Priscilla looked hard at his face to see if he was joking. She really wanted him to be joking. One of the reasons she didn't like meeting new people was because of the potential for moments like this. She had no idea if she should laugh or answer sincerely. When Viv made a joke, Priscilla knew. How out of it was ole Vegetable Jedley? Was she being unfair? She didn't want to embarrass him. She didn't want to embarrass herself. He broke the silence.

Because when they send people up there, they can converse with them, right? There's a dialogue?

Inside, Priscilla winced.

Yeah, there are coordinates and satellites and instruments helping it get there, she said. Computers. Said there were like three cameras on there.

For sure, for sure, that makes sense, for sure, he said. They find anything? Extraterrestrials? I'm guessing there weren't any creatures scampering about or else we'd have heard by now.

I'm sure they'd keep that from us. There have to be aliens. If we're all there is, that's so depressing.

The Bible doesn't mention aliens once.

It doesn't mention cafeteria-style buffets either but we're sitting in one.

I think it'd be awesome if it was just us. It would mean we were number one. The strongest, coolest, and smartest in all the galaxy. It would mean God did the best on us, which means He tried the hardest on us, which could only mean He loves us the most. Sometimes in movies when aliens are smarter than us, I get mad. Because if God made them smarter, that would mean He loved them more, you know? That they were number one?

If we're number one it's only because we ain't played nobody. Anyway, NASA said they stuck the landing. *Pathfinder*'s shaped like a pyramid and they weren't sure how it'd hit so they gave themselves all this time to get it on its butt once it was actually on the surface. Got to have your feet under you before you can stand, I guess. But the thing came in hot, boom. Slams into the rock. Bounces fifty-some feet in the air three times, tumbling, tumbling, until it finally comes to a rest—and Priscilla tapped the table—upright, perfect, already ready.

That's wild. Mission control was stoked, I bet. You see any fireworks yesterday or were you on Mars all night?

There's a show at the football field every year. Usually watch from the backyard.

We always hang with my cousins on my mom's side. Mo's my dad's sister. Mom's brother, Uncle Toose, has a commercial license. He's got some connect in Little Rock, so he gets these gnarly suckers. Professional grade. We usually do a lot of Roman candle and bottle rocket fights and continued in that tradition yesterday.

He would sometimes slip into language far more formal than the language that preceded it. The flourish had bothered Priscilla at first, some strange attempt to mask his intellectual insecurities, but as time ticked by she found herself not minding as much. Gene brought the drinks.

And are we ordering à la carte or dining via the buffet this evening?

Buffet all the way, Jed said.

Huzzah, Gene said. You'll find the tableware at the maw of the line. Attack when ready. Holler with anything.

A thousand thanks, chancellor, Jed said. And may God bless you. Hard.

Priscilla didn't want to be so judgmental of Jed. He'd been very kind so far. She wanted to give the date a chance to go well. Certain things were facts. He was unattractive. His clothes were ugly and did not fit. If she saw him on the street, she would probably laugh. But she wanted to be better. Looks don't matter. If his heart was in the right place and they had things in common . . . She raised her glass.

I cheers you, Priscilla said.

What? Jed asked.

Just, whatever, cheers.

They touched glasses.

I just didn't understand the words you used, Jed said.

I fumbled them, Priscilla said. I fumbleruski'd them. How's your relationship with God at the moment?

Good good good. Tip-top of the line. Not without its frustrations, not perfect, I am fallible, I bleed, but all in all He and I are stellar. Going through the Beatitudes right now. Getting after it. Felt His spirit in a major way of late. Caused me to focus so much on others, which has been rad.

Blessed are they who mourn, for they will be comforted.

Blessed are the merciful, for they will be shown mercy.

My quiet times have had me in Habakkuk.

Habakkuk. That's one of the tiny ones.

She nodded, held up three fingers.

Three chapters, she said.

Habakkuk, he said. You don't hear a lot about Habakkuk. Habakkuk. Unbelievably fun to say.

Yeah. Habakkuk. Sounds like a camp or a sneeze or something. Habakkuk.

Habakkuk.

Habbakuk. But it's like Habakkuk—have you read it recently? Habakkuk?

Habakkuk's not really one of my go-tos. What happens in it? I usually like the parts of the Bible that make me feel good or if it's funny like that one in Song of Solomon where they call boobs gazelles.

Yeah, I've been meaning to tell you your hair was like a flock of goats, leaping down the slopes of Gilead.

That's what I told my haircut lady. I said I want the goats leaping, Vera. Not flowing. Leaping.

Priscilla subdued her laugh, kept it to a giggle, didn't want him to feel too good.

But Habakkuk, she said. It's basically Habakkuk talking to God being like Why do all these bad things happen? What's the deal? And God's like Dude, Habby, chill. There's a lot of stuff going down that's over your pay grade. I'm above time. Be patient. I got you. At least I think that's what it's about. Sometimes my mind tries to trick me. God loves telling people to be patient. Or sometimes it's like He says it by not saying anything? Like, He implies it through His silence? He'll talk when He's ready? Or maybe He's talking all the time and I'm a bad listener. I don't know, I've just been concentrating on trying to listen only to Him. Trying to make sure I remember everything He's done for me and that I operate in accordance with His will and not my own.

Right, he said. Hard to know what He wants sometimes.

It can be. Some moments He feels distant, but that's my fault.

Think that's normal. I go through that.

It makes me upset with myself.

I'm enraged by my imperfections as well. Scolded them this morning.

I know He's just, but sometimes He don't feel that way. Sometimes it's like I'm battling the entire universe and not winning even though I deserve to.

When I'm closest to Him, I feel real big.

I'm bothered by my vulnerability. I think I gave it to you too early.

Oh. I'm sorry. I wasn't trying to—

No. It's not . . . it's okay. It's not your fault. You did nothing wrong. I'm just not, you know—I don't think you earned it.

I'll work hard to.

I don't want to talk about this anymore. I'd like to talk about something else.

Okay. Um . . . do you like . . . animals?

Do I like animals?

Yeah. Do you like animals?

Yes. I like animals.

That's cool. I'm with you. Animals are sweet. Should we get food?

Let's do it.

Oh, I was trying to tell you before. You missed it. You'll get a kick out of this. This was hilarious. Did you see the little girl that ran by with that space shuttle?

—

She let him pay. Outside, a busker played guitar, something sad she did not know. Neither tipped.

Where are you? Jed asked.

That white one there, she said.

An '86 Mitsubishi Debonair. Pearl white. One hundred eight thousand miles and counting. Viv's husband, Tucson, had an old karate buddy who sold used cars at Buck Fontelli Motors. He hooked it up. Priscilla bought the vehicle with money made working at Flower Heads of Yaya, Cosmic Cattlesauce, and several basketball camps throughout her freshman, sophomore, and junior years of high school. Driven ragged before she got it, the automobile was now in the midst of a renaissance befitting its name, the executive sedan having developed certain suavities under her care, a disheveled elegance.

I'm the red Impala next to you, he said.

Nice dice, she said.

They're musical notes. From the art of music. Would you like to sit in my car and talk?

She rolled her eyes.

So thought out, she said.

I plan nothing, he said.

I'm not kissing you.

Me either. I'm not kissing me either. I'm yucky. I have cooties.

He opened the passenger door and she slid in. The car smelled like rain and was spotless save some change in a cup holder. She rubbed her hands on the dash. He got in.

You got this detailed today, she said.

Yeah, he said.

For the date?

I like stuff clean. Frees up my head.

To think about music.

I'm more than my music.

Gross. What else you think about?

I don't know. My family. The Cardinals. Hunting.

You hunt?

I don't look like I hunt?

Not at all.

How do I look?

Like you work at Claire's.

She looked at him and smiled. He smirked.

Pretty good, he said. I did get my ears pierced there. They did a good job. Made me feel comfortable.

Totally, it's where I buy all my butterfly barrettes.

Priscilla opened the glove box. There was the owner's manual, an unopened hairbrush, and a *Sports Illustrated* from late April of that year, Sunday red Tiger on the cover. Headline: *The New Master*. Priscilla touched the brush.

Is this for your streaming flock of goats? she asked.

Yeah, he said. That's for the goats. It's only break in case of emergency, though. Don't really need it. My hair's naturally lustrous. Looks good whether it's combed or not.

Those highlights aren't natural.

I'm saying lustrousness. Lustrousity. Not a word now, but maybe one day. Regardless, the hair shines whether the blond's there or not.

Liar.

He stuck the key in the ignition and turned it back. The radio clicked on. Garth Brooks, "Two Piña Coladas."

Requests? he asked.

Garth's good, she said.

Garth's all that and a bag of fries. Test passed. You want gum?

No, thank you.

Priscilla bristled at the test comment. The idea she was lucky she gave a certain answer, like she was battling for his affections, was absurd to her. He opened the console and pulled out a pack of Diamond.

I like gum, he said. It freshens me.

She smiled and pointed at him.

You still think you're getting kisses, she said.

I don't know what you're talking about, he said.

Getting the breath right. Worried those onions from the burger have you stinking. Tsk tsk, you glass door. You were trying to flirt on the phone the other day.

It was nighttime.

I remember.

Tuesday.

You were trying to be slick. You weren't good at it.

Please. I'm a five-star flirt, okay, world class.

You're not. You're clumsy.

Do you think it should be called Tuesnight when it's Tuesday night?

No. I think that's stupid.

Has anyone had that idea before?

Probably. Everyone usually just says the same stuff. Doesn't sound like a special idea to me, anyway. I could've come up with it if I wanted to. Honestly, it sounds like a child's idea.

Cool. Do you have dreams?

I never remember them.

No. Life goals. Hopes. Things you want to accomplish.

Do you?

I'm going to be on the radio. I have a band. No Longer Bulls. I'm lead vocals, lead guitarist, and lead songwriter as well. Not sure if you've heard of us. Well, I bet you've *heard* us but maybe not heard *of* us. We're definitely around. More on the cusp of the zeitgeist than the middle but that's where the outlaws live. Played Soup Fest last year. Kepty Barndance. Got forty-five minutes at Yaya Days. Lots of people, like my mom and dad and some of the other guys' parents, a lot of them said we were actually the best musical act there. So we're for sure good. But it can get really political with local venues as far as stage time is concerned. And we're a brash bunch and don't make any apologies about that. I'm not going to kowtow to the powers that be in the name of seniority when I'm the worthier talent. I made a decision last year. I'm kind of through opening for people. So big shows are kind of touch and go, but that's cool. We'll play smaller spaces. Coffee shops, well-chaperoned parties, that sort of thing. We just leave it all out there. It's about Him. It's about Him and the music and connecting with the people. Trying to get our foot in the door at the Yapley in Corder. Would be huge for us. Though I do think my future professionally is as a solo artist.

Ah, so you're a diva. You said it was Christian music? What kind?

How you mean?

I mean are they proper praise and worship songs or more contemporary?

Second one. My influences are like Steven Curtis Chapman, Jars of Clay, Jaci Velasquez. DC Talk, Rebecca St. James, Avalon. Carman was huge for me. Phillips, Craig & Dean. Pretty much anything you hear on KXOJ. I just want to be a vessel for God. I'm very fortunate. The Lord has blessed me with an absolutely nuclear set of pipes. My voice, sophomore year a judge at region-als said it was unassailable with a character all its own. It's actu-ally quite high, but I don't have to go falsetto or anything so it's still a very full sound. I lead worship for the youth group Wednesday nights and some people get mad because I'm not afraid to take a song up an octave or two. I'll play in the clouds, you know? Among the birds. Obviously, precious few in the congregation have the kind of range I do and I get that that's frustrating for them—if I were in their shoes I'd be pissed too, I'd kill myself if I sang like them—but in order for me to sound my best it's just got to be done at that higher octave. If worship's about praising God with our voice, then I'm going to make sure mine sounds as good as possible. He's given me so much. I owe Him my maximum. That's a line from my song "Taking It to the Max." It's how I approach my craft. I am always taking it to the max. Right now, this very moment, I am taking it to the max.

Priscilla pretended to snore and smiled at her joke. Jed was undeterred.

And if my taste is more evolved than theirs, if I trot out a vocal people aren't ready for, that's on them. That's a them thing. Ain't got nothing to do with me. There's plenty of music around town. Go find some you like. I'll be here playing the good kind. The ability to compromise is crucial, but some things are too important to compromise. Do you have dreams?

A diva and a dictator.

Those guys are always failed artists. I'm actually talented. I make the world better. I'll be fine. I'm a star. Do you have dreams?

I'm good at harmonizing. Typically go lower, though.

I'd have guessed that. Do you have dreams?

Yes. Yes. I'd like to be a preacher.

Oh, heck yeah. That's—

I want people to love Him as I do. I just want everyone to feel good and be safe and go to heaven. People need help. They're lonely and sad. If we believe what we believe, then we believe anyone who has not accepted Christ as their Lord and Savior will burn for eternity. Fire lakes. Screaming. Why aren't we evangelizing every moment? Why isn't that our whole life? We have the answers people need. We have to do everything we possibly can. These are good people. They're fallen, yeah, they've done bad things, and they need to do a better job, they need to straighten up, but they deserve a chance to really hear about Him, to know Him. They deserve a shot at perfection same as us. And of course some will say—what'd that girl say to Barkley in *Space Jam*? Be gone, wannabe, be gone. But I have to try. Sometimes I have a hard heart. Sometimes it's real black inside and I hate certain things and people and want nothing to do with them. I don't understand how anyone could even look at them, much less like them, and I pray and ask God to forgive my coldness. I often think about sin and forgiveness, how it all works. Like, say somebody dies at forty-three and they haven't accepted Christ. Someone witnessed to them once, told them about Jesus, and it didn't take. They go to hell, yeah?

As I understand it.

Okay, so then let's say there's another person. This guy lives to be ninety-eight. First ninety-two years of his life he was objectively awful, a deeply broken man. Beat his wife. Lit forest fires. Drove drunk through a red light and ran over an entire youth soccer game. Both teams.

He got them both?

Both. I'm telling you. This old man sucks. He shot pandas. Strangled eagles. Started wars.

Sheesh. This guy's the worst. I don't like what he stands for.

But after all that bad, he's walking through the nursing home one evening and comes up on this little church service in the courtyard.

How's this guy not in jail?

He's not real.

I'm just saying, we've got more than enough to prosecute.

Stay with me. This old guy's tired and it's nice out so he sits on a chair in the back and listens to the sermon. And God softens his heart right there in the courtyard. For the first time in his life he hears the words and understands them, feels them in his soul, and it happens: he sees the light. Takes up his cross. Truly and sincerely. Means every word. Gets baptized at ninety-two. Lives the final six years of his life a selfless, moral man. Where you think he went?

Probably heaven, I guess.

Is that how you'd do it?

It ain't on me. God's got that. Oh wow.

He reached into his back pocket and pulled out a small reporter's notepad.

What's happening? she asked.

I'm writing down God's Got That, he said. Killer song title and would look rad on a shirt. How could it . . . God's got that / He's where it's at / To Him I'm always faithful / I am Jehoshaphat. Bars. Could be, like, first person from Jehoshaphat's perspective? Fourth King of Judah / My father is Asa / Jerusalem good boy / Down with Asherah. Ooooweeee. Jed went and caught a heater.

Never write lyrics in front of me again. This is not the direction the conversation was pointed in and I'm taking the wheel back. Answer the question. Heaven or hell for the old man? Where's he going?

Based off all that info and everything I've learned, seems like old dude would head north.

Do you think it's fair the one guy didn't get to live that long? Who's to say he wouldn't have made the same decision sooner and done even more for the kingdom?

God never said life would be fair.

I understand that, but shouldn't fair be the ideal? Isn't that what we should be striving for? Fairness? What if the person who tells someone about God does a bad job?

What do you mean?

I mean what if they sucked at explaining everything or got something wrong and that was the person's only chance to really hear about Jesus? Or they got it all right but they did it in a boring way or they did it too fast or something, it was confusing? Whose sin is it to hold? The person being witnessed to or the person doing the witnessing?

Jed stared at her for five seconds, held his body like he was about to burp. She scratched her forehead. He rolled his window down and tossed out his gum.

I don't know, he said.

I'm not asking what you know, she said. I'm asking what you think.

I'm not smart enough for all that.

There's no right answer. What do—

I think that's a bunch to think about on a Saturday after dinner. Saturnight.

Thank you for using it in the wild like that.

I feel nasty. Do you smoke?

No. Do you?

Yes.

You can smoke in here if you want. Just open the window.

I'm fine.

Why don't you go be a preacher if you want to be one so bad?

Can't afford school. Seminary's expensive. And shoot, not like churches are falling all over themselves trying to hire lady preachers, whether they've gone to seminary or not. Some of these places, Mary herself would have a hard time getting a word in. They'd try to stick her in the nursery. When's the last woman head pastor you saw in any kind of Protestant, evangelical, Baptist-y church around here?

But you're trying for it anyway.

I'm a tad stubborn.

You could be a children's minister?

What? 'Cause I'm a girl I've got to be a children's minister?

I don't mean it like that. I mean you start there, prove yourself, move your way up.

I don't have the skill set. You have to be so good at telling stories. I'm not good at stories. I get lost, forget what I was saying. Children's ministers are all so joyful too. Don't think I project the right kind of warmth. I also just don't like arts and crafts that much and I get self-conscious if I have to read in front of people or do hand motions while I sing.

Youth pastor?

Never. High schoolers are awful. You know. You were one like five seconds ago.

So were you, grandma.

That's how I know. And now that I finally don't have to be around them all day, I'm going to pick a career where that's the whole job? I'm good. And again, when's the last woman youth minister you saw around here?

You could be a missionary?

For the people led to do that I'm impressed and forever grateful, but that's not me. I don't need to go hunting for lost souls in some far-off place. There's plenty around here. No, I'm sticking local for now. DDU in the fall. Get my basics, live at the house, start saving. Figure it out from there. You know what you'll major in? Or wait, did you say where you're going?

OSU. Don't know on the major. Don't much care, to be honest with you. Maybe business. I've always been unbelievably entrepreneurial. Had a lemonade stand for a week one summer whenever I was like eight. But after college, mark it down. Nashville. Christian radio. And just stack Doves. I'll be rubbing elbows with 4Him.

That'd be wild.

That's cool you want to preach. You always known you wanted to do that? When'd you get baptized?

Oh, we're doing testimonies? Jed. The Pry Guy.

He laughed and put his hands up.

Only if you want to, he said.

No, I'll tell you, she said. I didn't go to church when I was little. Parents weren't into it. They didn't grow up with it. My mom's best friend, Viv, I call her my godmother, she was all about it. Always trying to get us there. Mom never went. Dad took me a couple times. Think he was sort of trying it on, you know? I remember fragments. He wore slacks once. He never wore slacks. Had a hard time finding the songs in the hymnals

because nobody gave us a bulletin so everybody would be singing and Dad would be flipping through like crazy, looking
around, trying to sneak the hymn number off the page of someone close by. But we were a happy family. In my head it was
always lots of laughing and playing. Sometimes I can't remember as much of those days as I want. I wish they'd lasted longer.
There's no good transition. When I was five, I watched my dad
die. He got shot.

Oh, Priscilla, I'm so sorry. I had no—

I know, it's okay. Obviously that changed everything. Mom
had a real hard time. Messed her up. You know how you look at
some people, it's like their eyes have nothing in them? Talked her
into rehab a couple times, got her to a few meetings, but everything was just too much. Dad had people in San Jose, but I'd
never been. Wasn't trying to live with strangers. It was Viv who
kept me safe. Her and her husband, Tucson, they took me in, got
me to church. That's how it happened. They brought me and I
just loved it. We'd go four, five times a week. Tuesday prayer
meetings, Wednesday nights, twice on Sundays. And I was
always listening, reading my Bible, praying. I remember when I
realized I was ready. I was ten. They used to do these Sunday
evening services some summers where there wasn't a sermon,
it was just music. I loved those nights. I remember singing
"Come, Thou Fount of Every Blessing" between Viv and Tucson.
And when I got to those lines Here's my heart, O take and seal
it; Seal it for thy courts above—when I sang that, I meant it so
much. I felt warmer than I'd ever felt and wanted to feel like that
forever. I sat in the pew and shut my eyes, just focused on my
body and my heart and the way it was beating. It was so slow.
And I asked God to save me. Got baptized the next week. Not

sure how much I understood then, but it's been the main focus of my life since, trying to know Him more.

Wow, that's, wow. I'm so sorry again. That's so heartbreaking about your dad. And your mom. Gosh. So, so sorry.

That's okay. Thanks for listening.

Of course. Viv sounds like an amazing person.

Yeah, without her, who knows? Could've got ugly.

Neither said anything for a bit. The parking lot was mostly empty. Priscilla rested her head against the window, played with the frayed pocket of her jeans, wondered if she said too much.

Sorry if that was a lot, Priscilla said.

No, he said. Don't apologize. That's your journey. Each path is different. All are beautiful. I don't think I was a strong enough kid to be able to go through something like that. You must be very strong. But sorry, we don't have to— I'm glad you came. I've had fun.

Yes, she said. You've been a gentleman.

It's my nature.

I've been trying to be a better woman lately.

That's awesome. Me too, but a guy.

That means not lying.

Yeah, lying's bad. Don't do it.

I lied earlier when I said you were handsome. I'm not attracted to you.

The car got quiet. She looked at him. He looked at the radio.

K, he said.

There's more, she said. I'm feeling called to be radically honest with you. While I'm flattered you dressed up for me tonight, I find your whole look to be a little silly.

Silly?

Silly and kind of plastic.

Silly plastics?

There are good things, though. As the night has worn on, you've worked your way back to neutral. Your personality's positive qualities outweigh the negative. I have to block out all the, you know, stuff. The amount of accoutrements overwhelms in a bad, bad way, but I don't think you're ugly.

I'm hot?

No. Neutral. As an overall experience, you're just above neutral.

Do you want to see me again?

No. This will go nowhere.

Please reconsider.

I'm thinking of kissing you.

Wait. This is confusing.

I'm a woman of twists and turns.

Are you for real thinking of kissing me?

Yes. I told you. Radical honesty. Sometimes I don't have as much fun as I should.

I agree wholeheartedly.

Don't start thinking you're cute.

I won't. That's mean, but I won't. I want to kiss you too.

I don't want to be your girlfriend, though. I can't see an us. I'm not feeling you like that.

It's one date. It's only been a few hours.

I can tell. It's easy to tell.

But there's something here. We're getting along.

Just because I'm nice and liked some of your jokes doesn't mean there's something here.

I'm a good guy. I treat people well. I'm always hoping everyone's happy as long as they're not hurting other people. I often stand up for women or small men in public if the situation calls for it.

You need to keep your eyes on the prize, Jed.

Did you lie about other things? Do you really like my shirt?

You're a bad listener. I never said I liked your shirt. I said it looks comfortable.

What about my pants?

I hate your pants. They have racing stripes. Those are for cars, not jeans.

You seem sad. You're one of those sads. You shouldn't be sad. You're all that and a bag of fries. I should write a song about you, about your spirit.

I'm pure of soul and close to God.

He brings me joy.

Me too.

Do you like making out?

I do.

Will you make out with me for fun, please?

Will you remove all your jewelry?

All that I can. This thumb ring's been stuck here since 1993.

I shouldn't kiss you. We're not together and never will be. It's important to not place yourself in tempting situations that could lead to disappointing God.

What I'm suggesting—

Is what?

Light smooching. Fellowship.

She lit a cigarette.

You smoke? he asked.

Again, Jed, hun, you really are a bad listener, she said.

I love my rings. They're my children.

Swing and a miss. I like guys that are hard to figure out. I know everything you're going to say.

What am I going to say?

You're going to ask about my first kiss.

When was it?

I was eleven? So, six years ago. In a garage in the woods during a game of truth or dare. Scooter Bardell. Looking at it now, pretty good kiss.

Thought you just graduated?

Late August b-day. You're eighteen?

Nineteen in two days.

Look at you, old man. Happy early birthday. You having a party?

My parents are throwing me something Saturday. You should come.

You don't have many friends.

I don't think that's what I said.

I know, but it seems like I'm probably right.

You've got a booger right here.

I don't believe you.

It's there.

I refuse to check.

Okay. May I kiss you?

You may.

They kissed slowly. He held her chin with his hand. She touched his knee.

You taste like smoke, he said.

It's the cigarettes, she said.

You're not a good kisser.

Neither are you.

For ten minutes they made out. Their hands did not wander.

His stubble made her mouth red. She leaned back and sneezed into her elbow.

May God bless you so much, he said.

I'm good at singing in general, she said. Not just harmonizing.

Huh? What's that matter?

I wanted you to know. I'm good at singing. Like, I can sing the main part too.

Oh, melodies? Nice. You must not have many friends either. Maybe that's how you could tell I don't.

You didn't offer to pray over dinner tonight.

Neither did you. You want to keep kissing?

She nodded. They kissed harder. Her face was warm. Her chest was light. A burning in her forehead. His eyes were closed. She couldn't smell anything. He sighed. Her feet were numb. His hands were dry. Her cheek twitched. His lips were cold. He touched her stomach. Blood fell from her nose, a red avalanche. She couldn't feel it. It ran down her philtrum and onto their lips. He couldn't feel it either. They kept kissing. Her fingers in his hair. His hand on her thigh. Then the blood hit his tongue. He leaned back and saw her face. She opened her eyes. Her vision was blurred.

Your nose, he said.

What's happening? she asked.

Your nose, he said. Blood is falling from your nose.

The words hit her slowly, hung foggy in her head. He looked made of clouds and sounded like a garbage disposal. She rubbed her eyes and looked at her lap. A grinding somewhere. She heard elephants. Her vision cleared. He came into focus. Blood on his mouth. She gasped and touched her face. Blood on her hands. Blood on the Impala. Blood on her jeans.

Oh, no, she said. My blood's on you. Oh, no no no. My blood's on you. I'm so sorry.

It's okay, he said. I get them too.

My blood's on you.

It's okay. Tilt your head back.

Wait. Why aren't you mad? My blood's in your mouth. You should be mad.

What?

You're being weird. Why aren't you mad? My blood's in your mouth. You should be so mad.

Pris—

My blood's in your mouth. It's not supposed to be there. It's supposed to be in my body. I'd be furious if your blood was in my mouth. Why aren't you mad?

It was an accident. You didn't—

I hate my body. Stupid chunk of meat. How's this happen? *I can't have any fun?* I have to go.

She got out. Jed grabbed tissues from the middle console and set them on the passenger seat.

Wait, wait, wait, he said. It's okay. Don't leave. Take these.

You should be mad, she said. Why aren't you mad?

It really is fine. Don't worry about it.

Thank you for a nice evening.

Priscilla, please, it's cool. It's okay.

I'm a good person. Please don't tell Mo. I'm so sorry. I'm so sorry I bled on you.

Priscilla took the tissues and shut the door, could barely hear him say I like you so much, please don't go.

CAINRAISER

LADY WOULD LEAVE THE CLASSIFIEDS on the toilet, high-light jobs she thought he'd like. Table wouldn't look. He suc-cumbed to the funk. The money dwindled. Their water heater broke and they had to get a new one. Sonic closed for two weeks to remodel. Shortly after reopening, Lady stepped weird off a curb and rolled her ankle hard. She couldn't put any weight on it for a few days, couldn't work for a week, and limped for a month. Things got dire enough that when they ran out of toilet paper, Table went to the Ox Convention Center to steal more. New Light Baptist Church held their traditional service in the main auditorium on Sunday mornings and the entire concourse level was open and almost completely empty during the sermon. He tiptoed into every men's bathroom, emptied a few stalls of their TP, and stuffed the rolls into a green duffel. When he fin-ished, he went to the auditorium to rest. He sat upper level in the middle of an empty row. His neck hurt. His hands hurt. His back hurt. He felt dominated, didn't want to get to this point again. The preacher was white and a wispy forty-something. A hair taller than the pulpit with a face like a meerkat and a voice like an auctioneer. His yellow hair went to his shoulders and his goatee shone gold. He got after it.

And so you come to me, you say Brother Rufus, I'm hurting. Please, give me guidance. What's the Lord say about the hard times? Well, first, I'd lay hands on you. Pray with vigor. Tell you you're loved. Because here's the truth: you are. So much. Then I'd give you the word of the Lord. I'd say, from memory, Isaiah 43:2. King Jim's version says: When thou passest through the waters, I will be with thee; and through the rivers, they shall not over-flow thee: when thou walkest through the fire, thou shalt not be burned; neither shall the flame kindle upon thee. Verse out. Y'all will be like those stunt guys they set on fire for the movies but then they wind up, you know, it's cool, they're all good. They walked through fire. They were not destroyed. Top to bottom, Keds to heads, unscathed. My brother slash sister in Christ, the Lord is with you. Rejoice! God is always at your side. Loving you. Holding you. Then I would say—again, without consulting my Bible, I have this memorized—Romans 8:18. For I reckon that the sufferings of this present time are not worthy to be compared with the glory which shall be received in us. Verse out. I want every eye. Do you understand what I'm saying? Pain's temporary, y'all. It has an end. And when our lives are over, we'll ride into Paradise and nothing will hurt again. Bow heads. Prepare hearts. Father—

Table heard none of this. He was looking at a mural some twenty feet wide and ten feet tall on the far side of the auditorium. Wild mustangs sprinted away from a thunderstorm. White bolts of lightning dove jagged from clouds. The painting made Table feel cold and he did not know why. Brother Rufus shouted the name of Jesus. Table looked back at the stage, the pastor on his knees.

—because we are sinners, Lord. We are nothing without You. I want everyone to look around the room. Yes, I give you permission to open your eyes during a prayer. Gasp. Pastor's being weird. Move on from it. We linger on weirdness too much as a society. What's normal to one is odd to the other. Let the strange be strange. They ain't hurting you none. For instance, I sometimes like to eat chips and salsa in the bath—

Table heard music, "Jesus Was a Capricorn." He looked around. There were no musicians onstage. No one else seemed to notice. He stretched his neck and looked again at the painting. The horses smiled at him. He flinched. The song got louder, made his arms shake. He palmed the back of his head. His face was cold. His chest hurt. He felt far away and looked at the ground. His right shoe was untied. He was too tired to reach down. There was the sensation of a chair crashing against his back and he turned to find nothing there. A stinging in his ribs and the music stopped. There was Solomon on the ground and his daughter beside him and the blood and glass like blades of bright grass. Lately, Table felt a constant gnawing inside, like someone was brushing his nerves with sandpaper. An overflow of worry filled him, an anxiousness about his entire life. This sometimes led to stillness. He wouldn't know what to do so he wouldn't do anything. He'd sit and stare. Usually at the floor but sometimes a door or a tree or a wall.

—hold you accountable. Keep looking around the room. Every person you see's done so much wrong. They're a sinner. Look at them over there, sinning it up. They're sinning it up! No, we can joke and have fun. Y'all know I like to raise a little Cain. Your boy's a Cainraiser. Jesus had a great sense of humor too. He was actually a wonderful physical comedian. Quick example I've always found fun. We know of Thomas, do we not? That Doubtsman. From King Jimmy's version, John chapter 20, when news of the Resurrection reached him, Tommy said Except shall I see in his hands the print of the nails, and put my finger into the print of the nails, and thrust my hand into his side, I will not believe. And when the Lord did appear and Ole Tombone stood before his redeemer, Jesus said to him Reach hither thy finger and behold my hands; and reach hither thy hand, and thrust it into my side: and be not faithless, but believing. And friends the good book is canon and written on its walls are every truth the world has to offer, but in my studies on religion and philosophy and academia I have come across texts, scrolls, etchings, various

correspondence from the day which say—and these are corrobo-
rated reports from multiple sources, learned men of reason for
whom honesty was the only option—these texts say when
Thomas did reach his hand into the Lord, Jesus at once closed the
wound and trapped Tom's hand inside. You can imagine the
scene. Pandemonium. Thomas is freaking out, wrist deep in
Jesus's ribs, God's only begotten son and the rest of His disciples
hooting and hollering. Thomas is screaming Get it out! Get it
out! Get it out! And then the Messiah, His voice even louder:
Hey, Thomas, give me a hand with this? Getting back to it, I joke
because I'm joyful and I'm joyful because I know my soul's safe.
I've been redeemed. See, I'm joyful in the Lord. I want to say it
louder and slower. I want it to sink into your hearts. I'm joyful in
the Lord. I walk with Him in my pasture each morning and we
swap stories over coffee. I tell him Thank you, Lord, thank you.
He says I love you, Roof, love you. Keep looking around the room.
You may be staring at somebody with whom you have a real
problem. You may find that person conniving, a big fat dud.
Well, lemme tell you something, friend, you ain't perfect neither and Jesus died for them same as you. He died for everyone.
He loves us so much. I'm starting the altar call right now. We
break away from the bulletin. I promise: living free feels good. If
you've not yet accepted Christ as your Lord and Savior, come.
He's waiting. I speak this way because of the passion that exists
within me. The Lord placed it there. It is good. Some of y'all
don't want to rock your own boat. Hey, rock your boat. Capsize
it. Let the sea bury it. Nothing good comes without sacrifice.
Ain't no boats in heaven. The lakes are in hell. What's a ship to
an angel? We'll have wings. I'm going to ask Brother Lee,
Brother Guy, and Brother Gooch to join me here at the altar. We

have people ready to talk to you, ready to love you. I love you. I want to dine with you in heaven. I want to sing with you in heaven. I want to dance with you in heaven. And I know this is the traditional service, but when the spirit moves, so do I.

Brother Rufus breakdanced to silence. He spun on his head and screamed Let's goooo.

The congregation watched quietly. The pastor was athletic, moved with grace. He toprocked and windmilled beside the pulpit. Table checked his watch and realized he had to get back, take Lady to work. He stood and moved quickly. Brother Rufus C-walked. Table was near the end of the row. Brother Rufus did the worm. Table started laughing.

Look at that little fucker go, he said.

Then Table stepped on his untied shoelace, screamed the word *shit*, and fell down the stairs. The entire congregation turned and looked. Table lay in a heap at the base of the steps. He moaned until a woman kicked him.

Their spending habits got tighter. Table hung around the house, talked about trying various things, did little. Lady left Sonic and took a job as a waitress at a sit-down Tex-Mex place in Ox called El Burro. She was good at it, got to work nights, weekends, made more money. It wasn't enough. Their refrigerator died and they had to get a new one. Table fell asleep with the bathwater running and flooded the hall. The carpet didn't dry properly. It started to mold. That had to be replaced. Table got the flu and gave it to Lady. She missed another week of work. An old coworker of Lady's gave Table a job clearing brush but he got in a fight with the guy the third day over whether you could win a Super Bowl with Quincy Carter as your quarterback and got fired. Table felt like you absolutely could. The guy disagreed. They started screaming at each other. Table called him racist. The guy called Table Shithead. Table called him a dumbass pussy ass panda ass bitch. And the guy hit him in the face with a two-by-four.

One night, Lady sat in the Ranchero and stared at their front door. It was 11:47 p.m. The saddle was hard under her, offered no comfort, made her back ache. She smelled like old fajitas and her shoulders hurt. Blister on her inner thigh from her jeans. Bruise on her arm from Table. She put her head in her hands and sighed. Every light in the house was on.

The saddle was so impractical, she said.

She went inside and hollered for him. No answer. She searched the house, slapped at the switches, and turned out the lights. He wasn't inside. She looked in the backyard. He was there, in a chair, in the dark. She pressed the bruise and opened the back door. He turned and raised a beer.

There she is, he said. How was work?

Fine, she said. What're you doing?

Sitting. Want to sit with?

Why were all the lights on?

What?

Every light in the house was on.

Talking about that Trace Adkins song?

No. When I got home just now, literally every light was on. We can't afford to have them on when we're not using them. We talked about this.

Table looked at the house, then back to her.

Oh shit, babe, I'm sorry, he said. You're right. I totally forgot. I won't do it again.

You've got to be thinking about this stuff. I can't be the only one.

I know. I really am sorry. I swear. It won't happen again.

She knew it would. He'd try hard while the new task was at the front of his mind. But days would pass and other things would pop up and he'd forget again and the cycle would repeat. She didn't want to be this cynical about him, but she couldn't help it. He was too susceptible to distraction. She looked at him there in the yard and wished he were stronger. His head beat him too much and he was quick to give up. Sometimes he knew he was lying. This wasn't one of them. Her face was cold. She put her hands on her knees.

Please help, she said. It's so much to worry about.

I understand. I'm sorry.

You make me feel so alone sometimes.

Table stood and brought her to the chair, held her. She curled into him. Her head was on his chest. He felt like he'd contained the situation and was proud of himself. He was being a stand-up guy, taking responsibility for his actions, swearing to change. And he was there for her, a pillar of strength and integrity. A grove of Flame Amur maples thrived across the creek, looked maroon in the dark. He wished he hadn't made her sad but thought in some ways this could be a breakthrough for them. He stared at the trees and kissed her cheek. Her cheek was wet. She pressed the bruise again. He kissed her hands. She wanted him to say something that made her feel taken care of.

I'm sorry, baby, he said. I don't like seeing you hurting. I love you.

We need you to get something, she said.

You're right. I will. I promise.

Okay.

You said it was a good day, though?

Said it was fine.

What happened?

Nothing. It was just fine. That's why I said it was fine. Wasn't good. Wasn't bad. It was fine. Been hard to have good days lately.

Well, I'm sorry to hear that.

You been knowing that.

Her body stiffened and her weight shifted forward. She hated when he acted surprised by something he already knew. He tried to lift her chin and she swung her face away. She didn't want to fight. She wanted to go to bed. Grinding in her temples. She looked at the creek.

Hey, he said. I said it won't happen again. I promise. I'll be a good boy from here on out.

She wouldn't look at him.

Hey, he said. I really am sorry.

Okay, she said. Let's move on. I'm t—

I love you.

I love you too. I want to get up.

She did. There was no energy in her face and her head felt heavy. Leaves slid across the yard. The Amurs leaned. She didn't move. Table wanted to say something that would put her at ease, show her he was responsible, emotionally intelligent. Her eyes stayed away, stared at the grass to the left of the chair. He looked down. There was nothing there.

They let you eat? Table asked. If not, I got a plate for you in the what's it called . . . And I was looking, just trying to be forward thinking, we'll be fine. We can stretch the casserole another couple days, long as we're smart. Plus, we still got the chips and all that. Should be paid up on shit by Monday if you have just a normal weekend. Then we're back in the black and rising.

Lady put her face in her hands and her shoulders sunk. She rubbed her eyes. Her nose burned. Her face stung. She flexed her quads without realizing and looked up.

What a chore you are, she said. Goddamn . . . errand.

What? he asked.

Your ears are just for decoration, huh?

She started toward the house. Table watched her. The grass was black. Her feet dented it. His mouth was open. His eyebrows were down. There was a tingling in his head and he looked at his feet. His chest hurt. He stood on concrete. Solomon was dead, his daughter beside him. Her eyes were red. Her eyes were yellow. Lady was at the back door. Her head was tight.

Fade, she said.

Table looked up.

What? he asked.

She stepped inside. The doorway framed her and the edges of her seemed to fray. Clouds passed over the moon. He could not see her face. She licked her lips. Her lips were cold. She pressed the bruise again.

You got me fading away, she said.

RITAS AT SILKHAVEN

SILKHAVEN LOUNGED on thirty-three acres of pristine Missouri woodland forty-five minutes west of downtown St. Louis, the surrounding countryside restful, mellow, lush. After two decades in the city, Roxanne and Methuselah Silk had grown sick of the steel, decided they wanted a little less bustle, a little more space. They knew the moment they saw the land, bought it on the spot. Designed in 1973 by American architect E. Fay Jones, the main house was constructed from 1974 to 1976. The Silks moved in July 5, 1976, a day after the two-hundredth anniversary of the adoption of the Declaration of Independence. Redd Foxx was at the housewarming, Phyllis Diller, Yogi Berra. They swilled Buds from cardinal-shaped goblets and roasted Dan Dierdorf until he cried.

It was five minutes from the entry gate to the main house, the road painted imperial red. Table had dozed off on the way up and was still snoozing. Lady took the curves slowly, tried not to jostle. The redtop wound through black oaks. It was a Technicolor autumn. Bright musclewood and eastern wahoo and bald cypress thick in the forest. Leaves of tiger and raspberry and honey, the Ranchero in shadows, until at last the wood opened and Silkhaven was there. Lady hit the brakes with her jaw dragging. The estate bloomed out of the side of a hill at the far end of the clearing. A ten-bedroom, twelve-bath, two-story behemoth. Forty-one thousand square feet and shaped like a horseshoe. A super-charged Prairie-style, ultra-Usonian remix constructed from native sandstone, agate, and the surrounding oak. She drove past stables and tennis courts, a helipad and giraffe enclosure. Retired Budweiser Clydesdales the size of Silverados grazed in the pastures. There was a pond, infinity pool, two putting greens, and a full-scale pink granite sculpture of a carousel. She couldn't believe it. He wasn't lying.

This was her inaugural trip to Silkhaven, but she'd hung with Methuselah before, been around him a few times. She enjoyed his company, thought he was out-there but fun. He was exceedingly kind to her and took every opportunity to put Table in his place, both big-time pluses from her perspective, but it had always been impossible to gauge just how real the money was. Paying for dinners does not a tycoon make.

They first met at a minor league baseball game, AAA, Oklahoma City 89ers vs. New Orleans Zephyrs. Lady and Table drove up for their first anniversary and Methuselah came down to party along. They sat general admission, drank too much, and hurled annoyances at Zephyrs left fielder Turner Ward. Ward was down on assignment from the Milwaukee Brewers and under fire all night.

Table: Ever danced with the Devil in the pale moonlight?

Methuselah: Are you on fire for Christ this evening?

Lady: When did you first know you loved me?

Methuselah got so drunk that by the middle of the sixth he was shirtless in the aisle double-fisting soft pretzels and dancing to "Sabotage." By the top of the eighth he was standing in his seat screaming. His voice boomed.

Waaaaaaaarrrrd. Goooooooouuuuuuuuurrrrd. Watch me rouse the rabble, you unrighteous beast. My bed's a Vladimir Kagan. My desk an Eileen Gray. Your dick's like uncooked bacon. My chairs are Jean Prouvé. Yes, I am Gaia the Earth Goddess. Look at my breasts. Teats galore. These feed the world. Hoo hoo hoo.

The Silkhaven trip was for Table's forty-sixth birthday. He'd wanted to spend it with Methuselah, asked if he'd be up for it. Methuselah said Yes, if you come to me. When Table brought the idea to Lady, she said We can't afford a trip to St. Louis. She only agreed when he told her Methuselah offered to foot the bill for gas and let them stay at Silkhaven.

Table never explicitly said so, but Lady knew the main purpose of the trip was to ask Methuselah for money. It wasn't that he didn't enjoy his uncle. He seemed to genuinely get a kick out of him, sometimes it even seemed like he admired him, but Table wasn't the type to initiate anything he had to plan. She didn't know how he'd do it, if he'd want her there for backup or not, but he would definitely ask. He was too lazy not to. Regardless, whatever happened, it would be obvious when he got his answer. If Table was bothered, people knew. His face was disloyal. He telegraphed his emotions like a soap star, was far more transparent than he realized. Her guess was he'd ask when she wasn't around. It wasn't his way to set himself up for public embarrassment. He was far too insecure. As for when it would go down, Table was historically impatient. He wouldn't ask right upon arrival, but after that, it could come at any moment. Might wait until Sunday, might ask that night. He was desperate and capable of anything. All behaviors were on the table. She hoped, for Methuselah's sake, Table would wait until later in the weekend, but anything was in play.

Lady had no idea what Methuselah's answer would be. After seeing just this much of the property, no doubt there was money to spare, but she wasn't certain he was a definite yes. How could he be? Table had surely asked for money before, most likely more than once. Just because Methuselah might have helped on those occasions, that didn't make it automatic he'd help now. It would almost make it less likely. And if he said no last time, why would he say yes now? They were close to the house. Table was still asleep. She popped him in the chest with the back of her hand. He opened his eyes.

Hey there, slumber bunny, she said. We're here.

He sat up and looked around.

I'm losing my mind, Lady said. This place is insane.

Told you he was loaded, Table said.

He has a giraffe.

What? Table asked.

He looked out the window.

Holy shit, he said. I didn't know about the giraffe. That's new.

Yeah, 'cause giraffe loaded's a whole other ball game. Regular loaded's, like, heated seats in the Rover. Giraffe loaded is, like, Hey cool car. Check out my fucking giraffe.

A copper roof spilled beyond the edges of the house into cantilevered overhangs ornate with trumpet honeysuckle, these tubular flowers, Day-Glo blooms. Candy-red, yellow-throated megaphones. The driveway doubled as a courtyard with a small fountain in the middle. Lady parked beside the water and a young white woman in a green pantsuit opened the front door. She waved, hinted at a smile. Lady rolled her window down. The woman spoke first.

Salutations and osculations, Mr. and Mrs. Table. Welcome to Silkhaven. Your uncle regrets he's unable to greet you in person. A prior engagement ran longer than intended. He's asked I extend the warmest of happy birthdays and escort you to the veranda for refreshments. You may luxuriate there until his return. Right this way.

She led them around the side of the house to a colossal teak table with a tray of watermelon, two margaritas, and a pitcher of refills. They grabbed their respective glasses and turned to thank her. She was gone. Table reclined on a chaise near the edge of the porch, looked out on the property.

What'd she say her name was? Liza?

She didn't say.

It's probably Liza.

She's too tall to be a Liza.

There was a screen door to Lady's right. She pushed it open and slipped inside. It was the living room. There were stained glass clerestories and stained glass skylights, a Schimmel Pegasus grand, and a painting—a 1921 Onderdonk original: *Mountain Pinks in Bloom, Medina Lake, Southwest Texas.* Under the art and built into the wall was an orange-cushioned couch opposite caramel leather sitting chairs and a silver bookshelf made from old aluminum bleachers. The floor was the same sandstone as the rest of the house, grand Turkish rugs and the late afternoon sun warming the rock. There was a sycamore lamp like a mutant pink coneflower and a block coffee table made of one-inch Murano glass tiles, each square the same blue—a brilliant cobalt with fused silver and threads of navy—the whole thing about the size of a storage trunk. On top were two framed photos and the same wooden mallard Table had at the Palazzo. One picture was of Methuselah with two men, one Black, one white. They were dressed like musketeers with straight-bladed swords and flintlock pistols. Their arms were around each other. They laughed with their eyes closed. The other photo was of a young Roxanne. She rode horseback in the Peruvian Amazon, reins in one hand, beer and a cigarette in the other. Smoke left her mouth and she mean-mugged a parrot.

On the far wall were sculptures by the late Missourian artist Donald Judd, two of his famed stacks. They bracketed the fireplace, vertical columns of identical, evenly spaced boxes, six by twenty-seven by twenty-four inches, jutting from the elm wall and climbing to the ceiling, ladders without rails. Ten in each stack.

The boxes on the left had brass sides, the tops and bottoms translucent violet Plexiglas. The boxes on the right had amber Plexiglas sides, the tops and bottoms stainless steel. They basked in their respective spotlights, glowed polished, their colors and shadows filling the wall. Lady wanted to stare at them all day.

Lady, Table said.

He was at the door. She didn't hear him, just stared at the stacks.

Lady.

Still nothing but stacks. He clapped and raised his voice.

Lady.

She turned.

Nice, right? he asked.

She went back outside.

Never seen nothing like it, she said. Nicest place I've ever been. Kind of messing me up a little bit. I just didn't know. Wasn't sure. 'Cause sometimes you . . . you know, you lie. I just didn't know he had it like this. Place is so fancy it makes me nervous. Worried I'll break something.

Won't happen, he said. I can tell. I have this feeling way down deep. This trip's only good. There's no bad here.

Once you've gotten off your ass and we have actual spending money, we should get some art around the house. Paintings or something. A sculpture.

Of what?

I don't know. Something pretty.

Me?

You're more scarecrow than sculpture.

I bet I'd be great at painting. Like, if I knew how, I bet I'd paint some crazy powerful shit.

You have got to start saying sentences in your head before you say them out loud.

They heard the chortle first. It waddled around the corner with a garble and a cough, Methuselah almost there, tickled about something. Three seconds later he appeared wiping his eyes with his biceps and shaking his head. Cordless phone in one hand, margarita in the other. Methuselah was bull-necked and well haunched, big-time stubby, a block with rounded edges. His fingers were potbellied and his palms were like burger buns. He wore the U.S.'s team shirt for the '99 Ryder Cup and olive plus fours, argyled cankles thick and on display. The polo was burgundy with a beige collar and sleeve cuffs, covered in sepia pictures of American champions from decades past. His sunglasses were gold-lensed Gargoyles Classics and sneakers gray Velcro. They were the only shoes he wore. He bought them in bulk, went through a pair a month.

Methuselah had a lowing bray of a voice. A jolly smoker's moo. Small sacks of gravel in his cheeks that rattled when he laughed. Sometimes it sounded like it hurt to speak, but he couldn't help himself. He spoke like he was addressing a much larger, hearing-impaired crowd, as if he were in a play, unmic'd in some monstrous auditorium, using his whole being to pound the back of the room with every word. He presented his sentences. They were for everyone. He talked for fun.

Hoo hoo hoo, Meth said. Wolfy, you are en fuego. Terrific. Terrific. Chuckles with a confidant. The good stuff. Ah, and there is my shitheel nephew and his lovely wife. Refreshments in hand. Yes, the ritas will be flowing. Jubilation is imminent. As are tomorrow's headaches. Hoo hoo hoo. I had to bring out the flames too. Couldn't sit by and let you take all the laughs for yourself.

For now I must take my leave, but I shall speak with you soon, compadre. Our bond matters much, Shankapotomus. Treesus. Farewell, you crumb. Stay out of the cabbage!

Methuselah dropped the phone where he stood. It clapped hard off the wood and the rechargeable battery slid across the veranda. He held his arms out.

My Sylvia, he said. Happiest of birthdays, young man. Come and embrace me. Come give love to Uncle. Sound the alarm. Birthday love in store.

Table stood and they hugged.

Birthday love, Methuselah said. Birthday love.

Lady caught a blur in the corner of her eye, swung her head around in time to see the woman in the green suit disappear around the corner. The ground was clean, the phone and battery gone.

What's going down, Unc? Table asked. Appreciate you having us.

I forbid you to mention it, Methuselah said. Say any more and I'll have you shot. Instead, tell me, is there still shit upon your heels?

Methuselah burst out laughing, the chortle in full effect, body jiggling, a subwoofer come to life. The stroke made him stand like he was bracing for something, his left leg making up for his right. Before, he'd been spry in a used-to-play-fullback kind of way— thunderous thighs, twinkling toes, et cetera. Looking at him now, he didn't look slow exactly. More taking his time. He'd lost a step and clearly *something* had happened, but she'd expected him to look much worse based on Table's report. She'd expected decrepit. Lady felt disoriented and spread out, her thinking clouded, choppy. He'd told the truth about Methuselah having money. That was clear. But this was not a man hanging on. Methuselah shoved Table and hugged her.

And Our Lady of Perpetual Parties, Methuselah said. My darling girl. Ecstatic to see you. How's my niece?

I'm good, Meth, Lady said. Thanks so much for having us. Your home is unreal. Stunning. I can't get over it. You have a giraffe.

Yes, Silkhaven is a shrine to the sublime, Methuselah said. Towering achievement. Golden goose. How things should be. Cleopatra is a recent addition. Isn't she divine? Are you familiar with the American entertainer Wayne Newton? He's a great man with an angel's voice who, much to my good fortune, vastly underestimated the Broncos this past season. Every time I look at Cleopatra, I say a thousand huzzahs to Terrell Davis and that Denver offensive line. How was your voyage?

Oh, great, Lady said. Ole shit-for-heels here slept damn near the whole way. Didn't have to talk to him once. Was wonderful.

Methuselah threw his head back with laughter. Bass drum guffaws, hollering with glee.

She comes bearing arms, Methuselah said. Hoo hoo hoo. Lady, 1. Sylvia, 0. Terrific. Terrific.

How about you, though? Lady asked. You're looking svelte. Recovery must be going well. How are you feeling?

Oh, pretty as a picture, stubborn as a mule, Methuselah said. Slow going, but the white coats are pleased with the progress. Feeling very blessed. Blessed, but a smidge pongy at the moment, I'm afraid. Stinky boy, stinky boy. I've the course on me. I must divest myself of my knickerbockers and sportsman's top. Allow me fifteen minutes to perform my absolutions, make my toilet, become clean. After that I'll be ready for a chair, a refill, perhaps a story? Has he shown you the lagoon?

—

Neptune's Lagoon was a domed indoor pool decorated in the same cobalt tile as Methuselah's coffee table. The bright blue covered the sides and bottom of the pool, the floors and walls and doors. Only the ceiling was different. Deep black mosaic tiles with fused gold. Metagalactic space among them. Whirls of blues and reds and purples and oranges and splashes of stars among the colors and clouds of cosmic dust moved across the void. Neptune's moons surrounded the water. Fourteen, all pink marble, hand-carved by the reclusive sculptor Henri Cadieux in Biarritz, France. The pool itself was eighty-two feet long, forty-one feet wide, and doubled as a hot tub. There were jets in the walls and built-in benches in the corners. Wicker chairs poolside. They sat and drank and looked at stars.

Lady was reeling. Every new thing she saw was nicer than the last. It wasn't that she never thought she'd be somewhere like this; she didn't know places like this existed, didn't know it was possible to live this way, not in real life. Silkhaven made the world bigger. There was a feeling in her stomach that felt foreign, emotions cropping up she could not place. She was bewildered and excited and guarded and uneasy. Part of her wanted to say something about Methuselah looking so healthy. Part of her thought it was the wrong time. Table sat across from her looking distracted, in his thoughts. She knew he was thinking about Methuselah, how good he looked, how present. Salt and doubt on Table's face. Grains from the margarita clung to his mustache. Lady brushed them away, flicked his bottom lip. The door opened. Methuselah frolicked into the room carrying a refill and another pitcher.

The ritas are ready for prime time and so am I, Methuselah said.

Blood-orange terry cloth cabana shirt with matching shorts. Same sunglasses as before, plasma mirrored lenses. Methuselah danced as he walked, sneakers squealing on the tile. He refilled their glasses, leaned against the nearest moon, and pointed at his face.

Stepped on my last pair of regulars last night, Methuselah said. Fell asleep reading my diary and they slid off, landed in the floor. Round about one, my bladder woke me. Put my feet on the ground and crunch. You wouldn't believe how much it happens. Fortunately, my Gargoyles are prescription, so they can hold the fort until reinforcements arrive. Now then. Lady Lady, I wish to tell you of the lagoon's inspiration. May I?

Please.

I was in Los Angeles on business with the day off and nothing to do. It's depressing to admit I cannot now recall the exact year, but it was sometime middle of the last decade. Sylvia knows this, but any time I went out west I liked to get a bit naughty with my vehicles. This particular trip I'd secured the new Testarossa. Rosso corsa. Roaring Raris. No one calls them that but me. It will catch on one day. But that red, I simply cannot get enough. Virtues are important and vices doubly so. But as you can imagine, on these trips I was always hunting for reasons to drive. And with twenty-four hours all to my lonesome I decided, you know what? I'm having fun today. I'm going to Disneyland. And I did. I screamed south in that Testarossa looking for magic. Had one of the worst days of my life. Got a ticket on the way. My charms eluded the officer, a small, pathetic hamster-man who smelled like potato salad. Officer Dan Lawns. To this day, the biggest coward I've ever met. I hope to one day cheer at his funeral. Once inside the park it rained most of the day. One of the dry hours I spent in line for Space Mountain, which proceeded to get shut down for maintenance when I was but five riders from the front. The Matterhorn I did not like. The yeti was very scary and I ralphed my breakfast upon the platform at the ride's conclusion. Got stuck on It's a Small World for forty-five minutes because some teenager thought it would be funny to stand and pee out of the boat and accidentally fell in. Serves her right, but forty-five minutes is a long time to hear that song. Can it really not turn off? Is there no switch? Clearly there was at least one. Where are the others? Later I got turned around and found myself in the middle of the Main Street Electrical Parade. Park security accosted me, claimed I was up to something illicit, took me to their headquarters for questioning. I requested they go fuck themselves. Confusion is no crime. The only unadulterated positives during my visit were the three churros I ate while waiting in line for the Dumbos. But even then I dealt with stares. Judgmental ogles. How dare an adult enjoy themselves! How dare an adult have fun! What a freak! Let's all make him feel less than. Come now, everyone, let's all stare at him. I paid to get into the park same as them. And I'll remember the experience. Their children won't. Their children are stupid. And ugly. And weak. The vast majority are gutless and start crying in the middle of the rides anyways. Why are we catering to them? My good time matters more than theirs. I'm much closer to death. After the elephants, I'd had enough. The day had been a nonstop palooza of disappointments and I was ready for it to end. I got into that Testarossa dejected and without the juice. My usual sunshine, this star you see here, madame, night had fallen on Methuselah. I tooled around Anaheim like I was driving a hearse. In a bad mood, woe is me, wishing I'd made different choices. And then something happened, something extraordinary. The churros returned. My sweet treats, my only allies for the day, turned on me. And just as I had earlier, they were screaming south. Now, it was late late and nothing was open. I whipped into the closest parking lot I could find. Leapt from the car as it was happening. I squatted there beside the Ferrari in the dark, stomach on fire, my churros abandoning me. Then I saw it. I looked up and there it was, glowing, alluring, Neptune's Lagoons. A spa. On the front of the building, it said LUXURI- OUS PRIVATE HOT TUB & SAUNA RENTALS BY THE HOUR. And they were closed, but something about those two words— Neptune's Lagoons. Neptune's Lagoons. I shat there and stared. Neptune's Lagoons. Neptune's Lagoons. They were the only words in the world. And in a flash I had a vision: an indoor pool, elegantly done, appointed in all the finest trappings and decor, no expense spared, every stop pulled, with one swerve. Rather than design it to be an underwater kingdom ruled by a benevo- lent Roman sea god, it would be designed to give one the experi- ence of swimming on Neptune. The ice giant has melted and the water's warm. Float under stars in an impossible blue. Space is lovely this time of year. This is the energy. The next morning, I phoned the offices of Yance Vos, the iconoclastic Dutch architect who apprenticed under Nautarra and had just designed the New Cotence Opera House in London. We worked together closely for the better part of two years crafting the space, perfecting it. The heaven you see before you is the result. I say we, of course, to be nice. This is very much mine—my concept, my design, my aesthetic, my bloodsweat. If I could draw better and knew what things were called, I wouldn't have even needed Vos. A true charlatan. Wouldn't know cobalt if it jumped up and tore into his cockles. This barbarian, one day I saw him stare at a single tile for thirty-one minutes straight. Thirty-one. I didn't even interrupt. I was astonished. Finally, he putzed over to me, laid the tile on the table, and said I see azure. Well, Yancelot, I see the door. Leave through it.

I think you made something marvelous, Lady said. What a special blue.

I love it here, Methuselah said.

I've always dug the moons, Table said. Bold.

Pink Italian marble, Methuselah said. Rosa Del Lago direct from Verona.

You went and hit some today, Unc? Table asked.

The question carried an out-of-nowhere bluntness only achieved when the person asking is thinking exclusively about themselves. Lady thought she might have whiplash. Methuselah took it in stride, thrilled to talk about himself some more.

Ah, what I wouldn't give to say yes to that. Unfortunately, no. My vascular neurologist, Dr. Jimothy Molds, has forbade it for the time being. So, as it stands now, your dear sweet uncle is cartbound.

You go there and just drive a cart around? Table asked.

I have two tremendous amigos I accompany, Methuselah said. Wolfgang Mones, the mongrel you heard me confabbing with earlier—Wolfy, scalawag of the highest order, a true demon—and Bob "Zoo" Coiffs. A man who has not once, in the history of his life, said the words *I don't know*. They're a couple of lumberjacks and good for nothing but I love them still. Time with them has made the pain of losing Roxanne, it's not gone, but the hurt does not hold the power it once did. It's the damnedest, most wonderful thing. The three of us get together for Cardinals games, laugh so hard we think we might die. Wolfy's a fabulous mimic. Nader. Chili Davis. Marshall Mathers. Yes, we are brothers and I would kill anyone for them. Even you, my Sylvia. Hoo hoo hoo.

Methuselah's stomach interrupted him, a small rumble.

Hark, he said. The tummy talks and gives a warning. Sounds like chowtime. And my darling Lady, the decision is yours. Where will we dine?

Where? Lady asked.

We can eat anywhere on the property, Methuselah said. The gardens? Roof? Dining room? Here?

Lady looked around the lagoon, at the moons and stars and back at Methuselah. She smiled.

A huge grin spread on his face and he reached into his pocket. It was a small brass giraffe. He put the head in his mouth and blew. A short high whistle trilled and he screamed the name Roxanne. The door opened. It was the woman in green.

Yes, Mr. Silk?

Hello, Roxanne, Methuselah said. Lovely to see you.

Lady and Table looked at each other.

We have decided to take our dinner along the banks of the lagoon. Have the buffet set along the south wall under the windows, please, and bring up five bottles of the D'Angerville Volnay Frémiet. The '96. Let's do the fun little Hermès plates, please. Seashells, not circus. I am a big boy after all. For music, the new Dixie Chicks. I'm not sure if you heard, but they did it again. Another stone-cold classic. And I believe that's all for now. Thank you so much, Roxanne. There's a party on Neptune tonight.

They took their time. Fried baby lobster tails, toasted ravioli, duck fat mushrooms, and sautéed spinach. They got good and lacquered up. Ate until the wine was gone, then poured more. Lady told a story about the time she got a button stuck up her nose. I wanted to see if it would fit. Table did an impression of Dick Vitale having sex. This is awesome baby, with a capital A. Methuselah talked about his favorite places. A house in Big Sur, a river in Utah, a beach on St. John.

The sea turtles come right up onto the sand, he said. They're big enough to ride, but you don't because that's mean. I watched an octopus feed for an hour. Floated there in the ocean mesmerized. Tentacles flying about. Did you know octopus have three hearts? Or that some people think they're aliens? Did you know their blood is blue?

Blue? Table asked.

Blue as the tile on which we sit, Methuselah said. Blue as my beautiful eyes. Isn't that fascinating? I derive great pleasure from little oddities like that. We're certain it's one way. It's another. It's like how bulls can't see red.

What? Lady asked.

Methuselah put his hands on his head, made horns with his pointer fingers.

Bulls, he said. Can't see red.

Why's it make them mad then? Table asked.

It doesn't, Methuselah said. Cartoons have told us bulls hate red. Film. Television. Literature. These industries cannot be trusted. They trot out invented nonsense, spit fantasia, call it truth. They fabricate, invent, trick. It's how they keep roofs over their heads and food in their bellies. They lie to survive. They want all of your attention, all of it, so they can tell you a lie. It's why I only watch documentaries. Which reminds me, when we're finished here, I thought it might be fun to head to the theater room? Take in a picture?

That sounds amazing, Lady said. Tallyho.

Tallyho, indeed, Methuselah said.

I've seen clips of bullfights, Table said. The capes are red.

Yes, Methuselah said. The muleta is red, but not to anger the bull. The eye of a bull has no red retina receptor. They're red-blind. Dichromatic. They have the blues and violets, the yellows and greens, but no red. It's the movement of the fabric that concerns the animal, the matador's manipulation of the cloth, how it waves. That's what makes the bull charge. Well, that and being a bull. The cape's color matters not. Orange, green, yellow. Purple, pink, rainbow. The bull doth not discriminate. It attacks all.

Then why's it red? Lady asked.

The red masks the blood, Methuselah said. That's all. That's its purpose. It makes the whole affair a little easier on the eyes. Makes those watching feel better, makes the matador feel better, makes us feel better. It's a disguise, camouflage, another lie.

Crap fire, that's wild, Table said. Learn something new every week. Wait, is that right? Or is it day? Is it learn something new every day?

Lady and Methuselah, in unison: Not for you.

They burst out cackling. She howled and clapped and hit the table. He palmed his belly with both hands and shook with laughter, tears rolling. Table smiled.

Y'all are ridiculous, he said. Never been happier to have to pee. Where is it?

Back here, but if it's strictly liquid I've no qualms with you stepping out of doors, Methuselah said. It's a lovely evening and taking a tinkle al fresco is great fun.

I think I'll lift my leg under the stars then, Table said. Give the boys a taste of this Missouri night.

See, that's where you and I differ, Methuselah said. My balls are men.

Table left through the side door as Methuselah roared and refilled their glasses.

Thank you, Lady said. Surprised he lasted this long. He's got a bladder the size of a dime.

I remember his mother told me he peed the bed until he was sixteen, Methuselah said.

I know I shouldn't, but I believe it, Lady said.

"Cowboy Take Me Away" began. The stereo remote was on the table. Methuselah picked it up, held it like a conductor.

Oh, yes, Methuselah said. Crown jewel of the album in my opinion. Shall we get loud?

Please, Lady said.

Methuselah cranked it, had to raise his voice.

A triumph, Methuselah said.

So great, Lady said. How about "Goodbye Earl"?

What? Methuselah said.

Do you like "Goodbye Earl"? Lady asked.

Oh, a total romp, Methuselah said. Terrific. Terrific.

So fun, Lady said. Also, while he's gone, that was super generous of you, paying for our gas. Thank you so much.

What?

He leaned forward. She put her face next to his.

I was just saying thanks for paying for our gas this trip, Lady said. That was very generous. You did not have to do that.

Methuselah sat up looking puzzled. They locked eyes. He stopped the music and held his mouth like he was going to say something, he just wasn't sure what. Lady saw in his face pure confusion. He had no clue what she was talking about. She backtracked immediately and burst out laughing, pretended she was joking. Methuselah's face changed with hers.

He looked like he'd just opened a present he'd always wanted. And he rocked in his chair and chortled away. Table walked in looking confused. Lady was roiling and all the more furious she couldn't show it. She wanted to avoid any stressful drama around Methuselah. Just because someone looks healthy doesn't mean they are.

Dadgum, Table said. Y'all watching *Three Amigos* or something? What's so funny?

You should not concern yourself with the laughter of others, Methuselah said. It's their business. Not yours. And I would never watch *Three Amigos*. I only watch documentaries.

Just tell me, Table said.

Well pardon me, your majesty, but you can miss out on things, Methuselah said. You had to water the bushes and left on your own accord. We didn't force you. I did not come over there with my derringer and threaten to put two in your head unless you go potty. Lady and I are supposed to pause our evening and repeat ourselves, all because our bladders are stronger and more powerful than yours? I'm an old man and I've no time to compensate for your weaknesses. Honestly, how dare you? We're creative. Asking us to backtrack deprives the world of another wonder. I could've said so many interesting things during the time it has taken me to say all this. But those seconds are gone. You took them from me. Your pound of flesh. Bravo. This is life. Doozies come and go. You will hear them if you stay.

Yeah, y'all were for sure talking about me, Table said.

You wish, Lady said.

Methuselah nudged Table's chair with his shoe.

Sit, Methuselah said. Grow up. How was your trip outside? Everything come out okay?

Yes, a very powerful stream, Table said. I was thinking more about bulls. Them not seeing red? That should be a school thing. If I was teaching, I'd lead with that. Put it up there with boring stuff like numbers. Give it a little more verve. Pageantry.

The University of Table, Lady said. Great. I want to go to that school. First day's numbers, bulls can't see red, and how to steal cheap headphones from Kmart. Anne Sullivan ain't got nothing on you.

Cheap, Table said. You're just telling on yourself. No way you've used yours, because the sound quality is pristine. And who's Fran Sullivan?

Anne Sullivan, Lady said. Helen Keller's teacher. From that movie? Remember them at the water pump? Water. W-a-t-e-r. It has a name.

That mean teacher with the weird sunglasses? Table asked. She sucked. Anne Bancroft couldn't salvage that character and she was Anne Bancroft. Pam couldn't teach for shit.

What's the film? Meth asked.

Anne Sullivan, Lady said. Anne. Not Pam. And I agree her sunglasses looked weird, but I don't think it's a crime to look weird. At least you better hope not.

Lady, 7, Sylvia, 0, Methuselah said. A bloodbath. Did you say water has a name?

It's a line from the movie, Lady said.

The movie sucked too, Table said. Shitty movie about a shitty teacher.

I don't understand, Methuselah said. Of course water has a name. Water. What's the film? Is it a documentary?

No, Table said. It was a normal one.

Ah, Methuselah said. A narrative feature. I would not have seen it then. I prefer pictures with depth. Water has a name? Why is that a thing to say? This is why I only watch documentaries. What's the film?

The Miracle Worker, Lady said. It was based on a play. I read it in high school.

There's this shit little girl who's deaf and blind or whatever and her parents get her this teacher who shows her how to talk with her hands, Table said. Fucking stupid. The little girl and the teacher, both of them are mean as shit. Rattlesnakes. But besides all that, it was totally unrealistic. That could never happen in real life.

What? Lady asked.

The movie was unrealistic, Table said.

Oh my God, Lady said.

Oh, Sylvia, no, Methuselah said.

It's preposterous, Table said. A person like that could never survive. They'd be like the Elephant Man.

Well, Dr. Table, it did happen in real life, Lady said. The movie's based on a true story, you freaking idiot, you dumb, dumb ass.

Table leaned back in his chair and clapped his hands.

Wow, Table said. See, you're such a hypocrite. You just said it was based on a play.

Oh, Sylvia, Methuselah said.

I am sincerely blown away, Lady said. I cannot believe you exist.

Table saw their faces and knew he was wrong. He got incredulous.

That's a real person? In the world? Jan Sullivan?

Anne Sullivan, Lady said. Anne.

Table was stammering.

Anne Sull—but how did sh—wait, is the little . . . what's her name . . . the weird one who can't do anything.

Incredible, Lady said. Helen Keller?

The child one that can't talk, Table said.

That's Helen Keller, Lady said. It's a true story. She was real.

Table put his hands on his head and screamed.

She was real?

Pretty sure that's one of the movies where it literally says at the end it was real, Lady said. Like, words come up and it says their bona fides or whatever, what they did the rest of their lives.

Yeah, but sometimes they have joke ones or ones they made up, Table said. Like Unc was saying before. Lies.

I will enter the discussion at my own leisure, Methuselah said. Don't pull me in because you're drowning.

How did you not know Helen Keller was real? Lady asked.

By being cool, Table said.

Lady watched Table laugh at his joke, the unbridled ease on his face. No worries. He thought the money was a foregone conclusion.

Yes, Lady said. Stupidity is all the rage these days. Everyone's doing it.

That teacher was smacking the shit out of that girl, Table said.

You already forgot her name, didn't you? Lady asked.

Uh, no, smarty-pants, Table said. I didn't. Her name was Anne.

What was her last name? Lady asked.

Are you for real right now? Table asked. We just talked about it. You actually think I forgot?

I know you forgot, Lady said.

It certainly seems that way, Methuselah said.

Wow, Table said. Circling the wagons. This is incredible.

You don't know it, do you? Lady asked.

I absolutely do, Table said. I know it well.

What is it? Lady asked.

. . . Pelican, Table said.

Oh my God, Lady said.

I think your brain might be broken, son, Methuselah said.

No, it just runs like no other, Table said. But let's—I want to move on immediately and discuss the teacher no further. How are you doing, Unc? Your PT, everything. Seems like you're doing good. Trending the right direction.

I hope so, but I'm not counting any chickens, Methuselah said. I don't trust bodies. They have bad track records. Always getting hurt, dying. New models come out, last longer, run smoother, but inevitably, always, sooner or later, they fail too.

He paused for a drink.

It's strange, he said. I dream more than I used to. Guess I sleep more too. I don't know. I have dreams constantly. They're mainly sweet. There's one, I'm in a room full of trampolines. Those nights are gifts. I'm this age, but I can do flips and twists. Things even in my youth I had no hope of doing. I jump so high. Fly through the air like a luchador. I have them constantly. There's one where I'm lava. And I am sentient and present and completely content. I'm not all the lava. I'm a drop. I don't know what's going on with the other drops. I just know me. My spot. I have no face or arms or legs, no heart or voice or hobbies. I do not exist and it feels fantastic. I have them constantly. I have them and see Roxanne. And I'm so happy. So happy to be with her again. I missed her, you know? And I can't believe I get to see her again. I'm so lucky. She's back. She came back. And she's alive. And I get to hold her, and be held. Being held. My God. What a time. I wake up lower than ever. She's dead again and so are the pieces of me that died with her. And I have to learn again how to be in the world.

Lady scooched her chair over, rubbed Methuselah's back.

Thank you, darling, Methuselah said. I'll be okay. I have to be careful. I trend pouty. I must battle my brain. It'll be six years in October. It's high time I move on I suppose, but, I don't know, you just get used to seeing them.

Did I hear right earlier when you shouted for green suit girl? Table asked. Is her name Roxanne too?

Indeed, it is, Methuselah said.

Wow, Table said. Teeny, tiny world. What're the odds of that? Would've probably given Aunt Rox a chuckle, huh?

Yes, Methuselah said. It's wonderful. Her name's Roxanne. Her name's Roxanne . . . while she's here. At Silkhaven. While she works. Her real name is Della Bronson. She's at WashU actually. Getting her Ph.D. in aerospace engineering. Wonderfully smart. Warm. She—

Wait, Table said. Her name's not Roxanne?

No, Methuselah said.

But you call her Roxanne? Lady asked.

It started as an accident, Methuselah said. I was doing a crossword and came to one I couldn't figure out. I used to always pester your aunt for help and wherever she was in the house, she'd shout something back. But I'm doing the crossword and somehow, I don't know if I forgot she was dead or it was some kind of muscle memory something, but I hollered for her. Roxanne. And before I even knew what I'd said, Della hollered back Coming. By the time she arrived, I'd realized my mistake,

but it hit me—it felt really good. Saying that name. Her coming
in. I asked her if it would be okay if I called her Roxanne, just
while she's on the grounds. She was understanding but said no.
Then I offered her $10,000.

Wow, Lady said.

Why do you have to call her that, though? Table asked. You
can say the name whenever you want.

It's not just saying the name. I'd gladly mosey around all day
saying her name to empty rooms if that did the trick. It's the
response. The name responds. I get to talk with her again. Have
another conversation. I'm sure it's odd for Della at times, but it
makes me feel good. It's a lie, but it makes me feel good.

The theater room had three rows of seats, five seats to a row.
Stained glass sconces lined the walls, the same pink coneflower
as the lamp in the living room. Between the lights were posters
for some of Methuselah's favorite documentaries. *Hail! Hail!
Rock 'n' Roll, Antonia: A Portrait of the Woman, When We Were Kings,
Daguerréotypes, Black Rodeo, Maya Lin: A Strong Clear Vision*, he could
go on. Table stood in the back between the commercial grade
popper and soda fountain. He stared at the carpet and mumbled
to himself, ate popcorn by the handful from an upturned St. Louis
Cardinals baseball helmet. Lady sat in the second row wrapped
in a blanket with a box of Samoas. Methuselah stood down front
holding two DVDs.

Now then, Lady dear. Atención, por favor. You have two options,
both docs because that's all I watch. I have the new Freida Lee
Mock/Terry Sanders picture, *Return with Honor*. Originally aired
on PBS. American fighter pilots shot down in North Vietnam.

POWs for eight years. Will watch with or without you. Moving on. Option numero two—*Buena Vista Social Club*. Wenders's latest. Musica Cubana. Cooder's involved. Bound to be worthwhile. Been putting it off but only because I want to make it count. The boys went nuts for it. It's all Zoo listens to now. Will watch with or without you, okay? Don't make your decision straight away. A little percolation is always recommended. In the meantime, I'll fetch another bottle.

Table perked up.

I'll escort, he said.

And something in how quickly he spoke, the tenor of his phrasing, almost a gasp in his voice, Lady knew. He was asking tonight.

I don't need your help, Methuselah said.

We need two, though, Table said. Don't want to have to pause the movie to grab another.

Boy, I can carry two bottles, Methuselah said. I'm old, not condemned.

I'm coming with you, Table said. I want to talk to you about something.

They left. Lady shook her head and ate a Samoa whole. He couldn't help himself. God forbid he give it a day. If something was on his mind, he had to address it. He couldn't wait, try to find the right time. If he had a question, an answer better show up soon or things will get ugly. Uncertainty begat uncertainty and suffocated him. Better to just get it out of the way, let the rest of the trip be pure party.

He better pray for good news for a multitude of reasons, Lady thought. There was the financial side, dire enough already before these new lies. She didn't even want to think about the numbers lest she go mad with tears in front of Methuselah, blaze into a rage, and send Table into orbit. She fumed quietly. He'd now both withheld the real reason for the trip and lied about how it was paid for. She wanted to set him on fire. In these times she was reminded what a great actress she used to be. She kept her face straight, eyes gentle and oblivious. In this way too they were different. If Lady didn't want someone to know how she felt, they wouldn't. If Table didn't want someone to know how he felt, didn't matter. Take a look and know.

But the lie was chipping away at her. She hated him for it and herself for not expecting it. She hated how blindsided she was, how disrespected she felt. He won't get a job for money, but he'll spend hers to go beg Meth for more? Lady was steamed and trying to calm down. She touched the elephant charm, ran the beast on the chain, made trumpet sounds. Whispered, You know, Lady, I ain't trying to start nothing, but a bunch of people's saying you're the best thing breathing. Footsteps in the hall. She turned. It was Methuselah. He raised a bottle and smiled.

Have we decided on tonight's feature presentation? he asked.

Lady grabbed the first case she felt, held up *Buena Vista Social Club*.

Let's dance, she said.

Oh, the boys will be over the moon, Methuselah said.

Lady Frisbeed him the case. More footsteps in the hall. She turned. It was Table. His eyes were pale and low. White bottle-caps wrapped in gauze. His head fishtailed.

He sat in despair on the top row, muzz-faced, bottle in the seat beside him. Hangdog cheeks like primordial stage curtains, mangy and limp and unraveling. He was demoralized, sunk in doom. She wondered if he had it in him to cry around Methuselah. He did.

RHINESTONE STAMPEDE

HE STARTED TO STEAL. Change purses from valet stands outside the fancy restaurants in Juss's Gene District. Grocery bags from shopping carts in grocery store parking lots. Postgame concession stand bash and grabs at area high school sporting events. Nighttime runs into people's yards, lifted bicycles and dirt bikes and push mowers, pawned them two towns over. He went to the aquarium in Corder and combed through the strollers outside the dolphin show. He ripped power tools from construction sites and sold them at flea markets. Rarely were the takes big enough to put any kind of sizable dent in their debt. Lady begged him to get a job. He wouldn't. Didn't want someone over him, telling him how to be. He tried to think bigger.

The Ox Country Club had a golf course, four tennis courts, swimming pool, gym, and restaurant. Table put on khakis and a navy polo and snuck in dressed as staff. There was a small men's locker room tucked away upstairs. He slipped in and looked around. To the left of the door were stacks on stacks of white towels. He put two in his duffel. Beside the towels was a water fountain and beside that an automatic shoeshine and beside that a scale. Twenty wooden lockers the size of minifridges along the far wall, ten on ten, long bench in front with clothes and bags underneath. *SportsCenter* played on a television in the corner. Wind in Sal Paolantonio's hair. Pictures from decades past lined the walls.

The dance floor during the club's fourteenth annual Arabian Nights Party. Swaths of purple and gold. Persian rugs and sequins and pillows. There were shots of women poolside in floral swimsuits and sun hats the size of truck tires, their diamond-crusted, fat-knuckled fingers groping lime-wedged, umbrella'd margaritas. Photos of long-dead, mustachioed galoots wearing cable-knit

sweaters, Clubmasters, and exquisite tans. They played domi-
noes among putter-shaped michelada towers and laughed their
heads off.

The whole place smelled like bleach and oranges. He stepped
to the middle of the room and looked toward the showers. He
couldn't see anyone. He couldn't hear anyone. He faked a sneeze.
No response.

Heywhaddayasaythereboy, he said.

No response. He felt brilliant and got to work, rifled through
pants and jackets, bags and shoes. Sweat dripped off him and wet
his thumbs. His breath was heavy. He moved quickly. Wallets,
jewelry, cash, cell phones. He went to the sink. Aftershave,
cologne, Q-tips, combs. He kept going. Hair gel, mousse, hair
spray, razors. The television went to commercial. Table sang
with the jingle. Mathis Brothers Furniture—your style, your price.
The door creaked. He scrambled, started washing his hands. His
bag wasn't zipped. It lay collapsed at his feet, the fabric folded
over itself, the contraband hidden.

A young white man in purple Nike shorts and Ox Football
tank stepped into view. His chest preceded him. Five foot five,
early twenties, plump stump of a kid with hogshead body and
biceps the size of pineapples. His head was shaved. His beard
was black. He looked inflated and made of ham. Table wanted to
get out of there immediately.

Club open Friday? the guy asked.

Yes, sir, Table said.

Including snack bar?

No, sir. Unfortunately not.

Well, crap on a stick.

I know. I'm sorry. We're bummed too. That's where we eat
if we don't bring something. Can't get enough of them chicken
fingers.

The guy sat on the bench, tried to stretch his hamstrings.

They are good, he said. You're new, yeah?

Yes, sir, Table said. My name's Mark. I'm not from here but I
live here now.

Towers of green washcloths beside the sink. Table took one
and dried his hands. He tried to be relaxed about it, pretended
to yawn. The guy took his shirt off. He'd shaved his carpet-thick
chest hair into a cross.

I'm Pat, the guy said. Welcome to the party. May God bless
you so hard. Toss me one of them?

Table grabbed another washcloth and stepped over the duffel,
handed it to Pat.

Didn't want you to have to walk it over, Pat said.

No big, Table said. This the kind of flawless service you get
when you're dealing with Mark. I stay thinking—

Table turned in the middle of his sentence with the duffel under
him. He stepped inside the bag, lost his balance, and hit the ground.
Half the loot scattered onto the carpet. Table's eyes bulged. They
were like snowballs. Pat looked at the haul. Table tried to stand.

At ease, Clark, Pat said. Chill on your back for a sec.

Pat put his hand on Table's chest. His fingers were hot links.
Table watched him survey everything, gold bracelet at his feet,
a smattering of wallets and cash. Two wedding bands spun and
rang against the bathroom tile. Pat picked up one of the wallets. He opened it, showed the inside—a prom picture of him
and his girlfriend.

Table jumped to his feet. Pat came with a right and hit his neck, came with a left and missed entirely. Table scooped up the bag and turned to run. Pat lunged, got the strap. They struggled for the duffel and screamed at each other. Over and over, Pat told Table he'd kill him. Over and over, Table called Pat a bitch. The handles dug into Table's hands and there were sharp pains in his palms. He saw he was too weak to win. He let the bag go. Pat fell and said Dadgummit. Table knew the bag was lost and turned to bail. Pat dove, got the back of his polo, and pulled. The shirt whined. The slow stretch of polyester. Table couldn't get away. He was growing a tail. The shirt too was lost. He bent his body and slid out of it. Pat fell again.

Stop making me fall, Pat screamed.

I am your God, Table screamed.

Table turned to leave but the door was closer than he thought. He slammed into it. Blood dove out his nose. Tears in his eyes. Things were blurry. He got the door open. Blood kept pouring. His mustache went red. Pat grabbed Table's foot. Table kicked him in the face. He watched his shoe stomp his jaw, his nose. Green shards of glass beside Pat's eyes. Blood on the shards. Blood in Table's mouth. Blood on his soles. Visions of menacing chickens. He kept stomping Pat's face. The birds punched heavy bags. Pat started crying. His head sounded like a football. More blood off the shards. Table stomped him again. Solomon's jeans in the air, blood on the denim like jam.

No, he said. That wasn't there.

And he ran out the door. A member stood in the hallway. She was pastel white and said Oh my goodness, are you okay? He ran past her, sprinted half-naked down the stairs. Pat burst out of the locker room and screamed Stop the mustache guy. Table ran out

the front and through the lot and onto the empty drive. His eyes
stung. He kept blinking. His thoughts frustrated him. He wanted
to clean his mind. He wanted to take the top off his skull, remove
his brain, and give it a bath. He'd scrub hard the ridges and valleys
of the gray matter, get rid of the unwanted stuff.

He turned to see if he was being chased. Pat was at the edge
of the lot with his hands on his knees, two employees beside
him. They said something to each other, sprinted across the lot,
and jumped into a crimson Ford Lightning. Table's nose poured.
Blood on his chest now. He kept running.

The golf course neighbored Sutter Wildlife Reserve, a 57,000-
acre home to free-range buffalo, elk, prairie dogs, and white-tailed
deer. There were biking and hiking trails, places to fish and picnic
and rappel. Table never visited. He'd hidden the Ranchero there
among the elms and ran into the woods near where he'd parked.
He looked back. The Lightning was coming. He dove behind a
tree. The truck had a spoiler and Tiger Woods car flags. It crawled
along blaring Steven Curtis Chapman's "Speechless." Sticks and
stones on Table's chest. Roots scraped him. He tried to shrink.
After thirty seconds of staring, they drove on.

Table ran again. Sutter was quiet. He heard his feet landing. He
could see the Ranchero. He ran faster. His brain was cold. He felt
run over. A rock got in his shoe and stabbed his heel. The ground
was uneven. He started to stumble. The vehicle was ten yards
away. A fallen limb tripped him and his face dented the door.

That night they sat across from each other at the kitchen table.
The bruising had already set around his nose and eyes and he
counted the money they had left.

Twenty-two, twenty-seven, $28.34 to last us till the fifteenth, he said.

That's not enough, she said.

That's what we got. I'll go to Harp's, get a bunch of ramen, tuna. We'll be fine. I got some stuff in the works anyways. Ideas. They're actually really good.

This ain't no way to be in the world. Tuna sucks.

You're wrong about tuna.

So sick of this.

We'll be okay. I know you don't want me saying it so I won't, but Meth—

Stop right now.

The money lay between them like a pile of trash. Table shook his head and went to the kitchen. His face ached. He felt like he'd been stepped on by an elephant. His failure replayed in his mind. And the taste of the car. And his throbbing nose. And his chipped front tooth. He made plans to go back to the club and bust out the Lightning's windows. Lady watched him think and knew she wasn't on his mind. He leaned against the refrigerator, ran his boot over the imperfections in the tile. She walked over and stood beside him. His arms were crossed. He looked at the faucet. She held to the handle of the fridge and closed her eyes, thought about what to say. The window over the sink looked out on the front yard and beyond that the pasture and above that the black that went on and on and did not stop until the casino in Tunero in its violet. He stared into the dark.

Feels like you're not even trying no more, she said. Not really. We ain't paid the gas since when? It's going to get shut off. We've got to see about the roof soon. The car still nee—

We'll be okay, he said. We stretch this $28 a few days and it'll—

Get a job. You're supposed to work. That's how the world goes. You work.

Ain't nobody ask me to be in the world. Just got put here. Fucking . . . born.

She took a step back, half smile on her face.

You're upset at being born? she asked.

Peer pressure, he said.

What?

It's dadgum everybody being a bunch of followers. Oh, they have a job. I'll get a job. Oh, they had a kid, why don't we? Sheep.

Her mouth was open. She shook her head.

I sincerely don't even know where to start, she said.

Adam and Eve didn't have—

Kids? Yes, they did. Cain and Abel.

Jobs, if you'll let me talk. They didn't have jobs.

Yes, they did. They had to take care of the garden and all that. The animals.

She walked toward the bedroom. He followed her.

You really think they were out there in the jungle with the dragons or bears or whatever? he asked.

Absolutely, she said.

Shut up. You're insane. They'd be mauled and burnt to a crisp.

She stopped in the hallway and put her finger in his face.

Don't call me insane, she said. I've told you that a bunch.

Get sane then, girl, he said.

Get a job then, boy. Talking about don't be a follower but then the next breath let's do something these other people did. Literally probably the two most famous people of all time—

No way.

—and quit telling me shut up, you six-year-old. Ever since we met. Shut up. Shut up. You shut up. Turd.

She went into the bedroom and lay down, took off her shirt. Table slumped behind her, sat in the chair in the corner. There was a floor lamp beside him. He turned it on, looked at his hands. The light made him yellow.

Get over here, she said.

He didn't respond. She tilted her head to the side and snapped twice.

Hey, Adam, she said. You said you'd have sex tonight. Get over here. I'm ready for bed.

Can't afford no kids right now, he said.

Whose fault is that?

Well, besides that, maybe I'm not trying to have sex with someone who calls me Turd.

What?

Maybe I'm not trying to—

I know what you said. I was exclaiming. It was an exclamation. You're not serious?

I'm incredibly serious.

No. Stop. Get over here and have sex with me. You promised you'd have sex with me tonight. Tonight's the especially good night. I showed you the chart.

I don't feel like it now.

You don't feel like it now?

Yeah, no, I don't feel like it now.

He wiped his mouth. She looked out the window, saw nothing. Her voice was gentle.

I'll do all the work.

He stared at the carpet.

I don't want to, he said.

You're being mean to me, she said.

You're being mean to me.

Table, please.

He didn't answer.

Table, she said.

I love you, baby, but you're wasting your breath, he said.

She got out of bed and walked toward the bathroom.

Table. T. Hey.

He looked up. The bathroom light made her glow. She saw all of him.

I've always thought you were small, but I see now, in this light, you're also ugly.

Table parked outside the Dunta Beers & Fun with the six-shooter in his lap and a grinding in his head. His eyes hurt behind his sunglasses and sweat hit his lips. He tasted his salt. His face was a wasteland. His face was static. He opened his flask, took a drink of Voon's, stared at the gun. Dull silver now, the steel marked up and faded. He made fists and squeezed. Cuts appeared on his fingers. They striped them, seemed to ripple and curl at the knuckles. He thought of Solomon. He coughed. His stomach wagged. He closed his eyes. Green shards of glass like cash-colored lanterns hung bloodied and frozen in the black, constellations of rest. He took another drink and tried to light a cigarette. Adrenaline made his hands shake. His thumb slipped off the Bic.

Fuck off, he said.

His thumb slipped again.

Fuck you, he said.

His thumb slipped again. The collar of his T-shirt groped his throat and he yanked at the fabric and stretched it out. He focused his hands, tried the lighter again. The cigarette lit. He took a long drag and tried to trick himself into confidence.

And the crowd goes wild, he said. All right now, T-Nuts. You're fine, you're fine. You're so hot. You've conquered fire. You hold it in your hands. All good things. All good thoughts. Them little fudge brownies with the nuts. Nut up, old man. Let's go.

He put the gun in his jacket pocket. His head was tight. He stretched his neck. His chest vibrated. A light rumble in his throat. His gums hurt. Sweat like icing on his desert-red face. He turned the key back and the radio came on. "Amazed" by Lonestar played. It was the middle of the song, when Richie McDonald sings I want to spend the whole night in your eyes. Table drummed the air around him with the barrel of the gun, pumped himself up, sang the words he knew. He watched himself in the rearview. His face hardened. He faked like he was about to punch his reflection, screamed the word *pussy*, and got out.

The only vehicle in the lot was a yellow cabriolet dominated by bird feces, white-black spots everywhere. Table could see his breath and the dew had not yet gone from the grass. The jacket was Lady's, light purple, yellow rhinestones stampeded across the chest. Spread on the back was a cartoon buck on its hind legs. The animal was the color of sand and brawny. It wore aviators, smiled, and gave the deer version of a thumbs-up. Table's legs were stiff. He stretched his quads and breathed heat into his fists. There was a scraping in his chest. A Tacoma drove by. Fishing poles clapped off the tailgate. He wanted to leave. He faced the store. A Plott hound was tied to a post beside the front door. She slept in the sun by the freezer of ice bags. He went inside.

The man working the register was chalk-line white with Christmas-sounding brown hair. It stopped at his shoulders, strings of small bells and feathers woven in like wind-chime chandeliers. His name tag said Oz. His shirt said I KNOW I LOOK LIKE WILLIE NELSON.

How we doing? Oz asked. What do you say? What do you know?

Oh, less and less every day, Table said.

How's the mood striking?

Table looked at the display of bottles behind Oz, picked one on the top row.

Want that fancy Turkey, Table said. Kentucky Spirit.

He's got style, he's got grace, Oz said. Always felt they missed on the name. Could think of a hundred names better than Kentucky Spirit, but my God does it perform its necessary duties.

I like the name.

Well, you must die then. Nah. I'm joshing. You can live. It's cool. It's about forgiveness, kemosabe. That's what it's all about. Let me get the stool. We keep the good shit close to God.

Oz looked for his step and Table scanned the store, tried to calm down. Neon beer logos glowed in the window next to ATM Inside and Drink Up. A grove of inflatable elm trees rose up in the back of the store, gave shade to a display of Lone Star six-packs. The white-tile floor was slick with dirt and across it, in random patterns, were thousands of bare orange price tags. Fifty-some Dallas Cowboys helmets hung from the ceiling, their silver like bright mercury. Oz rattled off potential whiskey names.

Old Man Chambers, Oz said. The Sweat of Ralph LeBeau. Sun . . . how about that? Sun. Center of our solar system, which to me is the best of all the solar systems.

I agree, Table said.

That's a tough drink order, though, huh? You walk into a bar and say Oh I don't know why don't you give me three fingers of the damn sun.

I absolutely love it.

They high-fived the way bikers do. Oz found the stool and turned to the display for the Turkey. Table reached for the gun. The barrel rested crossways in his jacket pocket and the tip caught the edge and would not come clean. A Magnavox in the corner played Dolly Parton's "River of Happiness." Table was panicking.

So, this Y2K's cuckoo, huh? Oz asked.

Oz grabbed the bottle and turned, saw Table fumbling with his pocket.

You good, brother? Oz asked.

The gun came free and Table wobbled a bit, pointed the barrel at Oz. He was off-balance and widened his base to steady himself. Adrenaline had his movements wrinkled and chopped and his boot bumped a stand hawking six-packs of Corona. Bottles fell, shattered in splashes of lion yellow. Table looked at the beer. Oz pulled a hunting knife from under the register and threw it. The blade clipped Table's right arm. He made a noise like a tea-kettle, dropped the weapon, picked it up again. Oz chucked minis three at a time at Table's head and screamed You're lucky I forgot my gun today. Table slipped in the spilled Corona and screamed Stop being such a dick about this. A display case of Hennessy went flying. He stood again. An airplane bottle of Jack hit his trigger finger with the barrel facing down. A hole exploded in his boot and feathered at the edges. Blood came. The tan went scarlet. Table crawled, dragged a red path. Veins sprung in his forehead. He thought of Lady. He looked at the floor.

I don't want to have done this.

The Plott hound barked at the door, slammed her head against the glass. Oz threw a handle of Razz and missed. The bottle shattered against the row of rosé just above Table. It seeped to the floor in punch waterfalls and Table rolled in the wine. Jeff Gordon watched all this smiling, holding a Pepsi, blue-inked dick and balls headed into his mouth.

Table looked at the silver of the helmets and the stars shined and blurred and merged, shaking blue, a strange ocean above him. His brain fluttered and there was a pang where his spine met his neck. Streams of rosé in his eyes. His hair looked like pink yarn. When he was a boy, his mother would sing to him a song she made up. The last line was You look like a turtle. Table stared at his bloody foot. He was reeling. He started screaming. Primo shrieking.

I am the beefcake and I get to win. I am the beefcake and I—

A bottle of George Dickel got him, shattered against his cheek, stopped his howling. He smelled chicken. The light was red. The light was yellow. Blood fell out of him and it was like melted peppermints on the ground.

SOMETIMES RELATIONSHIPS GET ILL

PRISCILLA'S HEAD FELT EXCAVATED and she drove through Wahoo, Oklahoma. Penny eyes hidden behind aviators. The frames were tortoiseshell and the lenses blue. She found them in the bathroom of a Wendy's on the Kansas border. They'd been left on top of a hand dryer and said *Acapulco* on the earpieces. She wore a camel-brown velour jacket over a green dress. Pretzels in the cup holder. Point of Grace in the tape deck. Keep the candle burning. The Debonair went slowly through town. Her eyelids itched and she rubbed them. She'd not been sleeping. The night before, she lay in bed smoking cigarettes and watching *Tremors*. Now she pulled into the parking lot of Lamb of God Community Christian and stared at her church. Pillars on the steps, swan-white steeple, marquee out front: MOSQUITOES KNOW THERE'S POWER IN THE BLOOD. Straight-lipped men and women in black and navy and gray walked in with their heads down. Priscilla looked at her reflection in the rearview. Circles under her eyes the color of ash. She yawned, lit a Newport. Her Hakeem Olajuwon action figure was glued to the dash. The colors had worn over time and his hair looked dead. Her right knee bounced. It was 3:07 p.m. She walked toward the church and prayed with her eyes open.

God, Kones seemed kind. Seen him give Betsy Hointon a Werther's once and he was real sweet with her. Thought that was cool 'cause she's obviously a rough draw just, like, as a person. Know I didn't know him but figured nice to come. Please be with the family and everybody mourning. Alonzo Mourning. Sorry. Sometimes my head's too much. I love You. Be funny if I was trying to flirt. Oh, hey, God. I love the Alps. You did those all by Yourself? Sorry for having a hard time lately. I've been feeling cold and strange. A little . . . detached. Please be with Viv. Amen.

She tossed her cigarette and went inside. In the foyer was a sign promoting the Lamb of God youth group's Ultimate Frisbee/

Extreme Cornhole Extravaganza and two mammoth pictures of the late Randall Altephus Kones. One of him in the Navy when he was young. The other when he was older, on a dance floor, barefoot in a blue suit. His tongue was out. He pointed at the camera and shimmered. Below the picture was his name, 1918–2000, RIP SNOW.

Priscilla grabbed a program and took the stairs to the balcony. The service had already begun. She went down the aisle, stared ahead, searched for a seat. A few people looked at her. She got anxious anytime she walked in front of a crowd. Her right leg itched. She started to sweat. First her back, then her temples, then her butt. She thought about taking her coat off. She decided not to. She thought about leaving. She decided not to. There were a handful of seats together near the top and she sat there, three empty chairs to her left, and two below. Ron Nudie, Lamb of God's music minister, led the congregation in a mid-tempo version of "How Great Thou Art." Priscilla roll-tapped the nails of her right hand against the nails of her left and sang along. The sanctuary smelled like pine. She looked at Jesus.

A stained glass depiction of Christ in the Garden of Gethsemane hung over the purple-curtained baptistery. His eyes were open and heavenward, burgundy triangles of blood pocking His cream-white face, His hands. The night sky was violet. Silver stars like bioluminescent lockets above Him. The disciples were in the background, robed and lounging, string of z's overhead, sandaled feet resting on boulders. To the right of Jesus's head was a speech balloon. In red: . . . NOT AS I WILL, BUT AS THOU WILT.

The stage was covered in candles and bouquets of flowers and wreaths and more pictures of Kones and the casket was there too and it was closed. "How Great Thou Art" ended. Nudie left the stage. A middle-aged white woman walked to the pulpit in a plum dress and black heels. Her brown hair was short and spiked with the tips bleached blond. In one hand was a water. In the other was a sheet of paper. She said Hello into the microphone and stepped out of her shoes, put the bottle on the ground. Priscilla was confused, felt unsettled, out of place. The woman coughed twice and began.

Sorry, I've never talked before. I apologize for taking my heels off but I don't like dressing up and my feet hurt. I'm Nayna Kones-Boller. Randall's, Dad's, oldest. I wrote what I'll say. Felt that best. I'll just read it to stay on point and not wander around all helter-skelter saying whatever. It's nice so many of y'all came. Dad would've acted like it wasn't a big deal but later on he'd have been Pretty neat all those people there, huh? Then he would've . . . I don't know . . . asked how my car was doing on gas. He was always making sure I had enough gas. Casket's closed for y'all but we'll open it for family. Think that's everything I was supposed to say. Lottie? That's it? All right. Lottie says that's it.

Nayna stepped away from the pulpit and took a drink. Priscilla sneezed with her mouth closed, swallowed the sound. She wanted no attention. Nayna continued.

I loved my father and I'll miss him. Lottie and J.L. feel the same. He was always honest with us and fun and made us laugh. I don't think I ever saw him be mean to anybody who didn't really deserve it and even then he was just stern with it, up-front. Never behind the back. I was always proud of him and it felt special to me he was my dad. I liked to tell people he was my dad.

Priscilla put her feet on the seat in front of her and tried not to think of her father. Wrenching in her stomach. Her head was hot.

My favorite memory with him is from my twenty-second birthday. We drove to the Grand Canyon. I'd never been there and wanted to go so he took me. It was great to be in the car with him, talking, listening to music. We camped at night, ate fast food. He'd ask me questions and actually listen to the answers. And he'd have something to say about the thing I said and I'd have something to say about the thing he said and it went on like that. They were good conversations. I don't have very many good conversations.

Priscilla folded her tongue, scratched her jaw. Her dad on the concrete. She looked at Nayna, tried to only see her.

One day on the trip he had to go pee real bad. He thought he could make it to a gas station but couldn't so he just drove off onto the shoulder and ran in the grass to piss. He was peeing for a while and all the sudden he started jumping around, freaking out. I was like What's going on? He fell down, got back up, sprinted to the car. His little tush out the whole time. He was shouting Ants. Fire ants. They got ants out here, Nanners. Big ole pee stain on his pants. Hardest I ever laughed. Dad let me take a picture of him with the stain there. He pointed at it, gave a thumbs-up. Mom framed that. It's up here somewhere.

Nayna took another drink of water. A slow gathering of tears in Priscilla's eyes and she stretched her neck.

After I took his picture we realized the spot we were in was real nice and we just sort of stood there awhile. Regrouped. Dad liked to say things like It's a beautiful day even when it wasn't. We'd get on him like There's clouds out, it's not that pretty, but that time he said it and he was right. He liked sunsets a lot. He was so cheesy and stupid.

Priscilla cried quietly. Her throat burned. She sat on her

hands, flexed her calves, and checked to see if anyone was looking at her. No one was.

Dad liked to go out to eat. I'm guessing he went to Red Lobster with more than one of y'all. He loved those cheesy biscuits. Always took a ton home. What you do, Nanners, is right before the meal's over, ask for more. Then when you get the check, you ask for a box for the biscuits you just ordered. Get to take a full load home. Was very proud of himself. Thought he'd gamed the system. They're already free. When we visited he'd bring them out like hors d'oeuvres. They don't age great. He loved OU. I know he'd want me to say Boomer.

And a great multitude shouted Sooner.

Texas, Nayna said.

And that same multitude shouted Sucks.

Priscilla coughed. Her cheeks were damp. She wiped them. Her lips tried to shake and she whispered Come on.

He was proud to be a rancher and loved to work a hard day. I don't care what you do, but try at it. That was his message for us. When he retired he'd go up to the school and help out with the FFA. He'd always talk about how kids today were very special, very smart. One of his favorite things to do was go to the VFW and drink with his friends Gary Ray Fetters and Ron Mkoppins. G.R., Kopp, he'd have wanted me to mention he was a better fisherman than both of y'all put together. Prettier too. Dad loved this state and was always proud to be an Oklahoman. He was honored to have served his country. Said he felt stronger for having done so. He was never shy about letting folks know he was a Democrat, a fact that never ceased to bowl people over. I'm sure plenty of y'all got into some lighthearted political discussions with him. Most of them very reasonable, no doubt.

He wasn't Snow to us, he was Dad. His hugs were legendary. If you were ever fortunate enough to be brought into the Kone Zone, you know that's true. For y'all unfamiliar, the Kone Zone is what he called it when he hugged us. He'd wrap us up and squeeze and shout Kone Zone, you're in the Kone Zone. They were just big bear hugs but they were fun. Mom said he tried calling it Kones Zone at first but Kone Zone was easier to say. Dad was about efficiency.

Priscilla rested her cheek on her shoulder and rubbed her chest. The room swamped on her. She tried to stay silent.

Him and Mom were married fifty-three years when she died. She was the love of his life. He was always real gentle with her and they loved to dance. Both of them treated us real good. We kids talked about it and we all felt very loved.

I'll end with this. Not really a story. Just something that happened. After they let Dad leave the hospital he'd spend the days in bed and he was in a lot of pain and it was hard to see him hurt. But there was a time this last Wednesday where he had his spirits running nice and we played chickenfoot and mainly talked about things that didn't matter at all. Hotels with indoor/outdoor swimming pools. Andre Agassi. J.L.'s ugly belt. Dad smiled a lot that day and it was special because we knew it was maybe the last of all that and we just told him all day that we loved him and he said it back a bunch. I loved his voice. It made me feel safe. When we put him to bed that night he said I had me a day today, girls and boy—I wasn't sick today. Next morning he was hurting again. My dad was a good person. He was a good friend, brother, husband, and father. He's in heaven now, undoubtedly watching, loving how tore up everyone is. Thank y'all for coming to celebrate him. We're just happy we got to have him around for so long. Love you, Daddy.

There was a peeling in Priscilla's stomach. She closed her eyes and the black was bright. It felt like her skull was shrinking. Stubble on her legs straightened and her teeth hurt. The neck of her dress rubbed her strangely. She scratched her throat. Her French tips striped her. Her elbows tingled. She took them off the armrests and opened her eyes. Nayna sat front row. The piano started. Nudie came back onstage with a microphone and a smile. He said Why don't y'all stand with me? Boy I tell you what, that was some cool stuff right there. Thank you for your words, Nayna. I know they were a blessing to me. We're a few months into the new millennium and this season is one of change and transformation. In these tumultuous times, may we all bind our wandering hearts to Christ Jesus, just as our friend Randall did.

He started "Come, Thou Fount of Every Blessing" and the congregation joined. Priscilla couldn't believe this was the song chosen, didn't know what it could mean.

Are you mad?

She sang hard. Her head was full. Her knees felt flimsy. She sat down and closed her eyes, listened with her whole body. The hymn surrounded her. She felt trampled.

When the service ended, Priscilla waited in the receiving line. No music played. She spoke to no one. Her face was swollen, puffed cheeks pomegranate red. People cried with the family, hugged them, shook their hands. One white lady at the front had her palms on the casket and wailed like someone drilled a screw into her neck. Her dress pulsed with her heaving. A man picked her up like she was a baby and carried her away. Priscilla moved with the line and prayed.

Please be with that loud lady. And the Koneses. I'm sorry. There's been times lately I've felt alone and far from You. Then I feel guilty for feeling like that. I know You're always with me. I know You are. But sometimes it's like I don't feel You, I guess. I'm so sorry. I'm trying so hard to be close to You. Every day. I just don't understand what I'm doing wrong. Please help me focus on You better. Seen a video on the TV this morning of a gigantic Russian woman eating a fifteen-pound lobster. She had red hair and gold eye shadow, ate the thing with her hands. Lobster meat flying everywhere. Made me gag. Please help me get that image out of my head. I can't get it out of my head. Lord, please change my head. Make it different. The way it works. I'm sorry. I shouldn't be thinking about myself right now. I'm a bad person for thinking about myself. Please forgive my selfishness. Amen.

She was disgusted with herself and one away from the front. The family looked haggard, these drooped faces. J.L. touched his toes. Lottie stretched her quads. Nayna arched her back. Priscilla's chest was tight and her heart banged and there was the taste of metal in her mouth. She thought about bailing. She decided not to. It was her turn. She shook their hands.

My name's Priscilla Blackwood, she said. I'm awful sorry about your dad. I didn't know him but I'd see him around here at church and stuff. He seemed like a great dad. I guarantee I'll pray for all y'all. I have so much love in my heart. For each of you. So happy he got to live a long life. That's a luxury for all parties involved. I too lost my father and it's hard, you know? It's just hard. My dad was murdered. I was real young. Murked. Gun-style. Sixteen years ago. I was there. It was no bueno. He got murdered and then he passed away. One usually goes with the other I guess, but God's here, right? Do you feel Him? I hope you do. I certainly do. Very much. He is all over me. Hey, I'll say it: it sucks when people die. Flat-out. But I'll tell you something else: God's good. You had a beautiful message today, Nayna. Thanks so much for your words. I'll cherish them. Y'all take care.

Priscilla was standing at a distance between normal and close and didn't know how best to leave. She wasn't sure if she should shake their hands again or hug them or do nothing. She felt herself holding up the line and panicked, lost her head, kissed Nayna on the cheek. She regretted it instantly. Nayna leaned back.

I don't know you, she said. Please don't do that.

I'm sorry, Priscilla said. Don't know what I was—I promise to never kiss you again.

That was a super weird thing to do, J.L. said.

I'll never kiss anyone again, Priscilla said. It's straight hugs from here on out. Straight Kone Zone. No. I shouldn't say that. I have no right to be in the Kone Zone.

You're not even supposed to talk much during these, Lottie said. It's like a handshake and So sorry and keep it moving. Especially if you don't know any of us. What's wrong with you?

It wasn't—this isn't normal for me, Priscilla said. I'm usually another way. You're not even really talking to me right now. This is some anomaly—the exception, not the rule. Very sorry. Kisses. Stop, P. I don't say *kisses*. I've never said *kisses* before in my life. Well, I've said it. Obviously, I've said it. It's a pretty common word. But I definitely haven't said it in that context. I'm panicking again. Hope y'all have a great day.

Priscilla turned and looked at the casket. It was black, golden handles she saw herself in. Her whole body was stiff. She was embarrassed, furious she hadn't kept her composure. The sanctuary was silent. She tried not to wonder if people were staring. Her hands shook. She touched the box. The wood was cold and muscular. Her father's coffin had been white and plain. She didn't like that. It somehow made him all the more lifeless. Black was smart. The Koneses were smart. And the gold trim was swank. The box's beauty was undeniable. Priscilla wanted to compliment them, ask where they bought it. She'd always felt destined to die young and wanted to know where to go for a good coffin whenever time came she needed one. This would also be a way to get back in the Koneses' good graces. They could see she was telling the truth before, that she was thoughtful and kind. She turned. An old white woman hugged the family. They wept with her. Priscilla thought she could steal a page out of that playbook, dole out hugs with her apology. A sincere hug cannot be faked and they would feel Christ's love wrapped sweetly in her warm embrace. She walked over with her hands up.

Excuse me, Konies? I know. So sorry. Just, real quick. I love this coffin. I think y'all knocked it out of the park and I'll bet your father's tickled pink to head home in a ride sweet as this. This is primo transportation. What a lovely final gift. Supreme, if I can say such a thing. I've always planned on mummifying myself. Figured I'd either go sarcophagus or be placed in some type of tomb like Jesus, but seeing this box has me reconsidering. How much did it cost and where did y'all purchase it?

Everyone in the sanctuary was watching. Some were confused, some angry, some thrilled. The Koneses said nothing. They just stared at her.

I know y'all probably don't want one from me but I'd love to give each of you a hug. If you could get a sweet hug from me you'd see how sincere and kind I am. Can I give y'all a hug?

Please don't, Lottie said.

Priscilla felt like someone hit her in the brain with a baseball bat. She saw she'd failed to achieve her goals and knew they'd think she was strange forever. She was upset with her brain, felt betrayed. There was a grinding in her temples. Her stomach twisted. She said That's my bad, and left the sanctuary at a sprint.

The church was quiet. She ambled around. Down the hallway in the adults' Sunday school area, past the welcome table, in and out of the choir room, around the nursery, through the library, and into the gymnasium. It was dark and the air looked silver, the floor dead carpet without fluff and dime-colored. Huge fan in the corner. In her pocket was a paper clip and she touched it. Her feet throbbed. She sat at the top of the key and took her boots off. The reception was across the courtyard, in the Fellowship Hall. Voices, music inside. It sounded like a party.

The smell of ribs hit her and she left, went to the church office. There were turquoise diamonds in the wallpaper. She used the office phone, made a call. A woman answered.

This is Viv, Viv said.

Priscilla covered the mouthpiece, kept staring at the diamonds. There was music in the background. She couldn't make it out.

Hello? Viv asked.

Again Priscilla said nothing. Her back was wet with sweat and chills hit. She shivered.

Helloooo? Viv sang.

Still Priscilla stared at the diamonds. Still Priscilla said nothing. The music got louder. The Roots, Eve, Erykah Badu—"You Got Me." Viv said I've seen people caught in love like whirlwinds and hung up. The diamonds turned green. There was a Crimson Outdoors mug of grape suckers on the church secretary's desk. Priscilla took three. The heater kicked on. Her head felt smashed and there was a clicking in her ears. She screamed for seven seconds, walked home in her socks.

MONTAGE OF A PRISON TERM

I MESSED UP, TABLE SAID.

Where they got you? Lady asked. It was garbled when they said it.

Dunta.

It was bad?

Sort of.

You hurt anyone?

No.

You try to?

No, but they thought so.

Where were you?

Liquor store over here.

The Beers & Fun?

Yeah.

Jesus.

I'm sorry. I'll send what I can.

So, nothing.

Probably. I don't kn—

Please have your talk take a walk and go fuck itself.

What's the name of that Bowie song with the ice cream shop? Lady asked. The one where the Earth's dying.

What? Table asked.

Your race!

Oh, "Five Years."

Right.

How are you? I was missing you today. What're you doing?

Hanging up 'cause that's all I wanted.

———

We didn't need the money that way, Lady said. We needed you to get something steady.

I was trying to do something big, Table said. Jump-start stuff.

You should've told me what you were thinking. We're married. Ain't supposed to be secrets.

Didn't want to burden you. What kind of man I am I whine to you?

You whine all the time. It's your preferred method of communication.

You can't just come up here so I can see you? Table asked.

Would rather eat my own face, Lady said.

It'd be fun to talk on that phone they have in movies, though. With the window between us. Put our hands on the glass like we're trying to touch.

I'm not doing that.

It would be romantic, Lady.

Table. Enough. I'm not coming up there. Let's move on. You get a chance to decorate your space yet?

My cell?

Yes. Your cell. Your space. Your place you can never leave.

We were supposed to have a kid soon, Lady said. This hurts so much.

I'm sorry, Table said. What you got going today?

Stop trying to get me to think about something else. I'm

trying to think about children. Shut the hell up and let me think about children.

I'm saying—

Shut the hell up.

Lady—

Shut the hell up. I wanted to dress a baby up in a tiny powder-blue suit. Boy or girl. I wanted to get a big dog and have the kid ride around on it. It would be their little pony. They could name it something strong. Darren.

Darren's a shit horse name.

Well, if you were listening I said it'd be a dog and don't talk about Darren that way.

Your picture was in *Jailbirds*, Lady said.

How'd I look? Table asked.

Pelican-esque.

Had the bruising begun?

Yeah. You look half-tough, though. Kind of hot.

For real? Save me a copy. Two copies. Actually, just get a bunch. Fill bags with them.

Tried out a recipe for pan-seared salmon, Lady said. Supposed to be healthy. Wasn't good, but it was something to do.

You went away from me and left me alone, Lady said.

I was trying to help, Table said.

You left me alone. I was alone again. I'm alone.

I didn't want to. I wanted it to work. I wanted to come home.

I don't know that.

You think I wanted to go to jail?

I don't know that.

Baby.

You still haven't given me a good reason why it's ten years.

Well, it's compounded by young Table's record. That guy was kind of crazy.

What'd you do?

Lot of small-time stuff. Shit just adds up after a while.

One fella in here goes by Heat Lamp, Table said. Not the chattiest guy in the world.

You could send me a picture? Table asked.

Why? Lady asked.

Decoration. Want to be able to see you. You ain't coming here.

Change your tone.

Other guys got pics of their girls.

You're going in other guys' cells?

I see them when I walk by.

Well, I'm not sure. I've got to think about it.

Why? It's a picture. Not a glamour shot. Just send one you already got or put on a dadgum burlap sack and take one. You can wear sweats and a helmet. I don't care.

The woman who got left doesn't need to explain herself to the man who did the leaving.

It wasn't that kind of leaving.

Leaving's leaving, baby.

I hate this.

You're getting worse.

I want to see you. I miss you.

I'm not coming there. I'm not budging either. There'll be a day, years from now, while you're still inside, and you'll think surely she's over it by now and if she's in a good mood and I beg enough it'll happen. It won't. You should've cared more to make sure you were around.

I was trying to get money. I was trying to take care of us.

Job.

I was trying to take care of us.

Job.

Please come here.

I love you, baby, but you're wasting your breath.

People ever say anything? Table asked.

Did for a while, Lady said. Then they stopped.

Oh.

People ain't thinking about you as much as you think they are.

Okay.

They ask me about me. How I'm doing.

What do you say?

I smile and say Awful.

This morning I tried to lift weights to improve my upper-body strength but a bunch of the regulars started calling me Fabric Softener and laughed until I walked away, Table said.

———

I'm drunk, Lady said.

How'd that happen? Table asked.

I really should've acted. I wish I was different sometimes. Die for Mr. Jensen, kids.

What?

You blitz. All. Night.

Huh?

I have nipples, Greg. Can you milk me?

I don't know what any of that means. You're talking about blitzes or titses?

You take on a name in there?

No. Why? You hear something?

You did then.

Some people call me a name but I don't own it or nothing. If somebody uses it I take a long time to turn around like I didn't know who they were talking to.

What's the name?

I'm not telling you.

Coward.

I don't like it when people don't like me. I want to be liked very much.

You're one of them only think about the people who don't love you types.

I'm gone tomorrow through Thursday, Lady said. So we won't talk for a bit. Going away for a few days.

Where?

Branson.

Solo?

Yeah.

Well . . . okay.

Oh, I'm well aware it's okay.

I didn't mean that. I just meant I understand.

I don't need you understanding. Even if you didn't, wouldn't affect me none. I don't care if I make sense to you.

What's on the itinerary?

Shows.

Yakov?

Him. Baldknobbers. Jim Stafford. Whatever I want.

They sat me next to that Clinton boy.

What's that?

One of Stafford's punch lines.

Don't be ruining jokes for me.

Lot of shows sounds like.

Yeah.

Lot of money for them shows.

Lot of my money.

You working more? Get a promotion?

That's my business. Not yours. I'm hanging up.

Wait. Get me a Yakov shirt.

God.

They used to have one that said *Happily Ever Laughter*. Either that, or the *America's Heart* one.

I'm waiting on you to tell me you love me.

The human spirit is not measured by the size of the act, but by the size of the heart—Yakov Smirnoff. I love you. Happy trails.

—

Going out with Sheeri and Lana, Lady said.

What're y'all doing? Table asked.

Olive Garden. Then dancing.

Dancing queens.

I been practicing my dancing. I'm so much better than when you went in. My hips are now under my command. Been working out. I look good.

Jerked off to you yesterday.

I use Laurence Fishburne now.

Eat a breadstick for me.

I stare at the floor a bunch, Table said. Try to count the hairs on the backs of my hands.

It's hard to be alone, Lady said.

Sometimes there's a buzzing under everything and it's like nothing can be good. I feel like I don't want to stand. I don't know why. Just seems like the most impossible thing in the world sometimes, standing. I'm bald now. Been bald a year. Been avoiding telling you that. Head's cold all the time. What else? The other day, during lunch, somebody started humming "Jesus Was a Capricorn." I hate that song. Don't make no sense. I told him stop and he kicked me in the chest. He leapt into the air and with both feet, like a ninja, and kicked me in the chest.

Just tell me what it is, Lady said.

I don't want to, Table said.

Come on.

You can't use it.

I won't.

Fine. They're calling me Scrotum Face.

Yikes. Why?

They said it's because my face looks a lot like a ball sack.

I did five hundred yesterday, Lady said. Starting to see a hint of a line down the middle of my stomach. I'm eating so much grilled chicken and salad. Every day you're in there I become more beautiful.

I want a kid so bad, Lady said.

I've had a bad day, Lady, Table said. Sorry. I'm not trying to talk about that right now.

I don't care. That's what I want to talk about.

Look, I'm sorry, but my head's having a hard time. I don't feel like talking about kids.

Do I have to say I don't care again or is that just understood in perpetuity?

You're being hurtful and unreasonable. Would you please come up here?

I'll talk to myself then. The best things about babies is they're sweet and want you around. Their toes are small and fat and funny and when they sneeze they surprise themselves.

Please come see me. I hate this. Whole place smells like piss. I don't really have anyone I can talk to about stuff. It's been three years. I miss talk—

It's very funny anytime one of them wears sunglasses.

I'm begging you. Please.

Their little fingernails get long and you got to clip them 'cause they'll scratch themselves and get little cuts on their face. You gotta be careful.

People visit their spouse in jail all the time. You're the one being weird. I'm being normal.

Yeah, well, fuck your normal. We got different normals then.

I'm not playing around, Lady. You better come see me.

You think you're the hammer. You're the nail.

I'm throwing away some of your underwear, Lady said. Time you get out they'll all be dust.

Don't mess with my Gaucho ones, Table said.

I will absolutely mess with those.

They don't make them exact kind no more.

World went and got all smart.

Lady.

Escape and stop me.

They're funny for jokes at parties and I remember them being very soft.

You got jail jokes now. Break those out. Y'all wouldn't believe it. I had to diarrhea in front of people.

Go, therefore, and fuck yourself, Table said.

Don't get it twisted like that's my only option, Lady said.

Ain't nobody want that ancient pussy.

This thing inhale the dick. Men love it. Sing songs to it. Guy at Harp's yesterday came up and said You didn't ask and I see the ring but I absolutely would.

I love dreams too. I try to have one every night.

Cool. I believe I'll go drive around and be outside and do whatever I want today.

Bolo, Table said, my new friend in here, the one I was telling you about with the Robert Duvall tattoo. He told me when I get out he can hook me up with his cousin's business. Said they make bags. Like, paper bags for grocery stores or whatever. Plastic bags. Bolo said they're going to start doing something with totes soon. I guess these totes are blowing up right now.

That's great, Lady said. Bags will always be in demand.

They're a staple of everyday life.

What's the place called?

Bags of America.

That sounds very made up.

Yeah. Bolo said his brother wants people to know what he's about on sight.

I'm glad you made a friend.

How's things with Sheeri and Lana?

Ain't hung with them in a minute. They got boyfriends. Do a lot of double dates now.

Oh. That's—yeah. Bummer.

Thanks. That really makes me feel better.

Sometimes I hear myself talk and think that's not how I would've said it, Lady said.

———

You're all in my head, Lady said. If I don't have work I just sit in the house all day and you're here but not and I think of you. Years of this.

I'm sorry, Table said.

I love you. I miss you. I want to leave you, but I don't. I won't. And you know that. And I hate you know that. You suck for knowing that.

Lady.

You're the only person I ever want to be with. There's something wrong with me.

You gotta calm—

I weigh 151 now. Lost thirty-three pounds you being in. Don't none of my pants fit.

That's amazing, baby. I'm so proud of you.

I feel miserable. I told you that so you'd dream of me.

I'm sorry you're having such a hard time. I don't like hearing you sad.

I think about you a lot.

I think about you too.

I don't like it. What good is it? Thinking of you? Missing you? You ain't coming home anytime soon. I decided today to try and think of other things. Spent two hours on chairs. Just thought about different chairs.

Lady, plea—

There's recliners. Kitchen chairs. The tall ones, what're they? . . . Stools. Rocking chairs. Lawn chairs. Some of them are plastic, but then they got those, they're not cloth, but they're softer? Porch chairs. Wheelchair. Got wheels, but it's a chair.

A bench is kind of a chair. Canvas. That's what I was thinking of. Director's chair, like a director would have, or like a movie star's chair. Sort of the same thing, but . . . High chair. Desk chair. Office chair. Chairlift. Stair lift. Them tiny chairs like they have at elementary schools. A toilet's a chair. I'm having déjà vu right now. This is weird.

I don't think I know the right thing to say.

She sat on the couch, faced its back, and looked at the hydrangeas. Then, with his small breath on the other end, she took her eyes from the sofa to the aquarium to the Formica to the ceiling, her head going back, back, and there were no lights on in the room and the sun could not get past the shades. Everything gray. She was exhausted. She fell. The coffee table caught her. An *Us Weekly* landed on the carpet. A Gaucho spilled. The hutch of dishes jangled. The phone was on the ground. She rolled off the table and looked at the magazine and the beer and the scattered stacks of laundry and his boots she'd brought out to shine. There was a herd of Diet Coke empties on an end table and a to-go bag from Dot's under the television. Her back was soaked, the phone still connected. He said her name. She shouted into the receiver.

I'm the only one here to clean this.

Yeah, you're big and bad over the phone, Table said. Wouldn't say shit like that if I was there.

Well, stretch hard and swing then, bitch, Lady said.

Had this book delivered today to better my intelligence, Table said. Some guys made fun.

They made fun of you for reading? Lady asked.

It's a book on sewing.

Oh. Well, then, you kind of had to know that was a possibility.

Thought I might like to learn. My pants get holes.

I think that's great. Not the holes, but trying something new. I actually started knitting recently. That's kind of, you know, same general area.

They were calling me Martha Stewart at lunch.

Better than the other three.

Three?

Fabric Softener.

Right.

Scrotum Face.

I hate when you say it.

And Bitchard Dreyfuss.

Ohhhh. Right. I'd blocked that one out.

It's stayed with me. Thought it was very creative, very devastating. Think about it probably twice a day.

I'm getting tired, Lady said. Sick of this.

What do you mean? Table asked.

Mean I'm tired. Sick of this phone. Talking to you. You don't say anything.

I say stuff.

I might go. I might not want this anymore.

I'm not going to sit here and talk about you leaving.

You think you're in charge of this conversation?

Ain't talking about you leaving.

Then I got nothing else to say and I'm gone.

You've waited five already. You can't wait five more?

Listen to that argument. You've got no power here.

You don't love me?

That won't work.

I just thought you did is all.

I wouldn't't've hung on this long and you know that. Your act's played.

Please wait.

Why?

I love you. Please don't leave.

Now you're begging.

Please wait for me.

Do you deserve that?

No.

Least you're aware. I'll wait if you give me a kid.

Would have to be some Abraham and Sarah shit at this point.

Even if it's not you.

What do you mean?

I mean when you get out we live with the kid and you call it yours even if it's not.

Adopt?

No. I want a kid with some of me in them.

Sperm donor?

That freaks me out. Not knowing. Makes me feel weird.

We could freeze your eggs or whatever it is. Invictus.

You have any clue how much that costs?

So, wait, you'd go up under another guy?

I would. I love you so much and I would.

That hurts, though.

I know.

If I say no?

I'm gone.

You couldn't wait to try with me?

Might be too late then.

Come here. We could try here.

It'll be a good long while before I let you touch me again.

Please don't let it be anyone I know.

Okay.

And if it happens, I don't want to talk about it.

I'll talk about it whenever I want.

That's mean, though.

It's how it'll be. Or I can take off.

No. Do what you want, I guess. Just please don't go away.

Okay.

Okay.

I'll wait.

DINNER IN A
GAS STATION

WHEN LADY GOT BACK FROM Frank's Drugs, she tossed the ovulation test on the coffee table and got in bed. Her plan was to pee on the stick the next day, when she'd calculated she'd be at her most fertile. She tried to sleep. The moon came in the room and made shadows on the walls. Her whole body sweated. Thunder in her chest. She smoked a cigarette, reread the paper, and decided to carpet the bathrooms. Her head wouldn't quiet down. After three sleepless hours she went to the kitchen for a Gaucho and crackers. The radio in the living room was still on. It played *Coast to Coast AM*. A man said he was abducted by a colony of aliens who all looked like the Queen of England.

I believe you, Lady said.

She stayed up and drank and paced and stared at the unopened Frank's brand box. The crickets were deafening. Her feet were numb. At 5 a.m., a woman told a story about the Loch Ness Monster swimming laps in a reservoir near her home. Nessie wore culottes and spoke fluent German. Lady turned off the radio and talked to the test.

Me and Table were walking in the pasture once, just out there strolling with our wine slushies, and I told him about these racist customers I had once. It was at the restaurant. These guys asked for more sopaipillas and I'd already given them two extra orders. We can only give out so many so I said they could have them if they paid for them. They got all fired up, talking about this is why we should've just killed all y'all when the *Marchflower* landed here in the first place. *Marchflower* he called it. Jellybrained fucks. Thin goatees. Had no idea how far I could throw a chair. Table was a few yards ahead while I was saying all this. Not facing me, just sort of looking out at the afternoon. Thought he'd been listening, but out of nowhere he starts telling me a story about flamingos. Or not a story. Just, like, facts. Flamingo trivia. He said when they get hot, they pee on themselves to cool off. That's similar to this other bird, the marabou stork. Lives in Africa. It poops on itself to cool off. Poop legs. This is what he says to me. And I was just sort of watching him talking there, watching his mouth move, and he looked so proud of himself for knowing all that. Hey, I got so mad. Asked if he heard what I said. He said yes. I said What'd I say? He repeated back damn near every word.

She grabbed tortilla chips from the pantry and started eating.

I asked why he didn't respond to my story, why he just started talking about something else. He said he didn't know what he could say that'd make anything better. I said So you told me about some birds? He shrugged, said Thought I'd try to take your mind off it. Then he just turned away, started looking at clouds. Wouldn't have pissed me off so bad if it was the only time it happened but he'd been being more and more dismissive of me around that time. I'd told him a week or two before that I was sad my grandma didn't get to meet him before she died. Pretty understandable emotion. He said Don't be sad. That's it. Oh, don't be sad. No I wish I'd have met her too. No What was she like? Nothing. Just Oh, don't be sad, baby. What an idiot. What an absolute freaking loser. Comfort me. Give me a hug. Kiss me . . . But so he'd turned away, right, and I just lost it. Said I think the doctors messed up when they circumcised you, your weird little wiener. He goes How you mean? I said I mean I don't think it's supposed to look like a handicapped crawdad. He got maaaad. Told me if he divorced me I couldn't get nobody else so I better be nice 'cause if he bailed it'd be me fat and alone forever. Called me Lordess of Cheeseburgers or some such thing.

I don't know. I was steaming. Hit him so hard. Open hand. Wop. Flush on his ear. He went to his knees. Ain't a thing on Earth more delicate than a bitter man. It's amazing. I started to walk off. Didn't hear him get up. He just strolled right up behind me and pushed me down. I rolled over and stared at him. Something in the way he was looking at me, I could tell he thought he'd pushed me too hard. That made me all the more furious, as if any amount of pushing is okay? But he'd gone from angry to worried, his sad little rat face, and he reached out and touched my hand. Looked me in my eyes. In my eyes. He laid beside me and we kissed awhile. I reached down his shorts. Touched him. Stopped my kissing. Made him look at me. Had my hand on it. He was awful stoked. I spoke slow. I go Hey, Table baby. He said What? I took a look inside his shorts, then looked back at him. Never seen a man more hopeful in my life. I stared deep into his eyes, pulled my hand out, and said I was right. Hoo. I expected something back but he just went sad on me, whimpered a bit, and went inside. I just stood out there and looked at the fields. Everything was real open. The stars were right on top of me, went on forever. I felt powerful and small. Sort of wandered around the rest of the night. Just walked the pasture, talked to myself. It was so much fun.

She ate another chip.

I feel unbeatable right now but also hateful. I never do what I want. I want to do what I want. I've never done anything wrong. This ain't wrong. When I was a girl my mother would sometimes ask How long since your last kiss? She did that 'cause she wanted to be above me. I'm going to have sex with a man I don't care about and see if he can give me what I want. I want this on Table. I love him and I want him to know I went elsewhere. He wasn't all I had. God, I could make it to the moon right now. He'll take care of a kid that isn't his and he'll do it because I said so.

Lady went to the bathroom, sat on the toilet, and peed on the stick. Her knees would not stop shaking and all she did was stare at the test window and breathe. Her brain was a circus of hopes and fears. After five minutes she got her answer. She smiled.

In the early evening she stared at dresses. One black with no shoulders. The other orange, baby-blue waves in swirls along the bottom. She put on the black. Her biceps twitched. Her face was cold. There was a raking in her stomach and her eyes went to her breasts. She reached down the front of her dress and lifted them, whispered All rise.

A full-length mirror leaned against the wall and she sat on the bed and smiled at herself. Her arms were cold. There was a coat-rack by the door. She spoke to it.

Vodka tonic, she said. Immediately, Slim. If I have to ask again I'm gonna start snapping dicks.

She looked to her left. Her chest burned. An imaginary man sat down.

Oh, she said. You could pay, sure . . . It's Lady . . . Lady . . . Right . . . You too.

She held her hand in the air and grabbed at space, acted like she was holding a glass.

Just thought I'd come for a drink, she said. Little sip . . . Oh, thank you. Isn't it fabulous? . . . And I got it at Penney's, it's like stealing . . . I once walked in on my husband pretending his penis was a guitar. Can't remember the last time I flinched. I don't like this conversation.

Lady took off the black dress and put on the orange. Adrenaline hit her legs. She started bouncing. A purple coat made to look mink hung on the rack. She slipped it on. Her shoulders were loose. Her face tingled. She didn't have to look.

You lovely rose, she said.

She went to the kitchen for fudge sticks and a glass of Cavane. Her chest was warm and she stretched her neck. Black hair waving. Her head was light and clear. The living room looked beautiful to her. She stepped onto the carpet. Her stereo was on the entertainment center next to the television and she pressed Play on the CD Sheeri burnt her. J-Kwon's "Tipsy" started. Lady danced around the room, sipped from her glass, rapped along. The sun made the air orange. She jumped on the couch and screamed Homeboy trippin he don't know I got a gun. Her coat was like a cape. Her head sweated. She was keyed up, ready for the night.

When the song ended, she opened the front door. The breeze was gentle. A warmth bloomed in her chest. She sat on the couch and looked to her right. An imaginary man sat down.

Hey to you, she said. I'm fine. I have a job. I can buy my own . . . You first . . . Clay's a strange name 'cause it's part of the earth and you don't be seeing a bunch of guys named Soil or whatever . . . You here to flirt? . . . Got a sweet tooth, huh? . . . What about my face? My body? 'Cause that's why you sat down. Tell me how I look.

Lady closed her eyes and pretended to listen. She touched the elephant, bit her bottom lip, ran her fingers over the couch cushions. Loud from the speakers: Kwon, put out them trees. A gust came through the door and knocked a ceramic Jesus off the windowsill. The Lord landed unbroken on the turquoise carpet. Lady opened her eyes. She'd been awarded the piece seven years prior at the Florra Long John Silver's after winning a hush puppy eating contest. She ate twenty-three in ten minutes. The Son of God was dressed as a pirate. He wore an eye patch, cocked hat, and held chicken planks in each hand. On his apron: RAN OUT OF LOAVES AND FISH BUT BROUGHT YOU THESE PLANKS, WHICH I LOVE. WITH THEM I AM WELL PLEASED.

"Tipsy" ended and "One Time 4 Your Mind" began. Low sun now. She stared at her lap. Rays hit the orange, made it yam. She chugged her wine and looked back to her right.

That was nice, she said. Those were good words. I am beautiful. That's true. And yes. You may come home with me. I want to lay with you, and make love to you, and never see you again.

She was buzzed and alone when she walked into Sorno's 4.4 Forty Mart later that night. Her feet throbbed. She was hungry. The man working the register said You look like you went swimming with your clothes on.

I been dancing, she said. You look like a young my ex and I want some of them egg rolls.

Well, we've a great many flavors, the man said. Pork. Shrimp. Chicken.

Those are fillings, not flavors.

I think flavors and fillings are the same thing with regard to egg rolls.

I think you're mistaken.

Another option is you order a corn dog and we don't have to talk about this anymore.

The pork-filled then.

She sat in the booth at the back of the store. The table was orange. Egg rolls, a soft pretzel, and a tallboy of Husst in front of her. She ate looking out the window at the closed Supercuts across the street. The man working the register listened to WWLS The Sports Animal and a voice on the radio said There are planes that couldn't catch Adrian Peterson. A Sierra sped past the station. She began to cry. The man working the register sat down.

You and the table call each other so you'd match? he asked.

She wiped her eyes, looked at her dress, and touched the table.

This table's my very best friend, she said.

Tonight's my last night working here, he said. Moving to France. Houston, I mean.

He pulled a pack of Camels from his pocket.

Want one? he asked.

No, thank you, she said.

What a dummy.

He lit one. There was a tattoo of Mookie Blaylock on his left hand.

Read somewhere they were actually right back in the day, he said. Cigarettes are good for you. It's, like, a fact.

How old was that book? she asked.

Was a pamphlet.

And you believed it?

It's a pamphlet. I'd imagine there's a strenuous process with fact-checkers and things of that nature if you want to publish a pamphlet. I'm sure senators are involved.

Are you?

Anybody can write a book. You have to be qualified to write a pamphlet. Pamphlets are real official. They always have seals on them. Phone numbers and emails and shit. Astronauts.

What about them?

Some of them probably smoke.

I bet not.

On the ground I guarantee they do. They can't in space due to the sciences. Fire's not allowed. Saw it on television. Causes explosions.

I want to go to space.

Spacewoman.

Lady wiggled her eyebrows.

I've often smoked in here, he said. Makes me feel good anymore, smoking indoors. Get that I'm doing something wrong-feeling. It's good to be bad sometimes. Makes you powerful. Where you coming from?

Luffo's.

What'd you get into?

Just danced. Why are you moving to Houston?

Brother's starting a business, asked me to help.

I'll take the cigarette now.

He held the pack out and she saw silver shavings under his pinkie nail from lotto scratchers. Lady took a Camel and put it to her lips. He seemed happy and harmless and sparked his Bic. She waved him off, used her own.

It's this candy company, he said. He's big into candy. Makes it all himself. His specialty's this taffy lots of places are buying up. He asked me to come down, help out. You from here?

Florra, she said.

What do you do?

Waitress at El Burro in Ox.

Nice. Good tacos there. Well, good tacos everywhere. Hard to fuck up tacos.

Lady looked out the window.

I like burritos, she said. I like to eat burritos.

You like working there?

What do you think of me?

What?

What do you think of me?

He licked his lips and smiled, looked at the table. He was trying to be sexy and she saw she had him if she wanted him.

I don't know you, he said. We have never met before and are not friends.

I'm aware, she said. But based on the knowledge you have, how do I seem?

I can't tell if you're serious but I'll play.

None of my fingers are crossed.

What about your toes? The little piggies?

All the hogs are straight.

I think you're smart and sad. Maybe you're trying to make your face sadder than you really are, but you're definitely sad. Could be, like, a light sad. And you're nice. But your mind is not all the way here.

I like Olive Garden. Like going to the Hasting's to look at the movies. Sometimes I don't rent anything. Just stare. Walk down the aisles. Enjoy the colors. All the cases. I really love nachos.

Nachos are awesome. I like movies too. I like *Unforgiven*.

I didn't like how her face was all cut up.

Me neither. I think you're pretty too, though. That wasn't a smooth way to get there, but I wanted to tell you that. And I'm not saying that trying to make something happen. Not that I wouldn't be into it, you know, you're—he smiled again—fantastic. But it always makes me feel good when someone tells me I'm handsome. I'm not beyond that mattering, you know?

What kinda stuff you like?

Shoes. Sneakers, I mean. I hope to have a lot of money one day so I can buy a lot of sneakers. That'd make me happy.

I been meaning to make myself happy.

How you gonna do that?

Made up my mind to do something.

Yeah?

If there was, like, a squirrel in your yard, and you saw him crawling around 'cause one of his little legs was broke, would you nurse him back to health and return him to the wild?

He looked out the window. She watched him think. He started to nod.

Yes, he said. I would. I'd save him and make him strong again.

She decided she would sleep with him.

What's your name? she asked.

That squirrel would call me Hero, he said.

What's your name, though?

Doak. I have to use the restroom.

What time y'all close?

About now. Have another toll-free if you end that while I'm gone.

Doak slid his cigarettes across the table. Her bangs were in her eyes and her knee bounced. Her throat felt full. She wanted to relax. Her chest was heavy. She looked toward the road. The store's marquee said *Happy Birthday Switzer Lacer* on one side and *Freedoms Important* on the other. Lady thought of Table. Her jaw was tight. Cell towers winked red in the dark. A milky glow from the power plant in Lussana. She stopped thinking of Table and looked at the ceiling. The heater kicked on. She saw Doak light the cigarette. She saw him smile and say Fantastic. Her eyes were bright. She touched the elephant charm, ran the beast on the chain, made trumpet sounds. Then she whispered You know, Lady, I ain't trying to start nothing, but a bunch of people's saying you're the best thing breathing. She looked across the booth to where he would return.

My husband's in jail, she said. I have a husband. He's who I was talking about when I said you look like a young my ex. He's not my ex. We're together. I took my ring off tonight and now my finger's cold. His name's Table. He's sometimes hateful and makes me feel far from him. I came out tonight to find someone to take to bed. Someone kind. I mean, they don't have to be. It'd just be nice if they were. You seem kind. Could I take you home? I want to lay with you and make love to you and then never see you again.

Okay, Doak said.

Lady turned and he was there, drying his hands on his shirt.

You heard that? she asked.

Yeah, he said.

What part?

Think I came in around He's not my ex.

And you want to?

Yes, ma'am.

None of that.

Sorry.

It's okay. My name's Lady and you can call me that.

All right. Ask again.

And you want to?

Very much.

My pastures are pleasant.

I've no doubt.

Then let's go get you naked, young man.

DIANNA

I'M GOING TO TELL YOU ABOUT IT NOW, Lady said.

Fine, Table said. What'd you end up naming her?

Dianna. Wound up not having her before Friday so I had to go in for them to induce. Dr. Nacadat told me get there at three thirty in the afternoon but I was all charged up and nervous so I showed up early. Just sat in the car for an hour. Thought about her in my belly. Was just there quiet, looking at the steering wheel and my tummy almost touch. She was wiggling. I started thinking how I was gonna have to be laying down for a while so I got out and stood in the parking lot for a bit. Had my hand on my belly, rubbed it, talked to her. Told her I loved her so much and couldn't wait to see her. How smart and funny and strong she was. Then I got to looking at the building. Tried to describe it to her. Don't know why. Think I just wanted somebody to talk to. Wanted someone else to know what I was seeing, experience it with me. Told her the hospital was real gray on the outside, bunch of small windows. Real black and shiny. Looked wet almost. Green awning over the entrance. Glass bricks on both sides. Talked about the gardens by the handicap spots. Had these pretty purple flowers in them. Don't know what they're called. Said the place looked more like a office building than a hospital. Was very beautiful.

I went inside and they put me in the room. Was actually the room I'd seen on the tour as a example of what my room might look like. Thought that was funny. Or not funny but, like, fun. Lucky. Made me feel prepared. They got me in the gown and all that. Nacadat came in there, talked to me. I was so nervous about everything but trying to pay attention so it was like some of the words hit me but some didn't. Kept having her repeat herself. Made her a little frustrated but whatever it's a big day. I've got to look out for myself. Around five they put in the—it's called a Foley balloon. That kick-started things. Went from one centimeter to four in like six hours. My day nurse, Kim, she went to Bidido, had real pretty hair, told me everybody's different and sometimes it takes awhile to fully dilate and sometimes it happens super quick. Can't project it. Just sort of happens how it happens. Wasn't too bad at first. Little discomfort but nothing nuts. In the night it cranked up. Contractions coming quicker. My body you could tell was sort of like Dude, what's going on? My night nurse was Jessica and she was very sweet and funny, always checking in on me, trying to make me feel better. She played fast-pitch at Gutter Creek when they were winning it a bunch and she'd talk to me about me and the baby and she was just real thoughtful. They had that crushed Sonic ice there. She brung me cups of that. Felt like she was my friend. After a while the contractions were hurting a bunch and I ordered up the epidural. They brought the epidural guy in, whatever's he's called. He was real gentle with me, real soft. Said I couldn't move or sneeze during the shot. I said But sneezes are surprises. He goes Don't get surprised. They don't let you see the needle. I guess it's huge. Worried it'll scare you. Made me hunch over a pillow. Flinched a little, but he got the needle in. I was crying. It hurt a lot. Was like they were shooting ice water into me. I said I'm sorry, I think I moved. He said That's okay, I know you tried not to. Numbed me up good, T. Couldn't feel nothing. Then I was just by myself. Just in bed and looking out the window at this courtyard. There were these stone benches and people would sit out there and eat or smoke or read. Had these dogwoods in the middle and they were all white and nice and I liked to watch the leaves blow off them. Had her at 8:37 p.m. And nothing crazy happened, T. Nothing bad. Always thought there would be. She'd be wrapped in the cord or come out feet first or something, but everything was fine. I pushed and pushed and it was like I was coming apart, like I was breaking, but Nacadat and Jess and the rest of the nurses were all saying what a good job I was doing and cheering. Made me feel real loved. And I was how I wanted to be. Handled my business with strength and poise. They said they could see the head. I was so ready to be done. So tired and wanting her out and then Nacadat was like Just one more, you know? Just one more and the shoulders'll be out and she's here. I reared back and pushed like mad and there was this real wild pulling down in me, this yanking, and it was like my insides were twisting and everything so tight and I felt the whole world on me. Then it was over. And she was on my chest. And we were crying and I just held her. I was just soft with her and loved her and told her she was the most perfect thing. Had kind of a cone head 'cause my cha cha pinched her on the way out. It was hilarious. She was so gorgeous. Sort of rosy-looking and glowing. I just felt her on me and my chest was moving and so was hers and she was warm and alive and I touched her hands. She has big hands. Her fingers are elegant-looking and long and they make me feel strong.

RETURN OF THE COWDUDE

LADY WOKE EARLY, the winter sun on her face in thin shivs of light. She went to the bathroom and stared in the mirror, looked at her whole body. Her chin, arms, stomach, and legs. Her nose, lips, cheeks, and eyes—four hairs between them. They grew in the shape of a diamond and she shaved them away. Dianna appeared at the door in *Toy Story* pajamas and a home-made sash that read MISS PRISS. One of Lady's old purses was slung over her shoulder and she held a stuffed panther in her hands. She was five now and stout, sunken eyes brown, big copper hair. They smiled at each other. Lady curtsied.

Your Highness, Lady said. Breakfast time?

Dianna nodded.

Lead the way, Lady said.

In the kitchen, Lady opened the pantry and refrigerator. Dianna stared at the food. It was a quiet morning and bright. Lady made coffee. Her fingers were tight and she popped them, wondered what he looked like now. There was a rag on the counter. She stared at it.

How do I look to you? she whispered. Look good too—looking great—you're looking great. And you thought I was lying. If I'm lying I'm flying, and as you see, I'm still here. Well now you see me in all my—well now you see the fruits—well now you see how hot it can get. Nice to meet you. My name's Equator. Let's go to our bedroom—let's be—let's go home and make love—I want to make love to you. I want that too. It's the return of the cowdude. Drive fast. I will. Drive so fast. I shall. I missed you so much. I missed you too. Look at these jeans. The front. Stretching. Reaching out. My God, Lady. Look what you did to these jeans of mine.

The refrigerator closed. Lady turned. Dianna held milk and a box of Kix.

Thank you, my dearling, Lady said. Princess spoon or big girl spoon? she asked. How we feeling today?

In her right hand, Lady held a pink Cinderella spoon. It was old and faded, the princess's eyes gone. In her left, she held a plain tablespoon. Dianna pointed there.

Feeling grown today? Lady asked. All right, cool. Guess that makes me royalty.

They ate on the couch, watched Wile E. Coyote get flattened by a cement roller.

We gotta eat halfway quick, Lady said. Mama needs to get a pretty face on for today. Gotta get my hair done here in an hour at Sandy's. New nails. Something loud. Or some kind of pictures on there. Don't forget your nice picture for Daddy. Can't believe y'all are meeting. What a day. Oh, what do you think of this smile, D?

Dianna kept watching cartoons, said nothing. Lady took a bite of cereal. Her hand shook. She wanted Table and Dianna to like each other so badly. His face was in her head. She started sweating, sunk back on the couch. Her arms were heavy. Wile E. Coyote built a brick wall in the middle of the desert. On it, he painted a sunset. The sky was orange and pink, the highway a lie. The television blurred. Lady thought she might pass out. It was like she was inside an oven. She felt drunk and high, her pulse like a gong. Her cheeks rattled. The Road Runner was color and light. He sounded like a space shuttle.

The prison was small and gray and Lady checked herself in the passenger window. One of the straps on her dress fell to her bicep and she moved it back to her shoulder. She turned when the buzzer sounded.

Table stared at the ground and swam in his clothes. He'd lost weight and she could see the skin grabbing his cheeks, the bones in them sharper, more defined. His shoulders were slumped. She wanted things to be okay. She wanted him to be excited. The gate opened. He walked through.

There was a dull pain in her stomach. She was so happy to see him. She was so worried. He scratched the top of his head, adjusted the way his jeans fell around his boots. Then he looked up. There was no sound. They smiled.

Pretty jacket, she said. Little loud for a stickup. But pretty.

Thank you, he said. It's my wife's.

She has dynamic style.

She's cool. You'd hate her, but she's cool.

No, I'm with you. She sounds amazing.

That's a dress right there.

It's trying to be.

Little cold for all that. Got goose pimples everywhere.

I feel warm.

You'd like to kiss?

Very much.

She held his face and kissed him hard. He returned it with strength. After a bit he leaned away and she said Hey and brought his face back. She kissed his cheek, his jaw, his neck. He touched her face. She kissed his fingers. He watched her mouth. She leaned against the Ranchero.

The cowdude returns, she said. We're so happy to see you.

And then Table saw her, yellow bucket hat too big, brim just above her eyebrows. She stared back. Someone played a piano with a chainsaw. Lady wanted him to talk.

That's her? Table asked.

Dianna, Lady said. Your daughter.

Table shook his head.

Still can't believe you actually did it, he said.

I told you I would, Lady said. I'm a strong woman and intent on behaving as such. She's mine and yours.

Lady. Not mine.

I said she was.

Words.

I remember what you said.

Some other guy's seed.

Flower's yours, though.

Lady waved for Dianna and she got out. Her eyes were on the gravel now. She held a sheet of paper.

Dianna, this is your daddy, Lady said. Table, here go Dianna. Say hello.

Neither did. Dianna raised her head slightly, looked at his boots, the frayed hem of his jeans. His shadow covered her and she stepped into the sun. She wore yellow tights and a white Gap Athletics shirt. Red bandana around her wrist. The paper clapped in the wind.

You want to give Daddy his special gift? Lady asked.

Dianna handed Table his present. He looked at Lady. His chest was tight. He looked at the paper. An illustration: *Scenes from a Western Sizzlin' Parking Lot.* A stegosaurus between the Ranchero and a golden truck. Flamingos on the dinosaur's spikes with wings spread. Lady on the roof of the truck wearing a blue bikini and holding a rib eye. Table sat on the ground and looked at cracks in the asphalt. Dianna was dressed as a firewoman. She squatted behind the Ranchero with a porterhouse in her mouth and horns on her helmet. Table looked up.

I got no idea what to do, he said. How was I in your head?

You said thank you and checked yourself a little, Lady said. Made sure you weren't about to behave foolishly.

Oh, to be a fly on the walls of your brain, he said. Happy as hell in all that bullshit.

He stepped past them and got in the car. The vehicle smelled like lavender and cigarettes. He set the painting on the dash. He'd been excited to see Lady and had tried, in the lead-up to his release, not to think about Dianna. When Lady brought her up he'd listen for as long as he could, then try to change the subject soon as possible. Seeing Dianna now, he only thought of Lady with some faceless guy inside her. It was infuriating she expected him to act like it was no big deal, like she'd done something normal. His head felt squeezed. He was upset he couldn't enjoy freedom. Dianna's hat was stupid to him. Childish and dumb. Her picture she'd drawn was unbelievably realistic and seemed far too advanced for someone her age. It was museum quality. If it hung at Gilcrease or Philbrook, nobody would bat an eye. The detail on the vehicles in particular was astonishing. There were scuffs and mud stains along the truck's running boards and an airbrushed painting of the Mojave on the tailgate—cacti, a Gila monster, turkey vultures, assorted scorpions. He refused to admit he loved it.

Dianna was on the couch with a sippy cup of ginger ale and a battered copy of *George and Martha*. Her legs were crossed and she stared at the noise. Lady and Table were arguing in the bathroom with the door shut and the fan going. She sat on the covered toilet. He stood beside her.

—to dadgum freedom here you go right this way Mr. Table so that you can raise someone else's kid, he said. 'Cause your wife spread her legs for someone else. This is crazy. Whole world been talking about it probably.

Don't nobody think about you, she said. Besides, people don't know I didn't visit. They probably think I came up there like you wanted and she's yours. Which she is.

You gotta stop saying that.

What? That she's yours?

Yes.

She's yours.

Jesus.

I don't know what to tell you other than congratulations, Dad, it's a girl.

Your head's in another galaxy.

You knew about her. Why's it all the sudden a thing?

'Cause I just seen her for the first time of course. She's real now. It's not strange for me to have a problem with this.

I disagree, dummy.

He raised his voice.

Ain't in no joke mood, Lady.

Lady flinched at the volume and felt her body remember the feeling. She hated it.

Don't be shouting in here, she said. Be nice to me right now. We had so many conversations about her. You knew she existed. You heard her crying. I mailed you pictures.

I didn't look at those. She don't look like me. People will know she's not mine.

The fella was white and all y'all look the same so whatever.

We all look the same?

Bunch of cheese pizzas.

He moved his head from side to side like he was searching for words in the air.

I'm trying hard to think of something stupider, he said.

Trying to rob a liquor store and shooting yourself in the foot, she said.

Very hilarious.

She lifted the cover off the toilet seat and dropped her underwear, started peeing.

Lady, come on, he said.

Stick your head down here, she said.

You had a kid with someone else.

Getting worked up ain't doing anything. Calm down. I hid nothing.

Telling the truth about doing something bad don't make it all the sudden good.

She's not bad.

I don't know what to do about this.

She's yours too. She loves you. I tell her stories about you. How you changed the world.

I never did that.

I know.

She flushed and stayed seated. He got naked. His body was lean. Veins lined his arms. The hair on his chest had caught grays and he ran his fingers through it. He looked weaker to her. She crossed her feet at the ankles, her underwear in a tangle. He had a heavy farmer's tan and his stomach was wanting, his pubic bush lush and like silver felt, a bouquet of stainless steel sponges. He grabbed the shaft of his dick and acted like he was playing guitar. She scratched her calf. She scratched her chest. He pulled the curtain back and turned on the shower.

For real? she asked.

I don't like smelling all prisony, he said.

He stepped into the tub, left the curtain pulled back, let the water hit his shins. He spoke over the noise.

She's five? he asked.

Lady nodded. He closed his eyes and stepped toward the showerhead. Water on his face, hot and kneading. He felt like an emperor. She didn't want him to be mean.

What grade's she in? he asked.

Nothing yet, she said. Kindergarten next fall. Didn't do pre-school.

She got any friends?

Not really, but I'm her best friend.

You know, I hear your voice. You think this is all right. I'm really mad. This won't just magically become okay.

He didn't feel home. Her voice came soft and she took off her earrings.

Look, you're my one and only, but a woman has to flex sometimes.

Spare me the practiced lines. That came from you long ago. Staring in a mirror. Trying to be tough.

Think you and I both know there ain't no trying.

He turned off the water and got out. She stretched her neck.

That was quick, she said.

At a certain point you're as clean as you're gonna get, he said.

She tossed him a towel.

You put carpet in here, he said.

Yes, she said.

I liked the tile.

Cool.

Dianna and Table sat across from each other at the kitchen table. His nose itched. He didn't scratch. He thought it would make him look nervous. Lady smoked a cigarette and prepared chicken parmesan. Table had changed into a new denim shirt she got him. It was unbuttoned, sliver of the pale chest shining. A Gaucho made water rings on his knee. He pointed at Dianna.

So you're her? he asked.

She didn't answer.

Hey, he said.

She said nothing.

Dianna, he said.

What? Lady asked.

Trying to talk to her.

She ain't doing that yet.

What?

Talking.

She ain't talking?

Not yet.

Like, not to me?

Not to nobody. Not even me.

Don't seem like that should be.

She's unique.

You should take her to the doctor she's this old not talking.

She'll talk when she got something to say.

She's a mute?

She spoke once.

What'd she say?

No thank you. She was three. I offered her a french fry.

That's the only thing she's ever said?

Supposedly she insulted some white guy in Marshall's once. Called him Stinky Man. I didn't hear it. I'd lost her, briefly.

Why didn't you tell me?

'Cause it's not a big deal. People lose kids all the time.

Well, first, no they don't. Second, are you taking her to specialists and shit?

She don't need none of that. She's good. Supersmart. Already knows how to read.

How do you even know?

I see her lips moving and ask her yes-or-no questions based off the books. She always gets them right.

What? Lady, that—

Not now. I mean, not . . . don't be that way today. Let's be happy. I'm happy. You're out, so you gotta be happy. Let's act the way we are.

He shook his head and looked around. The house had barely changed, only differences the bathroom carpet, a newer television, and two paintings, both by Dianna. One was an exact replication of Seurat's *Horses in the Water*. The other was a self-portrait. In it, she wore the red bandana around her wrist and a blue dress with ruffles. Hair in a bun. Massive smile. Her face made him feel alone. He tried to remember the things he'd planned to say. He couldn't.

Guess you mainly kept it the same, Table said.

I like this house, Lady said.

The Palazzo's a cool spot.

Good to be out, though, yeah? Wear your own clothes? Get comfy? I missed you. We missed you. Oh, remind me. Your Bags uniform's in the closet. When you need new stuff you're supposed to go to the what's it called. That store beside the Mexican church, across from Long John's. They got an account there. You find out when you start?

Next Monday.

Well, yeehaw, cowdude.

She turned back to the chicken.

Dinner'll be ready in about an hour, she said. What you want to do after? Braum's? Movie? Rib Palace? Their bar's usually got deals. Good margaritas, weirdly.

Table pointed at Dianna.

Where's this going while we're out? he asked.

She ain't a this, Lady said. She's got a name. You know it. Don't do that. Sitter's coming at seven thirty, so we got time for whatever. And can you set the table, please, Table?

His comment hung in the air over dinner. They drank three bottles of Lindown and didn't talk much, some back-and-forth about her garden, the next day's forecast. After dinner, they went to Heater's and drank more. They sat at the bar and talked about the live band. Lady liked them. Table didn't. He told her he was concerned about the lack of playmakers in Oklahoma's defensive secondary. She told him sometimes she has dreams where she has no face. She has a head and hair and skin, but nothing else. No eyes or nose or mouth or ears. Her head's the same size, still head-shaped, it just has no definition whatsoever, completely smooth. The conversation turned stilted. He didn't want to talk. He wanted to go home and go to bed. She tried to think of something funny to say. She couldn't.

They sat hammered on their stools and watched people party. Table's cheeks sagged. Lady looked at him with the edges of her eyes. The band started playing Pam Tillis's "When You Walk in the Room." Lady smiled.

This came out the year we met, she said. I remember listening to this song at Sparrows and thinking of you.

Yeah? he asked.

Yeah.

That's cool.

She tilted her head to the side. He wouldn't look at her. She didn't want to fight.

Would you want to dance to it? she asked.

Um, he said.

And he was silent for a few seconds. He didn't want to move.

Sure, he said.

Jesus Christ, T, Lady said. What's your deal? I'm trying to have a sweet moment with you. Wake up.

Are you being for real right now?

Explain your wonky attitude.

It might be because you have a daughter and—

Stop.

—have to look at her.

Accept her. Accept her right now.

Shit don't work like that.

I told you what I was doing and you said okay. You got no right being mad at me.

You're so confusing.

I missed you. You ain't miss me? We're supposed to be good now.

Your mind's floated off. Words sound weird out of your mouth. You make words sound weird.

You're so hateful.

It's all gobbledygook.

Lady shook her head and looked at her wine.

You know, never understood why somebody'd throw a drink in someone's face, she said. I get the desire. Heated moment, want to do some light damage, notice the glass in your hand, bombs away. Such a waste, though. I'm a well-balanced woman. I will not surrender to dramatics. This wine's very good. I bought it. I'm drinking it. Ain't wasting it on your sad face.

She walked away slowly, floated into the mash of people on the dance floor. There were tears on her face and white Christmas lights fuzzed in the rafters. The band played Stoney LaRue's "Velvet." She dried her forehead with a napkin. Table stared at her. His eyes were murky. The room bent on him. Everything around her moved. Shadows slid on the wood. A hornet in his brain. He wanted to feel good and go to her. He wanted to touch her. He wanted to hold her. He wanted to scream. He wanted to relax. He wanted her to feel bad. He wanted her to apologize. He wanted to sleep. Lady stood still among the dancers. She sweated and drank and wiped her face, watched people kiss, watched Table leave.

They didn't speak for two weeks. The house was quiet, Table on the couch at night and gone in the morning by the time Lady woke. It was that way until he came home drunk one night, smoke thick on him. He'd been out with friends from Bags. Lady was asleep. He blew on her face. She opened one of her eyes.

You smell like butt, she said.

My butt's cute, he said.

Your butt ain't there. Never has been. Ghost booty with your invisibooty. Needing belts.

Have you finished your long-winded joke?

Why'd you wake me up? I was asleep. Dreaming.

About what?

She closed her eyes.

The beach, she said.

It was nice? he asked.

Mmhmm.

You was swimming?

Yeah.

Laying out?

No.

What'd he look like?

She opened her eyes.

My dreams don't have men in them, she said.

Don't mean the dream, he said.

She felt hot and took her shirt off, turned her pillow over.

Babe, he said.

What? she asked.

What'd he look like?

Who?

You know who.

I don't. Careful with the tone.

The man you were intimate with. Who placed, with his wiener, a baby inside you.

Why's it matter?

Because it does.

Table's hands were in his mutton chops and he fiddled with his mustaches.

I don't want to tell you, she said.

I know, but just tell me, though, he said.

That's not convincing.

I'm going crazy here every day. My mind's eating me.

Then think about something else. Think about lamps.

I don't want to think about lamps.

Lamps are great. They give light.

Baby, come on. I been trying to get past it—you and this man and your bodies and everything with sex—but you and him are just always waiting right at the edge of my mind. It's too easy for me to think about y'all.

Yeah, that ain't got nothing to do with me.

That's dumb. I'm drunk but that's dumb.

What good will it do? I tell you what he looks like, what's it change?

One less mystery in the world.

I don't want to tell you.

I've heard you say that twice now and both times it's really hurt my feelings.

You don't just be getting what you want, though.

I'll ask for the rest of my life.

I want to sleep. Look how sleepy I am.

The unknown's murdering me, baby. It's shooting me in the face. Just what he looked like. Ain't gotta tell me his name or where he's from or the dadgum state of his soul when he entered you. Just what he looked like.

She rolled over and buried her face in her pillow. He touched her shoulder. She looked at him.

He looked like you.

That's not what I mean.

Dude.

She put her face in her hands, tugged at her eyebrows, wanted to scream.

I mean *what* did he look like? he asked.

I just told you, she said.

No. What? Did he look like any thing?

I'm confused.

Did he look like any kind of, like, item? A product or thing.

Did you have every beer? What's it matter?

It just do.

That's such a weird ask. Why're you so weird? I don't know what thing he looked like.

You can, though.

I had a delicious cheeseburger for dinner and I'm full and want to sleep.

What'd he look like?

I need time to think.

Take time now.

Lady looked at the pillow on the other side of the bed and thought of Doak. He reached his lighter across the table. It had been ten months since she last remembered him. She'd been checking out at the Albertson's in Sammta, saw some taffy. Now she considered his face.

Table walked into the bathroom and turned on the light. His body hummed drunk. It started to rain. He peed for a while, splashed water on his face, and went back to the bedroom. Lady's eyes were closed. She thought of gardening equipment, rubbed her stomach, and knew her answer. Table found a left-over chicken nugget in his jacket pocket and ate it in one bite. Lady held her hands to the ceiling like she was stretching. He sat at the foot of the bed, kissed her feet over the blanket. A yawn hit her. Light spilled from the bathroom and caught her ring. She touched the spangled rock. They looked at each other.

Neoprene fishing gloves, she said.

Table put his head down, felt below the earth.

Oh, he said. He was beautiful.

Yes, she said.

Damn it.

Like you, though. Pretty like you.

Chest.

What?

He probably had a nice chest. Pecs. Glistening.

Yes. His chest was unbelievable.

Table sat in the chair in the corner. Lady lay there, stared at him. His face was in the half dark and she couldn't see his eyes. Rain ran on the window and he watched the shadows of the water move on the carpet. The floor swayed and twitched, a sad disco. He looked at the table beside the chair. A Halloween photo from last year. Dianna was a seahorse jockey. She wore a green swimsuit, jockey helmet, scuba mask, and water shoes. Number 7 pinned to her sleeve. Golden trident in her hands. Lady made the oxygen tank out of PVC pipe and a cardboard box. Table shook his head.

Seahorses aren't big enough to ride, he said.

Shut up, she said.

Which hospital you have her at?

You know.

They were good to you?

Yeah. Had that crushed Sonic ice.

I remember that part.

Nice room. I didn't die.

We met at Sonic. You remember that?

I do. You wanted to jump my beautiful bones.

She was crying when she came out? She was weeping?

Yeah. Think they all show up yelling.

Were you in love immediately?

Yes. She was so perfect. I'm so happy when I look at her.

You were by yourself?

No. Doctor and nurses were there.

But nobody else.

No.

You were alone.

His hands were on his knees. The turquoise carpet looked blue in the night. She realized he was paying attention. Her nose burned. His mouth was pink. He looked pretty when he was sad. She was so glad he was in the room.

Never told you, but when she was a baby I was so worried she'd die in her sleep, she said. Splurged on one of those video monitors. Watched her sleep on that. Would just be terrified, staring at the thing, trying to see if her stomach was moving. Sometimes early on I couldn't tell so I'd go hover over her crib. Put my hand real light on her belly, feel it move. First time she slept through the night I sprinted into her bedroom when I woke up. Thought she was dead. She wasn't.

She was just sleeping, he said.

Yeah. Even now, I think all the time about her dying. If I was driving and got in a wreck and she got all smashed. If she choked on something. If she drowned. Sometimes I imagine what I'd say at her funeral if she died this young. I'd talk about what a awesome person she is. Was. How she was full of the good stuff. Y'all don't understand the joy she brought. She was such a kind, sweet little girl. A dream, really. She loved minestrone, loved drawing. When she concentrated she'd lick her two front teeth. Best day I ever had was with her at Stanks Gardens. We sat by the pond and fed Fritos to the ducks. One bit her. It was so funny. I loved to kiss her chunky cheeks. I was never good at folding her T-shirts. Some nights she fell asleep holding my hand. Made me feel unstoppable. Guess I wouldn't be able to talk very long.

Lady wiped her face with the covers. Table lay beside her. She touched his hand. She was ecstatic.

Sometimes I think about what if I died and didn't get to watch her grow up, she said. I don't want to die. I want to live forever. We do puzzles and listen to country music. She's so great. I just like her so much.

He rolled onto his side and looked at her.

I don't want to talk about this, he said.

A flash of silver in her head like her brain got slapped.

You were asking, she said.

I don't like that I did, though. I take my question back.

You seemed interested.

I'm just not able . . . it's like, I'm not sure how you . . . lost my train of thought.

It makes you sad? Hearing all that?

Sad. Mad.

I like to talk about this stuff with you. It's good for me to tell you what's inside me.

I guess I don't care. It's too much to hear. I'm sorry. I love you. I'm not okay with what you did.

I love you. I don't think you have a right to be mad. I really don't.

Then where are we?
Are you leaving?
No.
Then learn how to deal with it.

STACEY DALES / LANEISHEA CAUFIELD

THERE WERE NEON-PINK SHEETS in the oak. They'd flown off the line in the night. Priscilla stood in her backyard and stared at the covers webbed against branches. It was 5:14 a.m. and the sky was mainly black with a navy east, blue shreds at the horizon. It had rained hard in the night and the ground was soaked. Charcoal-colored puddles gathered in the low corner of the driveway. A heavy breeze came. Water sprayed off the leaves. She wore boxers and her father's old Olajuwon shirt, ran her hands through her hair. Her house was by the interstate. Two sport bikes battled on the road like athletic Starbursts. She frowned at the noise, got her ladder, and fetched the sheets. They were muddied and drenched. Bark flakes stuck to the pink like chocolate sprinkles. Streaks of dirt and mud all on the sheets, handful of grass stains. They'd need to be washed all over again and still might not look clean. She scowled at the tree. The tree shrugged. She looked back at the sheets.

Her eyes stopped. Her mouth opened. Lightning in her head. A warmth bloomed in her chest and she could not feel her face.

On the fitted sheet, in the smeared dirt, she saw an image: Jesus checking His watch. His hair was long and swayed in the breeze. Her eyes glassed. Jesus scratched His head, looked confused. Priscilla did the same. Her mind was blank and full. The sun was inside her face. There were waves in the light. A tornado of rays. Melted stars in her hair. She closed her eyes to keep them from exploding. Tears on her lashes. More wind. Leaves clapped and the light dimmed. She opened her eyes. The tears fell. Jesus was gone.

Five hours later she was inside the sanctuary at Lamb of God, seven rows from the altar, gaze frozen on Christ. Pinned to her breast was a welcome team badge and her hands were tight. She blew heat into them. Blush-marigold cheeks and rust lips on the Christ in the stained glass over the baptistery. Moss eyes exhausted. His beard was dark orange and thin at the midcheek, fuller and fuller as it made its way down the neck. Priscilla rubbed the pew, looked at her wrists against the wood. Indigo veins, magenta veins. They reminded her of spiders. She looked again at Jesus. Her nose started bleeding. She tilted her head back and grabbed the Kleenex under the seat. Blood ran into her mouth. She stuffed tissues in her nostrils and said the word *interesting*. The sanctuary walls were the color of the moon. Blood glazed her tongue. She scraped it with her teeth.

Heavenly father, precious and beautiful God, let me be welcoming this morning. Kind. (And she made this word rhyme.) *Genuine. Were You in the sheets? Please answer. I wish I was more confident. I want to speak well and cool to people. I want to speak that way to You. There's an emptiness in me sometimes and it's like I can't get happy. My feet aren't on the ground and I worry about my soul. As You know, need to ask forgiveness for recently wishing I was better at clowning on people. I shouldn't want to roast folks this much. Help me see the world pretty. Give me a soft heart. Today, during worship, help me just sing and not worry about harmonizing loud to try and impress people around me. I know it's my vanity. But were You in the sheets? I'm often sad about my life. Don't know why it's not better. You're all I want. I'll do what You say. How do I feel better? Want to reiterate I'd like to know about the sheets. Amen.*

The congregation milled in the rows and the organist began "Sunlight." Priscilla turned to look at the rest of the sanctuary. Two little white boys ran down the aisles and pretended to shoot each other. They made gunshot sounds with their mouths, kept shrieking Never! One boy hit the floor and crawled under the pews. The other climbed over the seats in pursuit, caught him. The first boy screamed Please let me live, David, I got so much life left. David screamed Do you love Jesus? The first boy screamed Yes. David screamed I'm sending you to heaven then and shot him in the face.

"Sunlight" ended. "O Worship the King" started. Priscilla stared at the carpet the color of nuclear seaweed, rubbed her eyes, felt alone. She looked up. A chandelier made of deer antlers spread honey-amber light throughout the room. Beyond the antlers, on the ceiling, was a fresco: a polyptych of God kicking the Devil out of heaven. Satan fell through golden clouds, robes in tatters, huge wounds on his body. Muscles and tendons were exposed in his calves and hamstrings and biceps, deep lacerations on his chest and back, face sliced seven times, the cuts like tiger stripes. Gashes and holes in him and inside the flesh like metagalactic space. Whirls of blues and reds and purples and oranges and splashes of stars among the colors and clouds of cosmic dust moved across the void. Lava and vermilion pools dripped off Lucifer in sheets and all of him was bloodstained, completely red by the end, an onyx rectangle receiving and erasing him. God floated high over it all. He looked young. Long blond hair, clean-shaven, and tan, the color of Clydesdales. His stomach had an eight-pack and His thighs were the size of vans. His whole body glittered, thick veins like nautical rope, God's triceps flexed with great purpose. One hand pointed at Satan, the other at the stage. Priscilla looked that direction.

There were flowers on the piano. A dozen white magnolias. She walked over. The vase was red and strips of yellow shot down from the top like curved stalactites, opulent McDonald's arches. Priscilla saw her reflection in the ceramic. Her face sagged. She looked run-down. A dedication card stood among the petals. It was empty. She looked back at God's shoulders. They were like lions, slick with sweat and gleaming. A young white man walked up to her. He wore flip-flops, a black fleece pullover, and blue pajama pants. His breath smelled like tar and his glasses were on top of his head.

Have you seen my panther? he asked.

What? she asked.

He didn't respond. She felt bad for wanting to walk away.

How are you? she asked. Can I help you? My name's Priscilla. What's yours?

He didn't respond. Lines of blood dribbled out her nose. She didn't feel it.

Certainly nice outside this morning, she said. Though we're inside right now.

The blood hit her lips. She put her hand over her face.

Oh my gosh I'm so sorry, she said. It's . . . I've been going through some really hard, like . . . I think there's just so much pollen in the air right now.

He took his glasses off and rubbed the lenses against the fleece.

Cheers, he said.

And he walked away. Blood on her hands. Blood on her blouse. Blood on the sanctuary carpet. She shouted after him.

God's excited you're here today.

At 6:17 the next morning, she walked into the cart barn at the Links at Swallow Ridge, Wahoo Country Club's eighteen-hole golf course. A bear rug covered the concrete floor and the lilac inflatable chair in the corner was deflated, a sad pool of liquefied amethyst. She sat on the bear and blew up the chair, posters of Fred Couples and Chi-Chi Rodríguez staring at her. Both snack carts were at the back of the barn. She pulled them outside, sprayed them down. It was a quiet, empty course. Gray-blue light on everything. Priscilla kinked the hose and lit a cigarette. She wore her work uniform. Khaki shorts and white polo with her name on the front and SNACK CART CLERK on the back. Her brain hurt. She tried to massage it. Her skull got in the way.

She set up the carts—snacks, coolers, cigarettes—and went back to the barn. There was a wallet-sized King James Bible in her pocket, the leather pounded, slate colored, and cracked. An old ticket held her place in the middle of Psalm 74. It was from a 2001 Missouri–Oklahoma women's basketball game in Norman, Sooners stars LaNeishea Caufield and Stacey Dales on the front. Priscilla sat in the lilac chair, read verse nine through the end.

> **9** *We see not our signs: there is no more any prophet: neither is there among us any that knoweth how long.*
> **10** *O God, how long shall the adversary reproach? Shall the enemy blaspheme thy name for ever?*
> **11** *Why withdrawest thou thy hand, even thy right hand? Pluck it out of thy bosom.*
> **12** *For God is my King of old, working salvation in the midst of the earth.*
> **13** *Thou didst divide the sea by thy strength: thou brakest the heads of the dragons in the waters.*
> **14** *Thou brakest the heads of leviathan in pieces, and gavest him to be meat to the people inhabiting the wilderness.*
> **15** *Thou didst cleave the fountain and the flood: thou driedst up mighty rivers.*

16 The day is thine, the night also is thine: thou hast pre-
pared the light and the sun.
17 Thou hast set all the borders of the earth: thou hast
made summer and winter.
18 Remember this, that the enemy hath reproached, O Lord,
and that the foolish people have blasphemed thy name.
19 O deliver not the soul of thy turtledove unto the multi-
tude of the wicked: forget not the congregation of thy poor
for ever.
20 Have respect unto the covenant: for the dark places of
the earth are full of the habitations of cruelty.
21 O let not the oppressed return ashamed: let the poor and
needy praise thy name.
22 Arise, O God, plead thine own cause: remember how the
foolish man reproacheth thee daily.
23 Forget not the voice of thine enemies: the tumult of those
that rise up against thee increaseth continually.

The barn door was open and Priscilla lit another cigarette,
stared at the course. This was her favorite time of the day. The
perennial ryegrass looked silky and buffed. Sprinklers shushed
and wet the earth. She ashed onto the fur. The ceiling was covered with old paintings of oranges and apples. She eyed the fruit,
took another drag, swallowed the smoke. Killdeer trilled over
the sprinklers. She wrote notes in her Bible.

People love questions. I want a dragon. We could fly around. Light stuff
on fire. I'm always cold. I want to be warm. Sheets.

Priscilla rubbed her face, closed her eyes.

Were You in the sheets? I don't want to be crazy. The other day on the
Internet somebody seen You in a Cheeto. Why not this? There weren't

*watches when You were running around. Why You even need one? Don't
You just know the time? Didn't You invent it? You got a skinny face. You
ever braided Your hair? Would probably look pretty good, I bet. I should
stop. I'm getting in the weeds. I know my mind's been off lately. And I
know sometimes You feel me being bothered at You or whatever but that's,
that's not right of me. I'm just being a little idiot. Little sinful idiot. Sinning
it up. And it's wrong and disgusting and I'm sorry. I'm trying to get out
of this haze. Maybe I could get more friends or something? Please? I wish
I had the money to buy new pants. Every time I buy new pants, I always feel
really happy. Like, if they're beautiful, that's always so exciting for me.
I want to be a good woman and live for You. Amen.*

She tried to hear God's voice, listened to the room, the sky,
focused on every sound. Brakes in the parking lot. A leaf blower.
Still the killdeer shouted. Footsteps right outside. Flip-flops
clacked heels. She opened her eyes. Faye Lephoon walking.

Morning, pastor, Faye said.

Hey, Priscilla said.

How's God?

Chatty.

You front or back to start?

Front supposed to be, but I can take back if you—

I'll ride with what's there. That was you set up the carts again?

Yeah.

That's nice. Thanks. You don't have to be doing that.

You're welcome. I like doing it.

Faye carried a Vera Bradley purse. Violet, black, and red flowers mashed together like mutant hydrangeas. Handkerchief-
sized American flag tied to the strap. Pink gum in her mouth.
She played with it.

How you doing? Faye asked.

Magnificently, Priscilla said. God's good. How're you?

Fine. Ready for the weekend.

It's Monday.

About called in and told Daryl I was sick but can't really afford to. Place sucks.

It's a good job.

You ain't a good commiserator.

Sorry. I feel boring today.

Today?

Fat Hank was out of the trap and wiping sand off his haunches when Priscilla rolled up. She parked in the sun near the pond and lit a Parliament. He was dressed entirely in Greg Norman merchandise, blue shirt soaked, sweat pattern on his stomach the shape of Africa. Priscilla watched him waddle over. She didn't want to hate him, but she did.

How you feeling, F.H.? Got the Husst for a very reasonable price today.

Fuck a Gaucho then, he said. Two Hussts.

He walked to the back of the cart and stared at the laminated menu. She reached into the cooler for the beers. His shirt clung to his belly and he tugged at it, gave air to his stomach.

I'll start with the Donettes, he said. Powdered. What's the smokes?

Courts, D's, and Reds.

Reds then.

She grabbed the donuts and cigarettes, wiped sweat from her neck.

How's the Twixes today? he asked.

This type of question grated her. He asked things like this regularly, tried to be cute. She didn't want to be mean. She wanted to end the interaction. She played along.

Divine, she said.

Ooo, he said. Like wine? Gimme two. And that's it.

Priscilla looked at the items and did the math. $16.69. She panicked. He would make a 69 joke if she quoted that price. She hoped she'd gotten the total wrong, pulled out the calculator, added again. $16.69. Total and complete devastation. She could call it $16.70—he'd never know—but she hated lying. It made her queasy and bitter. She decided to quote the price using the word *dollars* and the word *cents*. This way, the last thing he heard was *cents*, not *69*.

Sixteen dollars and sixty-nine cents.

Sixty-nine. Nice.

Priscilla set her jaw, said nothing. She didn't want to get into an argument. He played all the time. She'd have to see him again. He'd talk to other members, lie. They'd start tipping less. She lived off her tips. She would not have her money messed with. She just wanted to complete the transaction and move on. He started talking like Borat from *Borat*.

Very nice. How much? My name-a Borat.

She said nothing.

Give me your tears, gypsy, or I will take them from you.

Can you please just pay?

Do your vagjin hang like sleeve of wizard?

Enough. That's gross.

What?

Vagjin? Sixty-nine?

It's Borat. It's a joke. It's funny.

Not to me. It's a primitive, kiddish way to be and it says a lot about you as a person. You're making these dude jokes all the time—

Dude jokes?

That's what I said. You're making these dude jokes all the time and you need to stop. Other day you're out here calling your cat a pussycat.

He is a pussycat.

Don't poop in my mouth and tell me it's a candy bar, okay? Just 'cause you're stupid don't mean everyone else is. They're bad jokes. Don't say them to me anymore.

Aren't you, like, thirty-something? What do you care? You're an adult. Grow up.

I'm thirty-one and I'm not playing.

I mean, thing is, I don't really be giving much of a shit about you.

A lot of us in the cart barn talk about you. We laugh at you behind your back. Because of your personality and physical appearance.

You must be in the fuck-a-tip state of mind.

Screw your 75-cent tip.

Would've been better if you'd said fuck your 75-cent tip. That hits. Yours lands soft.

I'm a woman of God and I don't say that word.

Ain't no cusswords in the Bible.

You're one of the biggest duds in the history of the world. One of the worst things there has ever been.

Actually, I got a baller ass spot on a nice piece of acreage near the river. Looks like a palace like they have in fairy tales. Infinity pool. My own personal laser tag course.

You look like a fat aye-aye.

No I don't. What is that?

A ugly lemur.

I am not a lemur!

Yes you are!

What you even know about aye-ayes? Probably not even real. Ain't no animal I ever heard of.

They're one thousand percent real. I read about them on BBC. com.

What's that?

A website.

I know that, Young Miss Hateful. What's BBC stand for?

British Broadcasting Corporation.

Well, that sounds pretty fucking gay.

A big fat hog with big fat cheeks, talking big fat words that do nothing at all.

Verbally abusive. Cantankerous. You don't seem like a happy person and I'm glad you're sad. Your sadness delights. Can't wait to tell Daryl about this. You'll be gone.

Tell Daryl. I been working here longer than Daryl.

Antagonistic. Quarrelsome.

Just shouting out words you think you know the definitions of.

DOING THE BULL DANCE, FEELING THE FLOW, WORKING IT

LADY SAT IN THE RECLINER with the *Ox News Sentinel* and read an article about Florra High School getting new band uniforms. To more perfectly symbolize Florra's Wilderness Explorer mascot, traditional helmets were being phased out in favor of a more authentic coonskin cap. Table lay on the couch in an Etan Thomas jersey and watched the Oklahoma City Thunder play the Los Angeles Lakers in Game 3 of the first round of the 2010 NBA Playoffs. A floor fan at the end of the couch cooled him. The Thunder were ahead. He coughed, pointed at the television.

Collison, man, Table said. Look at that dragon. Banging.

Rock chalk, he's hot, Lady said.

She wore a pajama top speckled with pink hydrangeas and a pair of sweats the color of corn husks. Dianna sat on the floor and played with a hot-pink pony. She wore a purple nightgown, jumped the horse over batteries. Scott Brooks clapped. Table mirrored him. Dianna tugged on Lady's sweats.

D, don't be yanking on Mama's pants unless you want to see your sad future, Lady said.

Table turned up the volume and Lady rolled her eyes. She moved to the floor. Dianna used her thigh as a pillow. Pau Gasol fell. Table laughed and said Fuck Italy. Dianna closed her eyes. Lady scratched her back. Table took his socks off and threw them down the hall. Russell Westbrook dunked.

Russ's like if Vince Gill could dance, Table said. Look at him. Doing the bull dance, feeling the flow, working it. Kevin Nealons. Happy Sandler.

I bet Vince is a good dancer, Lady said.

Dianna had fallen asleep. Table thought he had a drink on the ground and reached for it. It wasn't there. He tried to act like he was stretching. Lady noticed, giggled.

What? Table asked.

Nothing, Lady said.

Not nothing with your giggle britches on back there. What's funny?

Nothing. Go on about your business. Stretch it out. Cup's on the table behind you by the way.

So what? Why do I care where the cup is?

Well, I figured you'd want to know where it is seeing as how you were reaching for it.

Well, I wasn't reaching for it and I don't give a shit where it is.

Whatever you say, Stretch.

Maybe you should reach for a cup of shit next to you and drink it.

Always humbling to be in the presence of the quipmaster.

You know, you don't have to talk. Noise is not a requirement. It's well within your rights to just sit there and shut the—

His phone rang and stopped him. The timing of the call was disorienting. He got madder.

Who the hell calls during a playoff game? Table asked. What time is it?

Late, Lady said.

Shit.

He grabbed his cell off the coffee table and put on his readers.

Ladue, Missouri, he said.

Just let it go to voice mail, Lady said.

Don't tell me what to do.

He answered. Lady shook her head.

Aloha, you weapons-grade ass. I assume you called so late 'cause you can't fall asleep until someone tells you to go fuck yourself. Well, Ladue, go fu—

Table stopped, scratched his head, looked at the ground. Lady was smiling.

Wait, Table said. What's up?

His voice got lighter, more concerned. She stopped smiling. He stood. The room moved on him.

Oh, shit, Table said.

Lady muted the television.

How? he asked.

There was no energy in his face. She hoped it wasn't his job. The voice buzzed unintelligible on the other end. Lady carried Dianna to bed and came back. He was staring at the wall.

Okay, Table said. Right . . . Yes, sir, this number's fine . . . My wife does. I'll message it to you. I have text message . . . Well, appreciate you letting us know and, uh, yeah . . . All right, we'll talk to you.

Table tossed his cell on the couch and stared at Lady, pointed at the phone with his thumb. He looked like a hitchhiker.

That was a guy named Greg Layne, Table said. He's a associate of Meth's.

Oh, Lady said.

He said Meth died.

What? Oh, no. Oh, baby, I'm so sorry.

Happened in his sleep, I guess. This afternoon.

Oh, I'm so sorry, T. That's terrible.

Took him a little siesta and, uh—yeah. Funeral's Thursday in Ballwin, Missouri. I'm sending him your address for your electric mail. He'll send you the info . . . I feel weird.

He lay back down. His head was warm and there was a tight ache in his wrists. The edges of the pores in his cheeks waved.

His tongue shoved his teeth. His face was heavy. Lady lay beside him. He closed his eyes. She touched his hand.

Well, he said. We're rich.

The next night, Lady lay in bed with Dianna. Dianna's bedroom had lime stars on the ceiling. In the dark they glowed, exact replicas of the constellations, Aquarius staring at her. Lady brought Dianna close. They held hands and watched the stars.

A pool, Lady said. One of them slides for it that looks like it's just a bunch of fancy boulders, but it's actually a slide. And a hot tub with cup holders and lights that change colors.

They heard Table get home from the mall, walk in the front door.

I feel bad being a little excited about this money, Lady said. Dad's sad. Been bummed since the Meth news. Don't think he expected to be so down about it. I need to do something. Get him up.

Table turned on the television, watched an old episode of *King of Queens*.

I want to buy you movies, Lady said. All the ones I love. There's this one called *Babe*. It's a masterpiece.

Kevin James was screaming at the top of his lungs.

Wish I could've acted, Lady said. Wish my head would've let me. Being in movies would've been amazing. You get to look good mostly unless you're not supposed to and when you don't, people know it's on purpose. And everyone smiles at you and you get to do all this cool stuff and believe in fake things like giants or werewolves. That would be so fun.

She put her face next to Dianna's.

I should have more fun, Lady said. Sometimes it's like I'm too busy with my mind. Tell you what I'd like—a party. Someone should throw me a party. I don't have nobody that would, though. I can't make good connections with folks, can't talk to people good. I have to mainly be quiet and nod a lot. Sometimes I don't understand what people are saying but act like I do because the topics are basic things it seems like everyone should know. Someone starts talking about stocks and I'm like Yeah, stocks are that way for sure.

Lady kissed her forehead.

Sometimes I imagine you and I actually have a conversation, Lady said. That you ask me questions, and I give you answers, love of my life. And they'd be good answers you'd think on for always. You'd tell people My mama said some stuff now. Have you heard her stuff? She was brilliant.

Dianna yawned.

In one conversation we were in the car and you said Tell me about when you were a girl. And I said I had three shirts. One was just white. No sleeves. Had a stain at the bottom where I spilled some medicine. Another had a train on the front. Red train. It had a face. The third they gave out at the grocery store if you bought a specific orange juice. My mother got it before I was born. Logo all faded. Bunch of flaky oranges in the center. Said on there FLORIDA TASTES GOOD.

And after that you'd ask Did you have friends?

And I'd say Sometimes.

And you'd ask What's that mean?

I mean some people'd be my friend if we were alone, but other people being around made them change.

What'd they say?

Things about how I looked. My personality.

Why wouldn't they own the friendship?

Think it had a lot to do with them and what they had going on but there's parts of me that's difficult. I'm too sincere, I think, and particular, and sometimes . . . I don't know . . . it's like I don't know how to stand. Like, if I'm waiting in line to go in someplace, how do I stand? With my hands in my pockets? Behind my back? Cross my arms? My fear with that is, does that make me look unapproachable? And I think I'm just not, you know, classically, traditionally, I'm not a magnet.

People made fun of you.

They were always nice enough to do it to my face. D, if you're going to make fun of someone, always do it to their face.

What do you think I'll be like when I'm grown?

I hope kind. Smart. Funny. I want a good life for you. Want you to be able to do whatever you want. Want you to know you're loved.

You're so smart. You're like an encyclopedia.

I can't believe your voice sounds that way.

It does.

I know.

Okay. Well, all right then.

Dianna was asleep. Lady lay in bed a little while longer, watched the stars, held her hand.

Table was on the couch when she came out of the bedroom. He wore a new University of Oklahoma coach's polo, navy slacks, and black Lucchese ropers. His old clothes were in a Dillard's bag and his face dragged, light frown on his lips. He smoked a cigarette and watched a *Seinfeld* rerun.

Señora, Table said.

Fancy shirt fancy pants over there, Lady said.

Thought I could use some new, better clothes, Table said.

Very handsome.

She just go down?

Yeah. We read awhile. Had to read *Don't Let the Pigeon Drive the Bus!* four times.

I hate that bird. Fucking psychopath.

He's just trying to have some fun.

Lady sat beside him, watched the television. Jerry and Elaine were at the Seinfelds' condo in Del Boca Vista. Elaine complained about a bar on the pullout sofa denting her back. Table's shoulders were tight and he was nervous. He'd spent the entire day thinking about Methuselah, himself, Lady. He wanted to talk to her, apologize for some stuff. A palm tree on the screen. It stood in the sun like a mammoth feather duster. A few weeks prior he was watching a Corona commercial and came to the realization he loved palm trees. They calmed him, made him feel beautiful. That'd be his opening. He'd tell her he liked how palm trees looked.

I like how palm trees look, he said.

Yeah, Lady said. They're pretty. How was the mall?

Fine. Empty.

I'm gonna get an adult beverage. You want anything?

What're you drinking? he asked.

Mom's doing a little red tonight, she said.

Well, pour two then.

She stood and went to the kitchen. He rested his head against the top of the couch and smoked his cigarette. The popcorn ceiling looked like the moon. Early in the conversation he wanted to keep the mood light, ease into things. He licked his lips and looked at her.

So, what do you want to do about all this? she asked. The money.

The question surprised him. He hadn't expected her to have something she wanted to talk about. He tried to adjust.

Yeah, Table said. Been thinking about that. I don't know. What're you thinking?

I'd thought a new riding mower, Lady said. Wouldn't have to tinker with the beast no more. Maybe a bigger TV.

Yeah. That's . . . sure. That sounds good.

And maybe here soon we go to Juss? I can get the day off. Shop a little bit. Get some food. Have some fun. We can use the credit cards now.

Yeah. Cool. Sure. Be fun.

Anything you're wanting?

Smoke crowned him. He said nothing, just stared at the television. Elaine begged Mrs. Seinfeld to turn on the air-conditioning. Table's mind was turned around. He felt out of rhythm. Lady came back with the wine. His mouth was set like he was about to say something. She sat on the coffee table and faced him. His polo still had fold lines. He looked at the carpet.

What's up? she asked.

I wanted to . . . yeah, I was just thinking about, like, I'm sorry I'm not better at taking care of you. I should do a better job of that. I'm gonna.

Lady's head went back a little and she tried not to look surprised.

Oh, she said. It's, um—hmm. You're good, baby. I mean, you're mean. You are mean to me sometimes. And I'd like you not to be.

Yeah. I think we both treat each other bad sometimes.

You hit me, Table.

He nodded, piddled with the hem of his shirt.

I'm real sorry, he said. I know it's—I'm just real sorry.

Okay, she said.

Can I tell you I got you something? I know it won't change nothing, just want to give you a present.

He reached into the Dillard's sack and took out a box of Crystal Satin, a designer fragrance by GEOFF.

Thought you'd maybe like this, he said. I don't—sorry, I'm trying to—it's like, you make me mad and I love you. I get really frustrated with you sometimes and I don't like to look at Dianna. I know that hurts your feelings. I just want to be honest. I think I'm better than you think I am, but I know you have a hard time with me, and I know I struggle with certain things. I just want to try and do better. I want things to be good. I want you to be happy. I hope you'll be happy. I'm sorry if I make you not happy sometimes. I don't know. Feel like I'm not doing a good job talking.

He leaned forward, put his head in her lap. She ran her fingers up the back of his neck.

Well, there was a lot in that, she said. Thank you for the perfume. I'd like you to try and do better too, Table. I need you to. I need you to be better. I don't care if you don't like looking at her. Get over it. She's five. Be nice. And I love you so much, and you're my Table, and I think you can do anything, but—just because you bought me this and said these things . . . this don't fix anything. You understand?

Yes.

Sometimes you don't treat me very good. It's wild how sad you can make me. I hate it. I don't know. I love you.

I'm sorry. I love you. I'm not—I feel uncomfortable right now.
Don't hit me anymore. Not one more time.

I won't. I promise.

She lit a cigarette and scratched his back. He kissed her thigh.

The woman at Dillard's told me it's their most stately fragrance, he said. Guess it's real rare.

Lady sprayed her wrist and held it to her nose.

Wow, she said. Is it possible to bathe in this?

We're millionaires, Table said. Anything's possible. It's nuts.
I've lost a bunch of money before. I'm so good at losing money.
This the first time I've, you know, received a bunch. Have to say,
this is better.

Lady had an idea and turned off the television.

Let's throw a party, she said.

Table sat up.

A party? he asked.

Yeah, she said.

What kind?

Like a happy, fun party. For ourselves.

She drummed his knee.

Let's just be happy and fun, she said. A cookout. Just in the
backyard. Let's throw ourselves a party.

Who would we invite? he asked.

Whoever we want. It's our party.

Could just invite everybody we know and like. We don't know
and like that many people.

That's a good number. They could all fit. Get a picnic table,
more chairs, put them out there and make it pretty with lights.
Like the dangly icicle ones. You could grill.

I'd like to not cook if I'm partying.

Okay.

Cooking's work and I don't want to work if I'm, you know, making merry.

We'll order out. Pizza or something.

Delivery. Even carryout requires some work.

Okay, delivery it is.

How much do parties cost?

Whatever we want, but probably a lot since it's for us. We should just throw one.

Little soiree, huh?

Yeah. Little function.

I dig it. I don't dig those icicle lights, though. They're tacky. I prefer the multicolored. The multicolored is my preference.

I don't like it when you find a second way to say the same thing you just said. Stop doing that. We'll do both. Split the diff. Let's get back to the party.

When you want to do it? All I got's the car show in Tunero whenever that is. Need to look again. It's usually a Wednesday.

Let's do it, not this Saturday, but next. This Saturday we go to the city and buy stuff. We go to the city and be rich. Then next Saturday's the party.

Saturdays are good party days.

It's on, then. The bell tolls. Party time.

SAND BASS / CELEBRATION DAY

LADY SAT SHOTGUN IN THE Ranchero with her door open. She wore jeans the color of flint and a pink The Judds T-shirt. Table wore his new clothes he'd bought at the mall. He squatted like a catcher beside the coupe and put his hand on her knee. They were in the parking lot of the Crimson Outdoors in Juss. Lady shook her head.

It just feels weird, she said. She should be here having fun with us.

We wouldn't be able to have the kind of fun we want to have if she was here.

You wouldn't be able to have the kind of fun you want to have if she was here.

You know I'm right. You see the playground at that day care? Buckerooz is a goddamn Six Flags. She's good. Probably happy to have a day off from us.

You don't know.

Would you just come have fun?

She got out of the car. He clapped his hands.

There she is, he said. We need a day like today. Those are your words. You go We need this day.

She would've liked to have come is all I'm saying. She hasn't experienced the, you know, having of things—

Great Jesus's shaft, Table said. Look how beautiful.

Crimson Outdoors had a retractable roof and Arkansas River–themed bowling alley, its exterior the exact size and design of the White House, made entirely of oak, save the pillars, which were marble and dyed crimson. Parked just before the entrance was an army-green '57 Silverado, the store's name all over it in hunter orange. Packs of Arctic Cat four-wheelers stunted on either side of the Chevy. They'd been painted in camouflage prints, alternating Duck Hunter, Chocolate Chip, and Desert patterns. Unlit string lights hung in dull necklaces from handlebar to handlebar and the Crimson Outdoors logo hulked over the entrance. A rainbow trout broke a teal river, hook set deep through its left eye, the fluorescent-yellow monofilament line pulled straight across its body, and a mallard flew against a baby-blue sky. It was missing a wing and speckled flecks of blood shot off the body in splashes, the other wing in the river below, so it was like the fish and bird were in the air next to each other, dying. Redbuds lined the bank and in the lower sky a C like a horseshoe and an O like a lasso. The rope was yellow, the shoe silver. Their slogan over it all: *Nature's Ours*.

When the doors opened, they heard the waterfall. It started on the third level and dropped off the back wall, ended in a two-hundred-gallon freshwater tank on the basement level of the store. The floors were covered in Bermuda grass, gravel walkways weaving through each section. High above them hung the heads of animals—taxidermied elk, moose, mule deer, whitetail, caribou, buffalo. A mount of a mountain goat stood in fake ice grass. A mount of a mountain lion crouched on a rock. Eight canvasbacks flew in diamond formation. Odes to beauty and destruction. A thirty-five-foot-tall Chinese pistache stood full and green between MEN'S WORK PANTS and the free funnel cake stand. Lady and Table stood under the branches, stared at the wonderland.

I've always loved coming here, Table said. But now it's like I love it even more. Why?

We can buy whatever we want, she said.

I remember the first time we kissed I was so excited it felt like my teeth were shaking. I feel like that again.

I'm trying to decide how to present myself.

We're the best people here.

A handful of employees roamed the store dressed as twelve-point bucks. They wore orange hunting vests with I WANT TO LIVE on the back and every forty-five minutes a voice shouted Bathroom time over the loudspeakers. The bucks would pick a patron at random and swarm, mark their territory, sprinkle deer urine on their head.

What you want to see? he asked.

The lady things, she said. What about you?

Just want to go walk in it all.

I could run through a wall right now.

Meet at the fish tank in thirty minutes?

She nodded and went left. Half the eastern wall of the store was Viz's Downhome Buffet & Dancehall, a sit-down restaurant boasting an $8 all-day All-You-Want buffet that morphed into a honky-tonk at night. Men's and women's clothes made up the rest of the ground floor: shrines to Columbia, Jukit, Simpog, Guy Harvey, Lete, Bob Timberlake, Carhartt, Pelagic, et cetera. There were flannels, jeans, denim shirts, hoodies, cargo shorts, overalls, rain jackets, coveralls, work jackets, hiking socks, ski jackets, long johns, tights, on and on. Lady's chest did gymnastics. She got funnel cake bites and ate as she walked. Gravel swished beneath her. She followed FUR THIS WAY signs until she got to DRESS LEGGINGS and stopped there to lick her fingers. The sugar hit. The smell of ribs nearby. She was so happy.

I like the Judds too, a voice said.

Lady turned and a woman younger than her, Mexican, mid-thirties or so, stood framed between a display of Disney-themed lanterns and a body-length mirror. Her name tag said JOSEFINA.

Shame the show got canceled, Lady said.

It's bull crap's what it is, Josefina said.

Her hair was the color of an unlit lightbulb and her work vest was green. A button on the front. In red letters: ASK AND YOU SHALL RECEIVE. Her yellow sandals were like caution tape on her feet and golden rings the shape of cows garnished her middle toes. Lady smiled, felt comfortable.

I agree, she said. Total crap.

I'd love to help you with anything today, Josefina said.

I'm wanting a fur.

Need one. Need one. We all need one. What kind?

Oh, some kind.

You celebrating something? Announcing your arrival?

Little of both.

And you don't know what kind? 'Cause we got all kinds.

Pretty kind.

To the Pond then.

Josefina took a right out of DRESS LEGGINGS and led Lady through LUXURY NOODLING and WEIRD, TIGHT SOCKS to a wall made of glass. Lady touched it.

Bulletproof, Josefina said.

Why? Lady asked.

Bulletproof things are cooler than non-bulletproof things. Also, men are nuts.

Beyond the glass was a room the size of an NFL end zone with a small pond in the middle stocked with catfish. Fur coats lined the walls of the space, the outerwear on hangers and arranged by color, starting with red, ending with violet, every shade of the rainbow between them. Lady walked with Josefina. The room smelled like chicken liver and pine. They watched the coats go by.

Anything speaking to you? Josefina asked.

Lady reached out and touched the sleeves. Her hand passed from fur to fur, felt amazing. The colors faded up. She tried to imagine herself fancy.

I don't know, Lady said. Not sure how I want to be.

The pond had lights underwater like suburban swimming pools. They glowed purple, lit the fish. Lady stopped in front of the yellows.

Yellow's fun, Lady said.

Very, Josefina said.

What's this one?

Chinchilla.

Ahh.

I know.

One of the fancy words.

Yeah. It's like a cuter mouse. Like a combo mouse-hamster-squirrel. From Chile. They're endangered, so, you know, pretty big time. Try it on. Check out the view.

Josefina pointed her to a mirror. The fur stopped at her waist, made her shine. She posed a little, spun, looked over her shoulder. Her hands were in her pockets. She felt untouchable.

Very good, Lady said.

Very perfect, Josefina said.

I'll absolutely take it.

I'd've slapped you if you didn't.

I look so nice. Look how nice I look.

It's incredible. I'm so happy for you.

I'm for real drop-dead gorgeous right now. This is crazy. Look at my face and body.

I know.

I feel really, like . . . lavish.

You look that way. You still shopping or you want to pay now?

Still shopping.

Righteous.

This was a fantastic interaction.

It was. You were great.

You were too.

Want me to hold that up front?

I don't.

They high-fived the way bikers do.

Table was facing the aquarium when she got to the bottom of the stairs. The coat hung off her shoulders and a flute played through speakers in the ceiling. Lady looked at Table's body, jet-black in the lack of light, his outline carved into the cobalt of the tank. He stood alone, head going back and forth, following fish. Hundreds of them. Her eyes went from cluster to cluster. There were sand bass and bluegill and white perch and spotted gar and chain pickerel and redear sunfish. They came in waves and sprays of bubbles went up from them and glittered in the water. Lady put her arms in the sleeves of the chinchilla, brought the coat tight around her, and walked to Table. He grinned.

You buy that? he asked.

Not yet, she said.

It's nice.

Thanks.

Look like a gorgeous bumblebee. Attention will be paid.

Yeah, people will want to talk to me, they see me in this. You find anything?

Nothing yet.

A diver appeared in the water, red hair waving. She was built like a bodybuilder and they watched her feed the fish. A turtle swam alongside her. She touched its shell.

Read somewhere turtles been around for like two hundred million years, Lady said.

Seen a video of two of them having sex on the Internet once, Table said.

How was that?

Seemed to be enjoying themselves.

They went and stood beside the waterfall, got misted. Table threw in a dime. He hollered at her.

Hey hottie, he said. I wished for you eternal happiness and joy. No big deal. I'm a giver. It's a curse.

You're an idiot, Lady said.

I also wished for myself a stretch Hummer. You really do look amazing. I'm having fun. Let's go to the third floor.

After you.

The stairs were maple, and bur oaks climbed some thirty feet on either side. Table took the first step, looked up, and gasped. Lady looked. Next to the mouth of the waterfall, in an area labeled BEAR ZONE, a stuffed Kodiak stood on its hind legs atop a rectangular boulder painted like the American flag. Table put his hands over his heart.

And his dick grew three sizes that day, Table said.

She brought her mouth to the right side of her face and looked at him with the edges of her eyes. Her nose was scrunched. She rubbed her neck.

Table, she said.

I love that bear, he said.

It's nice.

It's new.

Good for them.

They haven't had it before is what I meant.

I understood.

I want it.

Well, no.

He giggled and ran up the stairs. Lady sighed and started after him.

When she got to the bear, he'd joined it on the rock. He pressed his fingers against each of its claws. Every time he connected, he said the word *ow*.

If it hurts stop doing it, Lady said.

This is so badass, Table said.

Table held the bear at the waist and swayed. He'd climbed over a fence to get to the animal, the area peppered with boulders, lined with mulch, small signs dug in telling people facts about Kodiaks. The bear was a little under nine feet tall and looked proud of itself and mighty and Table wondered if he was too old to start lifting weights again. He imagined bringing people to the Palazzo, acting like he'd bagged it. He imagined saying This monster was my brother, but I had to put him down. Was either him or me and I don't like dying. I grilled his heart and then ate it. Tasted horrible but now he's with me forever.

Lady worried someone would come over soon. The waterfall was loud. She had to shout.

Maybe don't hug her.

It's a boy.

Sure it is. You better get down before we get kicked outta here.

We're getting him.

I'm sure she's not for sale.

He's my bear. He's my bear and I will hug him. I will hug him whenever I want.

You told me your mama went nuts but I figured you had more time.

A white man in an unbuttoned Crimson Outdoors vest, no shirt underneath, and solid-black Air Maxes walked up. M Frame Oakleys hung off purple Croakies and his chest looked like two snare drums taped side by side. A tattoo of a young Dolly Parton bloomed on his twitching bicep. Veins crisscrossed the muscle like roads on a map. His name tag read TOPHER. His tips were bleached. He snapped his fingers.

Ay, yo, sir, Topher said.

Table, Lady said.

Sir, you can't be up there touching Madelyn Jean, Topher said.

Told you, Lady said.

Table kept his hands on the bear.

How much she cost? Table asked.

It's not . . . ain't able to buy her, Topher said.

Au contraire, Roids, Table said. I'm very able. I'm rich.

Table was looking directly into the bear's eyes.

Sir, Topher said. Get down or I'll have to, like, make you go.

I'll get down when I know how much this bear costs, Table said.

It's not for sale, dude, Topher said.

Twenty-five thousand dollars, Table said.

Hey now, Lady said.

Get down, sir, Topher said.

Thirty-thousand dollars, Table said.

Sylvia Table, Lady said.

It ain't like that, Topher said. Stop doing this.

Thirty-three thousand dollars for this beautiful Kodiak dream, Table said.

A truly insane amount of money to pay for a dead bear, Lady said.

Get down pronto or I embarrass you, Topher said.

I can't be embarrassed, you broke-ass crusty-ass Jeff Bagwell–looking motherfucker, Table said.

I embarrass you all the time, Lady said.

You got five seconds to get down, Topher said. I'm counting silently because I don't respect you.

I know about time, Canseco, calm the hell down, Table said.

I'm gonna fuck you up and tell all my friends about it, Topher said. You don't understand what you're getting into. I watch Kimbo Slice videos on WorldStar every night before I go to bed. I have anger issues I see doctors about.

I got money and I want something so I get it, Table said. That's how this works, ain't it? This America. Land of the no no no. I don't want to say that. Who do I pay for the bear?

You got one more chance to get down, Topher said.

Fuck your chance, Table said.

He gone, Topher said.

Topher hopped the fence. Lady grabbed for his arm and whiffed, screamed Table's name. Table ignored her. Topher took him by the waist and lifted him off the rock. Table tried to kick him, couldn't. Topher carried him toward the stairs. Lady followed. A group of kids at the shooting gallery had stopped testing out the compound bows and watched. Table looked folded, kept flailing.

That's too rough and wrestle-ish now, Lady said. Don't be all wrestle-ish.

Let go of me, Barry Bonds, Table said.

Table tried to get the kids to chant with him.

Let him go. Let him go. Let him go.

The kids just stared. One pulled out his phone and started videoing. Lady joined Table's chant, pulled a Nalgene off a shelf, and threw it at them. It landed in the grass at their feet and she flipped them off. Topher started down the stairs. Table stopped flailing.

Listen here, you Best Choice Giambi. I will rage so hard in ten seconds and it'll end with you in the tank and sad so I'll give you one last opportunity. Apologize and put me down or be prepared to go swimming.

Will you chill about the bear? Topher asked.

I will never chill about anything ever.

Then you're gone.

Topher slung him over his shoulder.

Like a continental soldier! Topher screamed.

People on the first level were watching now. Table was squealing, writhing. Lady grabbed a shirt, wet it in the waterfall, and tried to whip Topher. She missed and snapped it against Table's arm.

Crap fire, Table screamed.

Sorry, Lady screamed.

Three beeps rang out in the store. Bathroom time bathroom time bathroom time. Topher held Table like a newborn and the bucks converged. Twenty strong and completely silent. They engulfed the two men, overwhelmed Table, doused him with deer urine. He was red and stopped fighting. Topher laid him facedown in the grass. A crowd had gathered. People were laughing. Table was still and rubbery. He breathed in the dirt and made sobbing noises. Lady swung at Topher with the shirt and he caught it, ripped it away. She kicked over a display of travel coolers. More laughing. Table hadn't moved. She knelt beside him.

I'll swing for you, baby, Lady said.

She looked at Topher.

You want to be a human being right quick and not a dadgum rhinoceros? Lady asked. Look what you did.

Topher sighed and rolled his eyes, took a knee.

I apologize, sir, he said. We just, you know, got rules.

He put his hand on Table's back.

Hey, Topher said. Ain't no need to be crying and all that.

Topher brought his face closer. He was almost to Table's ear.

Sir, Topher said. Hey, come on, man. I'm sorry.

Table was smiling when he turned. Lady raised her eyebrows and clapped her hands.

Oh I love it so, she said.

Lady was laughing before Table's spit hit Topher's face. Topher grabbed her arm and picked up Table by the belt, carried him out of the store like a gym bag. The bucks applauded but their hooves were soft and made no sound.

Topher dropped Table face-first onto pavement. His cheek hit flush off a curb and opened. The store alarm rang. Topher held tight to Lady's wrist. His fingers dug in.

You're hurting me, she said. Hey. You're hurting me.

Table stood and squared up to Topher, eyes level with his nipples. He started growling. People had stopped walking to their cars. They stood in the parking lot and watched. A guy hung out the passenger window of an Avalanche and screamed Please fight. Blood dripped off Table's jaw. He craned his neck up at Topher.

You'll let her go, Table screamed. You'll let her go. You'll let her go.

More of a crowd gathered. The alarm kept ringing. Topher was distracted by all the phones videoing and accidentally loosened his grip. Lady ripped her arm away. Topher let go. She held her wrist, spit at his Nikes. Table's head was wet from the deer pee and the sweat and the blood fell on his boots. He flexed and screamed at Topher, acted the victor.

And that's just the trailer. Trust me. You don't want to see the movie. Blockbuster. Never be mean to the woman I love. She is my whole life. I will cut your legs off and eat you. Make me a little Topher stew. Hey everyone. Check out this dude. This dude's bullshit.

Topher got in Table's face and screamed Little boy! He strung the words out and pounded his chest like an ape. They saw the red-black back of his throat. The tendons in his neck shook. Table stepped back. The alarm dropped out. Topher pointed at Lady's coat.

You pay for that?

Five deer ushered them back inside. Customers stared as a cashier removed the security tag from Lady's sleeve. Lady stared back, bore holes into their skulls until they looked away. She'd refused to take off the fur. Why should she? It was hers now. She'll unbutton when she's ready to unbutton, several weeks from now, in the privacy of her own home. On the other side of the conveyor belt, above the candy bars, were two stacks of green ball caps that said I GOT PEED ON AT CRIMSON OUTDOORS. Table grabbed one and handed it to the cashier. Lady looked at him.

What? he asked. I did.

They went to F. Hughe Drew for dinner, a sixteen-table upscale barbecue spot in the June District. The restaurant had stainless steel walls and pinewood floors, tablecloths the color of bright bone. Muted televisions in each corner played, respectively, a reairing of the 2000 OU–Nebraska football game, an instructional DVD on how to properly roast a whole pig, *This Is Garth Brooks*, and the local news. Countless red bandanas had been fixed to the wall in elaborate swirls and pictures of Oklahoma-linked somebodies dotted the ceiling. Wes Studi, James Garner, Wanda Jackson, Clara Luper, Shannon Lucid, Woody Guthrie, Ada Lois Sipuel Fisher, the Selmon Brothers, Kristin Chenoweth, Ed Ruscha, Eric Coley, Shannon Miller, Ralph Ellison, Kevin Bookout, Mary Golda Ross, Maria Tallchief, Rocky Calmus, T.C. Cannon, Jeanne Tripplehorn, Reba McEntire, Todd Bonzalez, Wilma Mankiller, Crystal Robinson, Yvonne Chouteau, et cetera, smiled down on them.

They were seated by a window that looked out onto a courtyard with a stone fountain. Water fell from a lion's mouth and into a small pool. Lady and Table were thrilled to be there, felt special. Their waiter shuffled up. Norman. He was an older white man with a wrist brace, severe rosacea, and a Kenny Rogers beard.

We decide? Norman asked.

Half pound of pork butt, Table said. Pound of tri-tip, mac and cheese, fried okra, honey biscuits, and let's double up on the ribs and the fries.

Sweet potato or regular? Norman asked.

Table looked at Lady.

Yes, she said.

Appetizers? Norman asked.

Shredded onion strings of course, Table said.

Ranch? Norman asked.

Always, Table said. And how are the pulled pork nachos?

They are the tops, sir, Norman said. It's a big-time order. One of our elite dishes. Don't tell anyone but sometimes, when someone in my section gets it, I sneak a chip or two on the way to the table.

Please speak in a detailed way about them, Table said.

First, you've our world-famous pulled pork, Norman said. Responsibly raised. Locally sourced. We literally slaughtered the hog out back this morning. It was wild. I wish y'all could've seen it. Then you've got baked beans, tomato, bacon bits, red onion, jalapeños, sea salt. Obviously the chip itself, which is a tortilla-based chip. We make those in-house. Drizzled on top is both our original Drew's Sauce and our award-winning Four-Cheese Sauce. They're mingling, the sauces, and they get along very well.

Double your pleasure, Table said.

Double your fun, Lady said. And what are the four cheeses?

American, Norman said. Cheddar. Swiss. Drop a little Gouda off in there at the end.

Well, well, well, Table said.

He looked at Lady. She nodded.

Wonderful, Norman said. Reload the drinks? I'll send Brady, who I despise, to replenish your waters.

Please get us another bottle of Taureau, Table said. The way I want it is, when you notice that one's halfway gone, send the next. Repeat until I get stupid.

How will I know when that is, sir? Norman asked.

When I ask you to stop, Table said.

Norman said Woof and took the menus away. Table looked out the window. Lady watched him. His puffed cheek had already taken on purples and the light shone off his empty scalp and the neck of his polo was stretched and below the collar of his undershirt.

I can't tell if it's just I've gotten used to it or it's actually not that strong, but I'm having a hard time smelling the deer pee now, Table said. It was for sure strong at first but it feels like it's faded significantly. Can you smell it still?

She could.

No, she said.

Thank God, Table said. Not my pheromone of choice. Man, really feel like I got the better of that dude at Crimson. Creatine Craig. That vested fuck. Think I came out on top there.

I don't think I could say that's true, Lady said.

I mean physically he probably bested me, but verbally . . . like, with words, I was many moves ahead.

I liked some of the stuff you said.

I say good stuff.

They settled back in their chairs. The Swan Silvertones' "Heavenly Light" played.

You already got a nice little bruise, she said.

Yeah, I feel it swelling some. Need to ice when we get back to the house.

Lady blew fog on the window and drew a turtle.

From today, she said.

That jacket's nice, he said. Looks good on you.

I honestly love it so so much. Can't even tell you.

You warm?

Blazing.

Take it off.

Never. I'm a cartoon character now. Every day, same thing.

She took a long drink of champagne, burped, filled her glass again. Her shoulders were loose and she bounced in her seat.

Rather be murdered, she said. I look like a beautiful butterfly.

Table smiled.

It's soft? he asked.

Lady reached across the table, let him feel. He touched her sleeve and her eyes wandered to the walls. He whistled. She didn't hear him. She was distracted by bandanas.

Chinchilla? Table asked.

Lady said nothing.

Hey, he said. Señora.

She looked up.

It's chinchilla? he asked.

Huh? she asked. Oh, yeah.

It's like a varmint? Rodent? We should get some. Harvest their fur.

She was barely paying attention, eyes back on the bandanas.

Okay, she said.

They make sweatpants out of them? he asked. Where you buy them? Can you get them at a local pet store or do I have to drive to Corder?

They're endangered.

Oh. Well, that hurts our business model a little. I don't understand about endangered animals when there's a guy and a girl left. Why don't they just get them together and make them have a bunch of sex? Surely there's a way to make that happen. They should be trying harder to get those animals to fuck.

Wonder how Dianna's doing?

I'm sure fine. Giving Buckarooz all they can handle.

I miss her. I like to have fun with her.

Seems like that's mutual.

I feel bad. I didn't think of her enough today. Thought of myself too much.

I think that's allowed. A little playtime.

I feel like a bad mom.

And it was quiet for a second. Lady stared at the pepper. Dianna's face in her head. Table looked at her.

I think you do a awesome job being a mom, he said. She loves you a whole lot.

Still she stared at the pepper. Her nostrils flared and she scratched her cheeks. He watched her mouth. She began to cry. The Swan Silvertones sang about starry crowns. Lady stuck her tongue out and looked up.

Thanks, she said. For saying that.

She's a kind kid, he said. Good kid.

Yeah. She's—I'm so happy to have her. So grateful. I feel really lucky.

She wiped her face with her sleeves.

Come on, Lady, she said.

Brady appeared with water. He sneezed into the pitcher, said Shit, and walked away. Table reached across the table. They held hands.

Brady does seem like he sucks, Table said.

I hate him so much, Lady said.

When the meal was over they walked drunk into the courtyard for cigarettes and coffee. Lady sat on the edge of the fountain and Table sat beside her. They talked about socks. He thought about dancing. The music had changed to Smokey Robinson and the Miracles and was louder outside. They were in the half dark. The only light came from the restaurant.

I don't know what it is with my feet but ankle socks and I just don't get along, Lady said.

Table stood and spun. Her head went back. He danced. The drinks had his feet feathery. The brick was slick and moving was easy. He winked and blew a kiss. She whistled. He bowed.

Electric, she said. A smash. The show to end all shows.

Thank you, my dearling, he said.

Lady was so happy. Her face was warm. He was right in front of her. She cupped his butt and screamed That's mine. He laughed and untucked his shirt. Smokey said If you got the notion, I second that emotion. She lifted her cup and swayed. He lifted his and drank. His face was pink. He swung his hips, got into it. The coffee sloshed and burned his hand.

It's very hot but I don't care, he said. I am unfazed. Look at my face.

He put on a serious face and froze as best he could for a few seconds.

Resolve, he said. Resolve. It's as if nothing happened. A lesser man—hey, you look so good—but for real a lesser man would be sidelined by that. And I feel this deep inside so I know it's true: me, your mans, I've actually gotten stronger. Just in this short period of time since the spill, my body has regenerated. I am uncommon. Me and the grain have never gotten along. I'm always going against it.

You love yourself so much, she said.

Only sometimes.

He tried to clog.

God, I feel strong, he said. Look at my arms. And my calves as well.

He raised a pant leg. Lilliputian in scale, almost tranquilizing. She gassed him up.

How strong are you? she asked.

Not once have I died. How strong are you?

I adorn my toes with the rings of Saturn.

One of the things I've grown to appreciate about myself, I always go hard in the paint. No ifs, ands, or buts about it. Know what I bench?

A broom.

Clydesdales, my dearling. That's the kind of weight I'm moving. Dadgum Scottish behemoths.

They were laughing. He was by the windows.

You couldn't lift a Clydesdale's tail, she said.

The jumbo steeds of Budweiser, he said. Man. That jacket's cool as shit. Wish I'd bought me a cool jacket. I'm happy for you, though. Cool jackets are something I care deeply about.

"You've Really Got A Hold On Me" began. Table danced back to her. She smiled.

Where you off to? she asked.

Bathroom, he said.

Oh. So, it's actually pronounced fountain.

He put his mug on the ground and held out his hand.

Hold this for me?

They danced beside the lion in the dark. She laid her head on his shoulder. There was no moon. They kissed. A lifting in his chest. He spun her, brought her back. Smokey said I don't want you but I need you. She kissed his cheek and let go. They danced apart, got after it. Table was sweating and took off his polo. His undershirt was sleeveless and battered with bleach stains and holes. He ripped hard at the collar, tore the shirt down the middle.

She walked it out, swung her tresses. The elephant flapped. Table flexed his abs. Beluga-whale white. Nothing there. Smokey said Tighter. Lady sashayed around the fountain. Black hair waving. Tighter. They pointed at each other. The power in the restaurant went out. The music stopped. They couldn't see. No sound but the water. No light. They stretched out their hands and said each other's names. His shirt was like a vest. They came together.

BLOOD ORANGE AWNING

PRISCILLA ORDERED OUT FOR DINNER. It was a Wednesday. Storms had pounded the house all day. Rain came sideways. Thunder drummed her windows. She watched the sky move from her back porch, smoked cigarettes, felt off. Fuzz in her head. A stinging in her temples. She tried reading her Bible, tried working out, tried drinking. Nothing helped. She couldn't get to neutral. Now she was on the phone. She'd wanted Long John Silver's but the Wahoo location was closed for remodeling. She was furious, went with pizza instead.

Heavenly Pizza, a man said. Our pizza's heavenly. This is Terry. Delivery or carryout?

Hello, Terrald, Priscilla said. My name's Priscilla. I'll eat there. Just ordering now so it's ready when I arrive and I don't have to sit around waiting like a freaking loser.

I got you. What can I create for you?

Want a large grilled chicken and bacon. Light cheese, please. And cinnamon sticks.

What kind of crust?

Just, whatever, crust.

We got a bunch.

However it is usually.

Hand tossed?

Is that the thin kind?

No. That's thin. You want thin?

I don't. What's hand tossed?

It's slightly thicker.

I don't want thick crust.

It's the in-between kind.

Y'all ought to call it medium. Be easier for everybody.

We won't do that. That's a bad idea. What kind you want?

Medium. A large medium.

Come on.

You will know me by my orange shoes.

What a strange thing to say.

It'd been a hard month. Outside of work, she slept all the
time, stayed inside, wallowed in her gloom. On consecutive
Sundays she stress-ate too many donuts before worship and
threw up during the service. Chewed apple fritter in a white
woman's hair. Bear claw yacked into a purse. One night she
planned to go to Swallow Ridge for a party in the lounge with
some coworkers but couldn't decide between a white shirt and
a black sweater so she just stood there staring at her closet until
it was too late to go. And her listlessness grew. And she spoke
to no one. And each night before bed she'd lie awake, look at her
phone, and feel alone.

When she was awake her anxiety was at an all-time high. Her
mind banged around, ran into things. She was all over the place,
couldn't focus, would go from thinking about her soul to her job
to her car to her church to her childhood. She'd wonder what her
dreams were, then wonder why she didn't have any. She'd think
about what God wanted for her and how much she loved Him and
how much she wished she could feel better and she didn't understand why she felt so empty and found no joy in things. And
sometimes she would see her father on the ground. And her Bible
would get heavier. And she prayed hard but nothing got better.

Occasionally there were moments, little flickers of doubt,
when she'd wonder if maybe God wasn't real and she'd feel
guilty and hate herself and wonder how hot hell was. Images of
the Devil, dressed in blue. She'd think of her father. He was in
hell. He'd never been a believer. Priscilla found God a few years

after Solomon's death. She never got to tell him the beauty of the Resurrection, the sacrifice God made, how He'd sent His only son to die on the cross for humanity's sins. She would cry for her father in the dark. Visions of him on the bank of a lake of fire. Flames consume him. All day he burns. He doesn't stop. And he's trying to scream but he can't anymore. He's been screaming nonstop since he got down there and his throat's shredded and bleeding and raw. His mouth is open and crumbly. He barely makes sound. The wails somewhere between silent and hoarse. His neck looks filleted, threads of flesh hanging, wounds butterflying on his body. The floor's like fangs. It grinds, chops, rips him. Over and over and over. And every moment he thinks of his failures. And the fire gives no light. He burns in the dark. Feels only pain. Annihilated by an eternity away from God.

Priscilla hoped when she died God would let her advocate on her father's behalf, vouch for him, explain it was just a mistake and had he lived longer—like he should've—he'd have been inspired by the woman she became and because of that inspiration, because of how impressed he was with the way she lived, he would've asked God to come into his heart. Then he'd have gone to heaven when he died an old man.

She could go down to hell for a day, talk to him, prep him for what was about to happen, explain he's been redeemed, Christ was crucified, rose again, God is love, et cetera. Then they could head on up to Paradise, show God she was right, start forever. She understood this was in direct contradiction with Luke 16:19–31 ("between us and you there is a great gulf fixed"), but she had faith. And God is faithful to those who have faith. She'd take her heart out of her chest and her father's out of his and show God they were the same.

Priscilla walked tipsy into Heavenly Pizza with her Bible in her back pocket and her sunglasses on. She wore orange Nike Terminators, blue jeans, and an Oklahoma softball sweatshirt. Next to the door was a crane game filled with metal watches and silver necklaces. Priscilla touched the glass, pressed the button on the joystick. She'd thought her mood would take a leap when she arrived. It hadn't. There was a grating kind of nothingness in her. She put her forehead against the machine, felt hollowed out.

Come on, Dude. I want to be okay. I want to focus only on You. You're my best friend. I love You and I know You love me but I just don't ever feel, like . . . good. I just want to feel good. Or safe. I don't want to go to hell. I don't know what I'm doing wrong. Please help.

The restaurant was empty, save Terry, the man working the register. He was white and frail, mid-twenties with gauges in his ears, black Old Skools, and black jeans. His T-shirt was gold with the restaurant's name on the pocket. Three lady angels enjoyed a cheese pizza on the back. They were seated on a patio with Jesus tableside. He wore an apron and a smile. The angels were euphoric, spoke with full mouths, text over their heads: THIS PIZZA'S HEAVENLY! THANKS, JESUS! Terry sat behind the counter and watched professional wrestling videos on his phone. He looked at her feet.

Hello, Priscilla, he said. Cool shoes.

Terry, Terry, quite contrary. How does your pizza grow?

In the oven. It'll be right out. You can sit wherever.

Much obliged.

Jim Ross screamed For the love of God, someone tell me this is not happening, and Priscilla looked for a table. The walls of the restaurant were royal blue and aged, covered in acrylic flat paintings of Saint Peter wolfing down a slice of pepperoni at the Pearly Gates. A bronze cross the size of a vulture sat beside the soda fountain and cloud piñatas hung from the ceiling. There were off-white booths and tables, golden chairs, golden carpet. Priscilla's head hurt and she opened her mouth to stretch her face. Smoke on her breath. There were televisions in opposite corners of the restaurant. One on the local news, the other on TNT, closed-captioned *Anchorman* being shown. She sat in a booth against the wall and Terry brought out her pizza.

From the ovens of heaven, direct to your table, Terry said. One large hand-tossed grilled chicken and bacon. May I offer you some fresh parmesan or crushed red pepper?

No, thank you, Ter Bear, she said. You've done more than enough. Thank you for your service.

Well then, heavenly times to you.

Terry on my wayward son.

Terry bowed and left. Lady ate her pizza, read her Bible, Psalm 75.

1 Unto thee, O God, do we give thanks, unto thee do we give thanks: for that thy name is near thy wondrous works declare.

2 When I shall receive the congregation I will judge uprightly.

3 The earth and all the inhabitants thereof are dissolved: I bear up the pillars of it. Selah.

4 I said unto the fools, Deal not foolishly: and to the wicked, Lift not up the horn:

5 Lift not up your horn on high: speak not with a stiff neck.

6 *For promotion cometh neither from the east, nor from the west, nor from the south.*

7 *But God is the judge: he putteth down one, and setteth up another.*

8 *For in the hand of the Lord there is a cup, and the wine is red; it is full of mixture; and he poureth out of the same: but the dregs thereof, all the wicked of the earth shall wring them out, and drink them.*

9 *But I will declare for ever; I will sing praises to the God of Jacob.*

10 *All the horns of the wicked also will I cut off; but the horns of the righteous shall be exalted.*

She closed the book and watched the news. The Doppler radar was in the bottom right corner. A mash of green, yellow, and red went from left to right within the Oklahoma counties. Sister Rosetta Tharpe's "99 ½ Won't Do" played softly over the speakers. She took another bite and stared out the window. The storm had been sharp and everything looked stretched and wrinkled. Branches, trash, leaves in the streets. Wet roads. Black roads. Neon signs reflected off the pavement. Terry played *Cruis'n USA* in the corner, drove La Bomba through the desert. Priscilla watched *Anchorman*. Ron Burgundy prank-called Veronica Corningstone under the alias Dr. Chim Richalds. He lied to her, told her she was pregnant, called her pathetic. Priscilla looked at her table. Orange top cracked and faded, the word SAUCE carved into the plastic. She ran her finger over the grooves. Her shoulders were tight. She felt small. She took another bite. The air conditioner kicked on and made her look up. Some of the ceiling tiles were missing. Pink insulation showed. She looked out the window again. Her eyes stopped. A palomino stood in the road. The blond mane glowed like bleached honey. Priscilla's knee bounced. She looked back at *Anchorman*. Burgundy said the words *spiritual* and *existential funk*. Priscilla scratched her neck. A static buzz in her face like a snowy television. Brick Tamland wore a watch. The band looked brown and made of leather. She thought of Jesus's timepiece. She thought of Jesus's face.

I love You.

The movie went to commercial. Mathis Brothers Furniture. Your style, your price. She looked again at the road. The horse seemed bored. Hammers somewhere. A raking in her head. Priscilla rubbed her face and closed her eyes. Bits of almost silver in the black. The radio played a sad song she didn't know. A man with an acoustic guitar sang California's topographic luxuries are legion. She opened her eyes. Terry crashed La Bomba into a hot-pink truck. The palomino lay down. The sky started to drizzle. Priscilla sunk lower in her seat, her head below the top of the booth.

God, I want You to talk to me, please. Do me that solid. What do You want? I don't understand why I can't just feel good. Don't make no sense. I'm in a funk 24/7. I don't think I deserve to be. My heart's Yours. You're probably sick of this but I'll ask again about the sheets. Were You in them? What's the deal? Can You give me anything? Any sign? I'm having a really hard time. Please help. What can I do? I feel guilty when You don't bring me joy. The horns of the righteous shall be exalted. Sel— No. I feel weird. I'm sorry. I want to stop.

The restaurant phone rang. Terry didn't answer. Priscilla pressed the heels of her palms against her eyes. The room was cold. Terry shouted We ain't taking no more orders is why I'm not answering. Priscilla shouted Hey you got to do you. The movie came back on. Burgundy and the Channel 4 News Team were on their way to buy new suits. Priscilla said to herself It's weird to be the only person in a restaurant and ate an entire slice in three bites. The Channel 2 News Team with lead anchor Frank Vitchard confronted the Channel 4 News Team. The closed-captioning read DEAD PLACE. Priscilla went to the soda fountain and got a refill. On the way back to her booth, Terry won his race. A woman in a pink bikini top and purple skirt held a golden trophy.

Teronimo, Priscilla said. Congrats.

Thanks, Terry said. Yeah. Death Valley. I'm good at this one.

There's a horse outside.

Nice. That sounds sick.

They went to the window. Brian Fantana had a gun in his hand.

Storm must've busted up a fence somewhere, Terry said.

Yeah, Priscilla said.

Guess I should probably call somebody.

He went to get the phone and she went back to her seat. Champ Kind threw a man through a car windshield. The closed-captioning read [SCREAMS OF MEN, PONIES WHINNY, THE SHATTERING OF GLASS]. Priscilla took a drink and looked at the news. Video of that morning's Daisy Parade in Stortimer. Her nose itched and she scratched it. A banging in her head. A house fire in Pantts. Terry brought the cinnamon sticks. The phone was between his ear and shoulder.

Main strip out here, he said. Yes . . . a palomino . . . honestly stunning.

Wes Mantooth tried to stab Burgundy. Dorothy Mantooth is a saint. Priscilla went back to the front window. The horse was closer, in the grass between the road and the restaurant. A purple Cordoba drove by. Headlights made neon-white the mane.

A blood-orange awning wrapped the restaurant and Priscilla went outside, stood under it. She leaned against the building and smoked a Parliament. A green sign to the left of her head shined PIZZA. It stopped raining. She stared at the horse. Platinum-blond tail, lithe, stately. A yip of lightning in the west. There were no stars. Wind slid water off the awning. A brown Camry drove by playing Clipse's "Popular Demand." Pusha: Hollow tip dum-dums eat flesh like piranhas. Priscilla stared into the empty intersection in front of the restaurant. A Plott hound walked along the service road beside the convenience store. Streetlights glittered the black brindle coat. Priscilla felt jittery, wound up. Terry came around the side of the building. He'd changed into a purple polo.

Cops on their way, he said. Guess they got another call on it. Owner's coming with a trailer.

Priscilla nodded. They stared at the horse.

She's awful calm, Terry said.

She's cocky, Priscilla said. I don't blame her. If I looked like that, wouldn't even let people speak to me.

The town was quiet and strangely bright with the restaurant glowing behind them and the blazing orange neon of Gimmet's Pawn next door—electric guitars and AR-15s behind steel bars. She heard the stoplight click as it changed colors. A black Durango drove by blasting K.R.I.T.: Pocket full of stones, riding clean. Priscilla scratched her chest. She wanted to relax. The road looked silver. She offered Terry a cigarette.

Sure, thanks, he said. Pizza all right?

Very good. Thank you.

What about the cinnamon sticks? Trying to do a better job on them. One of my goals this year.

Them too. Real good.

Good deal. Didn't mean to go fishing. Yes, I did.

Y'all's shirts suggest Jesus made the pizzas.

Yeah, He's off tonight. You live here?

Yeah. You?

He nodded, took a drag.

It's Priscilla like Presley? he asked. Like Elvis? You named after her?

No way Jose, she said. Absolutely not. No. You know Paul?

Giamatti?

From the Bible.

Oh. Sure.

Wrote Romans. Galatians. Colossians. Bunch more. I was named after one of his helpers. She might've written Hebrews. Was part of the early church. Her and her husband, Aquila—

Her husband's name was Aquila?

Yeah.

Aquila the Hun.

That's incorrect.

It's similar in sound, though.

Priscilla and her husband Aquila were tentmakers and missionaries. They helped Paul found the church at Corinth. They were martyred.

No way. That's rad. Are you single?

Yes.

Want to go on a date? My cousin works at the casino. He's, like, a pit boss or parks cars or something, can't really remember, but he can get us in Nájera's, that new restaurant they got.

No, thank you.

All right. I fought hard, though, you know? Appreciate you letting me get the full pitch out there.

No prob. Isn't Nájera's a buffet?

Well, it's a casino, they have to have that option, but they also got a menu you can order from if you're not feeling the buffet. Wait, that's why you said no?

No. I love buffets, I'm not a loser. I said no for other reasons.

What are they?

I owe you zilch but honestly, physically, I just can't get there.

I can dig that. My face is an acquired taste.

Your purple shirt bothers me too. And it's weird, I usually like purple, but I don't like it on you.

Oh, I descend from English royalty.

What's that got to do with anything we're talking about here?

Purple symbolizes royalty. I'm royalty.

They dressed Jesus in a purple robe when they put the crown of thorns on His head.

Aren't you a dumpster of laughs.

Matthew called the robe scarlet. Mark and John said purple. Don't remember what Luke called it. He was long-winded. Sometimes I think you've got to shut up and listen. Man, I'm really angry with myself for not remembering what color Luke said the robe was. I was literally thinking about him this morning.

I won't hold it against you too much.

It's bad I don't know.

The horse sneezed.

God bless you, Priscilla said.

Your shoes are so orange, Terry said. They remind me of the fruit the orange.

Is Eduardo Nájera affiliated with Nájera's?

Not sure. Might just be an ode to.

Terry spit in the grass, leaned against the window.

Man, he said. I love horses. Don't you love horses? Ponies. Looking at them.

Yeah, she said. Horses are beautiful.

She went back inside and spent seven dollars to win a necklace. Marty Chisholm played over the speakers, a song of outlaws and backstabbing. Her face was heavy. A droning somewhere. It ate at her, not remembering the color of Jesus's robe in Luke. She wanted to feel better, imagined Jesus winking. It didn't help. Headlights distracted her. Cops rolled up, white Sierra behind them hauling a horse trailer. Terry waved and went out to meet them. The horse didn't move. Chisholm sang You fell for the outlaw's trick. She went to the front window to watch the horse get moved and caught her reflection. Her face drooped. She didn't want to look tired. She wanted to look strong. She overcompensated, flexed her abs, said Diana Taurasi. It didn't help. She was exhausted and her skin felt close to raw, like she was running marathons in clothes made of gravel. Her sweatshirt was heavy. She yawned. Terry, two white cops, and a white cowboy stood in the middle of the road. They laughed in unison. She looked back at the news.

Angelica Rothcoal smiled and spoke at the same time, '69 Camaro beside her head. Rothcoal sent it to their field reporter, Henrietta Drops, live at the 28th Annual Tunero Car Show. Drops walked and talked, strolled the middle of a shut-down street in Tunero's Upper 40s. Elephant-shaped streetlamps glowed overhead and multicolored Christmas lights were strung in zigzags above the road. A melted rainbow of a ceiling. There were food vendors on either side of the street. Smoke and steam rose up in puffs. Classic after classic, Drops walked among the vehicles. '71 Ferrari Daytona Spider in Venetian Red. '87 BMW M3 E30 in Sable Orca. Stork White '69 Chevrolet Corvette Stingray. Fire Blonde '73 Porsche 911 Carrera RS. A mash of people. Drops went up to an older white man standing in front of his vehicle. Priscilla studied the car: a 1968 seafoam-green Ranchero, upside-down longhorn rack on the grille, the horns crimson, and in white paint along them DEATH CAME FOR BEVO. The man wore a pure-white pearl snap, gray Stetson, and blue jeans. His eyes were in the shadow of the brim. Priscilla looked at his lips, his cheeks, gray hair covering everything except the chin. His sideburns were connected to his mustache and his limbs were like tent poles. He tilted the cap up. Priscilla saw all of him. Pianos in a woodchipper. Green shards in the air. A squeezing in her chest.

She went to the television and turned it up. The chyron along the bottom of the screen changed from EavesDROPS: 28th Annual Tunero Car Show to EavesDROPS: Sylvia Table of Florra. There was a scraping in Priscilla's chest and she shook. Her nails clawed her arms. Her face was hot. She couldn't feel her hair. Thin tears caked her eyes. She hadn't seen him since she was five, in the courthouse. She and Viv walked out of the women's the same time he walked out of the men's. They made eye contact. Table held his mouth like he was going to speak, but he didn't. He just stood there looking at her. Priscilla's eyes were wet and he was formless, refracted swoops of color, a smudge of a person. He walked away before her tears fell.

Now, in the restaurant, there was an ache in her right wrist. The edges of the pores in her cheeks waved. Jagged and green bits of glass in her eyes. She blinked. Something like a howl somewhere. Table held a Tecate and pointed with it. His face looked dilapidated. The howl faded.

—abnormally creative, Table said. And I wanted my vehicle to reflect that. See the horns? Guess I messed with the bull a little bit.

He paused for laughs, got none. There was a wrenching in Priscilla's stomach. Her mouth was open.

Well, it's certainly not my type of thing, Drops said. But it was clearly fussed over.

I appreciate that, Table said. All I am's a guy who worked as hard as I possibly could and now I get to enjoy the spoils of all my wars. The fruits of all my laboring. Sure, I've taken my hits, but I will never stop standing back up and doing what's right. My work ethic's too great. I'm the America that was promised. My pockets are fat as hell. They need to eat some green vegetables and go for a jog. You know how blessed I am? Fans on the ready.

He took wads of hundreds from his pockets, spread the bills in his hands, and fanned himself. Pandemonium inside Priscilla's body. Cyclones of fire and gasoline. The sun in her chest. Twisting in her face. Her face was wet. She started to sweat. She tasted blood. Her head was boiling. Her body was cold. Her teeth bit her cheek and it was like she was inside a comet. Table smiled. His teeth were little moons. Her father's jeans appeared beside the television. Glass shards on the back pockets like bejeweled Astroturf. Her fingers burned. Her eyes stung. She sneezed thrice. There were sirens. Another cop rolled up. The awning was red. The awning was yellow. She smelled chicken. Her head felt full. She looked back at the television. Table flexed. The jeans were gone.

Championship mettle, he screamed. Championship mettle. I'm not a star. I'm a galaxy.

Drops threw it back to the studio. Priscilla's mouth moved to scream. No sound came. She put her hands on the seat of the booth. A boundless ache in her stomach, a ripping. The carpet stabbed her knees. She heard elephants. Her eyes were like saucers and they roiled. Her pulse knocked in her temples. She walked to the window, put her forehead against it. The glass was cold. She looked at the road. The road fuzzed. The men were smudges. She wiped her eyes. She threw up everywhere.

God. God.

She was staggering to her car. Vomit stained her chest, rolled down the front window of the restaurant. She looked back at the road. The cowboy led the horse up the ramp and into the trailer. Priscilla wiped her mouth. Her teeth hurt. Her back hurt. She couldn't stop sweating. She threw up again. The men turned and looked. Terry asked if she was okay. She didn't answer. He asked if it was the cinnamon sticks. She screamed Yes.

In the car her eyes were loose. No star peeked. Her head felt crushed. Rumbles in her hands.

What is this? What do You want? Why are You showing him to me? I'm sorry. I should've been at church tonight. I could've worked in the food pantry or helped with the offertory or talked to the old people that get mad if there's guitars during the music. I could've made them feel less alone. People shouldn't have to feel alone. I'm so sorry I didn't go. That was so stupid of me. I'm such a freaking jerk. A freaking . . . I'm just not doing it how I want to be doing it. I don't like how I feel. What can I do? I know You know my heart. I know I have to be honest. I want to kill him. And that's a wild thing to say and against the rules or whatever, but I want to kill him like he killed Dad. I want to stand over him and shout around while he bleeds. I deserve this. Let me put him down. Selah. I think I feel

You saying go. All the horns of the wicked also will I cut off. This must be okay. Why the stirring in me before all this? Why this bad life? Yes, God. This feels right. Tell me Go to Florra. Tell me Handle my business. Go handle your business. That's You talking. My blessing's yours. I'm right beside you. Sometimes it's like my head collapses and I start crying and can't stop. Please tell me what to do. Your will, not mine. Give me a sign.

She listened closely. There was no new noise. Just wind in the trees, vehicles on the road. She pulled over and turned on the dome.

God, if I see a white car in the next thirty seconds, I'll know I'm supposed to go after him.

Sweat on her top lip. She licked it off. Her body was tight and breathing was hard. The color didn't come.

Think I might've stopped paying attention for a sec. Let's go again. God, if I see a black car in the next thirty seconds, I'll know I'm supposed to go after him.

For the next thirty seconds, she didn't blink. Headlights like pale grapefruits. A blue Ram. A white Cutlass. A brown Jeep. Nothing for a bit. Then a red Mercury. A purple Quest. A silver Maxima. Her heart galloped. Two U-Haul vans, a Walmart truck, and three khaki Humvees on their way to Camp Lona. Sweat rolled off her knees and she wanted to put her head through the windshield. The thirty seconds was up. She punched the steering wheel. Her knuckles opened. Blood dripped to her jeans.

Fine.

JESUS IN JEANS / POOLS (HOT TUBS)

THE NEXT MORNING AN EARTHQUAKE woke her. Her gray walls rattled and the Hakeem Olajuwon 1994 NBA MVP commemorative dinner plates clamored and fell, landed unbroken on the sun-colored carpet. The television rocked. A portrait of Jesus in jeans dropped off the wall behind her. It hit the top of the headboard and landed on her back. She screamed.

I mean come on.

The room settled. Priscilla lit a Parliament, waited for aftershocks. None came. She lay there and listened to the quiet earth. A raking in her forehead. She tried not to think of Table. Smoke clouded her, crashed against the light fixture. She went to the bathroom. In one corner of the mirror, a photo of Olajuwon petting a Venetian red Etonic. In another, Olajuwon dunking in an old LA Gear ad, cyber yellow UNSTOPPABLE huge above him. Fireball on his chest. Inferno behind him. A new freckle had appeared below her left eye. Table had seemed thin and weak on TV, but was clearly happy, flourishing. Didn't seem fair. Her head hurt behind her eyes. Her legs were cold. She turned on the heat lamp and brushed her teeth. Her gums bled. She saw Table's face, young and smiling. She shook her head. He went away.

She put on workout clothes and went to the living room. The radio was still on 98.9 The Horses, today's hottest country. She started her push-ups. When she got to four, she thought of Table again and stopped. She needed more noise. She turned on the television. *Charmed* was on. She cranked the volume and worked out in the cacophony—five sets of fifty push-ups, two sets of one hundred sit-ups, and fifteen minutes of jump rope. Her whole body sweated. She took off her shirt and lay on the floor. Her heart was loud. Her head knocked. Alyssa Milano rolled her eyes. Jake Owen from the radio: There's a whole lot that I just can't do. Priscilla went to the kitchen for water and looked into her backyard. A line of crows stood with their backs to her. Their feathers were like black crepe paper and they stared at the fence.

She took a shower and thought of Table the whole time. After, she stood naked in her room and let the fan dry her, thought of him some more. Her bedroom television showed a *SportsCenter* commercial. A copier gave Landon Donovan a yellow card. Priscilla got dressed and sat on her bed. Her sheets were hot. She smelled chicken. Her cheek twitched. Table flexed. Outside, two dogs yelled at each other.

Enough, she said.

She went back to the kitchen, opened again to Psalm 75, and stared at the ink without reading the words.

This is what was always coming. I'm filled with hate right now and need to know what to do about it. I don't deserve this. This guy's out there rich and I'm here praying to make friends? I want justice. What is this? Am I supposed to go to him? Is that what the earthquake was? A belated sign? A wake-up? It meant wake up and go, right? Surely. Should I drive there and stare at him and see what I can do? What—

Her head felt drilled. Her face was hot. She set the book on the counter, turned on the faucet, and held her head under the spout. Water wrapped her skull. She closed her eyes. The sink sounded like a hurricane. Her head wouldn't relax. She stood. Water dripped off her. She looked again at the Bible, read loudly in the middle of the kitchen. Her voice banged off the walls.

Unto thee, O God, do we give thanks, unto thee do we give thanks: for that thy name is near thy wondrous works declare. When I shall receive the congregation I will judge uprightly. The earth and all the inhabitants thereof are dissolved: I bear up the pillars of it. Selah. I said unto the fools, Deal not foolishly: and to the wicked, Lift not up the horn: Lift not up your horn on high: speak not with a stiff neck.

The kitchen was the color of Mars. She kept reading.

For promotion cometh neither from the east, nor from the west, nor from the south. But God is the judge: he putteth down one, and setteth up another. For in the hand of the Lord there is a cup, and the wine is red; it is full of mixture; and he poureth out of the same: but the dregs thereof, all the wicked of the earth shall wring them out, and drink them. But I will declare for ever; I will sing praises to the God of Jacob. All the horns of the wicked also will I cut off; but the horns of the righteous shall be exalted.

Her legs faded and she lay facedown on the tile. There were breadcrumbs around her head and she pulled her ears, tried to make them wider. Every muscle in her was clenched. Her breath bounced off the floor. She began to cry. The house was old and there were lumps in the floor. She felt them against her thighs, pushed her head harder against the ground. The tile whined. She heard her pulse. A charring in her throat. She wanted so much to kill him. Her face went from blush to plum. She realized she was holding her breath. She shouted.

I'm away. I'm away. I'm away.

She rolled over, held to the sides of her face. An eighteen-wheeler blared on the highway. Some jackhammering in her chest. Static in her arms. She coughed. A low hum in her ears. The ceiling waved. Her palms were wet. She stood and went back to the kitchen window. The birds were gone. Wind in the oak. Traffic on the highway. Big rigs crawled along the horizon like alligators. The hum left. Her eyes were sore.

If I see a blue car in the next thirty seconds, I'll know I'm supposed to kill him.

Tears kept her face cool. She searched for the color. It didn't come. The sun was behind silver clouds now. Green shreds in an Appaloosa sky. She sat on the floor. She said Fine.

All day she was in a haze. She went to the course, stared at things. The grass and the trees and the pond on 14. The ball washer someone ran over just off 7. Corona bottles and cigarette butts and tins of chew. The pines by the blues on 11. And every moment it was like she was in a fog. Voices came weak and dim to her and the golfers' bodies seemed to fray. She had half a bag of Tropical Skittles for lunch and threw them up on the thirteenth fairway a little after 2 p.m. An hour later she went behind the cart barn and wept. There was a banging in her head and every five minutes the sky snowed glass. At 6:17 p.m. she found herself in front of the video cameras in the entertainment section of Walmart. An employee walked up.

Ma'am, he said.

She just stood there, watched herself in the screens.

Ma'am, he said.

She looked at him. Her face was blank.

Need any help? he asked.

She looked at her feet, the floor, the man.

I'm not sure, she said. I don't remember.

What? he asked.

I didn't come in here. I'm not here.

Oh. Okay. Your shoes are cool.

I'm hoping to rendezvous with him later.

Priscilla went home. Orange sky over her backyard. She walked in the grass, listened to Nichole Nordeman, thought about Table the whole time. After dinner she watched the "Ice Worlds" episode of *Planet Earth*. She cheered for walruses to kill a polar bear, screamed Stab it with your tusks, thought about Table the whole time. The walruses failed. She was devastated. She went to bed. Her feet were cold. The highway was loud. The cuts on his fingers. She couldn't sleep. There was a squeezing in her head and she scratched her cheeks. Her eyes were milky and glowing. Pink lines on her jaws. His banshee voice. Every right to take his.

I will sing praises to the God of Jacob. I come humbly, Lord, asking for a definitive answer. I know You've been saying no but I feel like it might be okay now. You're understanding and within me and in the air around me. Selah. You see my soul. You know I don't do nothing bad. Look at my beautiful heart. Can you please see this is something I can't have happen? My father was going to make a good life for me and I'd have family and be happy. Now I'm just this person. I feel sad a lot. I understand the watch. You were saying You'd provide me a purpose, right? Sylvia. Take the doubts away. Yes. I feel like I'm supposed to go. Or at least start down the road. We'll keep chatting. Selah. Yes. I'm going. I'm going and I'm asking You, love of my life—what can I do?

There was a green duffel in the bottom of her closet. She threw inside a rain jacket, running shorts, her father's old Olajuwon shirt, three pairs of underwear, two pairs of socks, boots, and her Bible. Blood dripped out her nose. She tilted her head back and went to the bathroom. Blood in her mouth. She found the toilet paper with her hands and stuffed her nostrils. Her head settled. There was a flitting in her chest and it wrapped her, went up her back. She sat on the floor and put on her Terminators. Her face was damp. She opened the bedside table drawer and pulled out a wooden box. Inside was a pearl-handled Ruger Vaquero and a case of Hornady's 185 grain Flex Tips. Priscilla put them in the bag and walked into the living room. Glum, pale light limped in from the streetlamps and mixed with the night. The air was gray. Her furniture just sat there. The rain started again. Her nose burned. The room quailed. The room looked velvet. The room was dead. She touched her face. Her face was hard. Rain on the windows. Shadows of falling water on the carpet. The floor swayed and twitched, a sad disco.

My Lord is near me all the time.

She pulled out her phone and called Viv.

Hello? Viv asked.

Hello, godmother, Priscilla said.

Viv said nothing.

Viv, Priscilla said.

What? Viv asked.

It's Priscilla.

Is this a joke?

No.

'Cause if it's a joke it's messed up.

It's not a joke. It's me.

Priscilla? What—where are you? Are you okay?

I'm about to be driving. Should be in Nawb tomorrow evening, or I guess it's late enough I mean this evening. If you were around it'd be nice to—

Meet me at a bar named Pools.

Okay.

Priscilla?

Yeah?

This really you?

Yeah.

It's not a dream?

No.

Feels like one.

I'm real.

Sound different. Your voice.

It's probably the years.

Probably. I'll really see you tomorrow?

Yeah.

That's crazy.

Yeah.

I love you.

I love you.

Priscilla hung up.

I miss my dad. I think I feel him with me sometimes, beside me, and he'll put his hand on my shoulder. Think he's been in my house, watched a game with me. Think he's seen work, rode with me in the cart. We smoke together, watch the pond do nothing. And then there's times I'm alone at home and I'll look across from me and see some kind of something. It's this thing that doesn't have a shape or a name. It's a feeling and it's like I'm swallowing my head and it's tight in my chest and it all burns but I'm close to happy and close to mad and I taste smoke and there are wings in my mouth. I just stare at the space across from me and the air sits then turns and it's like it folds or something? It feels like him. He'd take his shoes off and sit in a plastic lounge chair on the porch. Drink margaritas. Read spy thrillers. Hollander Veach. Nights in Los Palmas. That wasn't the name of the book, but that was in there somewhere. Los Palmas sounds beautiful. Like a private island or a merry-go-round at a Mexican restaurant. It's not fair. If I met somebody now and they died five years later I'd be able to remember so much. I don't remember enough. I want to remember. How he'd carry me or how he smelled or what his favorite movie was. In my memories he's just his face and little else. He was so nice. He'd say Sure and it sounded like shore. Made me feel safe. I'd like to know about the car rides. Bet there was times when I was a baby he talked to me in the truck. He'd say There go my sugar back there. My sweet little dearling. I love you so much. You're so strong, so smart.

God, I'm afraid of so much. I'm afraid it's okay to kill him but I won't do it out of some worldly fear and I'll talk myself out of it even though You'd have been cool with it. I'm afraid it's my own selfishness that's motivating me and You'd never want me to kill anyone. I'm afraid I won't do it and I'll spend my life wishing I had. I'm afraid I'll do it and go to hell. I really don't want to go to hell. I once heard a televangelist with very blond hair say I talk to God every night and He tells me I did the best job on you. Do You for real say that to him? His suits have an overwhelming number of buttons. Why don't You say things like that to me? I want to be right. I cut the wicked's horns. Dad's sometimes in my dreams. There, walking up to me, but he's older than he was when he died, like my mind's projected him out, imagined what he'd look like elderly. We're in a house I don't know. Flamingos outside. He's still got his hair, but it's white, combed straight back. His face is weathered, tired-looking, like the ground's yanking at it. He moves slow. And even though he's old, for some reason I'm super young. One, one and a half. He carries me to the porch and there are orange trees in the yard. I point at them. He says Yeah, you see the oranges? I can talk. I say Oranges. He says Yeah, those are orange trees. P, can you say orange trees? *And I try hard but can't quite make the t-to-r transition, so it sounds like* orange twees. *He says Yeah, that's right. And he's holding me. And I'm warm. And our cheeks are touching. They really are. And my hand's up. And I point at the trees. I say Oranges. He says That's right, baby girl. And I feel him. And I'm there, in his arms—I am—and we just love each other so much.*

———

Pools shared a parking lot with Nawb's Prairie Motel. Priscilla pulled into a space near the ice machine and got out. It was dusk. On the hill behind the bar was a row of old chicken houses, dull silver and hulked, tin roofs, gashes in the walls and abandoned, these rusted-out spaceships. On one was a mural of multiple Barry Switzers. One was young and squatted like a catcher on the sidelines. BEAT TEXAS cap. Revolver in hand. Another stood in the tunnel in a white polo, crimson OU on the breast, hands on hips, '74, '75, and '85 national championship rings on his middle, ring, and pinkie fingers, radiant diamonds with shine lines floating off them. The last Switzer was older, drank a Coors in boxers, a fur, and nothing else. He sat in front of a locker and laughed maniacally. His neck flared. His knees had muscles.

Priscilla lit a cigarette and headed toward the bar. An older Black woman leaned on the tailgate of a royal-blue F-150 in the row nearest the building. She wore red cowboy boots, black jeans, and a souvenir sweatshirt from the Titan at Six Flags Over Texas. Her face was short. Her eyes were brown. Her hair was gray. There was a battering in Priscilla's chest and she considered turning around. She didn't.

Hey, Viv, Priscilla said.

Hello, goddaughter, Viv said. How are you?

You like roller coasters?

Hate them. But this was four dollars. You see how well it fits. Something hugs me this good, don't care if there's a picture of my dead body on it, I'm wearing the thing. You smoke now?

Mmhmm.

She'd hate that more than anything in the world.

Yes.

He would've loved it.

I know.

You look the same.

Yeah?

Not a bad thing. Just, you look the same. Never did look like her very much.

You been waiting awhile?

Ten minutes? Watched you park, stare at the Switzers.

Why you ain't get my attention?

Haven't seen you in eleven years. Wanted to watch you a little, see what you were like without knowing anyone's looking.

Pretty creepy. How'd I look?

I don't know. Bored, I guess. Where you coming from?

Panhandle.

That's a voyage. You living out there?

Yeah. Wahoo.

What's there?

Jack squat.

I see your car has testicles.

Believe those are called nutz, V. With a z. Where's Tucson?

Surfing the movie channels when I left. He'll probably just watch *Avatar* again.

What'd he say when you told him you were coming to see me?

Asked if he could come. I said I didn't see his name listed any-where on the invite. He said Well that sounds like bull but tell her hey anyway.

Tell him hey back.

Will do.

Priscilla put her hands in the back pockets of her jeans and flexed her shoulder blades, tried to pop her back. Gnawing in her stomach. She wondered if she looked distracted, unhealthy. Her palms itched and she scratched them.

So, you staying here tonight? Viv asked.

Not sure.

What's the other options?

Backseat. Or drive some more.

Backseat don't seem too safe.

I can't get hurt.

Priscilla's cigarette was a nub. She tossed it, lit another.

Back-to-back, Viv said.

Priscilla held out the pack.

Nah, Viv said. Stopped that . . . nine years ago?

Wow, Priscilla said. What for?

My body and face. My insides and outsides. And a little bit Tucson.

I'm very disappointed in you.

Priscilla looked at the street and tried to seem calm. Viv smiled, kept watching her. A Tacoma drove by hauling a kiwi Polaris. Priscilla coughed twice and spit.

I didn't forget you existed, Viv said. But it'd been a minute since I thought about you. Made my mind that way.

I can compartmentalize pretty good too, Priscilla said. I like your boots.

Thank you. Your shoes are very orange.

Felt like it'd be good to wear something that catches attention. Something memorable folks could comment on, open up communication between myself and strangers. Give me an opportunity to show God's love, evangelize.

Has that happened?

No.

Priscilla looked east. Sky there was sandstone, plum black. The early stars came out.

You know how some places you can buy a star and name it or whatever? Priscilla asked. I read they're selling stars to people and letting buyers name them. I don't like that. God already named all the stars. He doesn't need our help.

Selling stars? Viv asked. In the sky? Where'd you read that?

Maybe I didn't read it. But that seems like something people would do.

That's confusing and more than a little defeatist.

I'm a very positive person. God is good.

How many stars are there?

I don't know. A lot.

Viv took her sweatshirt off. Her undershirt was huge with a cartoon on the front—a thin Black body in a purple bikini. She tied the sweatshirt around her waist and checked her watch. Priscilla pointed at the shirt.

Got a weird-looking belly button there, V, Priscilla said.

Thanks, Viv said. It's an outie.

I love it.

Me too. So, where you headed?

Florra.

What's there?

Want to go inside? I'd like to drink.

Sure. Tonight's karaoke. Starts up here soon. Can be pretty entertaining.

Looked like a weird place when I drove by. What's its deal?

Hot tubs.

What about them?

They got hot tubs in there.

Inside the bar?

Yeah.

Oh. It's called Pools, though. Not Hot Tubs.

Want to hear something amazing?

What?

You won't believe it.

Tell me.

I can read too.

When they walked inside, the bar was on their left, twenty feet of oak with red-cushioned stools. All along the right side of the room were hot tubs, each with a different-colored light along the bottom, each named after that color. Orange, Red, Yellow, Purple, Blue, so on. There were twenty-one. Seventeen worked. Some people sat in the water and some soaked their feet. Some wore bathing suits. Some wore underwear. Others wore workout gear or the clothes they came in.

They sat at the far end of the bar and Priscilla swiveled around to look at the room. A massive shelf ran the length of the wall and held stacks on stacks of white towels. Windows were open to deal with the steam and stench of chlorine and it was thick muggy despite a breeze slipping in. The tubs varied in size. Some sat four, some as many as twelve. One of the eight-seaters brimmed with seven chodelike figures. Three were bald, two wore Crimson Outdoors trucker caps, and two more wore Oklahoma State football jerseys. All were white. All were laughing. Big-time guffaws. Priscilla pointed at them.

When a group of them all laugh at the same time it really comes off a little gloomy.

Chapfallen, honey. They all cry when they're alone in the car.

This place have food?

It's a bar off the highway with a bunch of hot tubs.

What're you saying?

I'm saying they have pretzels. You want a meal, there's a Denny's down the road. Little Caesars inside the Kmart. Subway attached to a Love's an exit away.

You look at some of these folks and it's clear they're peeing.

People love this place.

Priscilla faced the bar. A long rectangular mirror stretched behind the liquor. To its right was a blown-up cover of the 1994 *Sports Illustrated* swimsuit issue: Kathy Ireland, Elle Macpherson, Rachel Hunter, black bikinis, a pool behind them. There were writings on the bar top: *shit*; *hoss*; *Rashaun Woods touched God on fades*. A sixty-inch television hung in the corner closest to them. It was muted and showed an infomercial for adult diapers. The bartender walked over. They ordered two Gaucho Golds. The commercial ended. An ESPN Classic reair of Game 6 of the 1993 NBA Finals came back on. The Golds arrived.

This the Paxson game, Priscilla said.

Yeah, Viv said. I forgot about Oliver Miller.

Said the jerk. How could you?

I'm ashamed.

Four orange women sat in a booth along the wall to their right. They all wore the same dress (strapless, sequins) and in the glow of the table light the fabric looked maroon. One on the left side of the booth wore a veil. She clapped her hands and said Okay but avocados is not good for you, Erica. The many gold bracelets on her wrists jangled, sounded like someone running with change in their pocket. Priscilla looked back at the game. Danny Ainge wept openly.

Y'all got a lot of friends in town? Priscilla asked.

Yeah, Viv said. Got a good church family. Nice Sunday school class. Everybody hangs out with everybody. Most all them teetotalers, though, so it's nice to be out and drink with somebody I love that ain't Tucson.

I don't like my Sunday school class. Young singles. They go to fancy coffee shops a lot, listen to too many singer-songwriters.

That's white church behavior, Viv said. I don't know nothing about that.

Priscilla took a drink. Mark West went to the bench. Dan Majerle blew the camera a kiss.

Still the tannest white man I've ever seen, Priscilla said.

Thunder Daniel? Viv asked. Skin probably looks like beef jerky now. Who were you going for here?

Jordan.

Right.

I like winning.

Priscilla was sweating. She wiped her forehead, held the bottle against her cheek. The smell of chlorine began to agitate her. It was in her mouth. Her knee started bouncing. She wondered if she seemed nervous and looked at Viv. Viv stared at herself in the mirror behind the liquor. Priscilla palmed her forehead. Sweat dimpled her temples. Karaoke started. A white man in board shorts and a cowboy hat took the mic and the opening chords to Shania Twain's "You're Still The One" came trickling out. He began the spoken word intro. Several women screamed Yes. Several more screamed Okay. Couples went to the dance floor. Men in western button-ups with mountains on the chest and beers in their hands. Women in coated nylon pounding goblets of chardonnay. A disco ball sat on top of the karaoke machine. Shines bounced off the ceiling, the floor, the faces. There were diamonds on bodies. People twinkled, had so much fun.

Their joy annoyed Priscilla and she felt above them. Viv finished her drink, flagged the bartender, said Run it back. Priscilla looked at the bar top again. Near her hands: *Horses in the Water*. Beside that: *bullets are spurs*.

Sorry, Priscilla said. I need fresher air. Come stand with me?

Of course, Viv said.

The bartender brought their beers. Viv grabbed one and started toward the door.

They let you take drinks outside? Priscilla asked.

I let me take drinks outside, Viv said.

Priscilla sat on her hood and smoked a Parliament. Viv leaned against the driver's side door and watched the parking lot. The sky was still clear and Priscilla looked up, saw Taurus, saw Cygnus. The constellations seemed heavier, the stars closer. She raised the cigarette, dotted them with the fired end.

Where y'all stay? Priscilla asked.

House on the other side of town, Viv said. You should come over.

I don't want to.

Okay.

A cat ran under a Ram two spaces over and started licking itself. Viv pointed at the cigarettes on Priscilla's chest.

Give me one of them, Viv said.

Thought you ain't smoke no more? Priscilla asked.

I don't, but I'm getting wafts of that and it's making my heart warm so give me a ciggy.

When the cigarette lit, Viv's face went orange. She stood up straight, closed her eyes.

Like riding a bike? Priscilla asked.

Like riding a Cadillac, Viv said.

Priscilla lay back.

You used to be very passionate about cigarettes, she said.

Viv laughed. Priscilla wanted to take her picture.

You said passionate? Viv asked.

I'm wrong? Priscilla said.

I don't know about passionate. I'm passionate about Tucson. God. Hairless terriers. Not cigarettes.

Whatever. You smoked a lot.

I was . . . thirteen first time I had one? My friend Norma Klupp's older sister Betty smoked. She'd left the house to go to Tank's or wherever it was and we went into her room and got them. Lit up behind their shed. Made me feel real worldly. Real fancy. Then I threw up after.

It's very bold to smoke cigarettes. It's very cool.

I don't think those are the words.

You sound good. You seem healthy.

Last June I was back in Yaya for the first time in a minute. Tucson had team camp in Buck so I went through there on my way. Just sort of drove around, reminding myself. Klupps' place was gone. You knew about that tornado last year?

Yeah. It's wild y'all aren't there no more. Thought y'all'd be there forever.

I did too but, you know, God don't care much about plans.

Priscilla kept her face straight, made sure not to react. She sat up and scratched her shins.

You working? Viv asked.

Drive the snack cart at a golf course out there, Priscilla said.

Snack cart?

Golf cart with a bunch of snacks and drinks on it. I drive around.
Sell them to golfers.

You like it?

It's fine. Decent hours. Country club crowd, so tips are good.
Not a ton of stress. Get to be outside.

What about wintertime?

They got a nice little restaurant at the course. It stays open.
Waitress there. Seen you're still coaching. How's that?

No complaints. You think you'll stay out that way?

Not sure. Haven't really thought about it.

Liar.

I'm hungry. You want food?

Sure.

Think I'll get a room too.

All right then. I'll tab out.

Viv started to walk off.

And it's just them places you mentioned before? Priscilla asked.
There's not like a Long John's nearby?

No, Viv said.

Well, that really sucks.

They were in the motel room with the lamps on. Viv sat on the
bed. Priscilla lay next to her. There were two Little Caesars Hot-
N-Readies, an order of Crazy Bread, and a twelve-pack of Husst
on the floor. They'd ripped the tops off the pizza boxes and used
them as plates. A television sat on the dresser. The walls were
yellow. *Ladybugs* was on HBO.

This movie blows, Priscilla said.

So much, Viv said.

It makes me want to throw the TV through the window.

Dangerfield's eyes always bothered me. Reminded me of the guys that used to yell at me at the dairy bar when I was younger. Fill me up again.

Priscilla tossed her another beer.

So, how are you? Priscilla asked. I know I asked earlier but that question only gets a real answer if you ask later in the conversation.

You didn't ask earlier, Viv said.

Yes, I did.

No. I asked you. You didn't ask me.

Are you sure?

Very.

Okay. I'm sorry then.

It's all right. I'm honestly really good.

Good. Y'all like it here then?

Yeah. Moved, when, eight years ago? Seven. Got no concept of time anymore. Everything bleeds. It's a good setup, though. Not as much pressure to win. Good seventh-grade class coming up. Might have a shot. Told you about church, all the friends.

Priscilla didn't respond. She wandered through the channels without purpose, landed on an old episode of *Everybody Loves Raymond*. There was music outside and she went to the window. Two white guys in busted barn coats drove an old Gator down the aisles of the parking lot. They'd taken bungees and strapped a portable CD player to the back, blared George Strait's "Carrying Your Love with Me."

I don't think I want to live in Wahoo anymore, Priscilla said.

So don't, Viv said.

Been feeling sort of empty.

Yeah? I'm sorry.

I struggle to make good connections with people in conversation. Like, it'll feel like a lot of work, talking. Somebody'll say something, and then it'll be my turn, 'cause it's just me and them and no one else to pass to, and I'll just be in all the places in my mind looking for something good or funny or, like, a smart question to ask so they know I'm interested and want the conversation to go well. And I search and search but the good thing don't come. It'll just be that deadness and super quiet and I look at their face dying, hating it, and I'm hating it too. Like the other night I read tigers are bigger than lions. Wild, right? Seems like lions would be bigger. And I thought Oh, that'll be a good thing to bring up at work if I'm trying to make conversation with someone and don't know what to say. Lemme just slip in this tiger fact right here. And then hopefully that inspires a bond that will never be broken, an eternal friendship. Next day I was talking to the girl I work with and there was a lull and I got nervous. Couldn't remember what I'd planned. Told her I'd been meaning to ask her something but couldn't remember what. Started looking at the ground and there was just nothing in my head. When I looked back up she'd already gone. Sorry. I don't—I shouldn't be saying this. I don't want to make the night weird or whatever.

P, the ship sailed on normal the moment you called.

Sometimes I'll be at a party and in a circle of people that's having one of those, you know, group conversations, and it'll just be the worst thing I've ever been part of. There's like five of us in the circle and two people are doing a lot of the heavy lifting word-wise and don't nobody want it to keep going but nobody knows how to stop it without being rude so we all just deal with it until the two talkers tire out and the circle breaks. Then everybody sort of looks around, sees which new hell to join. I always sort of think, way in the back of my mind, that those situations only happen when I'm in them. That it's me mucking everything up—my energy or something—and if I was someone else it'd be different. Better. And I'd really facilitate the conversation and get everyone involved and it'd just be smooth and the group would be all This is great. We're a good combination of folks. We should all go get dinner or something. Plan a group vacation. Go to the beach, or the . . . beach.

Viv stared at her, took a bite of pizza.

I've always been jealous of people who are very themselves no matter what, Priscilla said. People with a consistent personality. I don't have that. I'm one way with one person, another with the next. I'm happiest when I'm the funny person people are excited to see but it's not weird when I leave a place early or just don't show up at all. I'm rarely that, though. Guess I can't remember the last time I was that. I don't want to be around people a lot of the time. I don't want to be me a lot of the time.

She grabbed another beer and sat on the edge of the bed.

You haven't asked again why I'm going to Florra, Priscilla said.

You ignored me the first time, Viv said.

I remember. Why didn't you ask again?

Didn't seem like you wanted me to.

Figured you would anyway.

Why? 'Cause I love you? 'Cause I miss you so much? 'Cause I was lying and I think about you all the time?

Yeah, those.

Why're you here?

I was driving through. Wanted to see you.

You ain't talked to me in forever. Disappear. Move without saying nothing. Never returned my calls. It about murdered me. I was so sad. So sad to not have you in my life. I couldn't talk to you and hear your voice. I wanted to hear your voice. I didn't know why you called. I didn't like it. Then I did. I just wanted to see you. I'm really mad at you even now and for a second when you phoned I considered giving you a tongue-lashing, but then I heard your voice and, I don't know, you're my baby still. Thought about going off on you when I seen you but I wanted tonight to go well. Wanted everything to be smooth and easy. Wanted to have a whole bunch of these nights. I don't know. I love you so much. Why'd you leave?

I just didn't want to be there anymore.

What happened?

It won't sound like anything and it'll make you madder.

I mean tell me something.

Priscilla put her hands on her hips and stared at the carpet. Her head felt punched.

It was at the Yarrow Parade, she said. I was just sort of standing there watching the people go by. The people, the horses, the cars and flowers and the band, just watching it all. Kids catching candy. People smiling, waving. All the floats. Nothing happened, really. Wasn't like it was this one thing. But I was just watching it all and something in me was, like, hurting so much and I just couldn't be there anymore. I'd been feeling bad for a long time, empty and sort of wandering, but hadn't thought about leaving. Didn't expect to want to. I did, though. It just hit me in this rush that . . . I just felt something in me screaming, like, you have to go. Right now. I think it was God. But I just had an ache in my whole body that showed me this place in my mind where I had to leave. And I just went. I left. I didn't want my life anymore. I wanted new things. And it felt like to get them I had to be totally gone. Completely clean break. I couldn't talk to you. Would've made me want to come back.

That ain't a good answer, P. You're saying you . . . I'm sorry. You're right. It doesn't make sense.

Some things don't make sense. They happen anyway. I know it'd be easier to understand if there was some big something that happened but it just—that's not how it went. It was . . . I don't know any other way to explain it. Just couldn't do it anymore. I had to feel different.

I'm not okay with that answer. Maybe I should be more under- standing, but . . . I just don't understand.

I get that.

I love you.

I love you.

I ain't even know if you were alive.

I know. I'm not sorry I did it, but I am sorry I didn't say any- thing. Should've, just . . . couldn't.

I mean, I forgi—I'm not gonna not forgive you. But I'm still— this don't fix nothing. What made you decide all the sudden to see me now? What happened that you were like Oh, maybe I should see my godmother who loves and cherishes me? I'm her precious princess. Maybe she'd like to see me.

I'm going to Florra.

You said that. What's there?

Sylvia Table.

Viv stood, put her hands on her face, sat back down. Priscilla took another drink.

What? Viv asked.

He's there, Priscilla said.

Okay. What you want to see him for?

Seen him on the news. At that car show in Tunero. Had this tricked-out Ranchero. Bunch of money. Cheesing. Apparently he's loaded now.

How you know that?

He was using wads of hundreds as fans, Viv. He was doing the geisha fans with the bills.

What's that got to do with you, though?

I'm gonna go see him.

Why?

It's not right. He don't deserve to have a great life, be rich. I don't even have a washer/dryer. It's not fair.

This is crazy.

Don't say that.

What's your plan?

I don't know. Have a chat. Maybe more.

More? What's more?

Priscilla said nothing.

You're gonna rob him? Viv asked.

No, Priscilla said.

What then?

Again Priscilla said nothing. Neither blinked. Priscilla licked her lips and tilted her head to the side. Viv mirrored her. They could hear each other breathing. Priscilla raised her eyebrows, told her with her face.

No, Viv said.

Stop, Priscilla said.

I ain't gonna hear that.

Didn't say anything for you to hear.

Didn't have to.

Don't be this way.

You're gonna kill him?

I don't know.

But maybe.

Maybe.

You can't do that.

I wouldn't do it if I couldn't.

That's confusing. Talk different.

Unless I got the okay from God, I wouldn't do it.

Viv raised her eyebrows and took a breath.

Wait, Viv said. What's up?

If God don't give me the go-ahead, I won't do it, Priscilla said.

So, you won't do it.

Depends what He says.

What are you talking about? He won't okay killing someone. Are you insane?

I said don't say that. God talks to people all the time.

I'm not saying He don't, but He ain't saying yes to killing somebody.

He may already have. I'm still sitting with Him. He's in my heart. I'm searching it, trying to see.

Thou shalt not kill.

I understand that's what He said in the Bible a long time ago, but something He'd say today would take precedence over that, wouldn't it?

God's perfect. He don't make mistakes.

He don't have limits, though, either. He can do whatever He wants, anything. He could change rules. He could let me kill him.

You're very different.

If you make the rules, you can change rules. You think God has limits?

I think you're scaring me.

Why can't I kill him? He killed Dad. Eye for an eye.

I'm still mad at you for disappearing and now I have to shift from that to this. This is so unfair. I should probably be understanding, but this is gross. I feel gross. Also, turn the other cheek.

My body rages against me I pray so hard. I'm this close to sweating blood. I taste it in my mouth sometimes.

Don't be so self-righteous.

The horns of the righteous shall be exalted.

I never told you, but after your daddy died, getting you to church, Amma being okay with that—when you got baptized, other than my wedding, that was the best day of my life.

I'm so grateful you did that for me.

And now your mind's like this.

You don't think God's capable of saying I see this guy wronged you and he deserves to die?

I don't think God's saying yes to you killing people. He's love.

God's killed a bunch of people, Viv. He sends people to hell.

If they've gotten to the end of their life and not repented. If they've heard His word and turned away. If they're bad. But He's not gonna say people can just up and start killing folks that did them wrong.

You're not inside me. You're not hearing Him.

I hear Him in my ways and I'm comfortable saying this is nuts.

He's a bad person.

So what? That don't mean you get to kill him. Also, you don't know he's a bad person.

I do. I see him and know.

God's the judge.

God's inside me and giving me the ability to know.

What if he's a Christian now?

Who?

Sylvia Table.

Priscilla scoffed.

I'm sure he's not, she said.

But what if he is? Viv asked.

Then I guess if I kill him, he'll go to heaven. What a gift.

So, it's about who he was, not who he might be now? What about forgiveness?

Stop trying to—that don't—what's your problem? If God says I can kill him, I can kill him.

What if he's not a believer?

What're you trying to accomplish here?

You kill a nonbeliever, you're sending him to hell. All that fire. An eternity of suffering.

He sent himself there by not accepting Jesus Christ as his Lord and Savior.

You could witness to him. Teach him about Jesus. How He died for us, gave us eternal life. You could save him. You could save his soul.

Stop. I don't want to think about those things. I want to kill him. I have a right to. I should get to avenge the death of someone I love. That should be totally cool. That should be cheered. You should be standing and clapping. I should be getting a standing ovation. Be ovational at me.

Why now?

What?

Why are you all the sudden worried about him now? It's just the money?

I blocked him from my mind. Did everything I could to avoid thinking of that night.

Why weren't you interested in hurting him before, though?

He was supposed to have a bad life. That's what I always imagined in my head. He wasn't good for anything and he was a bad, dumb person and I just thought his life sucked and would always suck. I could always invent a world where he was on the street or dead or something. He can be out there in the world with his bad life. But if things are amazing for him, that don't work. I can't just sit here with my life sucking the way it do and see this demon with all that cash, flaunting it. Money fans? I can't bear that. He killed Dad. He don't get to be happy.

There's something false about you.

I don't feel good.

You don't think God had a hand in him getting that money? What?

You don't think God has a hand in everything?

I do.

Then if you think that, you have to also think God wanted him to have the money.

Maybe He did. But that don't mean He wanted him to have it and be happy. Don't mean He wanted him to have it forever. Maybe He gave it to him so I could see him on the news. Maybe the whole point of him having money was so I could find him and go kill him.

You're gonna pull a muscle stretching like that and Satan's very near you now.

He's always close. I feel him all the time. I listen to God.

You're making your mind this way to convince yourself God's telling you something's okay when deep down you know it's not.

I'm not doing that.

Please don't do this.

I don't know if I'm doing it or not yet. I'm just talking to God, seeing what's right.

I understand that, but you've opened a place in your mind where bad things can fester. Made yourself soft to evil.

This isn't at all the way I wanted you to respond.

I'm trying to help and you're not wanting to hear me.

My life sucks.

You mentioned that.

I don't have nobody to talk to ever.

Whose fault is that?

My life sucks and it's been sucking and this isn't right. He doesn't deserve good things.

Waaa waaa. If you kill him, you will not feel good. You will not feel happy or fulfilled. You'll stay sad and mad and the world will close in on you and collapse and bury you.

I'm going to find him, look at him, and see what I can do. I'll tell him my name and watch his face and hear what he says and hear what God says and see what I can do.

How would you even do it?

What do you mean?

If God gave you the green light, which He won't, how you plan on killing him?

With a gun.

You have a gun?

Yes. I purchased it for protection from potential intruders.

And you'd shoot him with the gun?

That's how that'd go, yeah.

This ain't the Wild West, baby. You kill him, you're gonna have to pay for it.

God will protect me.

This the real, actual world, P. Concrete. This ain't some fantasy, imaginary thing that comes and goes with no consequences.

I know what this is.

Your life will crash down around you. You're in your hate and nowhere else.

I'm sitting here telling you I hear you.

This is obvious and I don't like this word, but killing somebody's some real shit. Don't be trying to hear what you want. You'll get caught. You'll go to jail. You want to go to jail?

Yes, Viv, I want to go to jail.

This is so sad.

You're not thinking about me. He ruined my life.

You think God will protect you.

Absolutely He will.

You're doing mental and spiritual gymnastics to justify a self-ish, evil act. You'll be so sad at the end of this. You'll feel so dead and so sad. I'm so worried for you.

Stop. I told you already, if I don't get the go-ahead, I won't do it.

You're already well on your way to convincing yourself it's okay. I see your face. I see your eyes. You're so far down the road already.

You don't know my soul.

I don't. I can only know what you say and do. Based off those, baby, you're in a bad, bad place.

I'm fearfully and wonderfully made. The eyes of the Lord are upon the righteous and His ears are open unto their cry.

God is not your puppet you get to make say and do what you want, and having Bible verses memorized don't make a person right.

I don't think of Him that way.

You're treating Him that way.

You're not inside me.

You need to know you're wrong. If you do this, you're wrong.

I'm not. Things have to be different. He changed my life. I want to be another way.

You're blaming him for everything. Your whole life.

I'm blaming him for killing Dad.

You don't deserve the generosity and care I've shown you here.

Yes, I do. I deserve the best.

I deserve more than you've given me. You didn't hug me when I saw you. You haven't hugged me once since you've been here. That's so weird.

You haven't hugged me.

You left! I'm sorry you've been sad. I don't want you to be sad ever. I want you to be so happy. None of this is good or fine or anything. My head hurts.

That's my every day.

I pray for you all the time.

I pray for you. I'd been feeling very far away from Him for a while. I was angry and upset. Felt like I was fading away. Then I saw the news. He's telling me beautiful things, Viv. I'm gonna do something beautiful in His name.

No no no. This is wrong. Stay here with us. Let me—I don't— just please stay with me.

God's right here. He's right here.

Please don't go. Life's not this way. You're losing yourself.

I have to give myself an opportunity to stand before him. To look at him. I have to see what's okay.

Just look inside yourself and be still. Just be quiet and think about the way you used to be, and the way you used to think, and go back to them. Please realize, somewhere inside you know this is wrong.

It's not. My father was shot and murdered. My mother sat around for the rest of her life sad and angry.

You gonna tell me my name now too?

I feel very close to Him right now. We are so tight.

I look at you and know that's not true.

Whatever I do will be right.

I think being a person in this world's hard.

What?

Those situations happen whether you're in them or not.

What're you talking about?

What you were saying before, about talking to people, about not liking yourself sometimes. Think that's an everybody thing.

That's . . . I don't know. I might be special. I really think I could be really special.

Don't kill him.

Blessed are they who mourn, for they will be comforted.

Blessed are the peacemakers, for they will be called children of God.

He deserves to die.

Your eyes aren't right. You don't believe what you're saying.

I do.

You're in the deep, deep end.

I'm a good swimmer.

They said it was self-defense.

Oh, did they? What a surprise that was.

Your sarcasm was disgusting when you were a child and it's disgusting now.

My sarcasm's amazing.

Change your mind.

Shut up. An earthquake woke me up yesterday.

So?

God's in charge of everything, right? So, He's in charge of the earthquakes. Shaking me awake the morning after I see Dad's killer for the first time in decades? It's a sign. He wants me there. I was sleeping and He was like Hey wake up. Go get justice.

You're reaching.

I'm not.

You can't kill him.

You can't say that. You don't know.

I do know. You can't do this.

I can do anything.

God don't want this.

He's cagey and strange.

You mean His ways are mysterious.

I mean the thing I said.

Please, baby girl, find your old heart.

Whoso sheddeth man's blood, by man shall his blood be shed; for in the image of God made he man. Genesis 9:6.

Look in a mirror and say that. You're not thinking clearly.

Shut up.

Say not thou, I will recompense evil; but wait on the Lord, and he shall save thee. Proverbs 20:22.

You're so arrogant to think you can know the state of my heart.

Why'd you even slow-play this? This was all you wanted. Why

the hangout before? Why not just ask me straight away what I thought of your plans?

I just wanted to sit with you and talk for a second like there wasn't anything wrong. Thought it'd feel good to do that, talk about nothing. Like normal life. Like before. I care about you. My mind's having a hard time. There are knives in my eyes.

You know this is wrong. You wouldn't have told me otherwise.

I wish I didn't think about myself so much. I want to be proud of myself.

Stay here. We'll wrap our arms around you. Just please be part of my life.

My chest, inside, there's this rattling. It's like any time I do something wrong it's—I don't know. Everything weighs so much. I'm exhausted. Anxious all day. Feel like I'm coming apart.

I love you so much. You're my darling and you're wrong. I want to take care of you. Please let me take care of you.

Sometimes I look at old pictures of myself and throw up.

Priscilla walked to the sink. Her eyes spasmed, relaxed. She stared at the backsplash—tangerine-and-turquoise tile, designs of lilies and muzzle-loaded pistols. The guns crossed to make an X and the flower split them down the middle. Together it was like some strange star. Viv was behind her. Priscilla looked in the mirror.

I wonder if it's possible to get, like, a new head, Priscilla said.

What? Viv asked.

Do you think I could get a new head? A person's head. Not any person that exists, but just like a brand-new, fresh-out-the-box head. I could take mine off and then I wouldn't have to be me anymore or have my brain anymore and I'd put the new head on and be a new person. And I'd think differently. And maybe I'd be smarter. Calmer. Funnier. Doesn't even have to be a cute head. So long as it's not me, I'm good. Could be an ugly one or, like, one where there's only one eye that works or no nose or something. Do you think that'd be possible? That'd be huge for me if I could get a new head. I've been meaning to get rid of this one.

I don't know what I'm supposed to say. Come to my house.

I lie about my name. I tell people I was named after Priscilla in the Bible.

There's a Priscilla in the Bible?

Yeah.

I didn't know that. I'll have to check her out. Come to my house.

I was looking at my palms the other day and could see inside my veins. It was boring. Wasn't nothing in there.

P. Please. Come to my house.

And do what?

Get right.

And Priscilla was in Viv's truck. The windows were down and let the night in. The town was dark. The town was still. They got to the driveway. Viv carried Priscilla's bag, held her hand. They went inside. The place was warm and golden. Blue carpet. Two walls filled with Precious Moments dolls. Three largemouth bass mounted above the television and on the screen the DVD menu for *Avatar*. Painting of the Last Supper over the fireplace. There was a black leather couch under the living room window and a white pleather recliner by the bookcase. Stack of quilts beside it. Their Christmas tree was still up.

Isn't it spring? Priscilla asked.

Definitely, Viv said.

Viv took Priscilla to the guest room and tucked her in, kissed her cheek. Priscilla lay there under the covers. They smelled like trees. Velvet sleep. Technicolor dreams.

When she woke, there was a cup of coffee on the bedside table and she smelled breakfast. Viv had made biscuits and gravy. They ate on the back porch off plates with turtles on them. And Tucson woke and hugged her and sat with her and Priscilla had forgotten how funny he was and the three of them played Trouble and Pretty, Pretty Princess and Monopoly and it was this way for years and she was their found child and her eyes were back. Then her hair was silver and they were dead and she was slow and sat under the oaks in their backyard with her Bible and coffee and the ground screamed and shook and the shaking made slits in the earth. An ocean of mouths singing Yes. The yard opened. The earth chewed her. Speckles of glass fell like death confetti. Operatic streams of silver. Crimson girders. Mangled steel fell. Dark and wooden halos. Crystal knives. The Devil painted a brick wall blue. Seventy-four televisions. On every one: flamingos flying.

Priscilla, Viv said.

She was back at the motel, staring in the mirror. Her face bent. Her hair looked like oil. She looked at Viv.

Come to my house, Viv said.

No, Priscilla said.

Viv shook her head, looked toward the window.

Then I think I'm leaving now, Viv said.

She grabbed her purse and went to the door. Priscilla turned.

I'm a good person, she said.

Viv looked at her. There were tears in her eyes.

I'm not sure, P, Viv said. I love you so much. I don't think you are right now. Steel yourself to the bad things inside you. Please don't let them win.

BEDLAM IN A VIDEO STORE

THE NIGHT BEFORE THE PARTY, Lady and Table got in a fight in an almost empty Hasting's over what movie to rent. They argued beside a broken television. Muted static fuzzed snow on the screen. He wanted to watch *As Good As It Gets*. She wanted to watch *Six Days, Seven Nights*. His immediate refusal of her choice and the condescension that came with it—he'd burst out laughing—made her want to prove a point. She'd been frustrated with him when they arrived, his countless party demands throughout the week, and in the aisle she felt his arrogance surge and put her hands on her head.

I feel like I haven't got to pick the movie in a while, she said.

The way Table looked at it, she always did whatever she wanted, said whatever she wanted, went wherever she wanted. It was his turn. He'd been thinking all week about how she'd gotten a cool jacket and all he got was some dumb hat and in the aisle he felt her rigidness and put his hands on his head.

That's weird because I literally never get to pick the movie, he said.

Now that's not true at all, she said.

You need to respect me more. I'm a proper breadwinner now.

Lady laughed hard, was over the top about it. She held her stomach and leaned against the television.

You're so selfish, Table said.

And you're a child, Lady said.

I loved you as Godzilla in *Godzilla*.

Your personality is a domestic terrorist attack.

You don't get to talk to me that way. You're nothing without me. I'm the one with the money. I'm the one with the juice.

Dianna looked at the carpet.

Be very careful, Lady said.

I'll be careful when I'm dead, Table said.

That line is bad and makes no sense. Don't—don't do this. Things should just be good now. Let's go backwards. I'm sorry for the hurtful things I said, okay? This is stupid anyway, let's just get both.

I don't know what you're talking about. Things *are* good now. I'm above you.

Table, stop right now.

You ain't shit.

You know, I saw—she pointed at Dianna and mouthed the words *her father*—the other day. Was coming back from work and stopped at the QuikTrip off Chaparral. Went in for a drink and there he was. Couldn't believe it. Last I'd heard he was in Texas. Must've been back visiting. He was bigger than he used to be. Not cut up but strong-looking and honestly, to make you mad, I was all about it. Never told you his name. It's Doak. Doak. Doak didn't see me but I just watched him there in the store and built this whole life for us. We lived in Galveston. Not near the beach but we'd go there sometimes. Play Frisbee. Drink a little. Eat a ice cream cone. And we would scamper along the shore like puppies. And I got my associates and became a paralegal. And it was beautiful. And fun. And he listened. And he was proud of me sometimes and funny others and he asked me questions about myself and told me how lucky he felt. He never thought he'd see me again but now he sees me all the time and it's great because of how hot I am. And fun. And I know things. Humans are the only animals with chins. Sloths fart out their mouths. Samuel L. Jackson demanded the studio keep *Snakes on a Plane* as the title because it was the only reason he accepted the role. And I'd tell Doak that stuff and he'd be like That's awesome. I thought for sure sloths farted out their butts. That really adds flavor to my, you know, being alive. And every day of our lives I looked in his beautiful eyes and told him how happy I was to be rid of you.

Table reared back, wanted to punch something, and opted for the television. The screened webbed and spasmed and the static warped. Lady shook her head. He shuffled around the corner holding his hand.

What happened, Mayweather? she asked. You break it?

No, he said. Let's go.

Dianna sat a few feet away, looked at the peacocks on her blouse. Lady stood with her hands on her hips, took some breaths, and stared at the ceiling. Oversized popcorn buckets hung next to papier-mâché Butterfingers and cardboard film reels. Her pulse knocked in her temples and she closed her eyes, tried to settle. Dianna stood and held her hand. The air-conditioning kicked on. Moans from the vents like barge horns, then someone whistling. Lady opened her eyes. It was just the noise for a few seconds, high and twisting, no song she knew, and the blank end of the aisle, and the movie cases, all the colors.

A woman turned the corner. She was young and Black, around twenty, hollowed out with headphones on. When she saw Lady she stopped. Lady watched her look at the television and Dianna and back at her. Table was at the registers hollering Lady's name. Dianna leaned against her. Table kept hollering. Lady nodded.

Hi, Lady said. What's—how's it going?

The woman seemed to wobble and it was like one of her legs was shorter than the other. Her eyes were full of light. They stared at each other. Table screamed Lady until he found her. He clapped. She flinched and was furious with herself.

It's been time, he said.

He walked away. Tears in Lady's eyes and she tried to stop them. She looked again at the white-tile ceiling, the fluorescent lights, the blank bank of televisions. Black screens like bricks of charcoal over their heads. Her feet were numb. The woman was still there. Lady tried to disappear.

He hits you? the woman asked.

Dianna kissed her hand.

I'm sorry, Lady said.

No—he hits you, the woman said.

I'm not sure what to . . . I don't know. I'm real nice. Smart. Fun to be with . . . I don't know . . . I don't know. I don't know. But I have made sure he feels me too.

LET ME
TELL YOU THAT
I LOVE YOU
ONE MORE TIME

THE FIRST THING PRISCILLA SAW WAS the Long John's. She was euphoric. The sign hung in the Florra sky like yellow gold and she wanted it to mean something good. She got the two-chicken plank combo and ate in the parking lot with the windows down and the radio low. Streetlamps winked on. The moths came out. She stared at the steering wheel and thought about Table—his nose, mouth, eyes. When he'd yelled on the television, he looked like he was smelling something awful, peak stinkface, his cheeks the color of slapped pig. She heard music and looked up. Across the street was a storefront Mexican church. Blue awning. White letters on the canvas reading MISION CRISTIANA NUEVA VISION: UNA IGLESIA ADVENTISTA DEL SÉPTIMO DIA. The front door was open. The congregation sang "Solo De Jesus La Sangre." Priscilla yawned and shook her head. Next to the church was a uniform store, Dickies and Carhartt logos prominent in the front window, WORKWEAR/SCRUBS written on white poster board and taped to the entrance.

Priscilla crossed the street and stood outside the store. Salt-white faceless mannequins filled the rest of the window, each dressed in a different iteration of work and medical wear: hi-visibility reflective safety vests, murdered-out Nike Monarchs, overalls, carpenter pants, double-knee construction pants, a vast Wolverines selection, rain slickers, flannel-lined jeans, lab coats, et cetera. One mannequin held her attention more than the rest. It was dressed in purple coveralls. Priscilla stood before the doll, stared at the fabric, touched the glass. She wore them out of the store.

The preacher was preaching now and the service mostly full. Six rows of orange chairs lined each side of the room, the walls Neptune blue. At the base of the altar was a towering yellow vase

full of fake roses with a painting of Jesus feeding the five thousand on the front. The preacher jumped and punched the air. He
was the shape of a triangle. Priscilla couldn't understand him.
The room looked soft. She tasted blood. On the back wall was a
fresco: an opening in a jungle, waterfall in the upper left corner,
red shrubbery on either side of the mouth, and the water spilled
down to a river, its banks lined with palm trees and myrrh and
above all that the sky, the same pure blue as the other walls but
with puffed clouds there too, and in the middle of the firmament
flew a dove. A stunning white with wings spread. Glow lines shot
off the body. It had no face. Priscilla's lips got away from her. Her
eyes were red. Two signs in English on the window in front of her.
One said JESUS IS THE WAY, THE TRUTH, AND THE LIFE. The
other said HE WILL NEVER LEAVE YOU. HIS LOVE IS FOREVER.

The preacher was on his knees. He hugged his Bible, said Y
los pájaros son hermosos y se elevan para él. Wind on her neck.
What? She looked for answers in the lights. None came.

She drove to the CITGO for gas, went inside for candy and
information. The woman working the register was white and old
with a buzzed head and energetic teeth. A false tan had her
chocolate-Labrador brown and there was a scab the shape of
Arkansas on her left cheek. Her name tag said LOBSTERTAIL.

Howdy howdy, Priscilla said. May I please have thirty on 6,
the Debonair? Plus the Skittles and a pack of Parliaments.

No prob, Lobstertail said. We'll get you fixed up.

She put the cigarettes on the counter and started scanning.

You rolling through? she asked.

No, Priscilla said. Visiting.

Tiny town to be visiting.

I'm here for the people. I hear they're cool.

As a valued employee of one of the busiest establishments in town, I can tell you that's as far from true as the east is from the west.

Priscilla laughed hard, wanted the woman to like her. Lobstertail basked in the laughter.

No way, Priscilla said. Zinger alert. I'm stealing that. Hey. Question. Do phone books still exist?

Phone books? Lobstertail asked. I believe so. Though they're going extinct.

Y'all got one here?

N— Um. Actually.

She squatted and looked under the counter. Priscilla thought she might cry.

Don't make phone calls much no more, Lobstertail said. I text my loves. There it go.

The phone book landed on the counter. Priscilla stifled tears and ripped open the plastic.

Thought I'd seen it, Lobstertail said. They send them still. Seems stupid. Usually just take them to the house, use them for kindling. Who you looking for?

Friend of mine, Priscilla said.

Who?

Priscilla looked up.

Small town, Lobstertail said. I'm a bit of a social eagle. Might be able to help.

Sylvia Table? Priscilla asked.

Lobstertail nodded. Priscilla's leg tried to shake.

He comes in here, Lobstertail said. Everybody comes in here. We're not friends or nothing, but yeah. I'm assuming you're here for the party?

Priscilla looked back at the book.

Yeah, Priscilla said. We go back decades but I've never visited. I'm a bad friend that way. I'm in the panhandle. Eons away. He doesn't know I'm coming. Wanted to surprise him, but lost the address.

I don't care much for him to be honest with you.

I can understand that.

He's not smart or cute and thinks he's both. Sorry. He's your friend.

It's okay. Depending on the day you ask, I might agree with you.

Oooooo. Girl, you're so bad. I love it. I think he lives in the super sticks. Out there at—

5 Mile. Thank you, my dearling.

Priscilla sat in her car on the side of the road. She was fifty yards past the entrance to the Tables' place. The only light was the house in the distance, one on inside, and a honey glow from the backyard. Faint music, mash of voices. She took out the Ruger and the bullets, felt their weight, and how they were cold. Her shoulders were tight. Her neck was stiff. Her head vibrated.

She loaded the gun in the dark. It was a country road, paved, lumpy blacktop. Fields all around. Moonlight leaked through iron clouds. She got out of the car and started toward the house. The driveway was wet and long and dented. She stepped over puddles. The party didn't deter her in the slightest. She was single-minded. The more chaos, she thought, the better.

Think I saw You in the forest once. In the deer woods out there outside Bidido. Had pulled off the road to go swim. Was a pond out there I knew.

And I'd been in the water awhile. On my back, floating, staring at the sky. And I don't know why, but I started thinking about Dad. Tried not to, but once I started, couldn't stop. Just got sadder and sadder. And I remember having the thought that today's a nice day, and I ain't have nowhere to be, no responsibilities, I was just some kid, swimming around and being free, and I hated I couldn't enjoy all that. That in that moment my mind could go to something sad.

Halfway there. Her feet were soft on the drive. The music came clearly now—The Band, "Atlantic City."

I got out the water and changed. Started back toward the road, going through the woods, and I heard something click in front of me. I looked up. Wasn't nothing there but just these two trees and the sky between them. I remember the trunks were real skinny and the sky looked huge. Very empty. And I just stopped and stared into the blue. Don't know how long I stood there, but at a certain point I saw Your face. Didn't have a nose or ears or eyes or nothing but You were there in the air in Your way, there and not. It was like some lines that made the shape of a head and they were kind of glowing and getting squeezed. Think I said Hey. In my head I did at least. I feel like I spoke it . . . I guess I'm not sure. Always regretted not saying more. I couldn't believe it was You, You know? I felt real small and light but strong too. I could feel my whole body, but it was that sensation you get when you're numb, that humming in you. I was just really there. I guess I don't—like, that was You. To me it was. And it meant so much to get to see You. But I was thinking about it the other day and got worried 'cause if it was You, I wouldn't have been able to look at You. You're too pretty, right? We can't take the sight? It's just too much? Maybe we could if You just made it so, though? Maybe if You made Yourself a kind of way and it was like You turned the brightness down? Maybe You did that day by the pond? I hope You did. Can You do it again? I love You so much. I'm so tired. Being this way. I want my mind to stop.

She got to the front yard, thirty-some vehicles parked in the grass. The music had gotten louder and she heard voices and laughter behind the house. She unzipped the coveralls and put the gun in the waist of her shorts. "Atlantic City" ended and Lefty Frizzell's "Shine, Shave, Shower (It's Saturday)" began. She moved slow. A white woman came around the side of the house with a Gaucho in one hand and her phone in the other. Half her face was painted like a zebra and she screamed Connie, it's a banger so get here.

Priscilla looked into the side yard. A white man in blue jeans and no shirt sat on a brand-new riding mower. He ate pizza and humped the air. She rubbed her eyes, heard water. There was clapping. Stoney LaRue's "Oklahoma Breakdown" started. A booming somewhere. She looked into the backyard.

Lady and Table stood on a picnic table near the house. Purple-and-orange streamers hung in waves from the gutters behind them. He wore a Brian Bosworth Seahawks jersey and poured two bottles of Taureau on himself. The champagne hit the fours, made them gold. Priscilla watched him laugh and her chest strained. She whispered.

I want to *I want to I want to. Please?*

Other guests popped bottles. Thuds rang out. Corks flew in the pasture. Table handed Lady a bottle, right hand wrapped and flush with bandages, and Lady tried to chug it. White jeans, red button-up, yellow fur. The crowd was hollering. She bailed on the chug. Champagne like a geyser out of the bottle. She started laughing. Priscilla felt like someone stuck a burning fork up her nose. Table stepped to the ground, offered Lady his hand. They lay in the grass. The party was drunk. Around them it surged.

Seven women in tie-dyed tanks double-fisted Roman candles along the creek bank. The fireworks feathered orange and spit sparks, colored the Amurs mango. A cherry-red Jet Ski sat proud and cocky on a flatbed near the water. Gaucho cans dotted the yard and ashtrays overflowed. Five coolers under the table, two kegs of Husst nearby. One of the tank-topped women ran to the center of the yard and lit an aerial repeater. Dashed, purple fire blossomed into stars, electric plumage, a fading canopy of drugged light coming down. A young Black man stood on a folding chair near the firepit. Cuban links like frosted paracord against his chest. He was clipped into a Bear Cruzer with an arrow set, half his face painted like a tiger, and he shouted the word *sounds*. A young white woman dumped Ronsonol on the point of the arrow and he dipped it in the fire. The flame caught. The woman stepped back. He shot a Folgers can packed with Black Cats. Operatic snaps let loose in the grass. The can yawned. Stoney LaRue's "Let Me Hold You" began and people slow-danced. Priscilla stared at Table. Lady's head rested in the crook of his arm and she smoked a cigarette. Table watched the cloud leave her mouth. They kissed. Priscilla put her hands on her knees and looked to her left. A wood board fence separated the backyard from the pastureland, eight live flamingos there along the fence line. They watched the party. Firelight played off their oxbow necks. They smelled like piss and fish and looked furious, pink-faced money rakes. Beside them was a kiddie pool filled with ice and bottles of Taureau. Priscilla opened one and took a drink. The song ended. A voice shouted Hey all y'all. She turned.

Lady and Table were back on the picnic table, Gauchos in hand, and people surrounded them. They clinked their bottles and drank. A purple hydrangea had been painted on Lady's left hand. Table kissed the flower.

Man, I guess you supposed to wait till the end for the cheers, but fuck it, Table said. Fuck all rules. Fuck everything I don't like.

He took a drink.

We're all some hammered hicks, he said. Let me settle. Want to say a major league gracias to all y'all for coming out and partying with us. I feel very good. Very strong. I'm rich as hell, man. I am excited to announce I have recently added a few aka's to my name. I'm Sylvia Table aka Big Noise aka Grandest Poobah aka Big Quiche. I'll answer to all. Don't forget we got Tina over there by the grill painting faces if you want some art on you. Tina, raise a brush. What up, Tina? We threw this little soiree to celebrate our newfound treasures and I just want to say I don't know shit about shit but this is a real nice thing, this evening. The future's blinding. Rest in peace to my uncle Methuselah, up there in the gold looking down on us. Unc, we miss you. We ain't happy you're gone, but we're gonna make it count. I shake your hand. So yeah, I love my wife, my Lady. She's warm—you're warm and kind and funny. You're such a beautiful person. Your heart. You're so beautiful. I deserve hell, but life with you is heaven.

Lady stuck her tongue out, pretended to throw up, and gave two thumbs-down. He laughed. She blushed, felt fifty feet tall.

To heaven, Table said.

They touched bottles and drank. Priscilla wanted to shoot him in the face. A digging in her brain. Redbone's "Sweet Lady of Love" began. Lady started laughing. Priscilla watched Table dance. His fingers waved. His hands framed his face. Lady popped, locked, and dime-stopped, sang hard. Priscilla took a long drink of champagne. Table pushed the air in front of him, then cupped his hands, brought the space back to his chest. Lady started giggling. Priscilla took her bottle and went to the creek. The tie-dyed girls played catch with lime glow sticks. She stared into the water.

Yes or no?

Her hands itched. She finished the bottle. A glow stick floated by, lit the water. The creek was up. Her throat felt full and her eyes were wet. She didn't blink.

Can I please?

Her head throbbed.

If You say nothing, I'll assume Your answer's yes. If You say nothing, I'm doing it. I'll go to my car, wait till the party's over, then shoot him. I'll walk up to him with my gun and look at him and shoot him. And he'll be dead. And the world will be better. Say something if I shouldn't.

She closed her eyes.

Where is Your sound?

The nerves in her arms stretched and swayed. Tears warm on her lashes. Her lips were apart. There was no new noise. She opened her eyes. The tears fell.

Okay then.

She coughed and scratched her neck.

Good . . . Great. Awesome. Thank you so much. I love You so much.

She got another bottle and went back to her car. It was a little after 11 p.m. The Ruger dug into her waist. The hammer kept poking her. She took the gun out, sat it in the passenger seat, and stared at the barrel. Blood out her nose again and she held the flannel under her nostrils and shrieked and the scream had chest and made the rearview shake. She stopped faint. Some ringing somewhere. Her muddled head. The twisting of air. There were stars in the car with her. She tried to touch them.

Her hands passed through the shines. Every color in her palms. She fell asleep. She dreamed of jaguars alone in cottongums.

A cow woke her up, had a moo like a weed eater. She touched her body, her arms and legs and stomach and face. A clouded dawn made a metallic sky and she stared at her reflection in the rearview. Dark circles around her eyes. Her face was dragging. She looked into her lap, let everything fuzz. Blood caked her lips and she licked them. Her knees bounced. The Taureau had spilled in the floorboard and her Terminators squeaked in the champagne. She put a handful of bullets in one pocket, the Ruger in the other. Her neck was sore. She got out of the car.

It was cool out and she walked slowly down the road. Light jangles from the ammo. Ripples in the grass. She raised the collar of her coveralls and went again down the drive. Red napkins littered the lawn. The breeze moved them. Her cheek twitched. She touched the gun. The handle was smooth. There were two vehicles left. One a stretch Hummer the color of the sun, the other the Ranchero. She looked at the house. The shades on the living room window were open and there was no movement inside. She tried the front door. It was locked. She went to the edge of the house and peeked around the corner. Nobody there. Her adrenaline made her shake and her chest was tight. She flexed her back. Her back clicked. She hugged the house. Clouds like cragged mountains, snowcapped, ashen. The sky looked like an oyster. Her face was wet. She looked into the backyard.

Lady and Table were there, in their chairs, facing the creek. Her tears blurred them and she wiped her eyes. Neither moved. A jerking in her neck. Her palms were damp. Her head poured sweat. Her fingers burned. Her legs burned. She shifted her weight from one foot to the other. Her back was wet. Sweat in her mouth. She put her fist against the brick and brought her hand down hard, scraped her knuckles. Blood ran down her fingers. Blood on her hand. Her brain fluttered and there was a pang where her spine met her neck. She palmed her nape and looked up. Blood on her neck. She pulled the gun and moved toward them, put the bead on his head. Hums off the creek. A wave of starlings left the Amurs, flew east in a spade. Priscilla could see their faces now. They were asleep, same clothes as the night before. Empty Gauchos in the grass. Table's hands were on his stomach, half-eaten brownie on his chest. Lady's hands were under her cheek, a smattering of pizza crusts in her lap. Priscilla pulled back the hammer. The click woke him up. He squinted, shaded his eyes with his hand.

Howdy, Table said.

Hi, Priscilla said.

What's your name?

Priscilla.

Hi, Priscilla. I'm Table.

I know.

He was still tipsy.

How you doing? he asked.

Pretty good, Priscilla said. How're you?

Fine . . . You got a gun there.

I do.

Their voices woke Lady. She saw Priscilla and the Ruger, thought she was dreaming. She tried to wake up. She couldn't.

What's this? Lady asked.

This is Priscilla, Table said.

What's happening? Lady asked.

We don't keep any money here, Table said.

Don't want no money, Priscilla said.

What's going on? Lady asked. Please don't do this. Please don't be here.

This doesn't have anything to do with you, Priscilla said. Didn't even know you existed.

Shut up, Lady, Table said.

Don't talk to her that way, Priscilla said.

Yeah, Lady said. Don't talk to me that way. Also don't talk to him that way. I can take care of myself.

What do you want? Table asked.

My name's Priscilla, Priscilla said.

You said that, Table said.

Priscilla Blackwood, Priscilla said.

A pop of light inside his face and he felt run over. He looked into her eyes, saw Solomon. Priscilla watched him remember. She nodded.

Oh, Table said.

He put his head down.

What's happening? Lady asked.

You never told her? Priscilla asked.

Told me what? Lady asked.

It was self-defense, Table said.

Please, Priscilla said.

What's going on? Lady asked.

He killed my dad, Priscilla said.

Lady looked at Table. Table looked at Priscilla.

Outside the Charlie's Chicken in Yaya, Priscilla said. He shot him. I was there.

It was self-defense, Table said.

Now who's repeating themselves? Priscilla asked.

Wait, wait, wait, Lady said. Table, you killed somebody?

It was before we met, Table said.

Y'all talk to me, not each other, Priscilla said.

This isn't right, Table said. What you're doing.

I'm going to kill you, Priscilla said.

Let's just calm down, Lady said.

I won't kill her, Priscilla said. But I'll kill you.

Well, I liked that first part, but the second half wasn't any good at all, Table said.

He didn't hang on like he was supposed to, Priscilla said. He's supposed to get to say stuff. One last thing. That's how it goes. Person's about to die. They have the strength to say one final thing. He didn't get to say nothing. I didn't get to say nothing. He was just dead. And my life's bad now.

No, Lady said. Now, just—what's . . . I'm sorry. I'm so sorry. What can—let's talk about—

I was five years old, Priscilla said. Five. You shot him. Why?

It was self-defense, Table said.

Stop lying, Priscilla said.

Look, Lady said. I don't— Please don't shoot him. Please don't kill my husband. Everything's good now. Everything's fine. We're all good. It's all good. We should just, like, let's get some breakfast. Get some food in us.

Priscilla still stared at Table.

You changed my life, Priscilla said. You changed my life.

When? Lady asked.

November 7, 1984, Priscilla said.

That was before we met, Lady said.

That's what I was saying, Table said.

I came here to see you, Priscilla said. To look at you. To see what I could do when I saw you. And I can tell, you're a bad person.

No, Table said. I'm not.

I don't like this, Lady said.

I don't either, Table said.

I'm right, Priscilla said. The Lord giveth wisdom: out of His mouth come knowledge and understanding. He layeth up sound wisdom for the righteous: He is a buckler to them that walk uprightly.

Seriously, you need to go, Table said.

Table, stop, Lady said. Priscilla, what can we do?

Nothing, Priscilla said. I came here to do this. I asked God if it was okay and He said it was totally cool so I'm doing it.

Jesus Christ, Table said.

Don't you dare take His name in vain in my presence, Priscilla said. And Lady, you'll be better off. You can be away from him. I'm sure he hurts you.

He loves me, Lady said.

I love her, Table said.

It's not wrong to kill someone like you, Priscilla said. The world will be better when you're gone.

Priscilla, you don't know us, Lady said.

I can still be right, Priscilla said. I'm His daughter. He loves me so much.

This ain't no way to be, Lady said. I see you. You're not sure about this.

I am, though, Priscilla said.

What good will it do? Lady asked.

You can't talk me out of it, Priscilla said.

Just don't point the gun at my husband, Lady said. Please? Hey. Please don't point the gun at my husband?

Listen to her, Table said.

You can shut up, Priscilla said. Lady, you don't see him. He's a bad person. He took my dad from me. Sent him to hell.

Point the gun at me, please, Lady said. Priscilla. Please point it here.

It's his, Priscilla said.

He's mine and I'm his, Lady said.

He don't get to have a good life, Priscilla said. He made me hurt. He makes you hurt. I see your eyes. I see your face.

Don't speak on my hurt, Lady said. I love him.

I love you too, Table said.

Shut up, Table, Lady said. I'm here and inside myself and I don't need no noise from you unless I say so. Priscilla, I take his bad. He is. I take it. Let it be mine.

It's not yours to take, Priscilla said.

Let me have it, Lady said.

I choose what I do too, Priscilla said.

Just don't do this, though, Lady said. I'm so sorry for what he did.

Thank you for saying that, Priscilla said. I appreciate that.

You're welcome, Lady said. Please stop.

No, Priscilla said. I'm a good person. I'm the good person.

So am I, Lady said.

He's a bad guy, Priscilla said. I'm supposed to win. I get to win. I can do anything.

It's hard when the people we love go away, Lady said.

What? Priscilla asked.

It's hard when the people we love go away, Lady said.

He changed my life, Priscilla said. He changed my life.

I know, Lady said. I'm so sorry. I'm moving toward my husband now. I'm gonna stand, take a couple steps to the right, and move in front of him.

You won't, Priscilla said.

I will, Lady said.

Lady pushed up off the armrests and Priscilla fired a bullet into the ground. Lady leaned away from the noise. Table curled into himself.

Don't be that, Lady said. Just don't be that. Please. I'm still gonna move.

Don't, Priscilla said.

Lady took another step. Priscilla fired a shot off to the left, put the gun back on him. Lady stopped.

I promise he's going to die, Priscilla said.

That will not happen, Lady said.

I've been with this for so long, Priscilla said.

This ain't the way, though, Lady said.

Lady, Table said.

In unison, the women screamed You've got to shut up.

He's not a good man, Priscilla said.

No, Lady said. Not really.

Then why protect him? Priscilla asked.

Lady looked at Table and saw he was afraid.

I don't know, she said. I love him. It's . . . um . . . I don't know. I just love him.

How? Priscilla asked.

It's— I'm not— I just do, Lady said. I love him . . . I love him I love him.

And I loved my dad, Priscilla said.

Priscilla, please, Lady said.

I'm gonna shoot him a few times now, Priscilla said. I won't kill him yet, though, so you'll still get to talk a little longer.

Please stop, Lady said. I'm moving in front of him, okay?

No, you're not, Priscilla said.

Priscilla took another step. She was close enough to touch him.

Girl, Lady said.

Table was frozen there. Priscilla put the barrel on his right shoulder and pulled the trigger. Lady backed away, shrieked. Blood rose up. Table wailed. Priscilla screamed *God*. Her lips were dry. She licked them. Her nose started bleeding. More shrieks from Table. She shot him once in each thigh, looked at the sky, and screamed again.

This okay? This okay?

Table slid out of the chair and into the grass. Lady sat next to him, brought him to her chest. Her claret-orange acrylics ran bright in the limestone white of his horseshoe cut. His blood was in her lap.

Shit ass, Table said.

Oh, no, Lady said. Oh no no no.

Shit ass, Table said.

You shouldn't use those words, Priscilla said. Those are cusswords.

Lady kissed his hand, held her lips there. Blood stained his jeans and jersey. It fell in streams, banded his legs. And the dirt got redder. Priscilla reloaded, spit blood on the ground.

Fuck all this, Table said.

I said don't use those words, Priscilla said. Don't cuss around me.

What's the point? Lady asked. What good does this do?

Told you already, Priscilla said. He don't get to have a good life.

Lady reached into her pocket for her phone. Priscilla put the bead on her.

No no, Priscilla said.

I'm just calling an ambulance, Lady said.

I'm not stupid, Lady, Priscilla said. Let go of the phone and take your hand slowly out of your pocket.

Lady did what she asked.

Please stop, Lady said. Please stop this.

Soon as he's dead, Priscilla said.

You're in the wrong here, Lady said. You'll feel bad about this.

I already feel like dancing, Priscilla said.

You're not dancing, Lady said.

I don't act on all my feelings and I don't dance to prove points, Priscilla said. This is about him messing up my life. Both our lives. He's probably super mean to you.

You don't get to decide how my life is, Lady said. You don't know me. My life ain't bad.

I prayed about all this, Priscilla said.

Lady moved Table's head to rest in the crook of her arm, put pressure on the leg wounds. His jersey was soaked. The fours went red.

I don't feel good at all, he said.

My head feels tight, Lady said.

Mine feels that way all the time, Priscilla said.

What can I do? Lady asked. What can I do to save my husband from you?

Jack squat, Priscilla said. You're helpless and control nothing. I understand that's frustrating, but that's reality.

I'll die if he dies, Lady said.

You won't, Priscilla said. God will be there for you. He's here. In the space between us. In my voice. And yours. This actually might even be Him speaking. He's probably speaking through me. I'm His vessel. Isn't that incredible? You can feel Him now if you just let yourself be still. Both our lives will be so much better.

I disagree with all that, Table said.

You're in the wrong here, Lady said.

I'm not, Priscilla said.

I'm bleeding a lot, Table said.

You're trying to tell me about me, Lady said.

You're trying to tell me about me, Priscilla said.

You're not in my head, Lady said. I'm not in yours. You're not in mine.

I am in yours, Priscilla said. I know it. God's placed me there. I've stopped feeling like dancing. I feel yucky now. I need him dead.

I don't feel good, Table said.

I need quiet, Priscilla said.

Shut up, Table, Lady said. Priscilla, being alone is terrible. I don't like my mind either.

What're you talking about? Priscilla asked. I'm not alone. *You hear that? She thinks I'm alone.* That, my dearling, is one of the funniest jokes of all time. Yes. I can be happy. My mind could be so pretty. The depths of His love for me cannot be put into words.

What? Lady asked. Just . . . what can I do? What can I do to save my husband from you?

Nothing, Priscilla said. You have no power here. I'm right. I know I'm right. I want to be somewhere else.

I don't understand why this is happening, Lady said.

What's wrong with me? Priscilla asked. What's wrong with you?

This don't make no sense, Lady said.

I'm too good a person to hurt like this, Priscilla said. Do you understand how nice I am? I go to funerals for people I don't even know. And I weep for them. He has to die. I'm working my butt off trying to make things better, but nothing gets better. Things stay bad. I never feel good. I haven't felt, like, happy or joyful in so long.

Fuck off, Table said.

Shut up, Table, Lady said.

I'm gonna have your brains and face everywhere, Priscilla said. Little bits of you in the yard. Bring pigs out. Have them roll in your leftovers— No. That don't . . . I don't feel right. Get out of the way, Lady.

What? Lady asked.

Move, Priscilla said. I have to kill him. Please get out of the way.

No, Lady said.

Now, Lady, Priscilla said.

No, Lady said.

I don't want to shoot you, Priscilla said.

Good, 'cause I don't want to get shot, Lady said.

I get to kill him, Priscilla said. I get to do that.

You don't, Lady said.

Move, Priscilla said.

No, Lady said.

Move, Priscilla said.

No, Lady said.

Move, Priscilla said.

No, Lady said.

Move, Priscilla said.

No, Lady said.

Move, Priscilla said.

No, Lady said.

Move, Priscilla said.

No, Lady said.

Move, Priscilla said.

No, Lady said.

Mama, Dianna said.

Everyone turned. Dianna stood near the house, about twenty yards away. She wore a green nightgown, red bandana around her wrist, rainbows on her cheeks.

Who is she? Priscilla said.

Baby? Lady asked.

What's happening? Dianna asked.

Oh my God, Table said.

Who is she? Priscilla asked.

She talked, Table said.

Dianna, baby, please go inside, Lady said. It's so nice to finally hear your voice again. I love your voice so much. I love you so much. Please. You have to go back inside.

I'm hungry, Dianna said.

I'll get you some breakfast real soon, Lady said. We're just talking with our friend. Why don't you go watch TV? I'll be in super soon.

Who is she? Priscilla asked.

Can I have waffles with honey? Dianna asked.

Absolutely, Lady said. I'll come make them in two seconds. Just go inside, okay?

Is she y'all's? Priscilla asked.

Lady kept her eyes on Priscilla.

Inside, D, Lady said.

I can't believe she talked, Table said.

Lady, is that y'all's daughter? Priscilla asked.

Lady nodded.

No no no, Priscilla said. No no no no no no no. This is not how this is supposed to go. This is supposed to go another way. Are you real?

Dianna said nothing.

Hey, girl, Priscilla said. Are you real?

Course she's real, Lady said. Dianna, please. Right now, baby. Go inside and close the door.

I still don't feel good, Table said.

D go D go D go, Lady said.

Table touched his bloody shoulder.

Why's this happening? Priscilla asked. This isn't supposed to be happening.

You can just go away, Lady said. You can just leave.

My dad, Priscilla said. He was my dad. He took my dad.

I know, Lady said. I'm so sorry. Please don't take hers.

I don't feel good, Table said.

I loved him, Priscilla said. I still love him.

It'd make you mad if I acted like I knew what you were going through, Lady said.

Priscilla looked at the sky and Lady saw Dianna was still there.

D, the house, Lady said. Please.

Dianna didn't move.

I never get to see him anymore, Priscilla said. I want to see him. He made me happy. I want to be happy.

This ain't no way to try, Lady said.

Those bullets were hot, Table said. Why'd you get hot bullets? I don't feel good. I feel like a fireplace. There are fires in me. I have fires in me.

Please leave, Lady said. Please leave us alone.

Priscilla spit twice, looked again at the sky.

Did y'all know it rains diamonds on Saturn? Priscilla asked. Always thought it was amazing God could do that. Diamond rain. I'd like to go there someday. Just be outside, stick my tongue out. Diamonddrops. On another planet. Even closer to Him. Catching diamonds on my tongue.

Tell me what to say that will make you feel better, Lady said. I'll say it. I'll call you every day and say it.

Priscilla stared at Table's blood.

I live by a highway, she said. I don't like it. Sometimes it gets inside my head, makes me feel dead. I don't like feeling dead. Wish I could hear this pretty water all the time.

She looked at Dianna.

How old are you? Priscilla asked.

Dianna scratched her cheek, held her arm straight out in front of her, and opened her hand.

Five, she said.

Priscilla let out wordless howls. Screams of agony. Guttural, ached banshee wails with her whole body seizing and bursts of silver in her face.

No no no, Priscilla said. No no no no.

Veins rose in her forehead and pulsed. Her arms were limp. A bevy of quail in her chest trying to get out. She fell to her knees and wept. Her eyes were like trees. She looked at Dianna. She dropped the gun.

I'm sorry, Priscilla said. I'm so sorry. I'm not shooting anymore, okay? Everything's okay now. Everything's good. Your daddy's safe. He's healthy.

Blood on Priscilla's cheeks. Tears in the blood. Dianna said nothing. Lady took her phone out.

Lady, Table said.

Yes, madam, Daddy's gonna be just fine, Priscilla said. I didn't shoot him anywhere important. Things are great. Think this will be a real turning point for all involved. We're at the dawn of a new age. The next chapter of our lives begins now.

Yeah my husband's been shot, Lady said.

Blood on the phone.

Lady, Table said.

Three, Lady said. Once in each thigh and once in his right shoulder.

Lady, Table said.

I don't know, Lady said. Six-shooter thing. Cowboy gun . . . She's still here but said she's done shooting.

Lady, Table said.

1698 6 Mile Road, Lady said. Florra. 74429.

Lady, Table said.

Right, Lady said. Yeah . . . No . . . Yeah, I know what that is . . . Okay. Enough.

She hung up.

We need to get tourniquets on you, Lady said.

I don't know, Lady, Table said.

Don't know what? Lady asked.

I don't feel very good, Table said.

No, he should be fine, Priscilla said. I'd give them a call back if I were you and explain it again 'cause everything should be fine.

Lady took her coat and shirt off. She bit at the collar of the button-up and ripped it in half, tied the shirt pieces around his thighs above the wounds. He tried to sit up. He couldn't. His face slumped. She made her fur his pillow, put pressure on his shoulder. She looked at Priscilla.

Come here, Lady said. I need your hands. Put pressure on his legs.

Priscilla shook her head.

I don't know if—

Right now.

Okay.

Priscilla knelt down, placed her hands where her bullets had gone, pressed down.

Lady, he said.

What? she asked.

It's a very soft coat.

She smiled.

Wish you hadn't got your blood all over it, she said. Pretty inconsiderate.

That's my bad, Table said. That's on me. Should come right out, though. Just run it under some hot water.

Yeah, he's fine, Priscilla said. He's flinging zingers left and right over here. May not even have to stay at the hospital overnight. D? You heard that? That's how fine he should be. One hundred percent. Your dad's a rascal. He'll not be down for long. Bet he's walking again, shoot, next week? What's cool is, a lot of times when people get hurt, they come back even stronger.

Dianna said nothing. Lady wiped Table's face. Again he tried to sit up. He couldn't. Her eyes were brighter than usual, caramel now, and he saw for the first time flecks of hickory and penny and sandstone and it was like there were threads of green in the irises. Blood on him like spilled paint. Blood in his dimples. Blood on her hands. He tried to sit up again, even harder now. She touched softly his chest. He was laboring. She kissed his neck. She kissed his cheek. She kissed his lips. They looked

at each other. The sky was in his eyes. Red crystals at the edge of the white. He blinked. The creek bed on her face. She watched him sink. Her face dropped. He shook his head.

I'm sorry, baby, Table said.

Oh no, Lady said. Oh God no.

What's happening? Priscilla asked.

Oh, Table, Lady said.

He opened his palm. He was crying. Lady put her hand in his.

Just be here now, Table said. Just be here with me now.

What? Priscilla asked. No. No no no . . .

Oh no, Lady said. Oh no no no . . .

. . . no no no no *please God. No. Save him. Please God just please save him? I'm sorry. Please take the bullets out? Just get them out and let him live, please? I'm so sorry to have to ask. I take them back. I take the bullets back. Get them out. Get the bullets out.*

Lady and Table were looking at each other.

I love you so much I can't stand it, Lady said.

I'd like to stay with you, Table said. I'd like it a lot to stay here with you. I'm in love with you.

I know, baby, Lady said.

I changed my mind! I changed my mind! Get them out. Get them out. Get them out right now!

He winced again. His whole body tensed up.

It's not, Table said. It's been a bunch. I don't know how to get there.

Table, Lady said.

No, Priscilla screamed. *God please. Make him okay. Please God please.*

It's sprinkling, Table said. They got elephants on the fence.

Get them out. Please. Please God please. Make him okay. I'm so sorry.

I'm so sorry, Lady. I'm so sorry, Dianna. Oh, Dianna. Oh no. I'm so so sorry. So so sorry. *I'm so sorry. I'm so sorry—*

I love you love love you I love you I love you, Lady said.

I'm saying, it's supposed to be the other one, Table said.

His chest settled, froze. They watched his eyes stop. Priscilla's temples throbbed and her eyes were numb and dead and wide and wet and she wiped her mouth. All the nerves in her head expanded. Dianna lay down in the grass. Lady was pale and swayed, hugged the body. Her neck felt shredded and it was like the pores in her face were being burned. She screamed.

Why's it this way? Why's it this way? Why's it this way?

Priscilla ran. Metal in her mouth. Her face was cold. She passed the Ranchero. Frozen cheeks. And the limo. The rumbling of a deep scream in her mouth. The dirt drive. Her car.

God. God.

When she got to the highway she was weeping. Screams of rage, the earth all quiet. Blood on the steering wheel. She wanted noise and turned on the radio. Wanda Jackson: He's got the pork chop, I got the pie. Priscilla's tongue clicked wildly in her mouth. She was the only one on the road. The sky was silver and she wanted it to fall. Chaos in her chest. Wanda hollered Looks like a thunder of love, better roll your windows down. Lifeless smile lines on Priscilla's face like gargantuan crescent moons. A tearing in her chest. Her head was heavy. Her feet were heavy. An ambulance and two cop cars went screaming in the opposite direction. Her tires roared. They rattled over the rumble strip. She thought she might faint and took the exit into Florra. More Wanda—the pistols are popping and the power is down. A steady ache in her throat. She pulled into the Sonic and jumped out of her car. Along the exterior of the building a sign featured piles of chicken

tenders in the shape of telephones and in the same font used on the album cover for *The Ramblin' Man* were the words SOFTLY AND TENDERLY OUR CHICKEN'S CALLING. She ran into the bathroom. There were writings on the walls: TZA; *hoss; the coyote of the desert always likes to eat the heart of the young and the blood drips down to the children for breakfast, lunch, and dinner and only the ribs will be broken in two.* She looked up. Dead crickets lay in the lights. She stared at her reflection, sweat in her hair, wilted face. Blood on the neck. Her mouth sagged. Hollow eyes like iced punch. Her gray face leaked. The lights droned. Visions of the Devil in a field of bluebonnets. She took off the purple jumpsuit, laid it on the floor, and looked in the mirror. A moaning somewhere. Veins like tiger stripes in her eyes. The moon smells like gunpowder.

She'd worn her father's old Olajuwon shirt under the coveralls and Dream stared back, thin mustache majestic, the neck stretched and crimson. His eyes were galaxies, unending and alien. He was beautiful and disappointed. She wiped away tears. She apologized to him. Her chest twitched. She was freezing. She sat under the hand dryer and turned it on. The blast of heat sounded like a missile. In her brain was a waving. Her hair was like vines and lightning. Comets in her head.

I'm so sorry. I'm so sorry.

The dryer stopped. She hit the button again.

I want to be warm.

She had no idea.

I'm so sorry. I'm so sorry. Let's just reverse time. Can we please reverse time?

She wept.

You're the love of my life.

The dryer stopped. She hit the button again.

*I want to be warm. Please forgive me? You're the love of my life. I'm
so sorry.*

The air was navy, beams of violet. The dryer stopped. She hit
the button again. She kept hitting it.

*I want to be warm. Please don't hold this against Dad. Please don't
hurt him anymore. Please let him up. Please. Please let him up. Please
forgive me. I'm so sorry. Can I touch You? I want to feel You so badly.
You're just real quiet to me and I'm so sad all the time. I'm just trying to
be good. I'm just trying to be good. What's the reason for all these bad
things? I have so much love in my heart and I walk around and feel none
of it. Will You have me? In the end? Will I get to be with You? Please let
me. God? I love You so much. Will I get to be with You? You're the love of
my life. Will I get to be with You? Will I get to be with You? Will I get to
be with You?*

Lady was still in the backyard. She held Table and kissed his
cheek. Dianna sat beside her. They made no sound. He was light
in Lady's arms, a small breeze now, and the smell of citrus came
faint from the Amurs. She stood. Clouds like great white sharks
in the sky. She put on the bloodstained fur. Hawks over the
trees. The flamingos just stood there. Her cheeks were cold.
They looked velour. A palatial surf in her head. Thorned waves
the size of mammoth castles smashed into the pink matter.
Coral stuck in her brain like horns. Her skull was a reef. The
center of the galaxy tastes like raspberries. Lady dragged Table
into the house and laid him in the middle of the living room.
Smears of blood and grass and mud on the turquoise. Sirens far
away. She knelt down beside the body, put her hand on his chest,
and began to cry.

Dianna walked to her mother. Great sobs from Lady and she
mounted him. His eyes were still open. She stared into them. He

looked like he was daydreaming. Her head thumped. Her jaw was set. Her knees squeezed his torso. She punched him in the chest.

You never made me catfish.

She punched him in the face. Smoke in her mouth. She punched him in the face.

Can you feel it? Lady asked.

She punched him in the face.

Can you feel it? Lady asked.

She punched him in the face.

Can you feel it? Lady asked.

She wiped her mouth and lay on the couch, looked at the room. There was the sword and aquarium and paintings and recliner. The cups he swore he'd clean. There was the place he first made her cry. His Crimson Outdoors hat. An open bag of Cheetos. An untouched bag of Fritos. There was the time he called cancer The Cance. A pile of dark socks. A bottle opener shaped like shorts. Napkins with roosters on them. A kiss by the window. His hand touching hers. There was an uneaten peach and a leaf by the door and Dianna on the floor and his leaking dead body and then the television. They'd left it on during the night. An Englishman spoke of buffaloes running. Lady stood in the living room and Table stood and Dianna stood and they were dressed for the party the night before. Lady took a drink of Taureau. Table took a drink of Taureau. Dianna started clapping. Table screamed I'm feeling it. You look beautiful and I'm feeling it. Wild horses the color of the moon on the television. They thundered through a lagoon in slow motion. Splashes of water fountained up from their hooves and their manes were like smoke. Lady sprayed the room with champagne and screamed I'm in the zone. I'm in the zone. I'm in the zone. Table brought her mouth to his. The kiss was soft. They were gentle with

you. I want to specifically mention the late, lamented Upstairs Gallery, the best theater in the history of the world.

Major thanks to Bill Simmons and all my colleagues current and former at *The Ringer*, especially my longtime running mate Jason Gallagher. Nonstop, Dirk-sized thanks for your friendship, veracity, and casting me in stuff where I get to make Stromile Swift jokes. Looking forward to hitting up the Wonka slots at WinStar.

Thanks to Fort Gibson, Charlie's Chicken, Oklahoma, and Russell Westbrook. Route 44-level thanks to JD Reeves for your honesty, for reading the book, and for being my friend.

Big gratitude to the readers of this book. Novels are expensive and long. Thanks for taking a chance on this one.

Lastly, thanks again to Blythe, June, and Adelaide.

June and Addy: My Ritzy and my Cheddy, the best girls in the world, I am so happy to be your dad. Watching y'all grow is the thrill of my life. You have my love completely, always, no matter what.

Blythe: I don't deserve you. Thanks for ignoring that and being with me anyway. And thank you for your strength and selfless support, your advice, your heart. This book's a shit heap without you. So am I. Love you.

ACKNOWLEDGMENTS

In the Acknowledgements of Roger Angell's *This Old Man*, he writes: "My steady feelings of thanks, which start with my children and my family and include a splendid range of cherished friends, are not reducible to a list." I'm with Rog. It's impossible. I'll try anyway.

First and last thoughts, here and always, are for my wife, Blythe, and our girls, June and Adelaide. I love y'all forever and will thank you again later.

Thanks to my sisters and parents for your love, support, everything. Sorry, Mom and Dad, for the language.

Thanks to Paul and Heather Haaga for your encouragement and generosity.

Thanks to Columbia's MFA fiction program and the classmates and professors I learned so much from. In no particular order: Sam Lipsyte, Rivka Galchen, Paul Beatty, Nalini Jones, Ben Metcalf, and Binnie Kirshenbaum.

Massive, Bunyanesque thanks to my agent Dan Kirschen for your patience, vibe, and friendship. Appreciate all the calls and your belief in the book. It doesn't exist without you. Go Bills.

Endless gratitude to everyone at Strange Light with special thanks to my editor, Jordan Ginsberg. The book improved enormously under your care. Thanks for your wisdom, confidence, and appreciation of Shai Gilgeous-Alexander.

I spent the better part of my twenties doing improv in Chicago. Thanks to that beautiful city. Impossible to list here the countless important friends, teams, and institutions that impacted me during that time, but you know who you are and you know I love